The Green

The Green

Troon McAllister

DOUBLEDAY

New York London

Toronto Sydney Auckland

PUBLISHED BY DOUBLEDAY
a division of Random House, Inc.
1540 Broadway, New York, New York 10036

DOUBLEDAY and the portrayal of an anchor with a dolphin
are trademarks of Doubleday, a division of
Random House, Inc.

The Green is a work of fiction. The characters and events exist only in the author's
imagination, and any resemblances to any real-life figures are purely coincidental and
unintentional. In those cases where real-life figures make cameo appearances in the
novel, they do so in a purely fictional context, and no representations of factual accuracy
are implied by the author or should be assumed by the reader.

DESIGN BY JAMES SINCLAIR

Library of Congress Cataloging-in-Publication Data
McAllister, Troon.
The green / Troon McAllister. — 1st ed.
p.   cm.
I. Title.
PS3557.R8G74   1999
813'.54—dc21   98-27469
CIP

ISBN: 0-385-49459-9

First Edition

1   3   5   7   9   10   8   6   4   2

In memory of Jim Murray

THE PAIRINGS

Friday Morning: Alternate Shot

United States		*Europe*
1—Jon Markovy		Juan Castillo Licenciados
Fred Asphal	v.	Andrew Firth
2—Derek Anouilh		Eric Swenborg
Mack Merriwell	v.	Fabrizio Migliore
3—Eddie Caminetti		Jürgen Kurzer
Enrico Senzamio	v.	Charles Woolsey
4—Joel Fleckheimer		John Wickenhampshire
Paul DeMonte	v.	Jacques St. Villard *(capt.)*

Friday Afternoon: "Best Ball"

United States		Europe
1—Eddie Caminetti		Eric Swenborg
Enrico Senzamio	v.	Jacques St. Villard *(capt.)*
2—Jon Markovy		Jürgen Kurzer
Fred Asphal	v.	Fabrizio Migliore
3—August Hookstratten		Eero Tukinen
Derek Anouilh	v.	Mieczyslaw Piranewski
4—Archie McWhirter		Helmut Braunschweiger
Tal Thomashow	v.	Andrew Firth

Saturday Morning: Alternate Shot

United States		Europe
1—Eddie Caminetti		Eric Swenborg
Enrico Senzamio	v.	Charles Woolsey
2—Jon Markovy		Jürgen Kurzer
Fred Asphal	v.	Fabrizio Migliore
3—Joel Fleckheimer		Eero Tukinen
Derek Anouilh	v.	John Wickenhampshire
4—Mack Merriwell		Juan Castillo Licenciados
Tal Thomashow	v.	Andrew Firth

Saturday Afternoon: "Best Ball"

United States		**Europe**
1—Eddie Caminetti		Helmut Braunschweiger
Enrico Senzamio	v.	Jürgen Kurzer
2—August Hookstratten		Juan Castillo Licenciados
Derek Anouilh	v.	Jacques St. Villard (*capt.*)
3—Archie McWhirter		Mieczyslaw Piranewski
Tal Thomashow	v.	Charles Woolsey
4—Jon Markovy		Andrew Firth
Fred Asphal	v.	Luc van Ostrand

Sunday: Individual Matches

United States		*Europe*
1—Robert Carmichael	v.	John Wickenhampshire
2—August Hookstratten	v.	Eric Swenborn
3—Paul DeMonte	v.	Charles Woolsey
4—Archie McWhirter	v.	Eero Tukinen
5—Tal Thomashow	v.	Mieczyslaw Piranewski
6—Derek Anouilh	v.	Juan Castillo Licenciados
7—Jon Markovy	v.	Fabrizio Migliore
8—Mack Merriwell	v.	Helmut Braunschweiger
9—Enrico Senzamio	v.	Jürgen Kurzer
10—Joel Fleckheimer	v.	Andrew Firth
11—Eddie Caminetti	v.	Jacques St. Villard (*capt.*)

"You men, you treat golf as an emergency.
Rain, wind, sickness, natural disaster . . .
it just has to be played, regardless."

—HELEN GRUENFELD,
APRIL 1998

Part 1

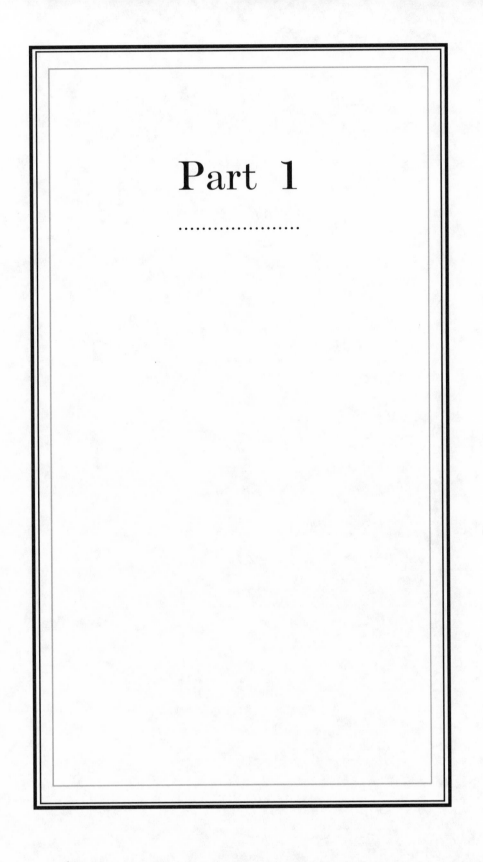

CHAPTER ONE

This is a true story. It just hasn't happened yet . . .

My name is Alan Bellamy. Of course you already know that, otherwise why would you be bothering to read a story about golf? But in case you've been held hostage by a terrorist organization for the past nine years, you should know that I've won the U.S. Open, the British Open twice, and took third and second at the Masters along with a slew of wins at other events of only slightly less prestige, including a second at the Tournament of Champions. I was the leading money-winner twice and Player of the Year three times. It may sound immodest, but those are the facts. Most important, though, I was captain of the U.S. Ryder Cup team last year, when it was played on American soil, and I was the one responsible for what happened.

What you don't know is *how* it happened, only that it was all my fault, but you don't know *why*, even though you think you do. You think, as does everybody else, that it was because I put one Eddie Caminetti on the team, a two-bit public-links hustler who never played in a single PGA-sanctioned event in his life, and who had about as much business being on a Ryder Cup team as Ilie Nastase. You think that's why things went a little haywire and, as a matter of fact, you're right, but not for the reasons you think.

First, a word about the Ryder Cup. If you're not familiar with golf, you might think it's just another of the dozens of barely distinguishable competitions that take place throughout the year, evenly spaced so it seems there isn't a weekend that goes by without hour after tedious hour of footage showing generally out-of-shape men alternately smiling, groaning, cursing, jumping into the air, holding their heads in their hands, holding those same hands up in triumph, berating their caddies and basically acting as though what they did was actually important in the greater scheme of things.

You'd be wrong. Not necessarily about your opinion of golf, which is shared by many, most of whom have never actually played the game but think they understand it better than the twenty-five million Americans who do, but about the Ryder Cup being just another tournament.

First off, there are only twenty-four players in the Ryder Cup and not a single penny of prize money. The results don't appear on any player's PGA record, nor do they count for his official statistics. The rules are often capricious, the playing format is brutal, and, for professionals conditioned to withstand the agony of participating in the loneliest and most individual sport on earth, the sudden plunge into team play is confusing and unnerving. Who wants to give advice, counsel and succor to people who spent every waking moment of the previous two years trying to kill you and who will do the same within days of the Ryder being over?

Yet there is no contest in the sport that the players take more seriously, and being on the team is the highest honor attainable, even though the subsequent scrutiny and the relentless pressure are almost unbearable. The strongest and most mentally hardened among the competitors have been known to sneak off into the woods in the middle of a hole to throw up from the sheer tension. Once in a rare while, a player with an erratic game even declines to play on the team for fear of having an off day at the worst possible time.

Why? Because the Ryder Cup is a biennial match pitting the best players in the United States against the best in Europe. It is played for honor, not money, and the players, like the Kagemusha of old Japan, are *our* designated warriors fighting *their* designated warriors on behalf of the entire U.S.A. Lose a major on the regular tour and you go home disappointed. Lose the Ryder for your team (as well as your country)—not an impossibility, since the entire three-day match can come down to a single putt—and it's warm-bath-and-a-razor time. In some ways, making damned sure you don't blow it for the team is vastly more important than winning it for them.

I know. I'm the one who blew it five years ago when we lost the cup at the Congressional. The tournament site alternates between Europe and the United States, and, while it's bad enough to lose over there, losing on your own soil is as bad as it gets.

Hang on a second. You didn't know I was the one who lost it. You thought it was Mack Merriwell, right? Missing his putt on the eighteenth during his match against Juan Castillo Licenciados with the entire tournament all square?

No. It was me. Everybody thought it was Mack because his loss came on the last day, and mine came on the first. But the fact is, Mack and Licenciados had fought an awesome battle for eighteen holes, trading the lead so often neither of them was ever ahead for more than two holes in a row. They not only tore at each other, they tore at the course, crushing the formerly invincible Congressional beneath their cleats. *Both* of them would have broken the old course record of 66 had they been playing medal format.

Again, for those of you unfamiliar with the Ryder Cup format, I should explain something. Just about every major golf event in the world is played according to the *medal* format, also known as stroke play. Nothing could be simpler: At the end of four rounds over four days, you add up how many shots each player took, and the one who took the fewest wins. Period.

What makes stroke play kind of interesting is that the players aren't really playing against each other, they're playing against the course. Most of the time, while you're out there, you don't even know for sure where you stand, at least not moment by moment, because it's possible that your nearest competitor is half a mile away. If you were all square, and then he made a birdie at the same time you made par, it might be several minutes before the news reached you. And even then, if you already played seventeen holes and he played only thirteen, he's got five more holes to try to improve his final score, and you're pretty much done. So you'll end up sitting in the clubhouse for an hour or two, helpless, waiting to find out whether you won or not without anything you can do about it anymore except pray, and, as any golfer will tell you, God doesn't listen to golfers. When He invented this game, He was 100 percent well intentioned but only 75 percent effective. Remember the old one about whether God can make a stone so heavy even He couldn't lift it? Well, when He invented golf, He created a game even He couldn't play. As Lee Trevino put it when someone asked him why he was holding a one-iron aloft during a lightning storm, " 'Cause even God can't hit a one-iron."

When you play in a tennis match or a bowling tournament, you have to beat maybe six or seven other people, which is the total number of matches you have to play. But whoever wins a golfing event under stroke play has to beat *everybody*, every other golfer in the entire contest, without actually playing *against* any of them. So how you play has nothing to do with whom you're playing against; you just try to get the lowest score possible all the time.

Except sometimes. And those are the times when the game gets truly exciting. If your closest competitor happens to be in your group, and your group is the last one playing, all of a sudden you have to pay attention to what's going on, because what the other guy is doing can have a huge impact on your game and how you play it.

If that's confusing, here's an example: About six months ago, I was playing in the Nissan Prudential Fruit of the Loom Texaco Open in Eau Claire, Wisconsin. (It used to be called the Valley View Open, but that was back before corporations figured out how to provide gigantic perks to their officers and customers while telling their shareholders that sponsoring golf tournaments was good for business because, even though it seemed to cost many millions right off the bottom line, the truth was that the resultant "image marketing" reaped huge benefits, which, while difficult to quantify, were nevertheless quite real, as the officers and customers would swear vehemently.)

The mercurial New Zealander Gerry Agnormo and I were in the last pairing on the last day. As we approached the seventeenth tee, he was leading by a single stroke, I was second, and Joel Fleckheimer, three holes back of us somewhere, was one stroke behind me through thirteen holes. Nobody else in the field was even close. That meant that Agnormo and I would be fighting each other down the stretch.

Now you might say, what's the difference—you're each going to try to get the lowest score possible, right? You could be on two different planets and it shouldn't affect how you play.

But it does make a difference. Because trying to get the lowest score possible is very risky. Sometimes, in order to score a birdie, you have to risk making a bogey, whereas if you simply go for par, it's almost a sure thing.

The seventeenth at the Valley View Country Club is a devilish parfour, 420 yards "from the tips," which means that the tees are set as far back as possible. The fairway is very narrow, thick stands of trees running down both sides of its entire length, but they're not the real problem.

The real problem is a lake sitting between you and the green. The front edge is 220 yards away, the back edge 260. So there are two basic ways you can play this hole. The first is obvious: Hit a long iron about 210 straight down the middle, laying up in front of the lake and leaving yourself 210 yards up onto the green and a likely par.

Then there's the other way: Smack your driver *over* the lake, so you can tuck a pitching wedge nice and close to the flag for a birdie opportunity. Nothing to it—so long as you can reliably whack your driver 280 yards, 261 of them in the air, and do it without hitting into the trees on either side. This is a fairly tall order for most golfers.

Which one should you do?

It depends. In my case, Agnormo had the honors and would hit off the tee first. Now, he was ahead of me by one, and he knew that the odds of my getting a birdie on this hole were very small, so he figured, why take a chance on going for birdie himself and risk mucking it up and losing his lead?

After pondering this for a moment or two, and weighing it against the pressure of several thousand of his fans gathered around in hushed anticipation of something spectacular, he yanked a four-iron out of his bag and stepped up to the tee box. He took a long time staring at a spot in the middle of the fairway, then seemed to put it out of his mind completely as he focused on the ball alone. With perfect control, he brought the club back and whipped it forward with a slight grunt, then watched as the tiny white pill rose into the sky and headed straight for the trees on the left. As the purely ballistic motion of the ball started to give way to aerodynamic forces, the dimples on the surface began biting into the air as they spun clockwise at a high rate of speed.

The dimples on the left side of the ball, moving toward the oncoming air, caused a lot more friction than the ones on the other that were spinning away from what aerodynamicists call the *apparent wind*. Gradually, this caused the ball to move to the right, just as Agnormo had intended. This is called a fade, and by the time the ball hit the ground, it had shifted a good thirty yards from its original path and come to rest dead center in the fairway, less than ten yards from the water's edge.

Agnormo couldn't have played this shot better had he been allowed to walk the ball out to the fairway and place it by hand, and the crowd knew it. He acknowledged the cheers with a big smile and a nonchalant wave of the hand—*Big deal, I do it all the time*—and tried not to gloat as he cleared out so I could hit.

Had Agnormo been *down* by one instead of *up,* there is little doubt he would have tried to blast one all the way past the lake in order to give himself a better birdie opportunity, which birdie he was not likely to get from his present position.

I, on the other hand, had no choice, unless I wanted to settle for a sure second place instead of risking a disaster in order to try to win this thing. If I could make birdie here, we'd be all square going into the last hole. And of course there was always the chance that Agnormo could put his next shot onto the green close enough for a makable birdie of his own. Even if I put the tee shot into the water, I told myself, I still had a chance of putting *my* next shot close to the flag, one-putting for par, including my penalty stroke.

To make a long story short, I put on my steely-concentration face for the benefit of the television cameras, took the driver, and, as they say, gripped it and ripped it. It was a mighty and awe-inspiring firecracker of a belt, about 290 smack down the middle and over the water as though the ball had onboard navigation radar.

Agnormo, being farther from the hole than I, hit next, a beautiful, soft four-iron that rose lazily into the sky and plopped onto the green about thirty feet from the flag. My nine-iron landed on the other side of the hole, about the same distance away as Agnormo's, and we both two-putted for par.

Net advantage to me for my risk? Nothing. He was still up by one. But I had to try, you see, and that's how a competitor can affect your game toward the end of the match.

Actually, now that I think about it, what happened on the next hole illustrates the point even better. Because just as we were walking to the eighteenth, a tremendous roar arose from somewhere in the distance. Agnormo and I looked at one of the tour officials scattered around the course. The man had a walkie-talkie at his ear, then pulled it away and said, "Fleckheimer."

Agnormo pursed his lips as I nodded my understanding at him: Joel Fleckheimer had just birdied the fourteenth. That meant he was now tied with me for second, one stroke behind Agnormo. I could see the gears working in The Kiwi's brain: He had only one hole left to play. Fleckheimer and I, between us, had five. What Agnormo was thinking was, somewhere among those five holes, either Fleckheimer or I was bound to make at least one birdie, which would place that guy into a tie with Agnormo for first, forcing a playoff. Two birdies by Fleckheimer and he'd have the tournament. So what Agnormo was thinking was, *I can't play the eighteenth safe and risk a playoff or an outright loss.* He had to birdie the hole.

The eighteenth is a classic finishing hole, a beautiful 560-yard par-five that sweeps gently from left to right, ending with a lake in front of the green that butts right up against it. Hardly anybody tries to reach the green in two, because plopping into the lake is too much of a risk. Even if you smack a 300-yard drive, there's still 260 to go, and it has to carry nearly all the way in order to get over the lake. Normally, The Kiwi wouldn't dream of trying it.

Normally. But now he was faced with the real possibility of blowing the Nissan Prudential Fruit of the Loom Texaco (formerly the Valley View) Open unless he pushed the outside of the envelope a little, since another player's game had now affected his own.

And the pressure was on me, too. Up until this point, I was alone in second place, and now I had competition from Fleckheimer. Would I have to try to get on the eighteenth green in two as well?

The question became moot for me, because at that point my caddie did something that both Agnormo and *his* caddie had neglected to: He looked at the leader board through his binoculars, and then he said something to me as discreetly and unobtrusively as he could, and I almost fainted. But he squeezed my arm in order to make me keep my composure and not give anything away, and I stood as still as possible as Agnormo addressed his ball.

Poised in his stance, The Kiwi let out a long breath and forced his shoulders to relax. Then he turned his head to the left and spent several seconds eyeballing his target, some tuft of grass or other landmark he had picked out on the fairway. Turning back to his ball, he took another moment to visualize exactly how this swing was going to look, then he hauled off and thwacked the ball just as hard as he possibly could.

The speed of the ball coming off the clubface was indeed a sight to behold, but the effort he put into his swing had thrown him slightly off balance, and the ball was heading to the left more than he would have liked. Since the fairway curved to the right, this added maybe twenty yards to the distance to the green for his next shot, even though the ball landed safely in the fairway with a nice, clean lie. The enthusiastic applause for his 310-yard blast betrayed the crowd's ignorance of what

Agnormo had intended to do: While his lie was quite good for getting on the green in regulation three, it was horrendous for reaching it in two. It would require at least 270 yards of pure carry over the water before it hit the ground. Agnormo, as keenly insightful about the game as any golfer alive, naturally expected me to try the same, but, as I said, my caddie had looked at the leader board, and so we both knew something that Agnormo didn't. So when I played a nice 260 pop safely down the center of the fairway, I could sense him shaking his head slightly in mild derision of my cowardice and willingness to settle for a possible third place.

The rest made the front page Monday, and not just the sports section. Mustering all his reserve, Agnormo took a driver out of his bag and tried to smack the ball onto the green. His shot was incredibly straight, but too low, and as the ball screamed toward the lake, everyone watching knew he was in trouble. His ball touched down in the water about fifty yards short of the greenside bank of the pond, and then, amazingly, took a huge skip and rose back up into the air. Several thousand hearts stopped beating as it appeared that the ball was going to land on the opposite shore, but it came down short again, and again skipped and jumped into the air, landing short once again, but this time staying down and dying beneath the rippling of the pond.

Agnormo closed his eyes and tried hard not to betray his dismay. I looked away, took hold of an eight-iron and laid my ball up about twenty yards short of the water. Agnormo took his drop, put the ball on the green and two-putted for a bogey six. I pitched up and two-putted for a safe par, now tied with him for first, and that's when Agnormo happened to glance at the leader board, the horror of it zinging into his brain with such force I thought he might fall over as he just learned what I had known back at the tee box.

Fleckheimer was still two shots behind. He hadn't birdied the fourteenth at all, he just parred it. But his second shot had gone into a bunker, with a rotten lie that afforded him practically no backswing, and he had hit an astonishing shot that dropped his ball onto the green, although still thirty feet from the pin. He then sank the putt to save par. That was what all the screaming from the crowd had been about, and Agnormo's failure to verify his assumption about what had happened had forced him to attempt a near-impossible birdie, leaving him with a disastrous bogey.

His glance at me at that moment was murderous. He knew instantly that I had been aware of Fleckheimer's status all along, which was why I had played the eighteenth safe. Fleckheimer never did make another birdie, and Agnormo and I found ourselves in a playoff for first place. The format was that we would both play the eighteenth over and over until somebody won it. Neither of us was willing to risk going for birdie, so each of us parred the damned thing four times, waiting for the other guy to make a mistake, which Agnormo did on the fifth go-around, missing an eight-foot par putt. I made my six-footer, and that's how I won both the Nissan Prudential Fruit of the Loom Texaco (formerly the Valley View) Open and the eternal enmity of Gerry Agnormo, who never forgave me for violating what he considered to be one of the gentlemanly canons of the game.

All that by way of illustrating how one man's play in this loneliest of sports can affect another's. I won, despite the fact that Agnormo was frankly the better golfer. Thank God he wasn't European and couldn't play in the Ryder to exact revenge on me.

How'd I get started on this? Oh, yeah, that's *stroke* play we've been talking about. But the Ryder Cup is *match* play, and that's an entirely different game. In match play, the favorite format of most golfers and fans, it's one player against another, *mano a mano*, and the overall scores don't count. They play hole by hole; lowest score wins the hole, then you wipe the slate clean and the next hole is a brand-new match. The one who wins the most holes of the eighteen available wins the game.

In stroke play, if you really screw up a hole, let's say four over par, you may never make up that deficit, and you have to play the rest of the game with that depressing thought stuck in your mind. Arnold Palmer himself once took a *twelve* during the U.S. Open at Rancho Park in Los Angeles (there's a marble memorial on what is now the eighteenth hole to commemorate the event, describing in detail how he got each stroke). But in match play, even if you hit twenty over par, all you lose is that one hole. Then it's history, and you start afresh on the next tee, down only one more instead of eighteen more, as you would have been in stroke play.

And in this format, what your opponent does, and where the match stands, has a huge impact on what you do on every hole. It doesn't matter if you take an eight on a par-four so long as your opponent takes at least that many himself or you already have a sufficient lead to absorb a lost hole. And once somebody's lead is larger than the number of holes remaining, the match is over. If you're up three and there are only two holes left to play, you can't lose, so the game ends and you win, "three and two."

It's the most thrilling format imaginable. The reason it's not used in regular tour events is that it would take too many rounds to determine a winner, and nine or ten days of golf is just too much.

But the Ryder Cup has only twelve players on a side. Not only that, there's no individual winner, just the team. Twenty-eight matches are played in all, each one worth one point. Ties are worth a half point. The team that wins at least 14½ points takes the cup home. If the whole tournament is all square at 14–14, the team already in possession of the cup from the contest two years prior gets to take it back home.

Damned exciting stuff.

CHAPTER TWO

Being captain of the U.S. Ryder Cup team is a once-in-a-lifetime honor, at least for an American (the Europeans tend to keep theirs on), but there is nothing honorary about the position. The captain sets all the pairings for the two-man matches, determines the order of play, is the only person allowed to coach team members once play has begun and has the absolute authority to make last-minute changes in who plays in what matches—or who plays at all.

And he's got one other little chore: The team consists of the top ten point-winners on the tour, points being awarded according to how they placed in events. The last two picks are solely at the captain's discretion. There is no decision more subject to criticism and second-guessing, which has little to do with whom he ends up choosing or why. It could be the winner of the Masters, an up-and-coming sensation, whatever. As soon as his decision is announced, a million self-anointed experts are sure to demand his banishment to the fires of hell for his bone-headed misjudgment.

Imagine what happened to me when, in addition to the no-brainer choice of Mack Merriwell, I picked Eddie Caminetti.

I first heard about Eddie during a corporate outing in Fort Lauderdale, Florida, some three months before the Ryder. An "outing" for a professional golfer means an excruciating day dragging three amateurs around a golf course for upward of five hours while trying to remember that they hadn't paid four thousand dollars each for His Eminence to act surly. The reward at the end of the day is another three hours or so of pumping the hands of half-soused, florid-faced, potbellied corporate types at the behest of the sponsor who set the outing up. I perhaps ought to mention that the other reward, at least for someone like me, is about fifty thousand dollars, which is not bad for one day's work, of which my caddie doesn't get his usual tour-event cut.

On this particular Sunday, the private course was filled with the usual onlookers gawking at our foursome, especially at me, the superstar who had deigned to honor their club with the graciousness of his presence. You might think such adulation is ego-satisfying, but it's really 100-percent pain in the ass, especially with no television cameras around. Answering the same old questions from this local Gang of Three as I get from reporters for network television is not only tedious but harmful: It's difficult to keep the sound-bites fresh after you've mumbled them a thousand times to people who don't count. If I had a buck for every joker that day who asked me whom I was going to pick as the final member of the Ryder Cup team, I could retire from the tour. Okay, I could retire anyway, but you know what I mean.

'Long about the twelfth hole, I noticed a funny thing. A lot of the people I thought were staring at me were actually turned away looking at something else, something on an adjoining hole. Even more amazingly, once in a while one or two of the amateurs in my group would kind of saunter off to take a look themselves. Now, what could be of more interest to a weekend duffer than playing a round with the Player of the Year?

My curiosity soon turned to annoyance. Sure, I hated outings and didn't need the attention from fawning locals carrying 25-handicaps, but I didn't expect to be snubbed, either. Finally, after I crushed an absolutely massive drive on fourteen and turned to savor the astonishment from the rest of the foursome, I found all three of them staring intently at the approach to the seventeenth green about fifty yards to the right of our tee box.

"Somebody want to tell me what—" I began with some irritation, but, surprisingly, *astoundingly*, Larry "The Hardware Maven" Dugelman held up a hand in my direction without even looking at me. I clamped my jaw shut before anybody could catch wind of my shock, not a likely occurrence since no one was looking at me anyway, and turned to see just what was so damned compelling over there.

The seventeenth is a par-four so long that it misses being a par-five by about three inches. Fifty yards in front of the green and off to the right is a sand trap, the back of which is a sheer wall nearly six feet high, shielding the green from whatever happens to be inside the bunker, which at the moment appeared to be an entirely nondescript man of average height, build and coloring and wearing clothes so ordinary that, to this day, I can't remember a single distinguishing characteristic of any of it.

Standing with him just outside the trap were two players decked out in considerably more dapper finery. At the moment my eye happened upon them, the two men were laughing and shaking their heads as they walked back up the fairway away from the bunker, where I spotted two golf balls lying about seventy and eighty yards from the slightly elevated green. I assumed they were both lying two, while the man in the bunker lay the same but at a considerable disadvantage.

"Lotta dough just went down on that little sucker," said the auto dealer whose name I couldn't remember, pointing to the bunker where I now saw another golf ball nestled at the base of that man-high cliff. Was it possible that this clown actually made a bet that he would win this hole? And even if he did, why would my three playing partners give a tinker's cuss in the middle of playing a round with—did I already mention it?—the Player of the Year?

I decided to watch with them, an easy choice since none of them was paying any attention to me anyhow. The guy farthest out on the fairway took a pitching wedge and lobbed his ball softly onto the green, maybe twenty feet from the pin. Not a bad shot at all for an amateur. The other guy tried a sand wedge but bladed it, sending the ball up over the green in a shallow ascent that put it in the rough more than fifteen yards back of the dance floor.

The guy in the bunker watched all of this without any outward sign that it affected him either way, then stepped toward his cart and reached into his bag for what should have been some kind of wedge. But it was over four feet long with a bright orange shaft as big around as a radiator hose. It also seemed to have telescoping sections . . .

"The hell's he doing with a ball retriever?" I asked, mystified. Surely he wasn't going to declare the ball unplayable and take a drop, costing himself a stroke? And even if that was his plan, why use a retriever instead of just hopping back in and picking up the ball by hand?

I grew even more puzzled when he did step into the trap and walk up to his ball, still carrying the retriever. As he surveyed the sand wall looming above him, I said to no one in particular, "Somebody want to clue me in?"

The auto dealer smiled, but still without looking away from the scene. "S'gonna play it," he said.

"What's the retriever for?"

The Hardware Maven turned to me, finally, a wide grin on his doughy face. " 'At's what he's gonna play it with."

At that point I lost all interest. Who was kidding who here? "C'mon, guys," I said in my most commanding, no-nonsense tone. "Let's finish up here."

"Why don't you come on over here and watch this," said Vinny Zworsa in *his* most commanding, no-nonsense voice. So I did.

The guy in the sand finished his examination of the bunker and stepped away from the ball, then twisted the flat part of the retriever head, jamming it firmly into the handle. He tilted the stick down and let the head slowly fall until it was in position behind the ball, being careful not to let it touch the sand, which would have incurred a penalty. When the whole configuration was stabilized, he took one more look at the wall, then locked his eyes onto the ball and stood as still as death for about five seconds.

Slowly, he took the club back, picking up speed as the metal head came into the air above his right shoulder. When he had it pointed straight up, he brought it back down so fast it became a blur. I couldn't help noticing that the only thing the guy was moving of his body were parts between his neck and his waist: Head and legs were so motionless they looked as though they'd been painted onto the landscape.

I couldn't see a single grain of sand come up from the trap as the retriever head slipped under the ball with the same kind of soft pinging sound a tennis ball might make if it were dropped onto a china plate. The ball flew almost straight up, seeming to follow the contours of the sand wall before it rose above the lip, and continued rising high into the late-afternoon sky. I couldn't actually see any horizontal travel, but by the time it finally ran out of upward trajectory and began dropping back to earth, it was hanging right above the green.

The dapper gentlemen on the fairway must have seen it, too, because I heard something roughly along the lines of "Holy Mother of God!" issue forth from one of them. As I followed the ball down, my eye caught the man in the bunker walking back toward his cart, not even bothering to watch his ball, said ball at the moment plopping onto the green, bouncing a few inches into the air and coming to rest on the same spot it had hit on its first touchdown, which was less than four feet from the hole.

My playing partners loudly exhaled breaths I hadn't realized were held, and then I did the same as they all turned wordlessly to watch my reaction.

"Lucky break," I said lamely.

"Yeah." The Hardware Maven snorted. "Was lucky the time he did it to me, too."

"Same here," the auto dealer threw in as Zworsa nodded.

He'd done this before? "Couple dozen times I know of," Zworsa said, as though reading my mind.

"Name's Eddie," The Maven said. "Eddie Caminetti."

All of a sudden, I wasn't so special anymore. "Where's he play?"

"Embassy. Over to Hallandale."

"Maybe I'll play him a little later."

"If you bet him," the dealer said.

"I don't bet amateurs," I answered huffily.

"Then you ain't playin' him," The Maven said as he walked back to the tee box and gestured for me to tee up.

"What're you, kiddin' me?" *I told you, I'm the Player of the Year, f'Chrissakes!*

"Man don't give a shit who you are," Zworsa said. "Only cares do you got money to play with."

I couldn't believe I was hearing this and decided to forget about it. On the next hole, as I stood over my ball ready to hit a seven-iron to the 190-yard, par-three green, I heard a sound like a brick hitting a concrete sidewalk from ten stories up and turned in annoyance, just in time to see a golf ball rocketing away from the eighteenth tee, this Caminetti character standing there still poised at the end of his follow-through. The ball was arcing heavenward, and I lost sight of it just as it finally looked about ready to start back down.

"Stick don't look right," I said, expecting a typical half-moon driver clubhead to be dangling beneath Caminetti's right shoulder.

"Was a putter," the auto dealer said, indicating impatiently that it would be all right with him if I decided to hit right about now.

CHAPTER THREE

After the boozy reception enabling about a hundred swaying business types to claim from now on that we were great friends, I made my standard little speech and then answered the standard questions, in addition to one that came from somebody's wife who clearly wasn't pleased at spending Sunday mornings with just the kids.

"Mr. Bellamy, can you explain how such a silly game can be so addicting?" A scattering of nodding heads told me she'd struck a sympathetic chord, but I also was pleased to note that the majority of the women in the room looked at her with real surprise, as though the answer should have been self-evident.

But it isn't, not to those who don't play. Trying to describe to a non-golfer what it feels like to hit a perfect shot is like trying to describe sex to a eunuch. There's no common comparative basis in the language other than to reference the act itself, so you find yourself locked into non-illuminating recursions, like *Hitting a three-iron 230 yards straight up the fairway is just like, uh . . . hitting a three-iron 230 yards straight up the fairway.* Attempting to communicate to a cynic why you love the game so much is a fruitless effort doomed to failure, so there's no sense even trying. It'll only invite ridicule, especially if you head off into one of those sappy, religion-aping paeans so prized by professional golf writers who have run out of more comprehensible things to say.

So I thought about her question and then said, in all sincerity, "No, I can't. I would only say to those who scoff that if twenty-five million people in America alone play the game, many of whom are passionate about it and think of little else between rounds, that unless you think every one of those twenty-five million is deluded, crazy, or engaged in a massive conspiracy to fool everybody else, I'd caution against being too vocal in your sarcasm, because if you have an open mind and any adventurous spirit at all, there's a good chance you'll wind up as one of them someday, sorry only that you waited so long before finding the kind of joy they've known all along."

Probably a little more strident than would have been appropriate, but she started it, and I thought maybe this was a good time to break things off. I shook a few more hands and then slipped off to try to go find the Embassy "over to Hallandale."

An hour later I found myself in the gravel parking lot of a pretty scraggly municipal course tucked behind a sprawling development of moderate-income houses. I walked into the small bar off the pro shop called—get this now, it's really cute—The Nineteenth Hole, and asked the bartender how he was doing.

"Real good," he answered, continuing to wipe glasses and singularly unimpressed with who was asking him. "How's yourself?"

"The same. Say, you know a guy named Eddie Caminetti?"

I thought I saw a slight hesitation in his wiping hand, but it might have been my imagination. "I see him around."

"Know where I could find him?"

Now I sensed some appraising going on, and I said amiably, "Trust me, I'm not a bill collector."

That got me a smile back. "Hangs here usually."

"Thanks," I said, dripping with appreciation and good-fellowship.

As I was turning to leave, he said, "Hey," and I turned back.

The bartender leaned forward and lowered his voice. "You gonna look for him now?"

"Yeah."

He was trying to tell me something, so I sat down on a stool and pointed to one of the taps near his elbow. He put down the towel and glass and moved over to draw me a beer.

"What's your name?" I asked him.

"Danny."

He set the beer down in front of me, wiped his hands on the towel and stuck out his right.

"I'm—" I started to say as I shook his hand, but he grinned and stopped me.

"I know who you are, Mr. Bellamy. You kiddin' me or what here?"

"You know me, then you call me Al, okay, Danny?"

"Suits me," he said, and resumed his wiping.

I took a sip of the beer and said, "Look, Danny, I'm not out to cause any trouble for Eddie, I just—"

"You wanna play him, sure. I understand."

It didn't seem to surprise him that one of the most famous golfers in the world would make an effort to hunt down some local muni-whacker and get up a game.

"Thing is," he began, getting quiet again, and looking around to see who might be in earshot. But we were alone. "Thing is, he's not there now. Prob'ly he's over to Stinky Peterson's."

That name sounded familiar. Where had I heard it? Something flashed in my mind, something I saw as I drove down through Boca on the way in to—

"That driving range?" I exclaimed.

"Shh!" Danny admonished me sternly, and I made an appropriate gesture of chagrin and apology.

"They got a range right here," I said, almost in a whisper, pointing out the window at the empty stalls a few yards away. "What's he need'a drive up to Boca for?"

Danny straightened up and shrugged. "Doesn't like people who know him should see him practicing."

I nursed the beer and shot the general shit with Danny, then threw a ten on the bar and stood up to go.

Danny made no move toward the money. "You won't tell him I said nothin', will ya?"

I crossed my heart. "No way. You take care now, okay?"

It took me about an hour to get to Stinky Peterson's, where I spotted Eddie pretty much by himself in the farthest hitting stall. I stayed in the shadows and watched for a while.

He was holding what looked like about a seven-iron. He had a nice swing, very relaxed, nothing you'd necessarily notice if you weren't on the lookout, but there wasn't really anything I could pick out that I would have criticized, either. The first shot I saw went up into the air a little higher than a normal seven-iron should, and came down about ten yards past the 150-yard marker and slightly left.

His next shot had about the same trajectory, and landed maybe ten feet to the right of the first one. The next looked the same, as did the next dozen or so.

There was nothing remarkable about any of those shots, nothing that would even warrant a second glance from a casual passerby. What *was* remarkable was what that passerby would have seen had he looked at the ground: Every one of his shots had landed within six or seven feet of the middlemost ball, an amazing feat of precision I couldn't have duplicated myself.

I stepped out into the glare of the tower-mounted floodlights and walked to Eddie's stall. At the sound of my feet he turned, took one look at me, and pursed his lips.

"Fuckin' Danny," was all he said, putting the seven-iron back into the bag and tearing the glove off his left hand.

"Don't give him a hard time, Eddie," I said as I came up to him. "I pressured him pretty good." Up close, Eddie looked even more nondescript than he had at a distance when I saw him out on the course, a little like Dustin Hoffman but with less prominent features, if you can picture that. I figured him somewhere in his late forties.

I offered my hand and, resignedly, he took it, not looking into my eyes. I looked down and saw that the hand I was holding was deeply tanned and leathery, while his left looked like a dead mackerel newly washed up on shore, white, smooth, unlined. This was a guy who'd been out in the sun with a golf glove on every day since he'd been weaned.

"Name's Bellamy," I said lightly, trying to reduce whatever tension Eddie had conjured up for himself.

"No shit," he snarled, but there was no malice in it, and we both smiled.

We let go, and I looked out at the range. "You always cluster 'em like that?" I asked.

Eddie shook his head. " 'S'why I'm practicin'. Get 'em closer."

Okaayyy . . . "I saw you out on seventeen today," I said as casually as possible. "How'd you do that?"

"Do what?"

What the hell *else* had he done on seventeen that I missed? "Knock it out the bunker with a retriever."

"Got lucky. Sometimes that happens, you're ahead, you get a little crazy. Figure, why not have some fun?"

He didn't know that the guys I'd been playing with told me he'd done it many times before. I let it go. "Like to play me?"

"I'll play anybody. What'll you gimme?"

"Just for fun."

"I wanna play for fun, I'll play alone. What do I need *you* for?"

I tried not to betray that this was probably the first time in my professional life somebody had turned down an invitation from me to play. "Okay. What do you want?"

He stepped back and scratched his chin with his thumbnail. "What're you, like a plus six?"

Most pros don't have an official handicap, but it can be estimated. *Plus six* meant I'm likely to shoot six under par on a standard course. "More like plus two."

He seemed to approve of that, my willingness to negotiate, to throw a little bullshit on the table. "I'll take five a side," he said.

"Hah!" I burst out, an involuntary reflex. I'd obviously wasted my time. "You nuts? What do you—"

"And I'll let you scramble four balls."

That quieted me up in a damned hurry. What he meant was that I could take four shots off the tee, then pick the best of them and hit four more balls from there, pick the best of those and hit four more, and so on until I holed out. I'd count only one stroke out of each of the four I took, as though I'd only played one ball from the tee. A birdie on every hole was a virtual certainty, and there was little doubt I could score eagles on maybe two of the par-fives.

Totally absurd. "What's the catch?" I asked.

"No catch."

"Because if it's one of those bullshit joke bets where you call up some cockamamy obscure rule or throw in a new condition later—"

He held up his hand. "You think it's a bullshit proposition, you can call off the round anywhere right up to the eighteenth and we walk away even. And we're talking match play. No spectators, either, and we carry our own bags."

I couldn't believe I was hearing this. "You're serious."

He stood there silently.

"For how much?" I asked warily.

He shrugged. "Five grand?"

Jesus! I tried to stay calm. "You sure?"

"Are you?"

I stuck out my hand, and he took it immediately. "Where?" I asked. "Not your home course."

He shook his head as he took his hand back. " 'Course not. Too short, anyway. I'm gonna play with a pro, let's play long as hell."

I thought about it for a second. "Tell you what. You ever play Seminole Hills?"

He laughed. "You kiddin' me? President couldn't get into the place."

"Well, I can. And it's seventy-three hundred from the tips. Tomorrow, six o'clock, all right?"

"Why so early?"

"So we get out before the citizens figure out I'm there and start crowding us. Also don't want the members to know I brought a slob like you to their club."

He grinned again. "Good by me."

I walked off, and when I was pretty much out of his sight, I turned to see what he would be doing to get ready for our match.

He had the seven-iron out again, hitting 160-yarders just as he'd been doing before I showed up.

CHAPTER FOUR

I arrived just before five-thirty and saw Eddie waiting for me outside the gate. He was driving a '67 Cadillac Fleetwood, which somehow surprised me. I thought a hustler like him would be driving something nondescript, something that wouldn't call attention to himself. He was standing outside the car with a three-iron hung across his shoulders, one hand on each end as he turned first one way, held it, then turned back and held it on the other side.

Once we got inside, he went directly to the range to hit some balls. He must have gotten to the gate by five so he could have his stretching routine done. I got through mine in about fifteen minutes, hit a few and then called out, "You ready?"

As Eddie had said, we were both to carry our own bags. It went without saying that I didn't want any caddies to witness me scramble four balls against a nobody. Both of us had brought carry bags, mine a leather-trimmed beauty I got as a gift from a sponsor, his an ultralightweight, apparently homemade job that didn't look as if weighed much more than the air it displaced.

The first hole at Seminole is a par-four that plays 475 from the back tees. Eddie took a moment to survey the hole, probably never having seen grass that looked like it had been cut with a nail clipper and a ruler. Seminole was like a postcard come to life, so impossibly manicured it seemed a shame even to set foot on it.

I let him have his look so I could have a moment to myself as well. I try never to tee off without first taking a few minutes to appreciate this game I play, and the physical environment in which I play it. On this perfect morning, the warm air was cooking the fresh-cut grass so that humid waves of its musty smell rose up gently like a heady perfume. The moisture in the air made things a little on the hazy side, a little heavy, recalling the dreamy laziness of summers when I was a kid. I find it hard to resist the serenity that seeps into me in these kinds of conditions, the kind that makes you want to walk a little slower, swing a little smoother, the kind that keeps pulling you back into awareness of the day so you don't get so caught up in the game you forget where you are.

I would have thought that Eddie'd be getting impatient by now, but he was standing quietly, maybe mulling over something of his own take on the day.

"You sure about this, Eddie?" I asked solicitously. "Not too late to change your mind. I wouldn't say anything to anybody."

He took a deep breath, then looked down at his shoes. "Deal's a deal, Al. Let's do it."

I stepped back out of his line of sight as he teed up his ball and took a few practice swings. Rolling his neck once to make sure it was loose, he sidled up between the black markers and took his stance, waggling the club and taking one more look down the fairway before fixing his gaze on his ball.

After about two seconds of stillness, he took the club back smoothly, brought it back down and hit the ball, keeping his head down, following through nicely and then looking up to see how he did.

It was a fine shot, almost perfectly straight, with only a hint of fade. It hit the grass and rolled, not as far as it might have a few hours later when the dew had dried, but good enough to end up about 250 yards away and right in the middle.

"Good shot," I said graciously as he stepped away to make room for me.

"Thanks," he replied, and got back out of my sight line.

I teed up and did my own pre-shot routine, not much different from Eddie's, and hauled off much harder than I normally would have, knowing I had three more attempts if it didn't work out.

My connection was very solid, and I, too, faded the ball a little, but I had started off more centered, so I drifted to the right of the middle. When the ball came to rest, I was at least thirty-five yards past Eddie, about halfway between the middle and the trees on the right, on the fairway.

"Beauty!" he said in sincere admiration.

I rocked my head a little. "Not bad."

Then I turned around, and as I pulled another ball out of my pocket, I said, "But I get to try again, right?" Thinking, *And here comes the bullshit.*

Eddie held out his hand, palm up, toward the tee box. "Be my guest."

I still had trouble believing this. I took another swing, this time as hard as I possibly could, knowing the first ball would play just fine and I didn't need any safe shots to protect me. This time I cleared over 300 yards, but the intended fade was more of a slice, and I was in the rough.

The next time I eased up slightly and got 290, but safely on the fairway, and my last shot was a real screamer that drew too much to the left, this time deep into the woods.

"You bring enough balls?" Eddie asked amiably.

"Plenty," I answered with equivalent good cheer.

We hefted the bags and took off. I dropped my bag down and walked to pick up the two visible balls I wasn't going to use, not bothering to hunt in the woods for the last shot.

Eddie waited for me, and we stopped at his ball. He had about 225 to go to reach the green. He chose a five-wood and hit a very pretty shot, landing three feet off the dance floor on the left side. It was a makable par opportunity. Then we went to the ball I decided play, the 290-yard drive sitting on the right side of the fairway. I had 185 to go.

First I placed a ball marker about six inches to the right of my ball so I would be able to tell where to put the balls for my other tries. I took out a five-iron and hit, ending up about ten feet off the green, on the side opposite where Eddie was lying.

"Crappy," I said, pulling another ball out of my bag. I placed it as close to where the first ball had been as I could, then hit the five-iron again. This time I hit the green, maybe twenty-five feet from the pin.

"Should be able to do better than that," I said, reaching for a third ball.

Eddie nodded enthusiastically. "Whaddaya got to lose?"

"Yup." I hit again, this time landing about ten feet from the flag. Then once again, ending up not much closer to the pin than my second shot.

"That oughta do it," I said, unable to keep the smugness out of my voice.

But Eddie was not to be dismayed. "Yup. Lookin' good, Al. Play this format a lot, I see."

At the green, Eddie chipped to within four feet, then went ahead and putted out for his par.

I took my time with the ten-footer, missed but saw the line, tried again and drained it. Birdie.

"Nicely done," Eddie said as he wrote down the scores on a sheet he'd pulled out of his back pocket.

I was up one.

Number two was a par-five, a 590-yard monster with a dogleg right about 320 out. One of the five strokes per side I was giving Eddie came on this hole, so I had to beat him by two to win it, or by one to tie. Eddie hit another nice drive, again about 250 yards, keeping it left so he'd have a way around the dogleg.

Not wanting to lose my head, I hit my first drive safe, about 280 and also slightly left. With a good one sitting in my pocket, I was able to whale away at the next three shots with abandon, doing everything I could to get past those trees. My second shot ended up in the woods, and the third, a cannon that actually put me just about past the trees, nevertheless ended up in the rough. The fourth was useless. It would be a tough call which one I'd play of the first and third.

Eddie hit a good three-wood that got him within 120 of the green. I knew after taking a look at the ball in the rough that there was no way I could put it onto the green, so I elected to be smart and play from my 280-yarder. I hit a three-wood just like Eddie had, but got myself within 70 of the green.

With nothing to lose now, I pulled out my driver and smacked my second try with everything I had. It hooked badly, splashing into the creek running alongside the rough over on the left. I hit the driver again, but took a little dirt, sending the ball less than 200 yards. For my fourth shot, I concentrated as hard as I ever have and hit the driver so clean and pure, damned if the ball didn't fly its way to maybe 40 yards in front of the green.

"Holy shit!" Eddie said, grinning like a schoolboy. "Wun'ta believed it, I hadn'a seen it with my own eyes!"

I turned around as casually as I could, slipping the head cover over the driver and placing it gently back in my bag. "Yeah, I liked that one."

Eddie easily plopped his ball onto the green with his pitching wedge. I hit four with my sand wedge and got one of them less than five feet from the pin. Once again, Eddie parred and I birdied, but because he got a stroke, we tied the hole. Or "halved" it, as we golfers put it.

I won the next one, which Eddie didn't stroke, so I was now up two after three holes.

This was getting embarrassing.

It went on pretty much like that for the next three holes. I birdied them all, Eddie parred them all. He stroked two of those, so I was up three at this point. I was having a good time, smacking hell out of balls without worrying too much about what happened to them, hitting enough beauties to ensure a birdie on every hole.

I started to notice Eddie's game a little bit more. It wasn't spectacular, but it was practically flawless. He didn't make mistakes and seemed to have a definite plan for every shot, always doing what he intended to do. He was deliberate.

Too deliberate. I was killing him, and Eddie was still being conservative, admittedly playing excellent golf, especially on such a long course, but I had this strange feeling I wasn't seeing his best game. Was he sorry now he'd made the bet, and too timid to pull out the stops and try to catch up to me?

"Eddie," I called out as we pulled up to the seventh tee and set our bags down. My back was starting to ache a little from all that whacking at the ball I was doing, as well as all the extra walking around to pick up the ones I wouldn't be using, so I sat on the bench alongside the tee box. "Wanna have some fun?"

"Fun, how?"

I thought about it for a few seconds. "You're down three, right?"

He nodded, not having to look at the scorecard.

"Look: Me making birdies and you pars, looks like I'm gonna be up about eight when we're all done, right?"

"Not if you get a couple eagles."

"And you could get some birdies. So what if I spot you five of those eight?"

He thought it over, probably realizing it gave him an outside chance of winning, whereas now it was completely hopeless as things stood. Of course, he also knew that I wasn't going to change the rules in his favor without some concession on his part.

Like upping the stakes. Which is what I expected him to inquire about next.

But he didn't.

"I got a different idea," he said, and I gestured for him to go on. He put his foot up on the bench and said, "Let's just double the stakes."

"And . . . ?"

"And nothin'. We just keep playing. For ten large."

I couldn't have heard that right. "What the hell are you talkin' about?"

"Just what I said. I'll even go you one better: Twenty grand says I beat you straight up."

I felt something cold crawl across my back. I literally shivered. "No strokes?"

"No strokes. Take 'em all back, 'cept what you already gimme. You start off up three on me."

I was clearly playing with a lunatic, and I realized that Eddie probably didn't have a pot to piss in and couldn't even pay off the original five thousand. "You plannin' to bolt on me, bud?"

He was ready for that, and walked back to his bag after laying his club against the bench. He reached into one of the outside pockets for his wallet. He opened it as he came back and counted off four bills, then pulled them out and laid them on the bench next to me.

They weren't bills. They were four cashier's checks, fully negotiable, for five thousand each.

"How many a'these you carry round?" I asked, buying time to try to cope with this madness.

"A few. Whaddaya say?"

I fingered the checks. "You wanna play me straight up for twenty large."

"That's the bet."

"And I'm already up three."

"Yup."

"And if you're bullshittin' me, I can call it off."

"Uh-huh."

He was starting to piss me off. "You got it."

I scooped up the checks and started to hand them back, but he turned away and said, "You hold 'em." Then he grabbed his club and walked back toward the tee box.

I got up off the bench, leaning left and right a few times to try to get the kinks out of my back and shoulders. I wasn't used to hitting that many woods and long irons—so far that I must've hit sixty or so as hard as I possibly could—and I needed a moment to work out the stiffness.

"Gimme a sec," I called out.

"Take your time," he yelled back. "I'm in no hurry."

The seventh was a par-three, 220 yards. I got one of my four tee shots within fifteen feet and sank the putt on the third try for a birdie. Eddie put his tee shot twenty feet out and two-putted for another par. I was now up four.

Eddie would have stroked eight and nine, but he gave those up when we changed the bet. I had an anxiety attack as he pulled out his driver at the number-eight tee box, thinking I'd been hustled and he was going to hit the damned thing 340 down the middle, but once again he hit a safe 250, just as he'd been doing all day. I only managed a par on the hole, and he halved it with his own par. I birdied nine, but so did he, and that was another half.

We finished the front nine with me still up four. I was now pretty certain that this clown's ego had cost him a whole bunch of money. I also thought that the reason he had to carry around cashier's checks was because he'd made so many dumb bets nobody would trust his markers anymore.

But, shit, my back was really hurting now.

I asked Eddie if he needed to stop in at the clubhouse as we made the turn, but he said no, so I said I didn't, either. The bag on my shoulder was getting heavier, like somebody had put cinder blocks in it, which is when I noticed Eddie was using one of those deals with straps like a backpack. It hung behind you instead of over a shoulder, perfectly balanced so you hardly felt the weight. I spied some pull carts near the starter's shack, and looked at them longingly, but if Eddie could carry his bag, so could I.

I shifted the bag to my left shoulder, and we trudged to the tenth. I didn't feel like talking, but I wanted Eddie to be yakking, maybe tire himself out a little.

"How come you never went on the tour Eddie? You got a pretty good game . . ."

"Not interested."

"You could make a lot of money."

"I don't need that much money. Too much work, not enough fun, too much time away from home sleeping in hotels and eating room service, forced to hang around with guys I may not like but have to be nice to anyway. Too many goddamned rules, too many bullshit traditions you gotta memorize."

"Sounds to me like you think you couldn't qualify."

"Think so?"

"Uh-huh."

Eddie told me why I was wrong about that, after which I sighed as I surveyed the tenth hole, another big par-five, and hoped Eddie hadn't heard my exhalation.

"You okay?" he asked.

"Am I okay? Whaddaya mean, am I okay?"

I popped the bag off my shoulder, trying to pretend it was weightless and I was an Olympic power lifter, jauntily reached for my driver and walked briskly to the tee box.

"You want, you can grab one'a them pullcarts," he said, no guile in his voice.

I snorted my derision at the notion. "What the hell for?"

I stepped smartly to the markers and teed up my ball, grunting slightly as I rose. I took a deep breath and tried to look effortless as I swung, but nothing felt right, and I hooked it badly to the left, right into some of that goddamned useless flower landscaping greenskeepers and beautification committees seem to find so freaking appealing.

"Fuck!" I hissed angrily.

Eddie was reading the back of the scorecard for the local rules. "Free lift," he said. "So you don't wreck the petunias, I guess."

Meaning I could drop it out of the flower bed without penalty. But it was much too far to the left, so I hit another one, shanking it barely 150 yards. Then another, hooking it *over* the flower beds and into a fenced area where power mowers were kept. Finally, I slowed way down and knocked one only 220 yards or so, but at least it was in the middle and playable.

Eddie politely said nothing, and I bit my tongue as he hit one of those goddamned exasperating, goddamned boring, goddamned 250-yard pieces of shit right smack in the middle of the fucking fairway. I couldn't even rouse myself to say, "Nice shot," but what the fuck; it was the same "nice shot" he'd already hit eight times, so what was the goddamned point anyway?

I hesitated before reaching down to pick up my bag, the damned thing looking like a fully loaded rail car to me now, but somehow I hoisted it onto my shoulder, then hustled to catch up with Eddie, who was already thirty yards down the fairway.

"Don'tcha wanna pick up your other balls?" he asked.

I didn't answer, but just kept walking straight ahead. We got to my ball first, and my automatic reflex was to reach for the driver, but I changed my mind and hit the three-wood instead, maybe 220 and a little to the right of where I would have liked. Eddie waited patiently for me to take my other shots, but I just stood there, then said, "Ah, shit, that's good enough," and put the club back in the bag.

Eddie also hit a three-wood, but his went 225 and, once again, dead straight.

My back was killing me. Muscles I never even knew I had were screaming at me. I guess I must have mumbled something about it, because Eddie nodded sympathetically and said, "The hell'd you expect, Al? You already played enough shots for thirty-six holes."

He was right. That's a lot of damned golf, and there were still eight holes to go. When we got to my ball, a sudden feeling of depression overwhelmed me and I got a severe case of the dreads. I didn't want to hit it.

But I'm a champion, and I roused myself, hitting a conservative wedge just so I wouldn't have to hit again. I landed on the front edge of the green and, again, declined to take my other shots.

Eddie also hit a wedge, a soft-handed, high-flying creampuff that landed less than four feet from the pin and checked up perfectly, moving barely an inch from where it had landed.

I two-putted for par, Eddie knocked his in for birdie, and my lead was down to three. It went down to two on the next hole, where Eddie parred and I bogeyed. Yeah, I'm scrambling four balls and I bogeyed, but I was in some real pain now, liberally laced with total exhaustion. I rallied on twelve and we halved the hole, then he beat me again on thirteen and I was ready to lie down right there on the green and sleep for three days.

Eddie won fourteen and fifteen to take a one-hole lead. I couldn't even see straight. That sonofabitch, without saying a word, actually carried my bag for me to the sixteenth tee, then set it down and said, "Uh-oh."

I was too weak to ask what was wrong, but he pointed somewhere to the northeast and said, "Somebody knows you're here."

With effort, I lifted my head and spotted a group of maybe ten or twelve people about 300 yards away. They seemed excited, and were pointing toward us. I hung my head again. "Shit."

"Wanna quit?" he said.

"I can't."

He knew what I meant. "Sure you can. We'll look all disgusted, like we been havin' a good time until those bozos came and loused it up." He looked over at me. "'Less you still think you can win this game."

Win it? I wasn't sure I could make it to the tee markers twelve feet away. I waited a few more seconds to make it look like there was actually a decision that had to be made, then nodded my agreement without looking at him, and took a few minutes to gather my strength.

When the mini-mob was only a hundred yards away, I stood up straight and hefted the bag, adopted an appropriately disgusted and annoyed look, then turned and walked off the tee toward the clubhouse, Eddie in tow.

" 'Course I don't got twenty large on me," I said, dipping into my pocket for his cashier's checks and handing them back to him. While I was willing to quit playing and forfeit the match, there was no way I could take advantage of Eddie's offer to call off the bet if I felt I'd been misled. He'd been a hundred percent straight up, no tricks, just like he said.

"Din't expect you would. Your marker's good with me, Al."

I wished I was dead.

CHAPTER FIVE

Next morning I felt like I'd been trampled by a herd of rhino. I had a massage scheduled, but I cried uncle five minutes into it, paid the guy and limped back to my hotel room. Things started coming back to me now, little things, like Eddie so casually saying we ought to carry our own bags and play a long course if we were going to bet serious money. It had felt like seventeen thousand yards to me, not seven thousand.

There was a message waiting for me, from Gregory Russell. I'd called his agent the night before and offered Greg the last spot on the Ryder Cup team. My conversation with him pretty well summed up the one I had a few minutes later with Jimmy Treville as well.

"We're all trained from day one to play for ourselves, Al," Greg said. "We know how to take disappointment, lick our wounds and come back for a second try if we blow it. Sure, it hurts, but there's no guilt, because the only ones affected are ourselves. But let the team down? Holy shit. No way we're prepared for that one. And with my game, there's no telling what I'll do on any given day."

Something about the tone of his voice told me that it would no good to argue with him. I did anyway, just to let him know he was appreciated and wanted, but my initial instinct had been correct.

"Can't do it, Al. I'm really sorry. Hope you understand . . ."

He'd given me a good speech, and entirely rational. But there's one little thing I may have forgotten to mention: The prevailing wisdom was that the Americans hadn't a prayer in hell of beating the Euros this year. They were fielding a team as good as any in Ryder history, a bunch of guys who'd dominated the sport for the past eighteen months to the extent that their top five guys combined had won more money than our top *ten* combined. And who wanted to play on a losing team? The ten qualifiers really had little choice, and also probably figured that they wouldn't get too much shit for losing if they put on a good enough effort, but the two discretionary picks?

It was months away, and already I was in deep doo-doo.

The round with Eddie continued to haunt me all morning. It wasn't so much that I fell for the cleverest hustle I'd ever heard of. I could chalk that off to an expensive learning experience and probably even win it back pulling it on some other unsuspecting pro. (We've been known, in exceedingly rare moments of weakness, to wager small denominations just for fun.) Besides, to be immodest for a moment, twenty grand was barely a rounding error on my balance sheet, although I'd have to come up with some explanation for my accountant that was less acutely humiliating than having lost it to the golfing equivalent of a bag lady.

It also wasn't how well this unknown played. It was hard to recall any heroics or evening-news replay shots but, through sixteen holes, he had played at three under par from the back tees. Without fireworks, he had methodically demolished one of the longer tracks in the state, one that he hadn't even set eyes on before stepping up to the first tee. He'd done it simply by not making any mistakes. Other than one or two approaches to the green that could have been closer to the flag for a better birdie opportunity, every shot he hit went just about where he wanted it to. Like that seven-iron he'd been hitting on the range. Pure precision golf. And, with what must have been a lot of money to him on the line, he hadn't gotten ruffled at all, at least not outwardly.

No, what really haunted me was that he *knew* he was going to beat me. Down four with nine holes left to play and he bets me another fifteen grand. He knew he was good enough to do that, even if I'd somehow managed not to crap out after the equivalent of four full rounds of golf. Not only that, he knew enough about me and my game by then to know I wasn't likely to pull off any miracles that would upset his plans. Or maybe it was that he knew his show of strength and confidence would put a kink in my own game, make it impossible for me to recover. Could he do that? Was he that savvy? And how would he know even before we started playing that it was safe to be caught four strokes down halfway through the round?

Hell, I don't know. A guy could go crazy trying to figure all of that out. Maybe that's the whole point, making the other guy go crazy trying to figure it out so he loses his concentration, loses focus. Maybe—

See what I mean? You just never knew with Eddie, and it was damned disturbing. God only knows what he could've done to me had we bumped the stakes up even higher.

I called the Embassy and got put through to the bar. Danny answered, and I said hello.

"Hi, Al. How you doin'?"

"Fine, thanks. Say, is Eddie around?"

"Believe he's out on the course. Wanna leave a message?"

I told him no, I had a plane to catch, but tell him I said so long.

"Okay. So you gonna play him?"

I stared down at the phone: Eddie hadn't even mentioned our round yesterday. Just another day at the office? "Don't know. Take care of yourself, okay?"

"Sure. Nice meetin' you, Al."

I hung up and dropped back—gingerly—against the padded head-board.

A truly insane idea was beginning to form in the back of my head.

CHAPTER SIX

Two months to go. I was getting big heat for not having chosen our twelfth man. While I hadn't yet announced my selection of the perennially optimistic and cheerful Mack Merriwell, I'd let it slip, on purpose, that it was a done deal, figuring I'd cut the lobbying in half once everybody knew there was only one slot open instead of two.

Some figuring. I was assaulted on all sides by managers, wives, girlfriends, golf instructors and lawyers on behalf of every starving pro who'd barely made it through the PGA qualifying gauntlet and could still swing a club without falling over. And that wasn't counting the agents representing the legitimate contenders, former superstars and tournament winners who'd simply had an off year and hadn't made the top ten on the points list. Those were the hardest to fend off, and it got so I was afraid even to show up at some clubs for fear of running into a guy I really liked, and who wouldn't say a word to me about "it" but whose eyes would say it all.

Toughest of all was Stephen "Boom-Boom" Harriman, a six-foot-four bear of a man who could hit the ball so hard you hoped he checked it before his next shot to make sure he hadn't torn the cover off. Trouble was, the ball sometimes crossed four fairways on its way to wherever it was going, which could easily be in a different area code.

That wasn't the only trouble, though. Harriman drank. He was one of those exasperating "functional alcoholics" whose skills didn't seem to get impaired when his blood-alcohol level climbed into the flammable range. Equally exasperating was his ability to lay off the sauce for days at a time without getting the shakes. Somehow, just knowing that he could have a drink if he wanted one was enough to hold him off for a while.

While Boom-Boom could still golf under the influence (sportswriters termed it GUI), the booze did things to his personality. If he duffed an important one, you didn't want to be occupying the same airspace in case he decided that this might be an opportune moment to break something close at hand. He had already settled three civil suits by fans who had objected to his indiscriminate imposition of blame on them according to some process only Harriman understood but which closely approximated random chance.

When he put his mind to it, Harriman was one fantastic golfer, capable of not only nuclear-powered drives but surprisingly soft and delicate approach shots. He was a thing of beauty around the green, that giant ape, lobbing wedges so gently you barely knew a ball had been hit. He'd won the U.S. Open and the PGA Championship once each and a handful of the lesser tour events. He had also quit midway through a number of tournaments and gotten disqualified from some others. He spent as much time under suspension as he did on active duty, but they couldn't ban him from the game because the citizens were absolutely gaga over the guy. Tournament organizers paid him huge appearance fees because he brought out the crowds, probably the same way pit-bull fights and hockey games did.

Most of his fellow golfers liked him. He was genial and generous, going out of his way to put younger players at ease, offering insightful tips to the veterans and generally spreading good cheer by dint of his expansive spirit.

But they were also nervous around him, because whatever it was that triggered his tantrums, its major component was unpredictability. You could razz Boom-Boom's ass with a barrage of vicious insults, kid him about his drinking, his temper, whatever, and he'd just throw it right back at you, or at worst get you in a headlock complete with noogy. He could even blow half a dozen easy shots in a row and just make stupid faces and laugh them off.

But once in a while—thankfully, pretty rarely—he'd mess up a drive or a chip or hear a camera click or some idle comment from the crowd and unravel right in front of your eyes. Usually he'd throw a club, or pound the ground with it, or break it over his knee, or once in a while he'd give his whole bag a mighty heave into the nearest water hazard. Sometimes he'd throw it at an official, or take out after a fan, or turn to a network camera pointed at him and hurl a stream of obscenities too fast for the guy in the control van to cut it off before a good number of them streamed out over the airwaves into homes all over America, as irrevocable as a SAC bomber without the right recall codes.

Boom-Boom was a damned fine golfer, all right, and he was welcome to behave like a complete schmuck when his own ass was on the line, but I couldn't see risking the Ryder Cup on the ungrounded assumption that, for this contest, he'd behave himself, and I generally let that be known, at least among the eleven players who already had their slots.

"I just can't believe he'd misbehave were he playing for a team and not just for himself," Fred Asphal said.

"How do you know?" I asked.

"Just a feeling." Asphal scratched the side of his patrician nose. "But I know Harriman pretty well."

He already knew how lame that sounded, and I didn't respond. Asphal himself was an exciting competitor and a well-liked guy on tour. Only five-foot-six, the little pecker could outdrive most guys half a foot taller. He had nerves of steel and the ability to focus with great intensity when the chips were on the line. An ideal Ryder Cup player, if you didn't count his penchant for taking totally insane chances when there was no real reason to.

Unlike his colleagues, many of whom had risen from modest circumstances and still liked to affect the air of working-class stiffs to counterbalance any lingering perception of golf as a snooty rich-man's sport, Asphal really was born with a silver five-iron in his hand. Pater, a partner in the stuffy New York law firm of Dewey, Fuck'em and Howe or something like that, was one of the original founding members of the Little Storping on the Swuff Golf and Polo Club in Greenwich, Connecticut. Mater, on the board of every important art gallery between Fiftyeighth and Ninetieth along Madison Avenue in Manhattan, portrayed herself a caring philanthropist of the first water, despite considering raising money for a new tennis cabana at the Yale Junior League Summer Camp to be on a par with the very best works of Mother Teresa.

Fred Asphal—in actuality Frederick Olmsted Asphal II, preferring to be called Frederick, so we called him Freddy—figured that if every downtrodden ethnic subculture in the country could invent a romantic history for itself and then proudly trumpet their roots at every opportunity, then he damned well could, too. After all, why should he be any more ashamed of his heritage than some potato eater freshly landed in the New World only in this century?

So Asphal dressed in expensive if understated clothes, attended the kinds of parties where the food was expensive but you had to grab a pizza on the way to keep from fainting of starvation before the night was over, and used his own 1937 Parker Duofold to sign autographs. He also made sure to speak prep school English at all times, even among his golfing buddies, most of whom thought Eton was something you did at mealtimes.

We were sitting, the few of us on the team who weren't up to our asses trying to squeeze a few last bucks out of the season doing corporate outings, in a private room of the clubhouse at the Crystal Canyon Country Club in Palm Desert, California, right next door to Palm Springs. Since the Ryder was to be played in the desert, we were trying to get acclimated to the dry heat as well as to each other. Also, desert courses got little play during the summer, so we had more privacy to practice. Crystal was well on the short side as far as tournament play was concerned, but it was a beautiful layout of twenty-seven holes demanding all kinds of shot-making ability. To work on the long game, we could head out to one of the courses at PGA West in nearby La Quinta.

But right now all we were working on was what to do about Boom-Boom Harriman.

Joel Fleckheimer, the greatest golfer never to win not only a major but *any* tour event, said, "I don't know the guy, so maybe it isn't for me to say, but with all the steady players who got their heads screwed on right, why go for Harriman? What's he bring to the party other guys can't?"

It was a good question, and there was an answer, but nobody could, or was willing to, articulate it. Stephen "Boom-Boom" Harriman was a kind of pet project to the tour players. Everybody wanted him to succeed, to kick the booze for good, to get a grip on his inexplicable self-destructive behavior. Every time he strayed, they forgave him and welcomed him back. Now some of them thought the Ryder Cup was just the ticket to complete his rehabilitation.

"Might could help us win," said Merriwell. "Sumbitch sure can play some golf."

Fleck was reluctant to argue the other side, much as I could tell he wanted to. He had just finished an extraordinary year, number one on the money list, but hadn't a single outright win. You could do that if you placed in the top five in nearly everything you entered.

Some of the other guys knew that Fleck had a legitimate point, and they appreciated that he felt a little out of place—Harriman had won two events to Fleck's none—although nobody thought it was warranted.

What they didn't know was that I was more than willing to sound them out on this issue, in the interests of team-building and because I did value their opinions, but the fact was, I'd already decided on the twelfth man. I really wasn't here to solicit their insights; I was here to sell them on mine. Even though it was entirely up to me, I didn't want to ram it down their throats by executive fiat. Unless I had to.

"Sometimes," Asphal said to Fleckheimer, "one must assume some risk, rather than play it safe all the time."

Thank you, Freddy! Biggest risk-taker in the sport. "Speaking of risk," I said, "I had an entirely different thought in mind. Little on the wacky side, but . . ."

I let it hang there for a second, knowing exactly what they were thinking, that the old man himself is going to take the last slot. But that wasn't it. I'd decided long ago that I couldn't play and captain at the same time. It was way too complicated and tricky, especially if I didn't play well in the early matches but still had to coach the others to do better. "There's this guy," I began. "He's not on the tour . . ."

That got their attention, and a few of them exchanged wary looks.

"What's his name?" Merriwell asked.

I cleared my throat. "Eddie Caminetti."

"I'm unfamiliar with the name," Asphal said.

"No surprise. Never heard of him myself, till just a little while ago."

"What's this about, Al?" Fleck had narrowed his eyes, trying to pick up on the real scoop behind this absurdity.

"It's about getting a guy on the team who can help us win, but who may not be a flash-bang superstar like you guys." A mild barb to get them off the track that said you had to be front-page news to be a good golfer.

Enrico Senzamio, who had come to the United States from Palermo for a tournament twelve years ago and never left, said, "What, Alonzo: You gonna sit there like-a some fokking mystery guy or you gonna tell us what'sa what, eh?" Rico hadn't had much trouble assimilating into our culture once his citizenship papers had come through.

"Caminetti, Caminetti . . ." Merriwell said to himself, frowning. "I know that name from somewhere."

"Pretty well known in Florida. Maybe you ran into him down there once."

Merriwell shook his head. "Not it. I know the name from somewhere, though. Damn . . ."

"I'll tell you what's what, Rico," I said, turning away from Merriwell. "This guy, the one down in Florida, I think this guy could whip half the guys on tour at a moment's notice, but he just never wanted to play in the show."

"Why not?" Merriwell asked.

I tried to explain, as Eddie had to me, but it didn't come out the way it had when he'd explained it, and I don't think they bought it. We argued back and forth, only Fleckheimer staying quiet. Merriwell scratched his head a little, still trying to figure out where he'd heard the name.

When we had settled down, Fleck said, "You mean you're really serious about this?"

The other guys had easily fallen into a spirited debate, but Fleck, ever thoughtful and analytical, just as he was about his game, and despite his penchant for practical jokes and the issuance of particularly scathing insults, had correctly perceived the real issue and could care less about Eddie Caminetti's take on the life of a pro golfer.

I nodded in response to his question. "Dead serious, Fleck." I didn't have to add that it was totally up to me. They knew that, but as long as I was inviting comments, they were happy to give me theirs.

"You saying he's better than Koovitz? Better than Russell, Treville, Delmondo?"

He'd just named four guys in the top twenty, acknowledged masters of the game and obvious front-runners, at least in the public's mind, for the twelfth position. Tony Delmondo had started the season late, following a rough ride with prostate cancer, but had come out of the gate well, and there was a reasonable chance he'd have been on the list had he played a full season.

Greg Russell, a somewhat erratic player, had taken off a lot of time to be with his dying father. Jimmy Treville had played in a series of events in which he had just one disastrous hole each, but enough to put him out of contention. In match-play format, like the Ryder, they would hardly have mattered at all. And Lester Koovitz had entered into a lucrative endorsement contract with a clubmaker, not realizing until seven events later that their clubs were all wrong for him. By the time he managed to negotiate his way out of the deal—he threatened to tell the whole world exactly why he kept losing—he was way behind on the money list.

All were exceptional golfers and good guys. Any one of them would have been a credit to the Ryder team. But while I wished Delmondo and Koovitz all the luck in the world, I couldn't see risking the Ryder Cup on inherently unknowable factors. Where was Delmondo's head and skills, and could Koovitz work the rust out of his old clubs quickly enough? The citizens would applaud my sensitivity and Christian charity for about a day, then would tear me to shreds in September if we lost the Cup.

And what my teammates didn't know, and what I was morally bound not to tell them, was that I'd already offered the spot to both Treville and Russell, who, shockingly, had turned me down, Russell because of the complete unpredictability of his game, Treville because, as he'd put it, who was to say that one disaster per eighteen wouldn't multiply into two or four at the Ryder?

Which was when I'd suddenly gotten desperate to find a twelfth player, which was less than twenty-four hours after Eddie Caminetti walked into my life.

"I don't know," I said in answer to Fleck's question. "But what I *am* saying, the man is not only a terrific golfer, he's steady as a rock. Doesn't seem to feel pressure."

"People like that are at risk," Asphal said, "often doing things like grinding their teeth at night. Pressure always requires an outlet."

"What do I care what he does to his teeth at night, long as he gets the job done during the day?"

"Whaddaya mean, he don' feel pressure?" Senzamio challenged me. "The guy ever play in front of a *pazzo* mob? Ever hadda put-a for two hunnerd g's?"

I recalled how Lee Trevino had once defined pressure when asked how he could stand up to the rigors of top-level competition. Lee said *real* pressure was when you were playing a five-dollar Nassau with only two bucks in your pocket. Imagine Eddie Caminetti, driving a decades-old car, putting twenty grand on the line.

The objections came flying fast now. "What inclines you to infer he's so good?" Asphal asked. "Have you ever observed his play?"

I nodded. "He was three under at Seminole through fifteen."

The room quieted noticeably. "What tees he play?" Senzamio asked. "The tips."

Fleckheimer started chewing a fingernail. "Really?"

"Gesù Cristo," Senzamio murmured.

Three under after fifteen holes at Seminole would have been a good day for any man in this room. Suddenly, nobody had anything to say. "So, whaddaya think?" I prompted.

There was a lot of scratching of beard stubble, shuffling of feet, throat clearing and the like, but no spoken responses. I knew what they were thinking, that it sounded a little less ridiculous now, but all they had to go on was my say-so on a single outstanding round. And that in itself wasn't enough to win them over.

Fleckheimer dropped a hand on the table with a loud thump that startled us all. "I got an idea."

He looked around to make sure everybody was paying attention, then he looked up at me. "Let him play The Kid."

CHAPTER SEVEN

The Kid, of course, was Derek Anouilh (pronounced "on-WE," like the playwright), a barely pubescent drink of water fresh off the boat from Borneo. He was destined to be the greatest golfer in history someday, but at one time he'd been convinced he already was.

That was before his breakdown.

Back then, The Kid hardly opened his mouth but what a sound bite programmed by his aunt didn't pop out. They had to stop scheduling him onto different talk shows in the same time period, because his adoring public was starting to catch on that he was a kind of human compact disc. People who watched him on all the shows, it got so they could mouth all the answers right along with Derek as he spoke them. He even giggled in the same spots, and would start yapping about "his dream" at the slightest provocation, like some Olympic figure-skating Barbie doll or a presidential candidate gushing "hope, growth and opportunity" even when he was ordering eggs.

So Auntie started spreading out his television appearances so they could custom-tailor each one and cut down on the repetition. America ate it up, especially after Auntie hired a public-relations psychologist from a political consulting firm, teamed him up with a pollster from Yankelovich and wired up The Kid to always say the right thing according to the prevailing social mood of whatever region he was in. For national spots, he'd say nothing, and make it sound so damned profound and wise and mature for a kid his age ("That's the thing about golf, Bob, you know? Any given day, no matter how good you been playing, it can leave you just like that. Keeps you humble, let me tell you [mile-wide grin] . . ."), he could start his own goddamned church—if he had the time and somebody paid him. It got so crazy they even had him make some social gaffes on purpose, just so he could publicly apologize and raise his Q ratings through the roof.

The citizenry sucked it all up, totally addicted to it. They knew it was bad for them, suspected some of the bullshit behind it, but they just couldn't stop. Hardly anybody asked any questions about a television special so laudatory you could get cavities watching the damned thing, even when it leaked out that it had been produced by his agent and scripted by Auntie. Even people who criticized him publicly secretly tuned in to watch him play.

America lapped it up, all right, but the pros on the tour didn't. They didn't like it when The Kid forgot there were other golfers on the course during his post-victory interviews, when he talked only about his own game, his own shots, as though it had been just him against the course, and wouldn't we all be a lot better off if they just cleared out the other competitors who were only slowing things down?

And they didn't like it when they started to find their careers and themselves being defined in terms of Derek Anouilh. "You were three behind Anouilh today, Bill. How you feel about that?" Or, "Think that drive on seventeen had a little Derek Anouilh in it, way it faded right with the wind?" Or, "Heckuva round today, Freddy. Think you'd be leading if Derek was playing in this tournament?"

At some point, and it's difficult to pin down exactly when, word somehow flashed around the tour, fast, like one of those chemicals dumped into your bloodstream by some gland in your brain, the kind that hits every cell at once. And suddenly Derek was getting a less obvious version of what they called "silencing" at West Point. Other guys barely spoke to him in the locker rooms, wouldn't give him the time of day on the course. No "Nice shot" or "Well struck!" or any sympathy on the rare occasions when he duffed one.

Nothing. Zippo. And goddamn if The Kid didn't even notice at first. How do you get to a guy, he doesn't give a shit about you in the first place?

Until he noticed that his occasional, obligatory attempts at some communication were being rebuffed with minimalist responses. He was used to people trying to get close to him, to be his buddy, people blabbering away idiotically whenever he deigned to dole out the barest snippet of his attention to them, however fleetingly. What he wasn't used to was people tossing a perfunctory "Uh-huh" or "Yup" or "Nope" and then walking away. He started to notice.

Auntie didn't, at least not then. But soon, every time a fellow pro was asked on television about Anouilh, all he said was, "Oh, he's so terrific." Didn't matter what the question was, the answer was always the same. "Oh, he's so terrific, Jim." Meaning, *Fuck you, Jim, what're you askin' me for?*

Really meaning, *Fuck you, Derek.*

Over and over again—*Oh, he's so terrific*—with a great big, sincere smile, so no one could ever accuse them of meanness or spite. "Why ya think he missed that putt on twelve, Greg?"

"Oh, he's so terrific."

Eventually, The Kid snapped. And, never having done anything half-assed in his life, he snapped good. Canceled out of three events, went into a near-clinical depression, almost killed his sports psychologist, whose job, after all, wasn't about ensuring that Derek Anouilh was a happy and well-adjusted human being, it was about making sure he won tournaments. The therapist's recommended cure for Anouilh was to get himself right back out there on the tour where he was happiest, goshdarn it, start winning again and reassert himself! It went without saying that Anouilh's contract with Exxon, which gave the corporation an out if he missed four events in a row, hadn't a thing to do with it.

Anouilh launched a few pair of spiked shoes at the psychologist, but therapists can take all kinds of abuse—after all, they're trained to treat all hostility as manifestations of some terrible shit in their patients and never take it personally—and this one eventually convinced The Kid, who roused himself and showed up for the Kemper Open. Just before the first round, he went to his locker, opened it and found every club in his bag snapped cleanly in half.

He stood there, in mortal shock, so blown away he didn't even hear the shuffling sounds behind him. He slowly reached inside the locker and picked up one of the clubs, looked at it closely and realized it wasn't his, just a look-alike knockoff. He picked up another one; also a knockoff, just like all the rest.

He stood there, rolling the half-shafted five-iron back and forth in his hand, and then, very slowly, the beginnings of a smile tickled the corners of his mouth. As he looked at more clubs, the smile widened, then he started giggling, and pretty soon the shuffling noises behind him turned into giggles as well.

One by one, the top players in the Open started to file into the locker room, Merriwell, Asphal, Fleckheimer and I among them. Without a word being said, they were soon pretty much doubled over, Anouilh himself laughing so hard tears started to flow down his face. Pretty soon he was able to calm himself for a few seconds, then looked out over the bunch and said, "Shitheads . . ." which touched off another round of debilitating hysterics.

The Kid went out and shot a 74, not all that terrible for his first day back and hardly any practice since his last event. Afterward, talking to a blissed-out congregation of newscasters, Anouilh said, for all the world to hear, "Most goddamned fun I've ever had playing this fucking game!" then sauntered away from the stunned worshipers to grab himself a beer and a shot with the guys.

Next three days, he shot 66–68–65 and won the Kemper, one shot ahead of Mack Merriwell. In the compulsory news conference that followed, Anouilh spoke at great length about how Merriwell had him scared, sweating, because Merriwell was such a strong player, you just never knew when he'd start pulling crucial birdies or the occasional eagle. And don't discount those other guys who were only a few shots back, he went on, because we've all seen what miracles they could pull out of their back pockets when they needed to. Remember Fleckheimer on the fourteenth at the Masters? Man oh man, don't ever write *that* guy off!

And so on. You'd have thought he took lessons from the President, the way he started looking everybody in the eye and asking personal questions. But he really did seem to care. Somehow, discovering there were other people in the world fascinated him, like opening a box of assorted chocolates and hardly knowing where to start.

Watching him play was like going to a Jimi Hendrix concert back in the old days. You never knew when he was going to be "on." And when he wasn't, it was a crashing bore. But you kept going anyway, because when he *was* on, it was positively transcendent. Same way with Anouilh: On a bad day, half the guys on the Botswana tour could beat him.

But when he had the magic, when you could almost see the rivers of electric current coursing through his body, it was as close as most of us are going to come to a truly mystical experience. In those hours and days, he ceased to be an ordinary mortal and passed over into some nether realm that language wasn't designed to describe. No golfer in the solar system could touch him. He got steely, solemn . . . not surly, not even taciturn, just, what was it . . . ?

Unconcerned. Yeah, that's it. Unconcerned with the ordinary affairs of the day and of men, as though his true abode were another plane of existence entirely, and his body were just stepping into this one long enough to hit a few golf balls while the rest of him, his mind or spirit or whatever, stayed on the other side.

Even died-in-the-wool racists were crazy about him, elevating denial to a high art by assuring themselves that he was no more than 25 percent African, which seemed to be some kind of threshold of acceptability. Tell you the truth, none of us knew for sure. Of course, half the minorities in America embraced him as their own, including every Malaysian, Tongan, French Polynesian, Hispanic and Inuit along with—get this, now—damned near every Caucasian as well. The Kid was a one-man melting pot, and if there was enough endorsement money in it, hell, he'd probably announce he was 2 percent Martian as well, and wrap up the bug-eyed alien demographic. I mean, who wouldn't? For all he knew, he could suddenly bonk some Tuesday morning and never hit a decent shot again in his life, so why not go for the gusto when he was hot? Lord knows I would.

There were times it got so intense you thought he'd crumble under the weight of it, and that's where Joel Fleckheimer came in. One of the few Jews in the upper echelons of the tour, Fleck couldn't be intimidated by Zeus himself. He could hurl insults so potent, Don Rickles was a hug therapist by comparison. Thing was, though, the guy was so lovable and lacking in guile that it was impossible to get mad at him. But anytime somebody got too pompous or full of himself, you could count on Fleck to restore his perspective in a damned hurry.

He was merciless toward everybody, but toward The Kid he was absolutely barbaric.

Fleck called Anouilh "Drek" instead of Derek, because *drek* was Yiddish for garbage or something close to that. And if The Kid had too many days in a row of fawning press and adoring fans and a sponsor-supplied phalanx of drooling sycophants, count on Fleckheimer to stick a pin in all of it.

Anouilh ate it up. It was like he was addicted to humble pie and Fleck was the only baker in town. When Anouilh ran around asking where was Joel, you knew Auntie had just given him another dose of you're-the-second-coming or some similar crap. Only Anouilh didn't call him Joel, he called him The Yid, and if you weren't clicked in, you'd've thought Harlem and Bensonhurst had declared nuclear war on each other, the way those two went at it.

Once again, Fleckheimer had managed to jump right to the logical conclusion. Nobody knew Caminetti, only I had seen him play, so stick him in the toughest match of his life and let's see how he does. Nobody expected him to beat Anouilh; they only wanted to see how he did.

From my point of view, I wasn't about to become a captain who'd started out holding the Cup and then lost it on U.S. soil. So I had no problem putting Eddie to the test.

It was an idea nobody could argue with, and nobody did.

I went back to my hotel room to phone Eddie. I was excited, like a father on Christmas Eve who's about to watch his kid setting eyes on that new bike after stringing him along for a month.

Without extraneous commentary, this is how it went to the best of my memory, which, in this particular instance, was photographic:

"Eddie. Al Bellamy."

"Hey Al, reccanized the voice. How you doin'?"

"Good. You get my check okay?"

"Yeah. Thanks."

"Well, you earned it, even if you did pull a fast one on me."

"Whud I do wasn't straight?"

"Nothing at all. Technically. But hey, I'm just jerking your chain a little."

"I know. So what's up . . . you want a rematch?"

"No way! Don't know what other kinda shit you'd spring on me! [Ha-has on both sides.] No, it's something else."

"Shoot."

[Pause.] "Eddie, how'dya like to play on the U.S. Ryder Cup team this year?"

"No thanks."

[Another pause, longer this time.] "Say what?"

"Forget it."

Forget it? "The hell d'ya mean, forget it!"

"I mean, I'm not playin' on no Ryder Cup team, or any other damned team for that matter."

"You can't be serious!"

"Sure I can."

"Eddie, listen. You sure you know what the Ryder is? It's the highest honor in the game! You'd be playing for the whole goddamned *country*, f'Chrissakes!"

"So what?"

"So what? What the hell do you mean, *so what!*"

"Al. Calm down and listen'a me. [I calm down.] I'm a hustler, 'kay? A hustler. That means I don't care about honor or fame or glory or prestige or bimbo groupies grabbin' after my ass."

"You telling me you don't got an ego?"

"Hell, I got an ego big as the moon. Just doesn't work the same way as yours, is all. My big ego shot, it's beating some guy, he don't even know he's been hosed. I don't care who else knows, see? So long as *I* know."

[Insert here about ten minutes of frantic and shameless pleading on my part, interlaced with stolid refusals on his, occasionally sprinkled with some indications that he's either weakening or just tired of arguing with me.]

"Tell you what, Eddie. Help us win, you get a hundred grand. Off the books. And it's all match play. Thought you loved it that way."

"Everything I win is already off the books."

"When's the last time you took home that kinda scratch for a couple days' work? Without any risk at all?"

"No risk? It'd ruin my whole hustle, I get famous playin' on the Ryder Cup team! Who the fuck'd ever play me again?"

"Jesus, Eddie, you don't hafta beat a guy by nine strokes. String the thing out and beat him just a little. Cut it thin as you want, so long as we win. It's all or nothing: We keep the Cup or you don't get paid."

[Pause.] "So, if I lose a match early, I just go home?"

"You can't do that."

"Why not?"

"It's the goddamned Ryder Cup, f'cryin' out loud! You can't just quit in the middle!"

"Says who? Who's gonna stop me?"

"Okay. [Pause.] You play four matches, you get twenty-five large for each one you win. Even if the team doesn't keep the Cup."

"What if I only play three? What if you don't play me one day?"

"You only get seventy-five grand."

"Uh-uh. Not enough. Now you're backpedaling."

"Okay, how's this: You win every match I put you in, I guarantee the whole hundred."

"So I can go home soon's I lose one."

"No! I told you, you can't do that!"

"And I told you: Who's gonna stop me!"

[Pause, teeth gritted.] "Good point. Okay, new deal. You play every match I put you in, you get paid, win or lose, but—only if we keep the Cup."

"Even if I don't play any matches."

"Right."

[Long pause.] "Okay. When do I show up?"

"Hold it. You ain't in yet."

"What the fuck now, Al? You been bullshitting me here or what?"

"No. It's just you gotta qualify."

"Qualify. I got it. Good-bye."

"Hold it! Don't you wanna hear how?"

"No."

"Play one round with Derek Anouilh."

[Pause, a long one, with the unmistakable sound of Eddie rubbing a thumbnail across the bottom of his chin.] "For how much?"

"For how— Eddie, there's ten million guys in this country'd *pay* twenty large just to be seen on the same course with that guy! Hell, every week guys cough up nearly that much to play *me*! You completely lost your mind?"

"You lost yours? 'Cuz I'm betting the game's in California, which is gonna cost me two days, and I'm also betting you ain't footin' my expenses, so I'm askin' you, Al: How much am I playin' him for!"

"You're playin' him for the privilege of being on the— You're playin' him for a shot at a hundred-grand payday."

"What's he givin' me?"

"Nothing. You don't even gotta beat him, just put up a good fight."

"According to who?"

"According to me and a couple'a my players."

"Forget it. You actually askin' me to pay to get to my own audition, then not tellin' me what I gotta do to pass?"

"Come within six strokes of him and you're in."

"What if he has one of those ridiculous days, you know, he starts pulling those eagles out of his skinny ass?"

[Insert sound of fast thinking.] "Play the course in two under and you're in, no matter what he does."

"Then why play him?"

"See if you can take the pressure."

"What's the slope?"

"One thirty-three."

"Length?"

"Sixty-five oh five. It's a cream puff."

[Pause.] "When?"

Tuesday morning, five-fifteen. It was close to the summer solstice, so the sun was already turning the stark desert landscape into a riot of deep purples and reds even though Ol' Sol himself wasn't visible yet.

The only people here were my guys and the club pro, Fitz Gleason, who let us in this early so we wouldn't have any citizens hounding us. As we headed out of the clubhouse, I saw Eddie on the putting green, along with a Hispanic kid around thirteen or so.

"Name's Jorge something," Gleason said. "Putts around and hits balls for a couple hours before school. His old man cuts the grass here."

I walked up behind them, then stopped. Jorge bent over his putter and hit a ball toward a flag about twenty feet away along the viciously sloping green as Eddie watched. The ball missed the hole by at least a foot. "Freakin' putter!" Jorge muttered, banging the head angrily into the ground.

Hearing the little guy blame the putter seemed to press a half dozen of Eddie's buttons. As I would come to learn, his disdain for golf-equipment hype contrasted sharply with that of most amateurs, who believed nearly everything the manufacturers told them. He was fond of telling people that, despite billions in "revolutionary" clubs, balls, gloves and even tees, the average national handicap had dropped less than half a stroke in the last twenty years. If you had a driver you didn't like, he'd offer to get it sold for you for a commission, and in a hurry. All he did was wait until somebody in his foursome blew a few tee shots, then told the guy his club looked all wrong, why don't you try this one, which of course Eddie had been smacking beautifully all along. He would never do this on the range, where the guy could take dozens of shots, but during a round, when he could take only one. Inevitably, the guy would wrap his hands around the grip, flex the shaft a few times, take a few practice swings and then wallop the living hell out of the ball, believing it was the club rather than the extra concentration and focus he was bringing to the shot, not to mention a good measure of relaxation since he knew flubbing the shot with a strange club would not reflect badly on him. At that point Eddie would exclaim, "Whud I tell you, pal! *That's* the stick you wanna get yourself!" Then he'd resist all entreaties to purchase the club—"No way I'm gonna let you have that monster in the middle of a money game!"—and continue to hit it straight and far the rest of the round until the guy was practically on his knees begging for it as they walked off the eighteenth. Not only did he get top dollar for the club, but the round was also his once the guy believed that his own stick was the single most evil thing in his bag. By the time the novelty of the new club wore off and the guy had settled back into his usual crappy driving off the tee, it was way too late. If he complained, Eddie just reminded him of that awesome shot he'd hit the very first time he'd had the thing in his hands, no warm-up, no nothing. Do it once, how come you can't do it again? Sure as shit can't be the club.

With some rare but notable exceptions, Eddie thought most of the equipment hype was complete bullshit, and got particular pleasure out of "long ball" claims. In this, I was with him. It's ridiculously easy to make a ball that will travel much farther than any in existence today, but the USGA has a mechanical hitting machine called "Iron Byron." If more than a small percentage of a brand and model of balls travels farther than a preset limit, the ball is illegal for regulation play. Period. So the manufacturers aren't really trying to make the ball longer, what they're doing is trying to get it as close to Iron Byron's limit as they can without going over it. The advantage to the player, if any, is less than that from a breeze so gentle you can't even feel it.

As Eddie liked to say, It ain't the hammer, it's the carpenter. So young Jorge cursing his putter was the kind of challenge he relished. "What're you aiming at?" he asked.

"Whaddaya mean, what am I aiming at? I'm aiming at the hole!"

Eddie watched as the frustrated kid missed three more putts, then said, "Hole's twenty feet away."

"No shit, mister." Jorge set up another ball. "So what?"

"So, never aim at anything more than three feet away."

Jorge stood up and gave Eddie a look. "You want me to move the hole closer?"

"No. Aim at something else."

"Like what?"

"Like something three feet away."

"Mister, how long you been standin' out in the sun?"

Eddie knelt behind the kid's ball, took his putter and held it up, plumb-bobbing the line. "How far to the right of that hole you figure you should be heading?" he asked.

"I figure maybe four feet," the kid answered.

Eddie nodded his agreement. "Okay. C'mere."

The kid, obviously skeptical, knelt down beside Eddie and looked at the club hanging from Eddie's fingertips. Then Eddie took hold of the bottom of the putter and tilted it slightly. "That's your line to four feet right of the cup."

"Yeah . . . ?"

"Now bring your eye back until it's looking at something about three feet in front of the ball."

"Like what?"

"Like whatever the hell happens to be there."

" 'S only grass."

"Then pick a piece of grass. Or dirt, or birdshit. What the hell ever."

"Okay. I got sumpin'."

Eddie stood up and handed the kid the putter. "Aim for that."

The kid took the putter and stood over his ball, looking back and forth among the hole, the spot of grass and his ball.

"What're you lookin' at the cup for?"

"That's where I'm aiming, ain't it?"

"No, it ain't. You aim for the cup, the ball ain't goin' in. You aim for four feet right, you'll never get it there either." He pointed to a spot about three feet in front of the ball. "That spot of grass you picked out. Aim for that."

"Wasn't grass. Was gooseshit."

"Fine. Aim for the gooseshit."

The kid did it, lining up the putter behind the ball.

"You got it?" Eddie asked.

The kid nodded.

"Okay. Now look at the cup."

"What! What for?"

"No other reason than to get the distance so you know how hard to hit."

Jorge looked at the cup, then back at the ball.

"Now, make sure the putter is lined up with your spot, then look at the ball and hit it, and don't pick your head up or even look away from where that ball is right now until I tell you."

The kid drew the club back, and Eddie suddenly shouted, "Hold it!"

Startled, Jorge froze without looking up.

"What're you doing?"

Now the kid looked up. "I'm tryin' t'hit the damned ball! What're you hollerin' for?"

"Why'd you twist the club? How come you brought it back curved 'stead of straight?"

Jorge looked back at the club, then at the cup. "Don't know. Didn't know I was."

"It's because you think you need to try to make the ball go in a curve to get to the hole."

The kid shrugged.

"Two things you gotta keep in mind, son. One, you can't make the ball do anything with a putter other than go faster or slower. You can't draw it or fade it, you can only knock it off line."

Eddie pointed at the ground and moved his hand in an arc. "Second, you gotta let the green do all the work. You hit it straight, let the ground move it around. That's one of the reasons you keep your head down. Once you line up on your spot, your only job is to hit the ball right to that spot, on a straight line. That's it."

The kid thought about it for a few seconds. "But I don't think it's gonna go left enough."

"Okay, then." Eddie smiled and nodded approvingly. "That's the real problem. So you figured maybe you'd help it a little, right?"

The kid shrugged. "Guess so."

"What you gotta do, you gotta pick a different spot. Pick one you *know* you can hit straight to without trying to help the ball. You don't think that green is gonna move the ball left enough, pick a spot a little more to the left so it doesn't have to move that much."

The kid knelt back down and resurveyed the situation, then straightened up and addressed the ball again. This time, without taking his eyes off the ball, he drew the club straight back and hit the ball without moving the club off-plane. It headed well toward the right of the hole, then started drifting leftward as the tilt of the green began pushing it out of a straight line. It passed less than an inch to the right of the hole and stopped two inches beyond it. It was by far the closest he'd come yet.

He waited a moment, then another moment, then yelled "Hey!" and Eddie, who'd forgotten one of his bits of instruction, said he could pick his head up now.

Jorge's eyebrows rose after seeing where his ball ended up.

"Just a touch too hard," Eddie added gently. "Took some of the break out. Tad softer, you'da drained it."

The kid looked at Eddie. "How 'bout that!"

"Always go a touch on the high side anyway," Eddie told him as he turned at some sound and spotted me standing there.

"Whyzzat?"

" 'Cuz if you're off a little, there's always a chance it'll fall down toward the hole." As he began walking away, Eddie said over his shoulder, "Ain't a chance in hell it's ever gonna fall *up*. That's why they call it the pro side."

"Hey, wait a minute!" the kid called out, suddenly anxious not to miss out on any more of this wisdom. "What about the short ones?"

Eddie stopped and turned. "What about 'em?"

"Tell me sumpin'!" *Anything!*

Eddie thought for a minute. "Always hit 'em a little harder than you think you should."

"How come?"

"Takes the break out. Lets you hit straighter instead'a trying to plot some kinda damned satellite orbit."

"But you miss, you're gonna be way past the hole!"

"But you're gonna miss a whole lot less often." Eddie started walking away again. "Long run, works out better, believe me."

"Whaddaya say, Eddie?" I held out my hand.

Taking it, he said, "Got in yesterday afternoon, damned near burned my shoes up just walking away from the plane."

"Drink as much water as you can hold, you'll be all right. Don't wait'll you're thirsty or it's already too late."

I love playing golf in the desert during summer. The heat is totally ridiculous, but there's something otherworldly and serene about it, maybe having to do with acre after acre of lush green grass thriving in what would otherwise be a hellhole. Every day you see guys crapping out after thirteen or fourteen holes, so dehydrated they think their heads'll explode.

The simple secret is to keep sucking down as much ice water as your belly can hold, once in a while mixing in some electrolyte replacement sports drink. You can play thirty-six holes on a 115-degree day that way, and feel just fine at the end. Long as your pee is "clear and copious," as the endurance athletes like to put it, you're doing okay.

I didn't want Eddie losing it because he didn't take care of himself in the heat, so I maybe went a little overboard drilling this into him.

"Hey, lighten up, will ya, Al?" Eddie said as he soaked down his golf towel with water from one of the many plastic barrels scattered around every course in the desert. "I play in Florida damned near every day!"

"Florida's humid. It's like playing golf in a steam bath. Humidity out here's so low that towel you're holding's gonna be bone dry after three holes."

"Ah, c'mon . . ."

"Hunnerd bucks says you can't get one drop out of it on the fourth tee."

Eddie looked up at me and broke into a wide grin. "You tryin' to get some'a your money back?"

"Just want you at your best. Promise me."

He shook his head and poured more water onto the towel. "Okay, I promise. Now where's Whatsisname?"

I waved over to my guys, and Whatsisname broke away. "Eddie, this is Derek Anouilh. Derek, Eddie Caminetti."

"Whaddaya say, Derek?"

"Good. You?"

"Been up since three. Jet lag, see?"

"So, you askin' for strokes now or what?"

They laughed and sized each other up, but only for a second. The Kid's life and golfing record were about as private as a stripper's behind, and there wasn't anything he was going to learn about Eddie that I hadn't already told him, which wasn't much.

The bunch of us jumped into carts and headed over to the first tee.

CHAPTER EIGHT

Crystal Canyon has twenty-seven holes, divided into three distinct nines. We were going to be using the Lake and Mountain courses.

Number one on the Lake is a pretty par-five with a pond just before a right turn to the green around a stand of trees. Right of the trees is out of bounds, so cutting the corner on your second shot to hit the green in two isn't a good bet. It was a lot easier to smack a good drive to the left of center and then take the next shot over the water.

Derek held out his hand for Eddie to take the honors. With little preamble, Eddie teed up his ball without even asking anything about the hole. I guessed that the real reason he woke up at three was to come out here and walk the course in addition to stretching. He took a few practice swings, addressed the ball and popped it straight as an arrow about 250 down the middle.

"Nice shot," Derek offered as he moved to the tee box. He took a few practice swings as well, waggled the club once or twice, then hauled off.

I'm not normally one to wax loquacious, but you have to stand next to this string bean when he's in the zone and playing his best to understand. Something shoots off of him that's downright intimidating, even for us grizzled veterans of both honest-to-God superstars and bullshit heroes-of-the-week. You feel like, if you were to say something frivolous or inappropriate, you'd break the spell and it would all disintegrate right in front of you, and the whole world would blame you, like the lady from New York who stuck a penny in a fuse box at the exact moment the great Northeast power blackout began and was convinced she caused the whole grid to collapse. It's that fragile, that tenuous and even frightening. Here was a virtual baby who could crack dumb jokes and play video games all night long, changing into costume in some cosmic phone booth somewhere and emerging totally transformed, a Jekyll-and-Hyde metamorphosis that took your breath away. Watching him swing was like watching a bolt of silk unfurl.

His opening drive of this match sounded like a howitzer going off in the early-morning silence. At the top of its trajectory the ball caught a glimmer of the sunlight that was starting to peek out from the mountaintops to the east, and looked for a moment like a meteor burning up in the earth's atmosphere. It went 330 at least, leaving The Kid with less than 225 to the green.

"Good one yourself," Eddie said as we shook ourselves back to reality and got back into the carts—nobody in his right mind would walk this course once the sun was in the sky—and drove up to his ball. He took a seven-iron, hit it solid and laid up just to the left of the lake, leaving him maybe 120 to the elevated green.

The Kid blasted a two-iron onto the right side of the dance floor, putting him about thirty feet from the pin. Eddie got his wedge within ten feet.

The rest of us stayed in the carts and watched as Derek hit a beautiful putt to within two feet. Eddie sank his, then conceded Derek's.

They halved the hole with birdies. No blood, and we moved to number two, a 336-yard par-four with water on both sides. This time Derek went first and cracked an awesome shot that damn near rolled up onto the green, murmurs of *"Fuck me!"* burbling up from the normally jaded pros looking on. Even Eddie seemed momentarily stunned, but I was impressed when he wasn't sucked into playing outside himself, and hit a clean, safe shot that left him about 90 out.

This time, Derek took a seven-iron and chipped it so close to the pin it was a gimme birdie. Eddie hit a nice wedge, but two-putted for a par. The Kid had a one-hole lead.

They both played just beautifully. Not a bogey on the next seven holes, but as we made the turn past the clubhouse, The Kid had five birdies to Eddie's two, putting him up three for the front nine.

"Gotta tell you, Al," Merriwell said when Eddie was out of earshot. "Sumbitch can play some golf."

Mack Merriwell had come up the hard way. He'd been to Q-school four times, and three times he'd failed to make the cut. Finally, seventeen years ago, he squeaked through by the slimmest of margins, owing to some fluke that escapes my memory, and joined the tour. Mack was a grinder, a not uncomplimentary term for someone who, with steady golf rather than flash-and-sizzle, consistently stays comfortably on the money list, even winning an occasional event.

In Mack's case, owing to a relentless work ethic and keen desire to fine-tune his game, he had climbed steadily, almost unnoticeably, from the top fifty to the top forty and then, this year, to the top twenty. He never took any of it for granted, ever appreciative of the life he had, thanking his personal deity daily for the strange good fortune that had allowed him into the tour in the first place so many years ago. He was a brick, this guy, unflappable under pressure and likely to be the most reliable member of the Ryder Cup team. He was also, without question, the most preposterously happy human being I'd ever met. Nothing could faze him, not even the game of golf, which has been known to make cardinals utter the kind of expletives that had to be deleted from the Watergate tapes. That's one of the reasons I'd picked him to be our eleventh man.

I nodded at his evaluation of Eddie, not wanting anything I said or did to be construed as either gloating or boosterism. But two under for this course, for a guy who could play the way I knew Eddie could, wasn't such a big deal. I thought he could do better.

We tried to hide our faces as we passed by the clubhouse on the way to the first hole of the Mountain nine, but it was too late. There were at least a hundred people gathered around the tee box, so everybody in our little entourage tried to look grim and hostile as we pulled up, hoping that the citizens would back off a little and not interfere with us.

They didn't, at first. In fact, they were looking past us, and I turned to see Eddie and Derek standing alone on the cart path about fifty yards behind. They were engrossed in conversation, and I was glad at least to see they were getting along. That was an important part of being on a team, that kind of easy camaraderie, and even though both of them knew Eddie was in an audition situation, that didn't seem to stop them from shooting the shit. They even shook hands as they began walking up to us, and I sensed some movement from the citizens.

A couple of people in the back were moving away from the bunch, cameras and videocams at the ready. Merriwell, Fleckheimer and I, the three sturdiest-looking guys, stepped in front of them. I fixed the biggest of the lot in a glare and said quietly, but with unmistakable menace, "Don't you even think about it, mister. This is a private game."

The big guy blinked a few times, then decided to assert himself in front of his buddies. "Listen, nothin' says I can't—"

"*I* say you can't." Fitz Gleason had hopped out of his cart and was walking briskly forward.

"Who're you?" the guy asked.

"I run the course. Nobody's allowed on it unless they paid a green fee and got released by the starter."

"But—"

"But, my ass. You got a receipt?"

The guy shook his head. Asphal whispered something in Gleason's ear.

Gleason turned to the crowd. "Like the man said, this is a private game. You're all trespassing." He waited a second, then said, "If you all keep quiet and keep still, you can watch. No photographs, no autographs. One person snaps a camera, anybody yells 'You da man!' I'll have you all arrested."

The crowd murmured its collective agreement, thankful at not having been thrown off altogether. I grasped Asphal's thinking, that it would be good to have some spectators, see how Eddie did while a crowd watched. Derek had arrived by now, and he stepped toward Gleason and whispered in his ear, too. Then Gleason turned back to the crowd.

"Everybody behaves, y'get autographs and can take photos when we're done. We got us a deal?"

This time the crowd lit up all smiles and applauded. When Gleason waved them behind the tee box, they all rushed to comply and, true to their word, were the picture of politeness from that point on.

The first hole on the Mountain nine is a tricky par-five along a narrow plateau bordering an old arroyo that runs the length of the hole, with a narrow entrance to a green protected on all sides by bunkers. The Kid was up first, and tagged his drive for about 320, with a slight fade that placed it to the right of center and eminently playable. The citizens involuntarily gasped their astonishment, then one of them chanced some polite clapping, at which Derek smiled, and then they broke out in enthusiastic applause and shouts of "Nice shot, Derek!" and "Well struck!" The Kid touched two fingers to his cap and saluted, and then it was Eddie's turn.

Two-fifty, right down the middle. This was starting to get boring. We got into our carts and sped toward Eddie's ball, but when we got there, Asphal said, "Let's wait until our little gallery catches up. That way they won't get frantic." It also meant that Eddie would have to hold off until the spectators arrived.

Once the citizens saw that we would wait for them, they relaxed, and hung back deferentially, our mutual pact some sort of symbolic communion between us. They'd be telling their grandkids about this day well into the next millennium and didn't want to risk blowing it. Eddie took a three-wood and hit a sweet shot about 225, putting him less than 80 yards from the money grass.

The Kid put a one-iron just off the back of the green. Eddie wedged to within fifteen feet. The Kid chipped up and two-putted for a par. Eddie holed out for a birdie.

Anouilh's lead was down to two. They each parred the next two holes, then came up to number four, the second of the three par-threes on this nine, which was really the thirteenth hole in this match. Eddie still had the honors because he'd won the last hole that hadn't tied, but he gestured to Derek to go on while he stretched his arms a little.

It was a fairly straightforward par-three, playing about 180 from the blue tees, but downhill to a very deep green. The flag was in the middle, and Derek took an eight-iron, figuring the net distance at about 170. Eddie was pulling at one of his shoulders as Derek wound up and swung, but stopped and watched the green out of the corner of his eye.

The ball flew a tad shallower than I suspect The Kid had planned, landing toward the front of the green and rolling rapidly toward the center. The odd topography of the surface grabbed hold of it and began pulling it to the right in a long, swooping curve that ended up nearly pin high but about fifteen feet or so to the right of the flag. A fine shot by any measure.

Eddie seemed to pause longer over his bag than he normally did, finally selecting a seven-iron. He teed up and then spent several seconds just staring toward the green, then up at the overhanging trees sheltering the left side, then at the green again. Finally, he planted his feet and addressed his ball, took one more look at whatever his target was and drew the club back.

It was not a pretty shot, not for Eddie, anyway. We could all see it was going to land way short, and way left, and some of us winced as the ball headed for the drooping trees on the left.

But a slight fade kept the ball from hitting any branches, and it seemed to be hugging the tree line as close as it could without touching anything. It was short, as we had suspected, landing in front of the green and bouncing onto it way on the left side, perilously close to a bunker that nobody had even considered as being in play. As it had with Derek's ball, the surface claimed Eddie's, pulling it severely to the right as momentum propelled it forward.

Except that Eddie's shot had started well to the left of Derek's, so instead of yanking his ball away from the flag, the shape of the green was directing it right toward it. Some breaths were held as we realized that Derek, in going first, had given his opponent a read on how the green was going to react, and it started to appear that Eddie had hit a perfect shot in exploiting what he'd learned.

Still the ball moved onward, on what was becoming clear was a collision course with the hole. Still carrying some inertia as it closed in, the ball clanked into the flagstick and bounced off, settling to a stop less than two feet away.

The simultaneous exhalation of all those held breaths made the on-lookers laugh before they broke into applause for Eddie's brilliant play. Derek joined in, smiling and shaking his head in disbelief.

When we got to the green, Derek sank his long putt, and the mob went nearly hysterical. When he conceded Eddie's putt, they went back to perfunctory opera clapping, having already forgotten the shot that had gotten him to that conceded point in the first place.

Two birdies. Derek was still up two, with seven holes left.

On fourteen, The Kid put his tee shot into the water. Eddie played his usual driver, dry and safe, if unremarkable. Derek smacked a three-wood layup in front of the strip of water guarding the green, and Eddie did the same. They both pitched up and two-putted, Derek for a bogey, Eddie for par.

One up, four to go. Derek miscalculated his drive on fifteen and overhit it, much to the delight of the crowd, which, like the rest of us, didn't realize he'd put it in the water again. Eddie—well, you already know how he hit his driver. He followed that with a brilliant nine-iron and a one-putt for birdie. Derek also hit a splendid wedge and one-putted, but his was a par on account of the water ball.

They were even. Interestingly, the crowd was still going crazy over damned near every ball Anouilh hit, largely ignoring Eddie. Even more interestingly, Eddie seemed immune to the onlookers, but Anouilh was playing to them. That last drive he hit into the water was a dumb mistake, born of his desire to smack the living shit out of the ball in front of all those fans, not even stopping to consider that it was possible to hit *too* far on a hole like that, and it had cost him.

On sixteen, the toughest hole on the course, Derek finally wised up and hit a three-iron off the tee, landing it just short of a largely hidden pond that extended into the middle of the fairway. Eddie, to my surprise, hit driver again, a wonderful shot that came down between the water and the right edge of the fairway.

Once more, Eddie took an unusual amount of time sizing up his next shot. I couldn't see what club he had selected. It looked like too much for the distance, but I held my tongue. Eddie lined up with the ball so far forward in his stance that his left toe actually pointed to the right of it. When he hit, a huge divot flew off the end of his club as the ball rose into the air at a steeper angle than I thought a low iron capable of.

It was easy to see the trajectory was taking it much too far to the right, to where it looked as if it would flirt with a bunker. Flirt it did, but it touched down just to the left, on a mound forming the bunker's left boundary. As soon as it hit, it bounced sharply left and sped toward the green. Toward the flag. Which it hit and, this time, it rattled once and dropped into the hole.

Now, much as it pains me to say it, an eagle on a par-four is always pure luck, as is a hole in one on a par-three. A top-notch pro uses skill to get the ball close to the flag, but only Providence will knock it in. That's why the crowd, surprisingly sophisticated, laughed as it clapped at an appropriate volume. They figured Eddie was lucky the ball didn't go into the bunker, and even luckier that it found the hole.

But I knew better, at least about the bunker part, and so did my teammates and Fitz Gleason. Eddie had set the ball down on the mound within inches of where he wanted to, knowing there was no way in hell that any shot sent directly to that tilted green could be controlled enough in terms of back- or topspin to stop it close to the flag. By using that mound to snap the left ball sharply left, and using that abrupt change of direction to take something off the ball's momentum, he let topography do what spin couldn't. Sure, that it dropped into the hole was luck. But that he got it close to the flag wasn't. That was genius.

As if any more proof were needed, Derek took a nine-iron and went directly for the flag. It was a truly amazing shot, landing as it did less than five feet in front of the hole. But even The Kid couldn't make that ball check up, and it skidded past the cup almost to the back of the green.

He didn't bother to putt it out. Eddie had already won the hole. My man was up one, with two to go. When Eddie put his club back in his bag, I took careful note of its position and quickly walked by to have a look at it before his cart started forward and rattled his sticks around.

Of course, I knew what I would find: a seven-iron. Same club he'd been clustering shots with that night on Stinky Peterson's driving range in Boca Raton.

It was pretty much the same story on the next hole, a 205-yard par-three over water. They both played it superbly, but the crowd noticed only Derek, to the point where they'd probably go apoplectic with joy if he even blew his nose. Eddie, they kept ignoring. Who could blame them? They'd never heard of the guy, and the fact that he eagled sixteen didn't sway them much. When both of them parred seventeen, they had no way to know that Eddie had just gone "dormie" on the most famous golfer on the planet, meaning that, being up by one with only one hole to go, there was no way he could lose. The worst he could do was tie if he lost the eighteenth.

The last hole on the Mountain nine is a wonderful finisher, a par-five with a long, gradual curve to the left around water that can't be seen from the tee box. At only 504 yards, it's reachable in two, but you have to land that first drive well to the right of center to keep it out of the water, and then hope that the flag was planted on the left of the green so the bunker guarding the front won't come into play. Otherwise, you'd have to launch a 200-yard approach shot high into the air to keep the ball on the green once you got over the sand.

"Color's the flag today?" I asked Gleason.

"Blue," he answered, then added with a mischievous grin, "Very blue," meaning, about as far back on the green as was legal. Not only would that add a good fifteen yards to the overall length of the hole, it also meant the target would be just a narrow neck of safety with little margin for error.

Eddie still had the honors and hit . . . again, you already know. Derek surveyed the situation for a few seconds and then hit driver straight toward the water, much to the horror of the onlookers.

But once the ball had gotten past its purely ballistic stage and began shifting into aerodynamic mode, the clockwise spin his outside-to-inside swing path had imparted to it began to do its thing, the dimples on the left side grabbing bigger chunks of air than those on the other side, pushing the ball to the right. It faded perfectly, descending down a virtual glide slope toward an instrument landing well to the right of the water, just in front of one of the larger "bays" that jutted threateningly into the fairway.

The usual swooning moan from the crowd issued forth, and we all trooped up to Eddie's ball. He had about 270 to the pin, and hit a classic three-iron right toward it that landed about fifty yards short of the vigilant bunker. The onlookers didn't even bother with token applause; there didn't seem to be anything particularly special about the shot, and they were hurrying toward The Kid's ball, hoping for some fireworks.

The deep fade had taken something off the shot, resulting in a drive of *only* about 290 yards, leaving him some 230 from the flag. Derek pulled a six-iron out of his bag, then toyed with it for a few moments, rolling the head back and forth over the ground as he looked from it to the green and back again. He made a clicking sound with his tongue, and then turned to drop the club back into his bag, pulling out his two-iron instead. The crowd murmured appreciatively as they realized Derek's strategy had just changed from safely laying up in front of the bunker to going right for the pin.

I thought the two-iron was too much club for this distance, especially for Derek. Maybe his plan was to go *over* the green, playing for a chip shot from the grass rather than a pitch over the sand? Then I watched him set up to the ball, and suppressed a smile.

He'd lined up so that the ball was out beyond his left foot. It was the same stance Eddie had taken on sixteen. Derek was going to try to shoot the ball high into the air, the excess altitude resulting in less horizontal travel, and drop it onto the green with little roll. I'd never seen him do that with a two-iron before. I'd never seen *anybody* do that with a two-iron before. In a tournament, it would have been a dumb move, but in this match of little consequence, why not give it a try? And who knew what this phenom was truly capable of?

To my amazement but not surprise, the ball zoomed up at a higher angle than I'd ever seen produced with a two-iron, but I soon realized that, in his zeal to achieve that trajectory, Derek had overdone it. The ball didn't look like it was going to reach the green. I looked at him, still poised at the end of his follow-through, and watched as he let the club drop off his shoulders and turned in disgust. He knew it, too.

Luckily for him, the sand in the trap was gravelly and didn't allow the ball to auger itself into subterranean oblivion. Unluckily, though, the ball took a little hop and ended up well toward the front wall of the bunker, leaving him little maneuvering room and hardly any green to play with.

Eddie revealed nothing of what was going on in his mind. He grabbed a sand wedge and elected to walk to his ball, slowly. By the time he got there, he knew exactly what to do and how to do it, and didn't waste time in the preliminaries. He settled into his stance, took only one look at his target, then gently lofted the ball high into the air. It came down so straight that it moved barely an inch from where it touched down, which was about four feet from the flag.

The Kid let out a sigh and walked to the trap carrying his wedge. He was good in the sand, and managed a damned fine shot from that difficult lie, not dissatisfied that he'd left the ball fifteen feet from the pin on the upslope side, meaning he'd have a difficult downhill putt. Too much speed without hitting the hole and he'd end up off the green. Not enough and he'd have pretty much the same putt all over again.

Eddie marked his ball and waited as Derek read the green from about nine different angles. Then he tended the pin, standing well off to the shadow side with his arm extended, grabbing the pennant as well so the flapping in the slight breeze wouldn't disturb Derek as he stood over his ball and got himself properly aligned.

"Pull it," Derek said without lifting his head. Eddie took the flag out and carried it well outside of his opponent's sight line. Derek put his head down a final time, took a deep breath and let it out, then took the putter back and hit the ball.

Too slow. Halfway to the hole the ball had decelerated to the point where it looked as if it was going to end up ten feet too short. But Derek had seen something the rest of us hadn't, a slight hump between ball and pin that was disguised by a lightening in the color of the grass that obscured the tiny dropoff. He had hit the ball with the intention of getting just to the top of the hump as the ball ran out of momentum, counting on gravity to pull it down the rest of the way without it picking up too much speed.

And that's exactly what it did. Poised on the edge of coming to a dead halt, it kept rolling as the little ridge took hold of it. The friction of the grass was exactly counterbalanced by the tug of gravity down the slope, so the ball maintained a constant speed on its way right to the heart of the hole. It was a miracle putt, so I wondered why Derek had dropped to his knees and buried his face in his hands.

I soon found out. The downslope didn't go all the way to the hole, but leveled out about three feet in front of it. That nice constant speed the ball was currently maintaining couldn't hold up, and the question was whether it would have enough residual momentum to reach the hole once the assistance it was getting from the little hill ended. Derek obviously didn't think so.

I couldn't tell. Would the grass have dried out enough by this late in the morning to reduce the friction and allow a little extra speed? Was the grain pointing toward the hole, the slight bending of individual blades acting collectively as an inducement for the ball to take half a turn more than it might have?

An encouraging cry rose up from the crowd, as though voices raised on high could provide that extra bit of inertia we all could see might be required. Two feet away the pill was still rolling, slowing noticeably but not stopping, getting closer and closer and still rolling despite everybody's intuitive conviction that it should have stopped by now, six inches away and still going, almost to a stop but still turning, one dimple at a time, right to the lip, where it hung with barely an eighth of an inch keeping it aloft.

Even the birds had gone quiet. Gleason looked at his watch to start timing. Derek, alerted by the sudden cessation of the moaning, took his head out of his hands and looked toward the hole, then jumped up and ran to the ball. Kneeling so his face was at ground level, he examined the underside of the ball in relation to the lip, then shook his head and stood up, tapping the ball in without waiting to see if it would fall.

It was a truly majestic putt and a damned fine par, and the onlookers, me included, roared their approval. Remembering their deal with Gleason, cameras, videocams, pens and papers sprouted everywhere as Derek picked up his ball and walked away from the hole. He put a finger to his lips to quiet everybody down as Eddie took his putt, which he holed with little fanfare as the people crowded together at the edge of the green pressed their lips together waiting for him to get it over with.

Derek was good, I have to hand it to him. As promised, he patiently signed autographs and posed for pictures. Eddie stood to the side and wiped down his clubs, tucked ball markers and tees back in his bag, and drank a little water.

Nobody except my guys and I seemed to have noticed that Eddie had won the match straight up by two holes, no strokes given, after being down by three at the turn. Which means he'd won five of nine on the back, while The Kid hadn't won any.

I added up the scorecard. Then I blinked and added it up again, finally handing it to Fleck to check for me. Gross scores in match play aren't all that meaningful, since there are occasions when you might deliberately play less than your most aggressive depending on whether an error by your opponent opened a safe door for you to walk through, or just the opposite if he kept putting himself in birdie country and you had to go for broke and risk blowing up. Either way, the net effect tended to work in one direction, usually adding strokes to your score rather than subtracting them.

Fleck's eyes grew wide as he affirmed my arithmetic. Eddie had not only won the match, he'd outscored The Kid on gross strokes, once we filled in a two-putt for the ball Anouilh had picked up after Eddie's eagle on sixteen. Derek had a 65. If Eddie'd had any anxiety about the crowd, it sure as hell hadn't affected his score, a 64.

It didn't make a difference that this was too easy a course for a pro. First off, Eddie wasn't a pro. Second, his score was better then Derek Anouilh's, who'd played the same course under the same conditions. As people in the crowd shook hands with The Kid for the last time and reluctantly drifted off, Fred Asphal came up and clapped me on the shoulder. "My word, Bellamy" was about all he could manage, speechwise. "My word."

The reaction was pretty much the same among the others. After they left me, they went over to shake hands with Eddie and bestow some heartfelt compliments, then they headed back to the clubhouse, leaving the two of us alone.

"Sixty-four," I said, shaking my head in wonderment.

"Sixty-four what?"

I looked up at him. "That's what you shot. Didn't you know that?"

"How the hell should I know? Match play, I don't keep my running score, just did I win or lose on each hole."

"You're kidding."

"When I don't keep score, it's usually the best I play. I don't get tense trying to recover from some bad shit, try to make up for it, or realize I'm shooting a career round and get crazy trying to keep it up."

"But then how do you enter your score for your handicap?"

"Entering match-play scores for your handicap is bullshit anyway. They're always gonna be higher than they should. You'll never go for a risky birdie if the other guy's gonna bogey and all you need's a safe par. Just raises your handicap too high, and that's not fair."

"Didn't you just say not keeping score makes you play your best game? How d'you figure that's gonna raise your score?"

"Al." I could tell he was thinking how thick I was. "My best game isn't necessarily my lowest score. My best game is when I do exactly what I want to do. Sometimes I may want to make a sure bogey, like if the other guy is screwing up and heading for a double." He winced and reached around to scratch his back. " 'Sides, I don't enter scores at all. Don't even have an official handicap."

"What? How do you match up with guys you're gonna play for money?"

"They all know me, know what to go for. Shit, you think any'a those guys I play are gonna believe some number in a goddamned computer anyway?"

Eddie pulled a cigarette out of his pocket, shook one out and held the pack toward me. To my surprise, I took one, and it tasted good in the oppressive heat I hadn't noticed until this very moment. "Whud you two talk about?" I asked him around a mouthful of smoke.

"Huh?"

"After the turn. Before we got to the tenth."

"Oh." Eddie took a deep drag, tilted his head back, and blew the smoke skyward. "Talked about making the game a little interesting."

My hand paused, and I let the cigarette dangle out of my mouth. "Don't you tell me you made a bet with Derek Anouilh!"

"Where's it say I can't?"

I slumped down on the cart seat, but then a thought leaped into my brain and I sat up straight. "How much?"

"Ten large." He smiled. "I told you, I hadda get my expenses back."

I almost hesitated to ask, but I had to. "Whud you get from him?"

Eddie rubbed his chin with his thumbnail, which I was starting to recognize as a characteristic habit of his whenever things got tense or he was thinking hard. "Three strokes."

With the tension of the match suddenly gone, and my professional opinion of Eddie having been vindicated in front of my teammates, I started laughing and couldn't stop. It was contagious, and soon Eddie was laughing along with me.

The crazy bastard had held back on the front nine to squeeze strokes out of Derek Anouilh that he ended up not even needing.

CHAPTER NINE

Later, washing my face in the locker room, I got to thinking about what had really happened out there today.

My initial assumption had been that Eddie had pulled a classic hustle, sugarfooting the front nine in order to set Derek up for laying down a bet and giving away strokes. That was why we'd had that good laugh together afterward, right?

But what if that's why *I* may have been laughing, but Eddie's mirth had just been over his beating Derek Anouilh?

No. You didn't need to know Eddie for more than five minutes to know how uncharacteristic that would have been. So what if he *hadn't* been holding back on the front nine? What if he really had played his best?

Then it was even scarier. How could he possibly have known he would beat Anouilh on the back nine, and beat him bad enough to first wipe out his three-hole deficit from the front and then get at least one extra to ensure the win? Had he somehow taken a look at the gathering crowd of onlookers and surmised that Derek, with nothing really to lose, would play to them, go for the hero shots and become vulnerable?

I changed over to cold water, filled my hands, and dunked my face in it. I was starting to obsess about this guy, now working myself up into some kind of delusion that he was psychic. He was just an ordinary guy, and a damned good golfer.

Which didn't solve the puzzle. If Eddie hadn't held back on the front, how'd he know before the tenth hole that he could still pull a victory out of it? If he *had* held back to set Anouilh up for the kill, then how'd he know even before the round started that he'd be able to beat him? And what made him so sure? Because what I'd been forgetting was the original reason for the match, Eddie demonstrating that he was good enough to be on the Ryder Cup team. Why would he risk his chance at a hundred-grand payoff by diddling around in his audition match, taking those kinds of chances?

I was left with only one conclusion that made rational sense: I may not know what he did, I may not know what he'd planned, but any way you sliced it, and after looking at it from all angles, the one thing I knew, as sure as I knew my own name, was that there hadn't been a doubt in Eddie Caminetti's mind that he would take the back nine, and take it by a lot. That was used-car-salesman kind of confidence, the pathological kind that didn't falter even if you'd blown ten sales in a row.

As I left the locker room, I bumped into Eddie coming in. With nobody else around, I said to him, "So what was it, Eddie: You soft-soap the front to set Anouilh up?"

He didn't answer, but shot me a withering look that said something along the lines of *You don't ask a magician how he did the trick.* Especially if you're another magician.

If there even was a trick. That's why he was starting to haunt me. If he could divine that much about people he'd only just met, what the hell did he know about me?

"Harriman's here," he said as the moment passed and he walked by me.

The force of those two words knocked me against the wall, where I leaned, helpless, just managing to squeeze out, "What?"

"In the bar," he said, leaning over the sink and adjusting the water. "Drinking grapefruit juice."

There could only be one reason Boom-Boom Harriman would come out to the desert in the middle of summer, to this particular club, at this particular time: to lobby for the last spot on the Ryder team. It was presumptuous and ran against all the unspoken rules.

I wasn't going to be intimidated into doing anything I didn't feel like doing. I steeled myself and walked into the bar, where I was greeted by a loud "Yo, Al!" and an expansive bear hug from Harriman.

"Yo, yourself, Boomer. The fuck you doin' here anyway?"

He let me go and swept his arm toward my teammates. "Figured to play me one'a these faggots what can't stand the heat, make a little beer money."

"So which faggot's takin' you up?"

"None so far, the pussies. Siddown, lemme buy ya a beer."

I ordered a grapefruit juice, same as Boom-Boom. The rest of my guys were as nervous as I was, and seemed grateful that a figure of authority had entered to manage the situation. After a few minutes of mindless banter, I looked at my watch and said, "You boys ready?"

They jumped up too eagerly, and I said to Boom-Boom, "Got us a meeting. You hangin' around?"

"Maybe the night, I dunno. Any chance of a game tomorrow?"

"Sure," I said without thinking. "They're gonna cook for us here tonight, we don't gotta hang out in town and get bothered. Join us, okay?"

Harriman, nodding, lifted his hands and let them drop. "Thanks, Al. 'Preciate it."

I waved so long, and the rest of us retired to a meeting room off the lobby.

"My word," Fred Asphal was the first to say. "Did you ever?"

"Man wants it bad," Merriwell said.

"Bad enough to behave himself?" Fleckheimer asked. "Get the job done?"

"No way to know," Merriwell conceded.

"Da' wass some goddamn show your boy put on there, Alonzo," Senzamio said to me. "Some goddamn show."

Derek Anouilh nodded. "He was on the tour, I still woulda been impressed. But a guy off the street like that . . ."

"Steady's what he was," Fleck said. "A brick."

He looked with mock accusation at Anouilh, who smiled sheepishly and reddened, a pretty good trick for a dark-skinned Indonesian from Borneo. "Didn't count, so I dazzled the crowd a little. So what?"

"So I don't think that Caminetti guy even noticed a crowd was there, Drek," Fleck answered, then looked at me. "Like I said, a brick."

"So now what?" Merriwell threw in to get the ball rolling. "That what this meeting's about, Al?"

"Yeah."

They had seated themselves at random on the chairs scattered around the room. There was no big table, just a couple of small desks here and there. I sat behind one and that made it the focus of the discussion.

"First off," Merriwell began, "why's a guy can play like that not in the show?"

"Doesn't like the publicity," I answered, a little too hastily.

"Then what the hell's he wanna play the Ryder for?" Fleck threw back at me.

I scratched the back of my head to buy time, but there was no avoiding this one. "On account of I promised him a hunnerd grand if he helped us keep the Cup."

"A hunnerd grand," Fleck echoed mindlessly.

"What's going on here, Bellamy?" Asphal said. "Since when does a player receive compensation for participating in the Ryder? And where is it supposed to come from?"

"From us. We're gonna pay him."

An awkward silence ensued. "Is it even legal?" Fleck asked, probably just to break the tension and keep things moving. He pointed to a copy of the rules I was holding.

I riffled through the pamphlet, which I'd already memorized. "Cup rules permit buying equipment, spending money on advice, sports psychologists, whatever."

"But do they say you can buy a player?"

"They don't say you can't."

"Maybe we oughta ask somebody," Anouilh proposed.

Fleckheimer nixed that one. "My old rabbi used to say, ask if something's kosher, answer's always gonna be no."

Merriwell, a sucker for any kind of iconoclasm, agreed. "Better to beg forgiveness than to seek permission. Let the Ryder Cup committee try to take away our championship on a bullshit technicality." As if we even had a realistic chance of winning this one against the Europeans, but Merriwell, like the rest of us only more so, was determined to stay positive.

"But what do we say?" Anouilh persisted.

"Let's just say he couldn't afford expenses," Asphal said, "and we simply covered for him."

I liked this. In the heat of trying to outwit the authorities, my teammates had already assumed Eddie onto the team.

Anouilh sneered at Asphal and said sarcastically, "A hundred grand worth of taxicabs and hot dogs?"

"What taxicabs?" Fleck added. "We even get our own courtesy cars, f'Chrissakes!"

Time for me to jump back in. "Hold it a second." I waved the rule book aloft. "Nothin' in here even says we have to tell anybody."

"You mean keep it a secret?" Jon Markovy asked.

Fleck shook his head and looked down at the ground. "Look, guy's takin' a week off from work, we're kickin' in to help him out, make up his lost income. What, we gotta file a report?"

Senzamio screwed up his face in confusion. "What's he do, he makes a honnerd g's a week?"

"The fuck knows?" Fleck shot back, scowling at this overly analytical and needlessly detailed turn of the conversation. "Point is, we don't needa bring it up. Nobody's damned business, anyway. Listen, you think the Euros are gonna squawk, we tell 'em we're bringing on a two-bit muni-hack and leaving Harriman home."

"Well, I don't wanna pay," Markovy said. "I'm not making dime one on this, why should I fork over ten g's to this guy?"

"It's not ten g's," I corrected him gently. "Twelve guys, thirteen if you count me, s'more like about eight."

"Whatever. I'm not giving him squat."

I was prepared for that. "Okay. Here's how it is: Everybody who wants to pay, those guys divide up the hundred large and foot it all. Simple."

"Hey, that's-a no fair!" Senzamio whined.

"Sure it is. You don't like it, bug out and don't pay. Your call."

More quiet, until Senzamio said, "So what-a you tell me, I don't pay, I cost evabodda else money?"

"Do whatever you think's right, Rico."

He looked around the room, everybody's face in turn. "Well, fock that. I'm payin'."

"Me, too!" Merriwell cried out, and that was the end of that part of the discussion.

"Has he even got a tour card?" Asphal asked.

I said that he'd had one once, and Anouilh asked how that happened. "Long story," I said dismissively, "but it's not a requirement anyway." Because it had never occurred to anyone to make it one. It would be like requiring that every baseball player in the World Series have his own mitt.

There was a lot of chin- and ball-scratching, some foot-shuffling back and forth on the rough carpet, until Ashpal finally said, "It still leaves us with the conundrum of dealing with Harriman."

"My big problem with Harriman," I said, almost as an aside so as not to push it, "is how do we know he's gonna hold together, the guy's wrapped so tight."

"Man was drinkin' grapefruit juice in the bar," Merriwell said, ever the optimist.

"But I'll wager he'll be drinking beers tonight," Asphal replied.

"How do you know?"

"He's under the impression he can handle it."

"Nine, ten bottles?" Fleck said. "That's nothin' to a guy can drink like Boom-Boom. Wouldn't even show up on a Breathalyzer, fucker's so big."

"I don't know how we handle Harriman," I said. "But you guys said let's test Caminetti, man flies himself across the country at his own expense"—I saw Anouilh wince at this—"sure as shit passes his audition, so . . . ?"

"Nobody's sayin' the man can't play golf, Al." It's a nice concession from Merriwell. "It's just, y'gotta be fair to the Boomer, know what I'm sayin'? Think it all out before you maybe do the wrong thing and hurt his feelings."

I knew what he was saying. Boomer's hurt feelings could turn into somebody else's broken bones.

I told Eddie what was going on. About how Harriman was a logical choice for the team.

"Guy's been suspended half a dozen times," Eddie said, leaning way back on a wicker chair out by the snack bar. "Forget about me for a second. This somebody you really want to risk your precious Cup on?"

Personally, I didn't. Far as I was concerned, Eddie was my man. But there was no way to prove Harriman might crack, just as there was no way to prove he wouldn't, and I explained to Eddie that this was the nature of the dilemma.

Eddie stayed quiet for a few seconds, then said, "He coming to dinner tonight?"

I nodded. "You're still gonna join us, though, right?"

He looked surprised. "Why, something change?"

I shook my head, then an idea hit me. "How'dja feel about playing him?"

Bad phrasing, and I said, "I know. For how much, right?" before Eddie could say it himself.

He grinned. "Precisely."

"For nothing. Just to see how you do."

The grin disappeared. "You mean a second audition?"

"Something like that."

"You know," he said, leaning forward in the chair, "some'a you guys really surprise me. Big bunch of hotshot fuckin' pros, I know guys without a pot to piss in keep their word better'n you."

"What the hell're you talkin' about?" I said, all offended, knowing perfectly well what the hell he was talking about.

"I'm talking about we had us a deal. I fly my ass out here, play this Dirk Whatshispuss, if I do good I'm on the team. Well, I beat his ass, din't I? And I still ain't on the team?"

I sighed and looked away. "My guys, they're a little worried. Not about you. They saw you play."

"Then what?"

"Harriman. Does he deserve a chance."

"Fucked up every damned chance you guys ever gave him."

"I know that. But he's turning around, you know . . . ?"

I couldn't pull it off in front of Eddie, defending such a lame proposition.

"So now you want me to play him, that it? So you can convince your guys to hold up their end of the deal you already made?"

"Something like that."

Eddie thought about it for a little bit. "Man's a crumbler," he pronounced definitively. "No way you can trust him, you think this Ryder thing's so damned important."

"I know. But I can't seem to get the boys to see it."

"Thought you were the head kahuna. Who gives a shit, they see it or not?"

"Tryin' to build some team spirit here, Eddie. They're playing the Cup for free, for honor. They don't need some asshole captain giving 'em shit while they're doin' it."

Eddie thought some more. "Tell you what," he said, standing up. "If

Harriman is up for playing me tomorrow morning, I'll play him. But if he's not, you put me on that team."

"How can I promise you something like that?"

"Threaten to resign otherwise."

I laughed mirthlessly. "The hell I will!"

"Right this minute, Al, you're a goddamned welsher. You're going back on our deal. But I'm giving you a way out anyway. You don't take it, then you got no right to talk about honor."

He was right. I hadn't known him very long, but I was certain he'd sooner go broke than go back on his word. So who was I to wax philosophical about honor? "Whaddaya mean, if he's willing? 'Course he'd be willing!"

"I said *able* and willing. Your guys think he's over the hump, think he's got some *cojones* now? Fine. He's got 'em, I'll go home and not squawk. Deal?"

I took the out he was offering. "Deal."

So what had Eddie seen in Harriman that the rest of us were missing?

CHAPTER TEN

As Fred Asphal had predicted, Harriman was drinking beers as I walked into the private dining room Fitz Gleason had set up for us. I was surprised to see that Eddie had arrived before me. I'd been sure he would wait until after I arrived, like he needed my protection or something.

But he was mixing in just fine on his own, standing off to the side with Derek Anouilh and Mack Merriwell, the latter two taking turns making motions with their hands that looked to me as if they were describing golf shots. Eddie seemed to be doing all the listening and asking, and none of the describing, and he also seemed to be having a good time. What he was probably doing was gathering intelligence in preparation for some kind of golf wager, but it was nice to see anyway. Whatever he could do to ingratiate himself with the team could only help our cause.

I sat down with Harriman, joining Fred Asphal, Enrico Senzamio and Joel Fleckheimer. I noticed that Harriman was nursing his beer slowly, even deliberately, as though he were pacing himself and didn't want to scarf down his allotment too early in the evening. A good sign, I supposed.

The seating arrangements weren't formal, just one table with twelve chairs for the seven of us. Dinner was served buffet style, so everyone just got up and helped themselves when they felt like it, then plopped down in different seats after each trip to the food-service table. It was a relaxed atmosphere despite my anticipation of complex lines of tension.

When I found myself alone with Harriman for a second, I pointed to his beer and asked him how he was doing, assuming he'd know what I meant. He was candid in his reply.

"Doin' good, Al. I was never an alky, y'know. I mean, don't get me wrong, I'm not sayin' I din't have no drinking problem, I ain't stupid, but it wasn't like an addiction or anything, know what I'm sayin'?"

I told him I wasn't sure.

"Means that I got a little nasty when I— No, that's not right. I mean I got a little, uh, high-strung. Yeah, that's it, like trigger-happy or somethin'. Didn't know what was gonna happen once I drank past a certain point, like I was standin' to the side watchin' somebody else who wasn't me, see?"

I nodded, hoping I was being encouraging. "And now?"

"Now I don't drink past that limit. I like the sauce, but like I said, I'm not addicted to it. Things are busy, I got stuff to do, I can go a week not touchin' anything. Shit, not even *thinkin'* about it, swear to God."

"So what's the limit?"

"Don't know exactly, but I can tell when I'm gettin' there. 'S'why I drink beers, see? Can knock back two sixes'a this shit 'fore it gets even close."

With that, he threw back his head and roared, slapping the table with his enormous mitt of a hand at his own cleverness. The Boomer's charm, like that of most denying alcoholics, was truly infectious, and I couldn't help laughing along with him, which was when I noticed Eddie standing behind us, waiting for a chance to jump in.

"Two six-packs?" he said to Harriman. "Shit, I drink three beers I'm laid out like road kill."

Harriman turned, the briefest cloud crossing his face upon seeing Eddie, but he recovered quickly, bound to show he was a good sport. A team player. "Hey, Eddie, siddown here, c'mon."

He pulled out a chair and tapped it a couple of times. Eddie dropped down onto it, then pointed to the glass in front of Harriman. "How many'a those you had already, Stephen?"

"My second," Harriman said proudly. "And this here don't look to be no more than mebbe ten ounces, tops."

"Huh" was all Eddie said, and I got a strange feeling in my stomach. Fleckheimer and Asphal returned to the table with full plates and took up seats near us. Fleck was about to say something, then saw Eddie rubbing his chin with his thumbnail, and something about it made him stay quiet.

"I wonder . . ." Eddie said. Anouilh and Merriwell had now rejoined the group.

"Wonder whut?" Harriman asked, all innocence.

Eddie didn't respond right away. None of the others had touched the food they'd set down on the table. I hadn't gotten anything yet, but found myself suddenly without any appetite.

"You interested in a little friendly bet?" Eddie said at last.

"You mean now?" Harriman looked toward the window. "Dark out already."

"No, no, not a golf bet. Something else."

"Sure, what the hell," Harriman responded, smiling and looking around the table. "What's the deal?"

"Hang on a second." Eddie stood up abruptly and headed for the bar, returning with an empty shot glass.

"Hey, I ain't drinkin' nothin' hard, bud," Harriman said with conviction, looking around to make sure we all caught it.

"Shit no, you crazy?" Eddie looked offended. "You think I'm gonna contribute to the delinquency of a golfer?"

Harriman laughed heartily; the rest of us laughed nervously.

"No," Eddie went on as he set down the jigger and resumed his seat. He put his elbows on the table and leaned forward, kind of hunched up, and pointed to the little glass with his chin. "What I'm proposin' here, I bet you can't drink one jigger'a beer a minute for an hour."

Harriman looked down at the glass and blinked a few times, his eyebrows knitted together in concentration.

"Ninety ounces, Boomer," Fleckheimer offered, but Harriman still didn't seem to comprehend. "Seven and a half cans."

"Oh!" Harriman said, then turned to Eddie. "You're sayin' I can't drink seven and a half cans'a beer in an hour?"

"Not sayin' you can't, but I'm willing to put a few bucks on it."

Harriman looked around at the others, then at me, then back at Eddie. "Listen, pal, I could knock back a whole six-pack time it takes you to go have a short crap, whud're you, crazy or sumpin'?" He looked around again, this time for some support, and got it in the form of quizzical glances at Eddie.

"Save your money," Asphal said to Eddie. "I've personally observed Stephen consume several times that amount in an hour."

"Seen him do a damned sight more'n that," Merriwell threw in.

Eddie looked down at the table and shook his head. "Listen'a me, Stephen. Not seven cans in an hour. One shot every minute. No more, no less."

"Same shit, ain't it?"

"I don't think so."

"What am I missin' here?"

Eddie just shrugged, so Harriman said, "What's the bet?"

"Whatever you want."

"Like . . ."

"Whatever you want."

"Okay, wise guy. How 'bout an even grand?"

All eyes were on Eddie. "Nope. Too much."

"Too much?" Harriman exclaimed. "Whaddaya mean, too much? What, you got no faith in your convictions?"

"It's too much because you won't be able to do it, and I don't want to take that much money from you."

Time for me to step in. "What's the catch, Eddie?"

"No catch." He took his watch off his wrist and laid it on the table. It was an old-fashioned analogue, with a sweep second hand. "You can drink the shot anytime you want to inside the minute," he said to Harriman. "You can drink the next one anytime inside the next minute. But as soon as that second hand hits twelve and you haven't finished the jigger and set it down on the table, you lose."

Harriman considered it. "So I can drink one right off, then wait until the end of the *next* minute to knock back another one."

"Absolutely. You can do whatever you want, just so long as one jigger's gone before each minute is up."

Harriman considered it some more. "Do I get to pee?"

"Sure. But you can't puke."

Harriman nodded vigorously at the fairness of that proviso. "How do we do it?"

Eddie started to get up again, but Anouilh beat him to it. "I got it," he said eagerly, going to the bar and returning with a six-pack of brew, two more loose bottles and another shot glass.

Eddie said, "Good thinking. We'll need two glasses to keep things moving. I'll pour 'em, Stephen, no head. You just drink 'em."

"What happens you pour 'em long?" Harriman asked.

"Good question," Eddie acknowledged, noting that there was no inscribed line on the glass to denote exactly an ounce and a half. "Tell you what: I pour 'em long, you're done as soon as the seven and a half bottles are gone, even if there's time left. And if I short 'em, you're still done when the hour's up. That way, no way I can cheat and screw you up. Fair?"

Harriman nodded. "But I still think there's a catch."

Eddie took no offense. "Okay. Anytime at all you think I tricked you, for whatever reason, you can call off the bet, no questions asked."

I was really starting to hate it when he did that. But there was no arguing with it.

"Boomer," I said as firmly as I could. "Don't do it."

"You kidding? Why the hell not!"

"I don't *know* why not, just don't do it!"

"Gotta gimme a better reason'n that, Al. Shit, you heard the man. I think he's bullshittin' me, I call it off." He turned to Eddie. "Right?"

"That's the deal. An' you got all these witnesses."

"Well, shit, what're the stakes then?"

Eddie held up his hands and let them drop to the table. Harriman said, "Hunnerd bucks."

"You're on."

"Fuck me, I'll take some'a that," Merriwell exclaimed, reaching for his wallet.

But Eddie waved him off. "Bet somebody else, Mack. I won't lay it off."

"Why the hell not?"

Eddie turned to Harriman. "Listen'a me, Stephen. You listenin'a me?"

"Yeah, I'm listenin'. What, already?"

"You won't be able to do it." Eddie fixed him with his eyes. "I'm tellin' you that up front so you won't say later I didn't."

"The fuck you talkin' about, Eddie? I'll have your hunnerd in my pocket in sixty minutes!"

"No, you won't."

"Ah, fuck that, and fuck you. Let's get started!"

"You sure?"

"Yeah, f'Chrissakes! C'mon already!"

They gave the others a few seconds to try to make bets with each other, but nobody laid anything off because nobody was willing to bet against Harriman.

I was tempted to—like I said before, Eddie Caminetti never made a bet he wasn't sure he was going to win—but I held back, because I knew deep in my heart that this was the last thing in the world Harriman should be doing.

This was not going to end well.

Harriman looked down at the laughably tiny shot glasses sitting on the table before him and shook his head with amiable derision. Ever fair, Eddie had filled them to only a quarter of an inch or so from the top, assuming that the true ounce-and-a-half line was somewhat lower than the brim. I had to admit, those itty-bitty snorts of amber liquid sure did look puny and inconsequential, especially in comparison to the thirsty hulk staring at them.

"Ready, Stephen?" Eddie had set his watch to high noon on the nose, leaving the stem out so the second hand would stay right on twelve until he pushed it back in.

"Hold it a second," Anouilh said, standing up and walking to the bar. He reached up and gently lifted the large white clock with black hands on the wall above. Seeing that there were no electrical connections, he lifted it off the picture hook holding it up and brought it back to the table. Merriwell positioned two candlesticks and propped the clock up so we all could see it, then set the hands to twelve. "When the second hand hits twelve, 'kay?" he said, and everybody nodded.

Harriman made some hand gestures reminiscent of Ed Norton getting ready to take dictation from Ralph Kramden, then cracked his knuckles a few times, all the while smiling broadly at Eddie.

"Ten seconds," Merriwell announced.

Harriman picked up one of the glasses in his thumb and forefinger, sticking his remaining fingers way out, like a cartoon character about to sip champagne.

"Okay, hit it."

With one supremely confident look around the table, Harriman brought the glass slowly to his mouth, then knocked it back like a shot of vodka. Smacking his lips a few times, he set the glass gently back on the table. "Gosh, that was a bitch, Mr. Camiletti! I don't think I can drink anymore."

Everybody laughed, Eddie included, and then we watched the clock as Eddie carefully refilled the glass.

"Why two glasses?" Asphal asked.

"Case he decides to drink two quick ones in a row?" Anouilh guessed, Eddie nodding that he'd gotten it right.

"Can he do that?"

"Only if one's inside'a one minute," Fleckheimer said, "and the other's inside'a the next. Right?"

" 'Zackly," Eddie said. The guys were catching on fast.

"Minute's commin' op," Senzamio observed. Harriman reached for a glass.

"Remember, you don't gotta drink it right away," Eddie reminded him.

"I know. But I'm thirsty."

"Can he drink *more* than a shot within a minute?" Asphal asked Eddie.

"No." That surprised everybody.

"How come?" Harriman asked.

"Because that's the way this game is played."

The second hand hit twelve. "Cheers," Harriman toasted, then drank it down. Eddie refilled the glass.

"Anything says we gotta let 'em get warm?" Harriman asked.

"Shit! Sorry, Stephen." Eddie jumped up and went to the bar, where he dumped the contents of a fruit bowl onto the table and began filling it with ice. "You watchin' the clock?"

"Got it." Once again the hand swept past twelve, and Harriman downed another glass. Eddie returned with the bowl, and Asphal and Merriwell stuck the remaining bottles underneath the ice.

"Better, Stephen?"

"You bet."

In the next five minutes, he drank five more shot glasses of beer, and some of us were starting to get restless. I raised my eyebrows inquisitively at Eddie, but his features remained calm and unperturbed as he pulled a fresh bottle out of the fruit bowl and twisted off the cap. I noticed that Boom-Boom had his chin pulled way in toward his chest, mouth open and flapping like a landed haddock.

"Time, Boomer," Anouilh said.

"Hang on a sec," Harriman answered. "Gotta burp here."

While he was struggling to expel some stomach gas, Asphal said, "Ten seconds, chum."

Harriman squeezed his eyes shut, and suddenly an enormous *Raaaalph* extruded out of him, causing all of us to lean back reflexively. A broad, satisfied smile crossed his face as muscles all over his body relaxed.

"Three seconds!" Anouilh warned. Harriman reached calmly for the next beer and slowly drank it down.

"Good man," Eddie said.

Harriman went through two more beers without incident, then screwed up his face again in preparation for another world-class belch. He had twenty seconds left in this minute interval and hadn't yet drunk a beer.

"Keep your eye on the clock," Asphal said.

"Shit!" was all Harriman managed to squeeze out, still trying to burp.

"Ten seconds!"

"Goddamnnit!"

"Come on, Boomer!" several of us yelled in unison.

"Five seconds!" Asphal said, panic in his voice.

Giving up on his effort to reduce the pressure in his belly, Harriman grabbed the glass and knocked it back, unable to swallow, holding it in his mouth.

"He gotta get it down?" Anouilh asked, distress in his voice.

Eddie thought it over for a second, then said, "Nah. Long's he don't spit it out."

Harriman's eyes were squeezed shut, and his breathing was labored. Finally he took some deep breaths through his nose and swallowed, then opened his mouth, gasping for air. He stood up abruptly and began jumping up and down, then stopped and let out a truly momentous belch, flopping back onto the chair as visible waves of relief washed over him.

Eddie refilled the glass while Harriman forced himself to choke out a few more burps. He drank his next glass easily, the next less easily. He went through the burping routine again, which didn't seem as troublesome as the one before, and managed two more shots.

"Don't feel so good," he said, leaning back in his chair and staring out at nothing in particular, then looking at the clock, then trying to focus on the two little glasses in front of him, finally closing his eyes.

"Fifteen seconds, bud," Merriwell said, reluctantly, it seemed.

"Fug." Harriman dutifully reached for a glass, waited until the very last second and finished it off. He quickly reached for the other one, waited for the second hand to hit twelve, then threw it back as well.

A few of the guys glanced apprehensively at Eddie: Had Boom-Boom drunk the beer before the next minute had started? Should Eddie choose to make that call, no one could really argue that he'd misread the clock.

"No problem," Eddie announced. "Ain't gonna screw him on a couple seconds here or there."

Soon it started to look as though he wouldn't have to. The clock read 12:25 and Harriman, white as a golf ball, his head rolling back and forth stupidly, didn't appear to be able to lift a glass, much less drink out of it.

"You wanna call it off, Stephen?" Eddie asked gently. "Never mind the hunnerd, we'll forget the whole thing."

The Boomer managed to stop his rocking head just as it was turned toward Eddie. "Fug no." He turned his bleary eyes toward the clock, sighed and drank another one. Then the pre-belch paroxysms began once again.

Much worse this time. Harriman was practically in tears as Asphal called out ten seconds to go, but he gamely drank the shot without having gotten any more gas out of his stomach. His head dropped as he let his arm fall back to the table, the shot glass hitting the surface and bouncing away. Merriwell reached out and caught it as Harriman began sniffling, his mouth full of beer, his glassy and red-rimmed eyes hunting about frantically for some help, which was nowhere to be found.

Twelve twenty-seven. Boom-Boom wasn't even halfway through. My teammates and I looked at each other in confusion. *What the hell was going on here?*

"You serious 'bout letting him off the hook, Eddie?" I asked, acting like a captain and trying to take control.

"Dead serious, Al. Fact, I wish you'd call him off."

"Yo, Boomer," Merriwell was saying to Harriman as he shook him, ripples running from the big guy's shoulders down through his belly unimpeded by any effort of his muscles to contract and slow them down. It was like shaking a bag of newly mixed cement.

"Ten seconds," Asphal announced. Somehow Harriman roused himself to some semblance of awareness and slid his arm along the table until his hand connected with the shot glass. He lifted it without taking his arm off the table, brought his head down and stared at it for a few seconds.

"Five seconds, Boomer," Merriwell said tensely.

Harriman kept staring at the glass, then set it down, gurgled once and slid to the floor, Asphal shooting out a hand to try to keep the big guy's head from smacking into the chair, which it did anyway, but only lightly.

Everybody was quiet for a long time. Finally Mack Merriwell leaned across the table and looked down at the inert form of Stephen "Boom-Boom" Harriman, nothing to indicate that he was even alive except the occasional twitch of a leg or cheek muscle.

"What in the holy flaming fuck just happened?" Merriwell finally asked nobody in particular.

Eddie Caminetti shrugged and said, "He lost."

Fred Asphal turned in his seat and considered Harriman's pallid face, lolling tongue and total inability to control himself, as evidenced by the thin line of urine streaming from his cuff. "Will he be all right?"

"In about two days," Eddie replied. "Till then he's gonna spend half his time afraid he's gonna die, and the other half afraid he isn't."

Which meant, at the very least, that tomorrow's match was off.

I turned to Eddie and clapped his shoulder. "Gentlemen," I said, standing. I waited until they'd all managed to take their eyes off Harriman and direct them toward me. "Meet our newest teammate."

The ensuing, somewhat reserved joviality was interrupted only by a juicy, prolonged, thunderous fart from the human peat bog piled on the floor next to the table.

CHAPTER ELEVEN

They were a savvy bunch, my teammates. Not one of them voiced a complaint that Eddie Caminetti had played fast and loose, getting Boom-Boom Harriman snockered and unable to play the most important match of his life.

They knew, as did I, that that hadn't been the point of Eddie's little demonstration. The point was that Harriman was weak and unreliable. Beset with delusions of adequacy, to such a degree that he blithely turned his back on a warning given to him by the very man who was making a bet against him, not to mention his potential team captain, what would he do when it came down to crunch time in the Ryder Cup and he just plain didn't like my instructions?

When Eddie looked him straight in the eye and told him not to take the bet, told him he couldn't do it, that was Harriman's cue simply to step back for a second and ask *why*. Eddie was ready to tell him: *You can't do it because nobody can do it; it can't be done.* And if Harriman expressed skepticism and pressed for an explanation, Eddie would have told him he didn't know, exactly, *But believe me, much bigger boozers than you have tried and failed, then spent a couple days regretting it.*

But he hadn't asked. He'd just plunged ahead, trusting only in himself when there was little basis for him to do so, driven by his ego and his arrogance and his childish sense of invulnerability. It might make a great story in a decade's time, one of those retrospectively romanticized perversions of the truth that added to the legend of a tragic and raffish rogue, but right now it was just depressing and ugly.

I'd had one other mildly uncomfortable moment that evening. As we were leaving the club, Merriwell, Asphal and Senzamio struggling to get Harriman back to his room, I found myself walking alone with Eddie.

"Just remember one thing, Al," he said.

"What's that?"

"I'm a hustler, plain and simple. Not a glory boy playin' for God and country."

"And therefore . . . ?"

"Don't be makin' any assumptions about what you think I might or might not do, see?"

"I get you. But what're you tryin' to tell me, Eddie?"

"Not tryin' to tell you anything but what I just told you."

"We have a deal, don't we?"

"Prob'ly know that better'n you, what I seen so far. I don't perform, I don't get paid. We both understand that."

"You got it."

"Okay, then."

And that was it.

I made the public announcement the following Tuesday at 10:00 A.M., and by 10:05 the *merde* had hit the fan and was spinning off the blades with dizzying ferocity, landing all over the place in great, slapping dollops, but mostly on me. I taped an interview with Barry Gambol for ESPN, to be aired that night, and watched it at Mack Merriwell's house on Long Island after having dinner with his wife, Juliette, and their three kids.

True to his word, Gambol hadn't edited the piece except for camera cuts, which was our deal going in. I'd been interviewed hundreds of times by the various forms of media, and never failed to marvel at how a skilled editor could make the same person look like a schmuck or a saint, depending on the angle the producers were after. They weren't about to give me final cut, so we agreed that there would be no cuts at all.

After Gambol's preliminary, scripted lead-in, he looked square at me and said, "Al, we been friends a good long time." I'd met him twice. "I know you well enough to know you wouldn't do something frivolous with an important decision like this." He didn't know me well enough to know my birthday. "So tell me: Who the heck is Eddie Caminetti?"

I smiled and pretended to take a moment to consider his straightforward question. "Barry, the thing you have to understand is that there are lots of guys out there who play splendid golf but aren't on the tour.

Just because you *can* doesn't necessarily imply that you want to." I can be a fairly articulate practitioner of the King's English when I'm on display rather than with my golfing buddies, who all have a tendency to lapse into a form of Okie dialect when just among themselves.

"Ain't that the damned truth," Merriwell said.

"Mack, the children," Juliette admonished him.

Merriwell put a hand to his mouth. "Sorry, babe," he said, then looked at his kids, all of whom were rolling their eyes skyward at Mom's naïveté.

"Okay, I'll buy that so far . . ." Gambol was saying on the screen.

I remember thinking, *I'm so pleased, Barry.* "Eddie Caminetti is just one of those guys. I've little doubt that he could more than hold his own on the tour, but there's nothing about that pressure-cooker life that interests him."

"Okay, hold it right there a second, Al. What *about* the pressure? What makes you so sure a guy like that, never played in front of a crowd, what makes you think he can stand up to Ryder Cup pressure which, as we both know, can be pretty intense?"

And how exactly would you *know, pal?* "That's a fair question. Part of it is just me knowing the guy. But he's played golf under pressure before, Barry. In fact, that's how he got his PGA card."

"Ah, I was gonna get to that. So he has his card, which makes him legal to compete."

"Sure does. A while back, Eddie decided to have a go at Q-school, see, and—"

"For those of our viewers who may not be familiar with that," Gambol broke in, "what Al is referring to is Qualifying School. It's not really a school but a kind of special tournament held each year to determine who will be allowed to play on the regular tour. The top twenty-five finishers get a one-year exemption from further qualifying."

"That's right, Barry. And as you well know from your years of experience in and around this sport, there's probably no event that even comes close to Q-school in terms of nerve-wracking, mind-bending pressure. These guys are playing for their professional lives, see, and it all comes down to six of the toughest rounds imaginable, against a couple hundred other guys who're just as driven to make the cut as you are."

"So how'd Caminetti do?"

I hesitated for a second to heighten the impact of my answer, then said softly, "He came in third."

Gambol raised his eyebrows and was speechless for a moment. "*Third?*"

"Yep."

"Wow. So how come we never heard of this guy?"

How come? Because Eddie hated every damned minute of it, everybody so grim, sweating over every shot, playing golf like they faced execution if they screwed up. Nobody wanted to lay a few bucks on their rounds, just to keep things interesting, nobody was having any fun, nobody was taking any chances until near the end, and then they did the dumbest damned things imaginable out of sheer desperation.

As Eddie told me during our round at Seminole, he just hunkered down, came in third and went home. A PGA official called to remind him that the deadlines were approaching for some of the season's opening tour events, and Eddie told him he wasn't going to be playing on the tour. The guy got crazy, asked him why in hell he went to Q-school when he had no intention of playing on the tour, and Eddie said he'd had every intention of playing on the tour until he *got* to Q-school, which is where he changed his mind.

The PGA had no policy for dealing with this, since it was unprecedented—like winning the Boston Marathon and then leaving town just before the award ceremony where they handed out the checks—so they huddled and decided to call up the guy who'd missed the cut by a single stroke and tell him he was now eligible for the tour. What I hear, the poor bastard almost had a heart attack and even thought some of his friends might have been playing a really malicious practical joke until the letter and his tour card arrived, by Federal Express, which he paid for himself just to make sure it got there before he worked himself into a full-scale psychotic episode.

"I think Eddie got a taste of what the tour might be like during Q-school," I told Gambol, "and just plain decided he wasn't going to like it."

I noticed that Merriwell had grown still on his lounger and was gripping the armrests so hard his knuckles were turning white.

"Happens a surprising lot, believe it or not," I was saying to Gambol on the screen. I doubt it had ever happened before or since.

"How 'bout that," he said. "So you're saying he took up a slot somebody else could've used?" That was Gambol, all right, always trying to find something evil and horrible in the most banal of events. Maybe that's why he was the highest-paid sportscaster on television.

Merriwell was sitting upright now, eyes concentrating on the screen so intently I thought they might pop out of his head.

"No, Barry, not at all. Eddie did the right thing. He informed the PGA in time for them to meet and decide to give the exemption to the guy who'd just missed the cut by one."

Merriwell started to gag and turn red. Juliette and the kids noticed and turned toward him.

"And that was . . . ?" Gambol prompted me.

"Seventeen years ago," I finished.

Gambol chuckled good-naturedly, trying to take some of the edge off his implication that Eddie had been guilty of something despicable. "Man, imagine what that guy musta felt like when he got the word!"

"Goddamnit!" Merriwell yelled, smacking the lounger's recline lever with his hand so hard he popped straight out of the chair and into a standing position. "God*damn*it! *That's* where I know that sonofabitch from!"

"Mack!" Juliette said sternly, noticing that the kids were smiling and giggling at Daddy's sudden outburst.

"Well, *shit*, Julie . . . !" He turned to me. "F'Chrissakes, Al, *I* was that fucking guy!"

"What fu— What guy?"

He pointed to the screen, finger trembling. "The guy who missed the cut by one!" Then he looked back at me. "I'm the guy who got the tour slot when Caminetti turned it down!"

I was having trouble absorbing this, and just stared at him for a few seconds before saying, "Well, I'll be dipped in—" A look from Juliette cut me off. "Well, whaddaya know about that!" I substituted, to her approval.

Discovering that his jaw was hanging open, Merriwell closed his mouth and slowly sat back down on the lounger. "Wasn't for him doin' that," he said, wonder in his voice, "I'd be selling knockwurst on the Lower East Side or somethin'."

"We goin' inta the city, Daddy?" the six-year-old asked eagerly.

"Get some knockwurst?" the nine-year-old added.

Merriwell looked over at the kids blankly, then got hold of himself and laughed. "Yeah, we're goin' to get some knockwurst, you bunch'a pudknockers!"

The kids whooped and jumped off the couch, swarming over Merriwell like bees over honey, him hugging them so hard I wondered how they could breathe, but they didn't seem to mind.

"Sometimes he just forgets himself with that mouth," Juliette said, shaking her head.

I weathered the storm over the next few days, knowing full well that something else would come along to replace it in the public's mind. The citizens would go purple in the face ranting and carrying on, warning of the end of civilization, and then get over it and forget what they'd been yelling about in the first place. You can get used to anything, given enough time—Americans being held hostage somewhere, floods making thousands of people homeless, drug and sex scandals among elected officials, people dying of epidemic diseases. All of it quickly becomes yesterday's news, although I have to admit, the Eddie Caminetti issue lasted longer than most.

For a lot of people, golf is more important than disease, scandal or other outrages against human dignity.

Part 2

· · · · · · · · · · · · · · · · · · ·

CHAPTER TWELVE

The big thing that happens when the team is finally in place is that we get an invitation to come to Washington and hang with the President. You'd think this was a great honor, but it's been a source of trouble ever since the Democrats conducted a sit-in at the White House in '92 and didn't leave.

Guys like Frederick Olmsted Asphal III were born exempt from any liberalism haunting their pasts, Pater being the kind of fellow who couldn't enjoy a meal unless he knew somebody else was hungry, but Fred was an exception. Many of the top moneymaking pro golfers were raised as Democrats, but later discovered the virtues of the Republican party, generally about the time they banked their first million. But while the lifelong GOP-ers still harbored some residual respect for the office of the presidency, the newly born, like people who had quit smoking, relished their enmity for the current administration and touted it in uncharacteristically uncharitable ways. Like putting up a struggle against the obligatory appearance with President Thomas Madison Eastwood that they threatened to take public unless I backed off.

It was the first time I put my authority to the test. I had the right to initiate proceedings against any player I thought would be disruptive to the team. There was a complication, of course, since it could be argued that the only one being disruptive was *me*, since the rest of them either were in complete agreement on this topic or, like Fred Asphal, chose to remove themselves from the fray or, like Eddie, couldn't care less either way.

The gods were on my side, however, and the players knew it. The PGA's position was easily predictable, since it would be based not on any silly and anachronistic sense of right or wrong but strictly on their Prime Directive, that of not doing anything that might embarrass the sport or themselves, not necessarily in that order. It wasn't hard to tell whose side the public would be on in light of President Eastwood's 64-percent approval rating and the traditional sense of awe that still surrounded the office in the minds of those citizens who hadn't spent too much time contemplating just why it should.

It ended quickly, and we all dutifully converged on the nation's capital one warm Tuesday in August. At an informal get-together just among ourselves the night before in my hotel suite, I saw fit not to comment on the excitement that had managed to infiltrate the team. Only a couple of us had ever been to the White House before, including Derek Anouilh after winning the Masters and me after my second Player of the Year award. Two others among us had played golf with Eastwood, a hard-core lover of the game and about a twelve handicapper.

The next morning, we trooped over to 1600 Pennsylvania Avenue and were ushered into an ornate salon that dripped all kinds of nineteenth-century symbolism, the type where, God forbid you should ask, you were likely to get a two-hour lecture on the toilet fixtures from some fanatical docent with no other life. We went through the standard photo op, in which Himself chats with everybody in the room for exactly twenty seconds, stopping at precisely the right moment to stare into a camera with his hand shaking yours, then mumbling something suitably innocuous before going on to the next guy and saying the same thing. Or so it seemed from a distance, until Eastwood got to me.

"Too bad about that shit-ass putt on thirteen at the British, Al," Eastwood said as he deftly positioned me toward where the camera would be as soon as the official White House photographer changed film. "What was it, a spike mark or something?"

"Tuft of grass, I think," I answered without betraying my surprise at his familiarity with this detail.

"Watched the tapes a couple times—ABC sent over the raw footage—swear to God the fucker was heading right for the heart when it swerved."

"I'd like to see that tape."

"No problem. Be in your hotel before dinner. Smile."

I did, just in time for the flash to blind me. I can't believe Eastwood's got any retinas left after all those years of industrial-strength strobes going off in his face.

"Lose by one, Jesus," he was saying as soon as the photographer's finger lifted from the shutter button. "How we looking for the Cup?"

Shitty was the honest answer, given the overwhelming dominance of the Euros these days. "Real good, Mr. President. It's a talented bunch and—"

"Their heads screwed on right?"

"Near as I can tell. They get along well with each other, and that's number one in my book."

"Mine, too. What's with this Camel Betty guy?"

Took me a second. "Oh, Caminetti? Good man. I think he's—"

An aide materialized out of thin air and, ignoring our conversation, which he probably assumed was standard mumbling for the cameras, tugged his boss away for the next picture. "Don't go 'way," Eastwood said to me as he followed the suit obediently.

Where was I gonna go?

As soon as the last picture was snapped, Eastwood whispered something to the aide and inside of three minutes the room was cleared except for my teammates and their President, who said, "Whadda you fellas say we step outside?"

So we stepped outside, finding ourselves at an exquisitely maintained putting green just off the Rose Garden, a card table loaded with beverages and fruit close by.

"Ike had this put in. C'mere, Merriwell," Eastwood called out to Mack. He picked two balls out of a bucket and dropped them on the putting surface about fifteen feet from one of the seven miniature flagsticks dotting the green, then grabbed two putters from a rack and handed one to Merriwell. "For a buck."

Merriwell grinned and took the putter, working the handle between his fingers and looking the shaft up and down.

"Don't worry," Eastwood said. "It isn't bent."

We laughed politely, then watched as both of them missed their putts, Merriwell having gotten it a lot closer than Eastwood. "Didn't give me a chance to study the green, Mr. President," Merriwell said lightly, and we all laughed again.

A few of the players took their own turns against the President. When Anouilh sank his, he said, "You owe me a dollar, sir," and Eastwood replied, "Deduct it from your next tax return."

More polite laughter, and a few more putts. Then Eastwood said, "So how's my putting?"

There was an eager chorus of "Just fine, Mr. President" and "You're doing great, sir" from the U.S. Ryder Cup team.

"Could use a little improvement, tell you the truth," one voice rang out.

The President turned toward the source of the voice, which was easy to locate because the rest of the players were inching away from it like vegetarians from steak tartare, leaving only Eddie Camel Betty standing by himself in the glare of the summer sun.

"Say what?" Eastwood said, squinting at him.

"Your putter isn't moving parallel to the path you want the ball to go."

Eastwood looked down at the club. "Feels like it is."

"It isn't." Eddie walked toward the edge of the green.

"But how do I correct something I can't feel?"

"Don't go by feel. Follow the ball with the clubhead."

"Meaning . . . ?"

Eddie took the club out of Himself's hands, demonstrating as he explained. " 'Stead'a hittin' the ball, pretend you're shoving it along. Keep moving the clubhead after contact, like you wanna guide the ball to the hole, and that'll make sure the clubhead is moving along the exact path you want it to go."

He handed the club back to Eastwood, who bent forward and took a few practice swings.

"More," Eddie said, shaking his head. "Like two feet."

Eastwood exaggerated the movement, leaning way left as he kept the clubhead going.

"That's more like it." Eddie reached out with his foot and kicked the two balls toward the President. "Now line up and hit 'em like that."

Eastwood did as instructed. The first ball missed by less than an inch. The second one went in. He straightened up and looked quizzically at the club in his hands. "How can what I do *after* I hit the ball make any difference?"

"Why do you follow through on a drive? Why not just stop the clubhead soon's you make contact with the ball and it's already on its way?"

Eastwood blinked a few times, then shrugged. "No idea. Too much momentum?"

"Partially. But why does it make a difference where the club ends up? Why not just let it do whatever it wants, straight up or over your shoulder or around your back?"

"I dunno."

"It's 'cuz knowing in advance what you have to do to make that club end up in the right place is what makes you swing it correctly in the first place, in order to get it there."

Eastwood's face showed he grasped the concept.

"It's like taking a divot," Eddie went on. "You think picking up a chunk of dirt makes you hit the ball better?"

"Always thought it did."

"Nuh-uh. But knowing you have to take a divot makes you hit down on the ball like you're supposed to. Fact is, you only dig up that chunk of dirt *after* the ball has already left the clubface." Eastwood looked at his putter, then at the cup. "What you do with the club after the ball has already left can't affect its path anymore. But *knowing* you're going to be following the ball makes you straighten out your swing plane before you connect." Eddie stepped over to the bucket, scooped out a handful of balls and dropped them unceremoniously on the green. "Hit a couple more."

Eastwood once again did as he was told and hit about a dozen more balls. Five went in, four missed by less than an inch, and three rolled right over the hole with too much speed, showing he at least had the line right.

He stood up, a broad smile spreading across his face. "Goddamn!"

"Well, there you go," Eddie said, then went over to the card table and grabbed an apple.

Eastwood came over to where I was standing. "That Camaletti?"

"Cami— Yes, sir, that's him."

He went over to the card table and said to Eddie, "You know how many lessons I've had?"

"Yeah, well, every golf instructor teaches the game different." Eddie bit into the apple and talked while chewing, as though he were chatting with a guy who was unclogging his toilet. "One says the key is to keep your head down, another says just keep it still, another says that it's the biggest crock-of-shit myth in golf altogether. One guy is obsessed with the swing plane, another guy couldn't care less so long as you hold your shoulders properly. One guy tells you that getting the grip right is ninety percent of the game, another says it's the stance. One guy tells you to remember fifteen different things as you're standing over the ball, another says to get your muscle memory in groove on the range and then forget everything and just let it rip out on the course." I could tell from the President's pained expression that he'd heard every one of those things at some time or another.

Eddie took another bite out of the apple. "Sometimes the simplest answers are the most correct. All these instructors are out there flinging bullshit left and right, and the problem is, each one thinks he's Jesus, thinks his way is the only way, and that everybody else is a complete schmuck who should have his certificate lifted. So every time you change teachers, you have to go through this fraternity hazing where you hit a bucket of balls while he watches, shaking his head and rolling his eyes and wondering what total asshole ever told you hit the ball *that* way, f'Chrissakes. Then you have to explain to him what the other guy explained to you, which is mostly a lot of New Age horseshit physics, and he laughs because it's such crap, and then he tells you exactly *why* it's utter crap, which he does by replacing it with his own brand of scientific horseshit, and that's about the time he says, Look, what we gotta do, we gotta completely take apart your swing and put it back together, unlearn all those harmful habits. Now, it's gonna hurt your game for a while, but you gotta be patient, and eventually blah, blah, blah and so on." He waved the apple around as he finished up, then took another bite.

"That's exactly what that asshole Firth said to me!" Eastwood exclaimed, naming one of the members of the European Ryder Cup team he'd met on a goodwill trip to Scotland.

Eddie nodded in sympathy. "So you start off your lessons with this clown shakin' his head like you're the dumbest damned creature in God's universe on account'a you fallin' for the first guy's line of bullshit, and you're embarrassed to even take a swing in front of this thirty-an-hour Nicklaus who's got you convinced you wasted the last three years of your golfing life."

It was as if he was plumbing Eastwood's deepest golfing insecurities and laying them bare right in front of him. "You ever teach anybody, Eddie?"

"Once in a while, but never for money."

"How do *you* do it?"

"I watch him hit a bucket. No matter how bad he hits, I nod a lot and grunt in approval. When he's all done, I says something like, Y'know, that's not bad at all, not bad at all. Couple adjustments here and there, you're gonna see a big improvement. You got any ice?"

Eastwood immediately turned toward a small door standing ajar near a rosebush on the other side of the putting green. "Manuel! Get some ice out here pronto, will ya?"

"Right away, Mr. President," came a reply, and Eastwood turned back to Eddie.

"So right away the guy feels good about the game, he knows I'm not gonna criticize the hell out of him, he's comfortable and eager. He won't cringe before his next lesson, afraid it's gonna be a half hour of me beating him about the head and shoulders and making him feel like shit. We're gonna have a good time, me and him, whacking balls, talking golf, me giving him some pointers and then helping him do it right and groove them into his brain."

"You telling me you don't have your own brand of bullshit?"

" 'Course. But mine is different for each student. If he's fixated on keeping his head down, I tell him fine, just don't get obsessed with it. If he's scared'a not bringin' the club back on what he thinks is a perfect plane, I tell him it's okay to be less than perfect long's he's got something else under control. So right away he relaxes. Which is half the damned battle right there, lemme tell ya."

"Fuckin' A it is." Eastwood looked down at the putter he still had in his hands, swinging it with that same exaggerated follow-through. "Huh," he grunted as he walked over to me. "Good choice, Al, that Camazetti." He pressed his lips together, swung a few more times and nodded approvingly, adding, "You done good," before he walked back to the green to hang with Camazetti some more.

The raw footage from ABC was already at my hotel by the time I got back to my room.

CHAPTER THIRTEEN

The Ryder Cup was being held at PGA West in La Quinta, California, part of the area colloquially referred to as Palm Springs, even though that term correctly refers only to one of a number of small cities clustered in the Coachella Valley. Drier than the Gobi and nearly as hot as Death Valley, this area is home to ninety-seven golf courses owing to a 150-year supply of fresh water in an aquifer just a scratch below the surface.

We'd be using the TPC Stadium Course, a 7,261 beast of a track that has been known to swallow golfers whole and is usually referred to by its victims as "The Bitch." Multi-tiered greens, pot bunkers everywhere, insidiously slanted lies and so much water you could practically surf on some of the larger lakes make it one of the toughest tests in the game, which is just what the members had in mind when they commissioned Pete Dye, who must have had some terrorist blood in his ancestry, to design it. Here's how I described one of the holes, the par-four number nine, in an article *USA Today* asked me to write a week before the tournament:

"It's only 381 yards long. Except that where there's supposed to be a fairway, there's a lake. The fairway is off to the left and it's about eight inches wide. That's because there's a bunker 130 yards long that separates it from the water on the right and grass mounds the size of small volcanoes on the left. Once you get in range of the green you've got a clear shot to it, so long as you don't land in the water on the front. But don't worry too much, because if you hit a few yards short, the bunkers will keep you nice and dry, as will those in the back and on the left. So the best place to land is on the right, because that way the twenty-foot-high hill will keep you in play by rolling your ball into one of the bunkers first, which—did I mention?—have sides so steep they're reinforced with railroad ties—laid *vertically*. Now, you could certainly hit it right onto the green, sure. Except that it's the size of a poker table, so firm you couldn't stop a ball on it if it were made out of sandpaper and so slick the best way to hit a long putt is to just sneeze on the ball."

True to our sense of sportsmanship, and unwilling to take advantage of the access we as United States residents had to the course, we didn't use it for team practice until the Sunday before the tournament, when both sides converged in the desert to begin their scheduled familiarization rounds. Of course, the TPC being open to the public, none of us had been precluded from simply showing up to play once in a while during the year, as all of us had, but no more than twenty or thirty times each; after all, we didn't wish to make a travesty of the tournament. Neither did our European brethren, who played it only when they happened to be in the States, which was during every PGA event held on U.S. soil, which happened no more than about forty times a year. Which pretty much made us all even up with respect to memorizing every blade of grass and grain of sand between the first hole and the eighteenth green.

Having arrived the day before the Europeans in order to make absolutely certain that everything was properly prepared for their arrival, we saw fit to inspect the course so they would have no untoward surprises their hosts might have been expected to spot in advance. The best way for a golfer to inspect a course being to play it, we saw no harm in going out for a few rounds in the afternoon once the administrative labors of the morning had been concluded.

Nobody was much surprised when eight members of the European team showed up as well. "Just getting a bit of an upsa-daisy on that jet lag bother, chaps," as Britisher John Wickenhampshire (pronounced "Wickemsher") put it. Nor did anybody care to mention anything about the absence of cross-cultural invitations to join in each other's play. We all knew why we were here, although a great deal of genuine, backslapping camaraderie did take place before and after our officially nonpractice rounds.

Some of it revolved around who wasn't going to be playing in the tournament. Our friends across the pond shook their heads in sympathy over my decision not to invite Boom-Boom Harriman, but none initiated any conversation as to why. The Europeans had little patience for the kind of shenanigans we in the States seemed willing to put up with from our superstars in all the major sports. Their transgressions tended more toward mass murder at soccer matches, shouts of "Kill the ref!" being less euphemistic than they are here.

"Jeez, what the hell's with him?" Eddie said as he walked off the driving range to get some ice water. He hadn't hit any balls yet, just done his stretching, but in this oppressive heat even that could wear you out.

"Him who?" I asked, and he jerked a thumb over his shoulder to where a player was hitting balls by himself.

Him was Robert Don't-Call-Me-Bob Carmichael. "You talk to him?"

"Didn't have to. Didn't get within twenty feet, he was yakkin' at Asphal about me so's I could hear."

Carmichael was one of the players who had been unable to make it to our gathering at Crystal. In truth, my invitation for him to join us at the retreat had been so halfhearted and insincere, a cinder block would have caught the message.

Carmichael's early arrival out here had little to do with any desire to groove with his comrades and more to do with grooving the course into his head by playing as many holes a day as his bad back would let him. Another reason was to be the first on our block to give me a ration of shit about Eddie Caminetti, his contempt for whom Carmichael made no effort to conceal.

I walked out to the range with Joel Fleckheimer, and we set our bags down on either side of Carmichael's hitting area. I asked him if he had a problem with Eddie.

"Problem? Me?" He took a moment to hit a very pretty wedge, landing it almost on top of the 125-yard marker flag. "Why should I have a problem when I busted my ass to be able to play for the Cup only to find I'm on a team with a con artist who needs tricks to win?" He hit another shot, nearly identical to the first. He watched it land, then turned to me, resting the clubhead on the grass and leaning on it. "Well, there aren't any tricks in the Ryder Cup, but why should I have a problem with that?"

"Man sure plays some pretty good straight golf," Fleckheimer assured him as he selected a club.

"My grandmother can play some pretty good golf," Carmichael retorted, teeing up a ball and then turning to Fleck. "But how's he gonna do with eight thousand people screaming in his ear? Toodling around the back nine at Bumfuck Muni with nothin' but a bunch of fuckin' sparrows lookin' at you ain't the same as the big time." Understand that, for Carmichael, this was one of his good days.

"He did pretty all right in front of a crowd at Crystal. Didn't seem to bother him."

"How many? Couple hundred?"

Fleck sniffled. "Maybe fifty."

"Fifty." Carmichael turned back to his ball. "A wonder they managed to fit them all on the course." He hit another one. "And what's this shit about me coughing up dough to *pay* the sonofabitch to play?"

At which point appeared one Eddie Caminetti a few positions away. I called out, "Yo, Eddie, c'mere. Say hello to Robert Carmichael."

Eddie walked up and extended his hand. "Glad to know you, Carmichael. Eddie Caminetti."

"I know who you are." Carmichael took Eddie's hand unenthusiastically and let go quickly, grabbing a five-iron out of his bag. "And I'm not gonna bullshit you, either. You don't belong on this team."

If that surprised or hurt him, Eddie's face didn't show it. "But I'm already on it, and there's nothing can be done about it, so why bust my balls?"

Carmichael set up his shot and took a look at his target. " 'Cuz the pairings haven't been made yet, that's why." Meaning I hadn't yet decided who plays during the first two days of the Ryder.

Turning his attention back to the ball, Carmichael lined himself up and swung. A sharp, clear *crack!* rang out as he connected, sending the pill an awfully long way for a five-iron, and awfully straight, too.

"Nice shot," Eddie said, meaning it.

Carmichael didn't bother looking at him. "Easy, when there's no pressure. Cripple can shoot twelve under on the range."

The thing you have to understand about Carmichael is that nobody on the tour can stand him. He's the only pro golfer who charges for his autograph, showing up at those sports-card conventions along with baseball players who make five million a year and aren't ashamed to squeeze ten bucks a pop out of little kids who worship them. Early on, people made excuses for him because he claimed to have a bad back and maybe it was the pain that made him so surly, but eventually even his own entourage gave up any pretense of trying to rationalize his nasty disposition.

Four months ago, on the final day of the Allied Sewage Recycling (formerly the Mountainview) Open in Baton Rouge, Carmichael had moved his ball a clubhead over on the seventh green to allow another player a clear line to the hole. Two holes later, an official asked him if he had replaced the ball in its original location before taking his own putt. Hesitating, Carmichael tried to think. This had happened to Davis Love III once, except nobody asked him, it just occurred to him well after the fact and he brought it up himself. He just plain couldn't remember whether he had replaced the ball or not, and neither could the other players or the caddies or the officials who had been there, so he penalized himself two strokes, and it cost him the tournament. A class move from a class guy.

At the Allied, Carmichael eventually remembered that, yes, he had indeed replaced his ball. I'd never prayed so hard for a guy to blow it on the eighteenth as I did that day, but he won the tournament, along with three hundred seventy-five thousand dollars. Bitch of it was, that squeaked him into tenth position on the list, and onto my team, by a margin of less than fifteen points.

By now Mack Merriwell, Fred Asphal and Enrico Senzamio had joined our little group. Carmichael ranted on for a while, and then we slowly drifted away and left him to himself.

Asphal was at the ice-water barrel. "Did he harass you?" he asked Eddie.

"Doesn't matter."

"He has his days, is all," Merriwell said. "Don't take it to heart." He turned and watched Carmichael hit a three-iron. "Looks like his back might be hurting."

"Good," Senzamio said softly, and we all laughed.

"What about that thing at the Allied?" Eddie asked Merriwell.

"Ah, you know what? I'm starting to think maybe he did replace the ball. Who the hell really knows, so why keep shitting on the guy? He's a prick, sure, but I just can't see any pro doing somethin' like that."

Eddie seemed to mull this over carefully. A few minutes later we were all back out on the range, clustered in toward Carmichael so we could control things and not let the Europeans see that there was any dissension on the team.

"Pressure, Caminetti," Carmichael said without looking at him. "You know what real pressure is?" *Whack!* with the three-iron.

"No. Why don't you tell me?"

"Can't tell you." *Whack!* again. "Nobody can tell you." *Whack!* Perfect as the last one. Carmichael turned, poked his club in Eddie's direction and said, "It's something you just gotta learn." He slammed the club into his bag and turned to wipe his hands on a towel hanging from the bag rack.

Eddie regarded Carmichael for a few seconds, then said, "So let's you and me play a match."

Carmichael *harumphed* and didn't even turn around. "I said *under pressure*. There's no pressure in a—"

"For fifty thousand."

The sounds of spikes shuffling and balls being hit ceased abruptly. Despite whatever crusty exterior Carmichael was bent on maintaining, no rejoinder to Eddie's gauntlet-throw was immediately forthcoming from him. It was put up or shut up, and all of us reconvening around the two of them, clubs still in our hands, were acutely aware of it.

"Seems a little rich there, Caminetti," Carmichael finally said, nobody missing the implicit *for you* he left out at the end.

"Idea was to put me under pressure, right?"

"Not so much pressure you don't got the means to pay it off."

"I got it," Eddie said calmly.

"Izzat so." Whether Eddie had that much money immediately available or not, what Carmichael had was five witnesses. He was really at a loss for words, and we started getting uncomfortable. I figured maybe I'd better step in and—

"You look a little worried, Robert," Eddie said.

"Worried, my sweet—"

"Hey, I can understand that," Eddie cut him off, as though he hadn't started speaking at all. "You barely made the money list, probably gone and used up all the dough just to pay off debts, right?"

Carmichael's face was starting to redden even more than would have been expected from the hot desert sun. "So I know what you're prob'ly thinking," Eddie was saying. "You're thinking, I know I can beat this asshole, but on any given day . . ."

He let his voice trail off. The *any-given-day* phenomenon was better known to golfers than to athletes in any other sport, although it applied almost everywhere. No matter how clearly superior one competitor was to his opponent, there was always a reasonable possibility that, on any

given day, he could lose. In golf, it could come from a couple of un-
lucky kicks from uncooperative fairways and greens, or from sprinkler
heads in the exact wrong spots, or lapses in concentration or any of a
hundred other factors the medical profession would label *idiopathic*,
meaning, *of unknown origin.*

"So I'll tell you what," Eddie continued, pretending to give it some
thought for a second. "I'll give you every green in regulation."

Fleckheimer raised his three-iron, laying it over his shoulders and
resting his arms on it. Merriwell pulled a groove brush out of his pocket
and began running it back and forth over his already pristine driver.

"Are you serious?" Carmichael asked.

"Uh-huh."

"What you're telling me," Carmichael said skeptically, "every hole
we play, no matter how I hit, I'm automatically on the green in two
under par?"

"You don't even have to hit," Eddie answered evenly. "Every hole,
you start putting at two under."

Carmichael turned his head slightly and stared at Eddie. "And in
exchange . . . ?"

"I get to put your ball on the green wherever I want."

"And I start putting from there?"

"Yep."

"You don't touch the ball again?"

"Nope."

"And . . . ?"

"And nothin'. That's it."

"That's it."

"Uh-huh."

"Can I lift the ball and clean it?"

"Absolutely. Set it back down just the way you like."

"Using my own balls?"

"Naturally."

Carmichael looked at Eddie for a few seconds. "I don't get it."

"There's nothing to get."

"There's a trick here somewhere."

"No there isn't. Only trick is, I'm gonna win."

Carmichael looked at the rest of us, who were doing an awful job of
trying to appear busy, then back at Eddie. "Bullshit."

Eddie nodded his acknowledgment of this reasonable conclusion, apparently taking no offense. "Tell you what, Carmichael."

Oh boy, here it comes again!

"You think I misled you in any way," Eddie went on, "you call off the bet."

"When?"

"Right up through the eighteenth hole." Carmichael didn't say anything. "Your call, Carmichael. Think I pulled some shit, bet's off. No questions asked."

Carmichael looked at me, and I said, "He means it. But don't do it, Robert."

"Why the hell not?"

"I don't *know* why not. Just don't do it!"

"Kind of an answer is that, Bellamy? What the hell're you talking about?"

"Man just told you. He's gonna beat you."

"So he told me, so what?"

I shrugged, helpless to try to rescue Carmichael from himself. "Means he is."

"He gives me eighteen greens in regulation, how's he gonna beat me!"

"I just told you: I don't know. But he will."

After giving me an are-you-completely-nuts look, he turned back to Eddie. "Anytime I think I was snookered, I can call it off?"

"That's the deal. Front'a all these witnesses."

As we nodded in acknowledgment, Carmichael hesitated, then threw the rag forcefully onto the ground. "Then what've I got to lose. Let's go!"

"Hold it a second!" I stepped forward and put my hand on his shoulder, turning him around to face me. "You can call it off, you think Eddie misled you. But if you just plain lose, you lose. Got it?" I pressed him some more: "Only if he snookered you."

"I speak English, Bellamy, okay?"

Now that the match was set, everybody began jockeying to join the foursome, yammering like nine-year-olds lined up at the ice-cream counter. "Hey!" I yelled. "I'm the captain, I'll pick the foursome."

They all quieted down and waited for me to make the decision. "Now, I wanna do this fair, okay? So first of all"—I hesitated a moment—"I'm in." This invited a chorus of derisive and obscene shouts hardly in keeping with the genteel traditions of the sport. "And Mr. Wizard."

Eddie hoisted his bag onto a shoulder and headed for a cart. Fleck came up to me and said, "Isn't he gonna warm up? He didn't hit any balls!"

I was way beyond telling Eddie Caminetti how to play golf. "Usually knows what he's doing."

I picked up my bag and went to load it up next to Eddie's. Mr. Wizard would ride with Carmichael.

"Mr. Wizard" was Jonathan Markovy, a serious, bespectacled man who looked more like a college professor than a pro golfer. Markovy was the best mechanic on the tour. Everything he did was scientific. He analyzed the golf swing endlessly, reducing every element of it to quantized bits and pieces until they could be broken down no further, then strung them back together in various combinations to produce exactly the swings he wanted.

It worked for him. His game was methodical in its approach and machinelike in its execution. When he blew a shot, he didn't get all crazy and bent out of shape, he just tried to figure out exactly what had gone wrong and then not do it again. The only thing that was a mystery to Mr. Wizard was why, at some point, he didn't just simply have the whole damned thing nailed. He was realistic enough to have realized early on that he was doomed to a lifetime of corrections, perhaps moving closer to the perfect game but never hitting it, like one of those wacky curves you learn about in high school geometry that keeps getting closer to the axis but will never touch it, not after a million miles or a million years. The mystery was compounded by the fact that sometimes he actually moved farther away, not closer. At first he assumed it was because he was getting older, and his muscles weren't cooperating, but then he'd suddenly improve, so that theory wouldn't fly.

As we drove to the first tee, I suggested to Carmichael that he go ahead and play from the tees anyway, just to get used to this course. Nobody, including Carmichael himself, would have predicted that he'd be on the team, and so he hadn't gotten in nearby as many rounds on "The Bitch" as the rest of the guys.

Pulling up to the tee, he leaned out of the cart and called out to Eddie, "Gotta warn you, pal. I been putting awfully good lately."

"Yeah, whyzzat?" Markovy said to him as he got out of the cart. "They make the clown's nose a little wider? Or just slowed down the windmill!"

I should have mentioned, rereading my description of him, that Mr. Wizard was far from being a geek. He had a great sense of humor and an easygoing affability that contrasted with his approach to golf, which, by the way, he happened to love playing for its own sake.

I tossed a tee into the air. It landed pointing to Markovy. "You're up first, Jon," I informed him. I came up second, Eddie third and Carmichael last.

PGA West named all the holes on this course, I suppose in some kind of attempt to capture the spirit of Scottish golf. But the Scots have lyrical and imaginative names that hark back to the history of the individual courses. Cruden Bay is a good example, with names like Bluidy Burn, from a battle fought there between the Danes and the Scots in 1012, Corchdane, translating as "Dane killer," and Slains, the name of the castle in Cruden Bay that Bram Stoker used as a setting for *Dracula*. TPC's are more like the kind you'd find on a miniature-golf course, like Double Trouble, Sand Pit, Moat and Second Thoughts, but they are fairly accurate descriptions of what you're up against.

The first hole is called Prelude, an intimation of things to come. It plays 440 yards, and is like I imagine a hole on the surface of the moon would be except in full gravity. It's a maze of man-high impact craters, sandpits and cute little hillocks whose sole purpose is to hide your ball from the green.

Markovy knocked a good one about 270, with a slight draw that landed him right in the middle. Mine was within twenty feet of his, and a little more to the right. Eddie, who'd been standing off to the side taking practice swings with his driver, walked onto the box and teed up. I started to yawn as he hit, but was shocked to watch him pull the shot badly, sending the ball much too far to the left. Luckily, it landed short of a sand trap. Unluckily, it came to rest at the bottom of a depression with a bush partially blocking his next shot.

Carmichael looked at me and then rolled his eyes upward, shaking his head. I tried to ignore him, and then it was his turn. He sure did look relaxed for a guy with that much money on the line, and I suppose it was because he was about as worried as Muhammad Ali would be before a bout with Olga Korbut. He hit a tremendous shot, at least 290, then tried to look nonchalant about it as he stepped away from the tee.

Eddie's tee shot still left him with about 250 to the green. I knew that he wouldn't risk using his driver off the deck, especially with a very narrow opening to the green, and he didn't, instead safely hitting a five-wood to within forty yards. Carmichael hit another beauty, an eight-iron, I think, landing on the front fringe and tucking the ball in close for about a twelve-foot putt. Eddie didn't get his wedge shot high enough into the air. The ball rolled along the Teflon green and left him a twenty-footer. I was on in two, about the same distance away as Eddie, and Markovy took three to get there but had the shortest putt.

"Nice shot," Eddie said to Carmichael as we walked onto the green. He walked past his own ball and stopped at Carmichael's, picked it up and started walking again.

"Hey!" Carmichael yelled out at him. Eddie stopped and turned, but said nothing. "I got on in regulation myself!"

"So what?" Eddie responded.

"So you said you were gonna give me greens in regulation so you could move my ball. I didn't need it, so you can't move my ball."

"You didn't even have to hit in the first place. You're only doing it for practice, remember?" He pointed at me, and I nodded my agreement. "Our game starts when we get to the green," Eddie went on as he walked away with the ball, "and what you do before that is your business."

Eddie was just being polite; no way was this news to Carmichael, the rules being so simple and straightforward. I just think he was surprised to watch somebody else pick up his ball.

Markovy was less polite. "Hey, Robert, what're you kidding here or what?"

Carmichael waved his hand dismissively and went to the front edge of the green, where Eddie was placing his ball. It was a good thirty feet from the hole, with a vicious hump along the way. "What the hell are you doing?"

Eddie had been kneeling and stayed that way. "Now what?"

"What kinda shit-ass lie is that? I thought you were gonna gimme something reasonable to hit at!"

"Now, why would you think that?"

"How do you expect me to putt decent from all the way out there!" Carmichael shouted back at him.

As Markovy and I looked at each other in astonishment, Eddie said, "Whole point was, I'm betting you fifty thousand that you *can't!*"

"That's not how I understood it!"

"Cut it out and hit the goddamned ball, Carmichael!" I yelled angrily across the green. "You knew damned well what the bet was!"

"Wanna call it off?" Eddie asked.

Carmichael looked back at the spot where his ball had first landed, then, pouting, set up for his putt.

It was an amazing one, especially considering his lack of experience on this course. He barely touched the ball, but it kept on going, missing the hole by four inches and coming to rest less than three feet past it. As he strolled up and bent over to mark it, Eddie said, "Pick it up." Carmichael stopped with his arm extended toward the ball and looked back at him. Who concedes a three-foot putt in a big-money game? "Pick it up," Eddie said again. Carmichael did so, and he was in with a par.

I two-putted, and so did Eddie, but that was bogey for him. Markovy knocked his in smoothly for par. As we walked off the green, Carmichael had a smug, shit-eating grin on his face. "Beat your ass anyway, hustler!" he said to Eddie.

"That you did, Robert," Eddie said amiably, already having forgotten Carmichael's petulant outburst.

"Jeez, maybe you shoulda warmed up, Eddie," I said as we got back in the cart and headed for the second hole.

He jerked his head around to face me, a scowl on his face. "Why're you tellin' me that, Al?"

"Uh, the way you hit that driver, maybe you—"

"What I'm asking, why are you telling me *now*? What do you want me to do with that piece of advice?"

"Well, there's nothing much you can—"

"Then why tell me!"

I hadn't thought of that. I felt terrible. Here was Eddie, down one after one hole, probably feeling bad enough already and knowing exactly why, and I was jumping on his face and—

He laughed suddenly, and just like that the anger was replaced with a *Gotcha!* smile. He tapped my leg with a fist. "Just jerkin' your chain, shithead. You worried?"

I was relieved that I hadn't just cost Eddie fifty large by playing with his head. I should have known that probably wasn't possible anyway. " 'Course I'm worried. You kidding? No matter who loses, it's still bad *juju*. For the team, I mean."

We pulled up, and Eddie stepped out of the cart. "Gonna be bad *juju*, Al, no gettin' around it, but you had it in the first place." He pointed a thumb at Carmichael, who was taking some practice swings, his ball already teed up since he had honors after winning the first hole. "Soon's this asshole showed up," Eddie said. He pulled out his driver and started walking toward the tee, looking back at me. "All's we're gonna do, just bring it out a little."

"Eddie!" He stopped, still looking my way. "Why *didn't* you warm up?" I said, lowering my voice so Carmichael couldn't hear.

"Didn't need'a. I could win this using nothin' but a baseball bat."

"Didn't look that way on the first hole."

He smiled again. "Relax, Bubba. Plenty'a golf to go."

The second hole, Craters, was a short par-four, just 373 to the green but with minefields all along the route. It requires a very accurate tee shot, and most players will hit off with a long iron or, at most, a five-wood. Carmichael damn near came out of his shoes trying to reach the green with his driver, and sliced the hell out of the ball instead. It didn't seem to bother him. The rest of us hit fairly decent, conservative shots. Markovy and I got on in two, and so did Eddie, but Carmichael took three.

"So I'm on in two anyway, right?" he said as we walked on.

"You got it," Eddie said, and once again picked up Carmichael's ball. Believe it or not, this green was forty-five yards from front to back. With the flag close to the front, I was sure Eddie was going to give Carmichael a 110-foot putt. Instead, he put the ball down less than twenty feet way. But there was a ten-foot-wide, saddle-shaped depression on the way to the hole, which looked to me like three changes of direction for the putt.

Carmichael did a pretty good job under the circumstances, but it was the kind of putt you have to see done a half dozen times before you know how to hit it. The ball settled in the bottom of the depression, and it took him two more putts to hole it out, for a bogey. Eddie made his par.

All even. Carmichael did not look amused.

On the next green, Eddie once again decided not to go for distance in placing Carmichael's ball. This green had several lobes on its circumference, making it look somewhat like a bloated amoeba. The flag was set in one of the lobes, and Eddie placed the ball in the one adjacent to it, so that there was about twelve feet of fringe grass, called frog hair, between ball and hole.

As I saw it, Carmichael had two choices: One was to try to putt through the frog, and the other was to deliberately putt away from the flag but at least have the ball end up with a clear shot for it.

As Carmichael saw it, he had a third option. He walked back to the cart and retrieved his pitching wedge.

"That legal?" I asked.

" 'Course it's legal," Carmichael retorted. "No rule says what club you can use where."

"Not so," Mr. Wizard said. "Local rules might."

"What're you talking about?"

You didn't argue rules with Mr. Wizard. "Like that green at Riviera that's got a pot bunker smack in the center? Members aren't allowed to use anything but a putter, even if that bunker's right between their ball and the hole."

"Yeah, well, I saw *you* hit a sand wedge over it!"

I remembered that shot. It was during a U.S. Open. "Because that rule is waived for PGA events, *Bob*," Markovy explained.

"Well, this is a match between PGA pros, isn't it?"

It was a weak point, but Markovy didn't take the path we thought he was going to, arguing that this was hardly an official PGA event. "Actually, Carmichael, no. Eddie isn't a PGA member."

Carmichael brightened. "Then how's he playing in the Ryder?"

"By invitation."

"Well, I invited him to—"

"Hang on a second," I said, and turned to go back to the cart. "Let's take a look at the scorecard and see what the local rule is before we start arguing the details."

"Don't bother," Eddie called out. "I waive the rule. Go ahead and use your wedge, Robert."

"You sure you want to do that, Eddie?" Markovy asked.

"Pipe down, Markovy," Carmichael said as he prepared to hit. "You his lawyer or what?"

It was a gem of a shot, plopping down four feet past the flag with so much spin it backed up about a foot. On any other green it would have spun back past the hole, but Carmichael read this one perfectly. Eddie conceded the par, then holed out his own putt.

Still even. Carmichael three-putted the next three holes, made a miraculous forty-foot birdie on seven, three-putted again on eight, and then, unbelievably, *four*-putted the vicious ninth green. In all fairness, though, I have to say that his putting was really quite superb. But there was no way, unless he was psychokinetic, that he could have consistently gotten close enough on his first stroke to produce makable par putts, not from those crazy-ass lies Eddie was giving him.

Eddie parred two holes, bogeyed two, then parred the last two. At the end of the front nine, he was three up on Carmichael, who was starting to look deathly pale despite the blazing sun.

We rode by the clubhouse on the way to the tenth and stopped for refills on the ice water. Carmichael went inside to hit the head. Markovy got out of his cart and wandered up to us.

"Tell me something, Jon," I said to him, taking advantage of the idle time to find out something I'd been wondering about. "How come, all this stuff you study, how come you're not off writing books and preaching the gospel?"

Eddie, uninterested, leaned back on his seat and closed his eyes. Markovy took off his straw hat and ran a damp towel over his forehead. "Because it isn't gospel, Al. Just *my* gospel. Works for me, but who's to say what good it'd do for somebody else?"

Eddie's eyes opened.

"Everybody keeps thinking he found *the* answer," Markovy continued, "like the golf god's been keeping it a secret for two hundred years and chose this moment to reveal it to a guy. Clear your mind, put this in your mind, stand this way and forget everything else, only the grip counts—all these guys think their way is the right way. The only way."

Eddie sat up straight.

"Now, a smart golfer, he'll try 'em *all* until he finds the ones that're right for him. To him, golf technique is a smorgasbord of possibilities that can be sampled, not a religion to be obeyed. And if he's lucky as well as smart, he won't run into too many teachers that start out by saying, Oh, Lord, who the hell taught you *that* piece of shit, we gotta tear it down completely and start from scratch, blabbity-blah. If you're already playing pretty good golf and you get a teacher says that to you, go find another one. 'Cuz it doesn't mean your swing sucks, it just means it's not *his* swing, and he doesn't know how to teach any other one. All the different swings are right, see? Every one. But there's only a couple that're right for *you*."

Markovy mopped his face again. "What you need is a teacher who takes the time to understand *your* swing, then helps you fine-tune it."

I now understood something about Markovy I hadn't realized before, why so many guys asked him for advice even though they didn't embrace the same methods. It was because, for all his scholarly dissection of the game, or maybe because of it, he had an uncanny ability to spot flaws in any kind of swing. A lot of guys could do that, but always in the context of their own game, not the one of the guy they're watching. So they'll see somebody drop his right shoulder too much, say something and wind up screwing him up completely. What they didn't realize was that maybe dropping that shoulder was okay for the particular way this one guy swings.

Markovy, on the other hand, if he saw that your swing plane was off a little, he wouldn't say anything until he carefully watched you hit a few dozen shots and figured out if it made any difference. Then he might come back and say, If you're comfortable with bringing the club that far back, delay rolling your wrists over just a tad and it should straighten out that fade. Where a hundred other teachers might tell somebody he's using too much wrist with his short irons, Markovy might tell him to bring his shoulders around a bit more, easing the strain on his wrists and giving him better control. What he was doing was fixing up *their* swings, not teaching them his. I think maybe that was the real reason we called him Mr. Wizard.

Carmichael came out of the clubhouse, made a beeline for his cart and dropped onto the seat, rapping his knuckles on the cupholder to get Markovy's attention. I think he wanted to get the hell away from the clubhouse before the group behind us came in and asked for the status of the match. Markovy made a face, then walked back as slowly as he could without it looking obvious.

Things didn't change much. After the first four holes of the back nine, Eddie had made two birdies he didn't need, and Carmichael had three-putted three times. Eddie won both of his birdie holes and halved the other two, and was now up five with five left to play. The very best Carmichael could hope for was to halve the match by winning all five of the remaining holes, and it didn't even come up to the level of a pipe dream.

Getting into his cart after the thirteenth, a totally insane, 220-yard par-three with only water for a fairway and a green sitting *alongside*, not behind it, Carmichael turned to us and said, "This is complete bullshit, Caminetti."

"What is?" Eddie asked him.

"I assumed you were gonna give me reasonable lies and let me play my own position if I got on in regulation. You didn't tell me you'd be laying down impossible putts nobody could make and stealing my good approach shots."

Eddie laughed and said, "Whadja think I was gonna do, make 'em all gimmes?"

I said, "Didn't seem to bother you when you won the first hole."

"You tricked me," Carmichael replied. After a moment he added, "And I ain't payin'."

"The hell you—" I started to say, but Eddie held up his hand and I stopped.

"I was shooting par, maybe even below par, some'a those shots I was making," Carmichael said.

Eddie again silently admonished me to stay quiet, and the message somehow made it over to Markovy as well. We played the rest of the round in near silence.

Coming off eighteen, I was still stunned, Markovy mortified. Eddie just seemed oblivious and untroubled about what had transpired. He shot a really wonderful three over, and Markovy and I both came in even. The three of us were aware that Carmichael had played much better golf than any of us, but it was wildly beside the point.

Carmichael jumped out of the cart before it came to a complete stop and stalked off, leaving the bag to be handled by the cart attendants.

Markovy walked over to us rapidly and said indignantly, "You gonna let him get away with that?"

"Get away with what?" Eddie asked as he calmly put balls back into his bag.

"Stiffing you, f'Chrissakes!"

"Whaddaya want me to do, Jon—report him to the PGA? Shoot him?"

"Shooting him would be good, yeah. I mean, *shit*, Eddie . . . !"

Eddie sighed and pulled ball markers and tees out of his pocket. "I never go back on a deal, Jon."

"What deal?" I asked him.

"I told him he could quit anytime he thought I was tricking him."

"But you didn't trick him!"

"I also told him it was his call, no questions asked. He made the call, that was his right"—Eddie zipped up an outside pocket of his bag—"that was the deal."

"Aren't you even angry?" Markovy, his voice plaintive, was almost whining now.

Eddie smiled benignly, trying to ease some of Markovy's distress. "Only woulda been angry if it'd been a surprise."

CHAPTER FOURTEEN

The Europeans had the course Sunday morning. I'd set it up that way in order to accommodate what I hoped would become a Ryder tradition, at least on American soil, and that was a golf clinic for inner-city kids.

Everybody thought golf would become an instant sensation among disadvantaged kids after Derek Anouilh sprang on the scene. It didn't quite happen like that, especially among the really hard-core downtrodden in the slums of New York, Chicago, Detroit and Los Angeles. These kids were too smart not to understand what a long shot it was to play basketball for money, despite seeing hundreds of black athletes making billions in the NBA. So they certainly weren't about to be kidded into thinking they had any kind of a chance doing it through golf just because one dark-skinned phenom had done it. Most of those minority kids we saw streaming onto golf courses in Anouilh's wake were the kind who already entered science-fair competitions and swim meets and did homework at night. They weren't the kids who needed rescuing, the kind for whom the acquisition of discipline and self-control were less than stellar inducements.

So I organized a clinic aimed at those who were clearly headed nowhere but at least hadn't dropped out of high school yet. We schlepped a couple dozen students out of South Central in buses, hoping the heat would tone down any excess rambunctiousness they might bring. They got off the buses already complaining about the weather, trying to look cool and not making a very good show of it, since short pants seemed to be out this year except on the basketball court. Speaking of which, four of them had brought basketballs along. They also brought with them a cynical attitude about the game of golf, which was not unexpected.

I made a little welcome speech about how we were going to give them an introduction to the sport, some lessons with the greatest names in golf, etc. One sour-looking kid started bouncing his basketball and talking jive loud enough for me to hear.

"Call that a sport, smack some tiny-ass ball wif' a stick?"

A lot of laughing, high-fiving and "Tell the mo'fo'!" ran through the bunch as the kid smiled snidely at his own performance.

"Look easy to you, pal?" I asked, showing no offense. The boy rolled his head contemptuously and looked away, still bouncing the ball. "C'mon over here, take a couple swings."

"Fag-ass game, I ain't hittin' *nothin'*!"

"Don't think you can do it?"

"Do it? You shittin' me? Bitch could hit it farrer'n you!"

More laughing, more shucking and jiving. I pointed a finger and wiggled it at him. He heaved a great sigh, tossed the basketball to one of his friends and walked up. "What's your name?" I asked, offering my hand.

"Napoleon," he said, slapping my hand and giving a sideways smile to the highly entertained group behind him.

"Well, okay, Mr. Napoleon. Take a stick and hit a couple." I handed him a five-iron from one of the rental sets the course had provided. Before taking it, "Napoleon" shrugged off his jacket. He was wearing a mesh-knit tank top that revealed a body Michelangelo might have used for a model, well-defined muscles rippling all over the place and a body-fat level that was probably too low to measure.

He took the club and hefted it for a second, then swung it like a baseball bat. I have to admit, the sound it made as it cut through the air was impressive. I kicked a range ball onto the center of a mat and said, "Go ahead. Right out there."

Exhaling loudly again, Napoleon stood next to the ball and swung at it as hard as he could, missing it completely and barely preventing himself from falling over, much to the amusement of his friends. He made a face and tried again. Same result. Then he hunkered down over the ball and actually looked at it this time. He finally connected but sent it zinging almost sideways. He angled the club so the head was near his face and stared at it. "End's crooked. How'm I supposed to hit it like that?"

I took the iron back and looked at the head myself, frowning. "Maybe you're right. Stand aside a second."

Napoleon moved over, crossed his arms and jiggled his head up and down as I addressed the ball. I hit it about 200 yards, and the jiggling stopped. I looked at the club again. "You're right. It is a little off. Want to try it with a different one?"

A few minutes later I had them all teamed up with some of my guys and a bunch of local teaching pros, two or three kids per player. That's when I noticed—and I have no idea how I could have missed him—one boy about five-foot-eight and easily weighing 250, none of it muscle. He was hanging back from the others.

"Who're you?" I asked him.

He pointed to the rest of his group. "They call me Fat Albert."

"What's your real name?"

"Albert, if you can believe it."

"Some coincidence." He really did look like the character from the old Cosby cartoons. "My name's Al, too. Want to give this a try?"

He just shrugged. Albert was sweating profusely, wiping his forehead with the shoulder of the worn white T-shirt he was wearing. I walked him over to the range and hooked him up with Fred Asphal, who seemed to have gotten three of the tougher-looking boys to tutor. I watched for a few minutes as Albert tried to hit a ball, not doing any better than Napoleon had. The others laughed loudly at each of his attempts, even though his tries weren't any worse than theirs had been. Sweat was running down his face now.

"Hey, kid," a voice said from behind me. "C'mere."

Albert turned toward Eddie, then handed the club to Fred and walked over. Eddie hadn't volunteered for this gig, and I was surprised he had shown up at the range. "Let's go on over here."

He led the boy to the last position on the right, then began talking to him. I couldn't hear what he was saying. He had Albert's back turned toward the rest of the group, I assumed so any taunting would be out of his sight line. Albert listened, his head hanging, looking only at the ground. Occasionally, he would nod.

I went back inside the (air-conditioned) clubhouse for a scheduled interview with a writer from *Golf Digest*. It was the kind of thing I could do with a quarter of my attention, and I periodically looked out the window to see how the clinic was going. It took about twenty minutes for the guys to get the kids involved, the challenge apparently having succeeded in winning out over chic disdain. Boys were taking huge whacks and sending balls scattering to the four winds. Every time one of them came even close to sending a golf ball somewhere generally toward the southeast and at least a foot off the ground, the pro would applaud enthusiastically and encourage the rest of his charges to do the same.

Things were different down at the end where Eddie and Fat Albert (sorry, I meant just Albert) worked alone. The boy had a mid-iron in his hands, and he was swinging it gently, bringing it back no more than about two feet and following through not much more than that. He was hitting some balls straight, some to the side, occasionally duffing one completely, but never getting one more than maybe fifteen yards out. As I continued to watch, the shots got straighter and more consistent, but with no increase in distance. After another ten minutes, Albert still wasn't trying to hit them any harder or take a bigger swing. I wondered if maybe Eddie wasn't in too far and needed some rescuing.

I begged a break from the writer—said I needed to hit a few to stay loose—and went out to the range, taking the position next to Eddie's. I grabbed a pitching wedge and started hitting some easy ones, but I mostly wanted to listen.

"You hear that sound?" Eddie was saying. "That nice click when you hit it right?"

"Yeah. When do I gidda swat the damned thing?"

"Soon. Hit a few more like this."

Albert had them all going straight and true by now, but he'd occasionally turn and glance with envy at the guys down the line, who were practically coming out of their shoes taking giant swipes. After another few minutes, Eddie said, "Okay. You're getting the hang of it. Now, listen'a me carefully." Albert set the clubhead, which I could now see was a five-iron, on the ground and leaned on it. I winced, hoping it wouldn't snap in two under his weight.

"I want you to bring the club back a little farther this time. Like this." Eddie demonstrated, the club coming back maybe three feet this time. "But here's the important part, you listenin'? Okay. Bring it back more, but *don't swing it any harder!* You get me? No harder! Same effort as you been doin'."

Albert nodded, set himself up carefully, brought the club back and swung it forward gently. The ball flew straight ahead, about forty yards this time. Albert jerked his head in surprise.

"Nice shot," Eddie said, but without overdoing it. "Again." Albert hit it again. "Again. Again. Another time." Albert's hitting was consistent, until he put a little more effort into it and shanked it.

"Okay, hold it. You see what happened?"

"Nuh-uh."

"You went to hit it harder, and it threw you off. What you did, *you came out of the shot*. Know what that means?"

"Nuh-uh."

"Means you screwed up that nice form you had going there. Now, hit it easy some more. Trust me, we're gonna be whackin 'em before you leave, 'kay?"

" 'Kay." Albert went back to hitting consistent forty-yarders.

Another dozen or so shots, then Eddie said, "Okay, Albert, take the club back about a foot more, *but don't hit it any harder!*"

Albert followed the instructions, and this time hit the ball seventy yards, dead straight. "Hot damn!" he exclaimed.

"Again."

Albert hit another twenty or so shots, at least sixteen of them the same as the first. Eddie nodded approvingly, then said, "Okay, take a break for a second," and took back the club. Albert wiped his face and shook out his legs, but he was standing up a little straighter than he had been before.

"Here's what's going on," Eddie said. He made the little two-foot swing. "You're swinging with a certain amount of force, right? Certain effort."

"Okay."

"Let's call it Little Albert effort. And you got it going for about two feet."

"Okay."

"So when the club gets to the ball, it's got two feet of Little Albert effort behind it, and it goes about ten yards. Get me?"

"No big thing."

"No, it isn't. Then you brought the club back three feet. So whud you have on it when you hit the ball?"

"Three feet'a little Albert."

"How far you figure it went?"

The boy shrugged. "Fi'teen yards?"

He was off by twenty-five yards, but Eddie nodded anyway. "Same effort, just did it for longer, right? Then you brought it back four feet."

"Four feet'a Little Albert, went mebbe fi'ty yards."

"Right. So what you did, you used the same amount of effort, but the longer you're using it, the farther the ball goes."

"Okay. So when do I gidda whup it?"

"Soon. But when you whup it, you don't keep that nice form you got goin', you're gonna hit it like those guys." Eddie pointed down the range, and his pupil looked back to see a hailstorm of random trajectories, some balls getting no farther than five feet from the tees, at least those that had managed to get hit at all.

Eddie handed him back the club. "Show me again. Mix 'em up a little, but don't change the effort."

Albert hit another dozen shots, ranging from twenty to sixty yards. On his own, he began bringing the club back more than four feet, concentrating hard on his form and not swinging any harder than "Little Albert." Most of them kept going straight, and when they didn't, he cranked down his backswing until he had his form back before ratcheting it up again. Eddie didn't say a word, and before too long Albert was consistently hitting about ninety yards. I couldn't see his face, but from the back it looked as if all of his considerable bulk had shrunk down to just him and the ball.

He didn't even notice that things had quieted down a little along the rest of the range. I turned, trying not to be obvious, to see half the other kids staring at Albert as his shots, one by one, popped gently into the air.

"Ready for a break?" Eddie asked.

"Fuck no!" Albert said defiantly.

"Okay. Go back to the two-foot swing."

"Say what?"

"Do it."

Shaking his head in disapproval at this apparent step backward, Albert did as he was told anyway, hitting about a half dozen of the kind of shots he'd started with. "Okay," Eddie said eventually, "now what I want you to do, I want you to go to Middle Albert. Bring the club down a little harder, not too much, but don't take it any farther back."

Albert chunked the club into the ground and the ball dribbled forward. Eddie said, "You lost your form. Try it again." Another chunk. "Okay, back to Little Albert." Four good shots. "Now a little harder."

This time, Albert hit it smoother and got the ball about twenty-five yards out with just the two-foot backswing. After another few of those, Eddie had him take it back to three feet, then four, and Albert was getting out about seventy yards or so. Once again, Eddie backed off and stayed quiet as Albert worked on his own.

He kept his swing effort constant as he brought the club farther and farther out, and every time he duffed one, he reduced the backswing until he recaptured his form.

Ten minutes later, Albert was hitting 130-yarders one after the other, and appeared to be using, at most, a tenth of the effort the other kids were using to get half as far.

"Okay, hold up, Albert," Eddie said, and it took the boy a moment to remember where he was and why. Eddie picked up a ball and set it carefully on one of the few flat pieces of grass still left near Albert's feet.

He backed off two steps and said, loudly, "Okay, kid, smack the shit out of it."

"Oh, yeah!" Albert hitched up his shoulders and set up over the ball. He took his time, even taking a few practice backswings. Then, without rearing back as I would have expected but staying well within himself, he pulled the five-iron back behind his head, hesitated for a split second, then smoothly whipped it down toward the ground, letting the club come through the ball of its own momentum and finishing up with it draped over his left shoulder.

The ball rocketed up into the air with a barely audible click, and Albert stared at it with his mouth open, blinking in disbelief. Roughly the same reaction had set in among his friends, nearly all of whom had stopped to watch when they heard Eddie's last instruction and saw him step away from Albert. When the ball dropped onto the ground about twenty feet past the 170-yard flag, Albert raised the club high up over his head in both hands and yelled, a kind of guttural *Aaarghh!* sound like some cartoon superhero might make after pulverizing the villain into his constituent elements. Then he turned around and did it again facing his friends, who were still staring in astonishment at where his ball had landed relative to their own.

"Damn!" Albert said to Eddie as he jumped back around to face him. He pointed the five-iron toward the driver in Eddie's bag. "When I gidda whup *that* mutha?" he demanded gleefully.

"In about six months," Eddie said. "Hit the five some more."

He did as he was told, shanking the first couple before he got hold of himself, backed off, and straightened them out. As I watched, I noticed that there was an athlete somewhere down beneath all those layers of adipose. His movements were smooth and assured, and he had great body awareness, able to tell when he was even slightly off the form that he had pretty much manufactured for himself. That he avoided hitting flat-out anymore, settling for consistent shots of about 150 yards, told me he had a certain level of maturity as well. And damned if he wasn't having a good time.

Eddie left him alone with a pile of balls and walked over to where I was standing. He pulled out a pack of cigarettes and offered me one. We lit up and watched the other kids on the range, me watching my teammates, Eddie watching the teaching pros.

"I love these guys," he said as he exhaled his first drag, "these Zen masters, they tell you to forget about all the mechanics, the fundamentals, just get up there, let your natural instincts take over . . . *Be one with the target,* f'Chrissakes."

He shook his head ruefully. "They're all full'a shit, those guys. It's the most unnatural goddamned thing in the world, the golf swing. Every kid, he watches golf on TV, he thinks, just lemme get up there and hit the thing, I'll show these overweight bozos what a long drive is."

He folded his arms across his chest as we continued to watch the students grunting and cursing on the range. "Few swings later the kid's practically in tears on account'a he can barely touch the ball, much less hit it anywhere, and for the life of him he can't understand *why*. Keeping your head down, the left arm straight, holding your body still so you don't sway into the shot, turning your wrists over—not a damned thing natural about any of it." Mack Merriwell jumped two feet into the air as a ball shot out sideways from the practice mat and threatened to break his ankle.

"But here's the amazing thing." Eddie stepped over to his bag and carefully—lovingly, I thought—pulled a five-iron out, caressing the grip until it seemed to come home and snuggle into his hands.

He waggled it back and forth, then took a few gentle swings. "You stick with it for a while, learn the fundamentals, start hitting the ball well, and after a while it starts to sink in, to make some kind of sense. And after another while"—he took a full backswing and whipped the clubhead down and up, staying poised at the end of his follow-through—"you realize that a golf swing is *the* most natural thing in the world, and you can't imagine hitting it any other way."

After watching his imaginary ball fly into the distance, he slowly brought the club down and rested it on the soft ground. "Problem is," he said quietly, moving the shaft back and forth, "there's just no natural way to come to it."

I watched him play with the club. It was as though he were giving it something to do, there being nothing sadder than a golf club not swinging at a ball. "But there are so many guys with such natural swings," I offered by way of weak argument.

"Such as . . . ?"

"Such as Senzamio." I pointed with my chin toward where Rico was hitting balls off the mat. We watched together for a few seconds as he smoothly hit a half dozen balls with his trademark fluidity.

"What do you mean by natural?" Eddie asked me.

I wondered if he was really serious, started to answer—"Well, obviously, I'm talking about—" and suddenly I was at a loss for words.

"You think the first time he hit a ball, he hit it like that?"

We watched as Rico took a swing with a seven-iron that looked so casual I doubted it would get past the ladies' tees. It sailed about 175 yards before hitting the ground.

"The hell he did," Eddie said before I could answer. "What you really mean by natural is that it looks effortless. And as any athlete in any sport will tell you, the only way to look effortless"—he lifted the five-iron and put it back in his bag—"is after years and years of more intensive effort than most people could muster up if their lives depended on it."

He hefted his bag onto his shoulder. "You don't believe me, ask Magic Johnson. Or Namath, or Navratilova, or any of 'em."

He began to turn away, then thought of something. " 'Course, that doesn't include Robert Carmichael . . ."

"Carmichael? What about him?"

"Now there's a natural swinger."

Surprised, I asked what *he* meant by that.

"Dumb sonofabitch does the right thing all the time," Eddie answered, "and has no fuckin' clue why."

As Eddie walked away, Fat Albert hauled off and walloped a five-iron, hard, but without losing control. He let out a whoop and whirled around to find Eddie, to make sure he'd seen it, flinging both arms into the air.

That evening, I took a walk with Juan Castillo Licenciados, the Spanish sensation who would have been more famous were it not for Derek Anouilh's explosion onto the scene that pretty much obliterated everybody else.

With two master's degrees in language and halfway to his Ph.D. in history, Licenciados was a deeply philosophical, quiet man who had taken up golf to relax and discovered a sport perfectly suited to his particular brand of contemplative introspection. As he brilliantly mowed down the competition in event after event, he seemed to take no special delight in besting his fellow players, but gauged himself only against his own expectations. Sometimes when he won, he'd shrug it off, as if it was no big deal. And sometimes when he lost, satisfaction would radiate off of him like beams of light. It all depended on how he thought he had played, not the position on the leader board in which he finished.

I liked spending time with him. He was somehow able to get me to step back and think about myself and my sport other than in terms of the money list or any of the millions of logistical details that comprised so much of a pro's life. And his English was near-flawless.

We walked along the ninth, tenth and eighteenth holes of the Stadium course. Licenciados likened it to a sleeping beast gathering its energy before spending the day happily devouring a meal of life forms arrogant enough to dare mounting a challenge. He asked me how I was enjoying my experience as a Ryder Cup captain.

"About like a troop leader would enjoy organizing a camping trip for a dozen gifted, billionaire nine-year-olds," I answered. As Licenciados listened patiently, I vented for about ten minutes on juggling impossible scheduling requirements, a demanding media horde and the countless tiny problems that I should have been smart enough to realize were a natural part of these kinds of undertakings but which seemed to me like a conspiracy to drive me nuts.

We paused on a hillock topping a sand trap and looked at the swaths of purple shadow that were sweeping across the desert to the north. "And I haven't even mentioned managing the fragile egos of guys who spend their entire careers scrapping as individuals and suddenly have to work together as a team."

Licenciados laughed and pulled a pack of Gauloises out of his shirt pocket, offering me one. We sat down and let our legs dangle into the bunker, a benign-looking piece of topography when you weren't trying to either avoid it or hit out of it.

"They are a special breed, athletes," he said after we'd smoked in silence for a while. "Not like ordinary people. Yes, of course, they crave the spotlight, love all the attention and hero worship, just as most of us would. But what makes them special is that small moment—it may only be a few seconds—that small moment when the competition ends and victory is sealed but not yet declared, that moment of *pure inwardness,* a radiance that pushes aside for a fleeting instant all the work, frustration, disappointment, rage and desperation, that moment of utter totality that only a victory at the end of a long and painful road can provide, and that only a rare handful can ever know. That addictive flash of perfect completion is what brings the special ones back time after time, no matter how rough the road, no matter how long the odds."

He took a long pull off the Gauloise. "And then for some, for most, it is only a twinkling before the emptiness starts to creep back in, the sense of something still unfulfilled, and the effort becomes a fleeing as much as a pursuing, as much a fear as a longing."

Licenciados ground out the stub of the cigarette and exhaled a cloud of smoke. "And that, Alan, is what defines the champions."

I wasn't sure I liked that last part, the intimation that some pathology underlay the psyches of elite competitors, and said so. "A little harsh, Juan. You think I do what I do out of fear and desperation?"

"Don't you?"

"No!"

"So why are you captain of the Ryder Cup team?"

"It's an honor—how could I turn it down?"

"So you don't care if you win or lose."

"Of course I care!"

"Why?" he asked calmly.

"It's an accomplishment! A once-in-a-lifetime opportunity!"

Juan nodded as he mulled this over, then said, "So when it's over, you will quit."

"Quit what?"

"Quit playing golf for a living."

"The hell I will."

"Why not?"

"It's what I do. I love it!"

"Then play on weekends at your club."

"But that doesn't count."

"What does count?"

"The big ones. Tour events, the majors . . ."

"How come?"

What the hell was he trying to tell me: that I was desperate, unfulfilled? Neurotic, deranged?

He drew his legs back onto solid ground and stood up, stretching his arms behind his back to relieve some stiffness, then stepped away from the edge of the bunker. "It is because you are a champion, Alan," he said, answering his own question. "One of the true ones."

As we began making our way back toward the hotel, I got the impression that he didn't necessarily think being a champion was a good thing.

CHAPTER FIFTEEN

I couldn't order it, but I asked the guys not to watch any real-time television or listen to the radio. I didn't mind them seeing the commentary, predictions, editorializing, handicapping and all the other varieties of bullshit that passes for sports "news" these days from people who don't know what the hell they're talking about.

What I minded was them hearing it from people who *did* know what they were talking about, some of the network guys who often knew a pro's game better than the pro did. I didn't want a Mack Merriwell hearing, "Well, Bob, if he pulls that three-iron on number twelve the way he did on fourteen at the Kemper, he'll never recover." Or a Joel Fleckheimer hearing, "You know that habit he has of opening the clubface too much on a right side-hill lie? Boy, if he doesn't get over that before the tenth, that pill's gonna be skin-diving for sure." Those are the kinds of swing thoughts that plant themselves so deep inside your head you can never get rid of them even if you hit two hundred perfect practice shots under duplicate conditions.

Instead, we watched footage of the Europeans' past tournaments on a four-foot screen. Not the edited-for-TV stuff that squeezes two thousand man-hours of play into ten hours of quick-cut television, but the raw stock, right out of the cameras scattered all over the course. Naturally, we had no way to know which of our guys would be playing which of theirs, but since there were only twelve of them and twelve of us, I saw no harm in the whole team sitting together and studying each of the opponents one by one.

This wasn't something you'd bother to do in a regular tournament, where you just went out and shot your best game, altering your style only if you were neck and neck with somebody for the last few holes, and then only *maybe*. But each round in the Ryder is match play, where your overall score is irrelevant, and what your opponent does has a major effect on what *you* do.

We watched John Wickenhampshire lose the British Open, right on his home soil, to our own Fred Asphal. Knowing what was coming, that Fred would eventually win it, there were a lot of whoops and hollers, the guys razzing the hell out of Freddy for every lousy shot. During the last four holes they yelled lustily, slapping Fred on the back, shouting "You da man!" at the tops of their lungs as Freddy smiled and reddened and smiled some more, watching himself turn a two-shot deficit with four holes left to play into a one-shot win with some of the boldest, riskiest, most magnificent shots you've ever seen out of one guy in one day. Everybody joined in the fun.

Everybody except Eddie, who sat at the back of the room staring intently at the screen, his thumb scratching at his chin. After Asphal holed out the eighteenth to win, pandemonium broke loose in the room. Even Eddie looked a little choked up, but he didn't take his eyes off the screen. He waited patiently until it was all over, then said, "Put on the Kemper, Alan."

"The Kemper? None of the Euros was even in contention for that."

"I know. But put it on, okay? Wickenhampshire's footage."

As I said, I had the raw stuff. Wickenhampshire wasn't ever really in the running after Day Two, but the cameras that were locked into position at each hole dutifully recorded him anyway. ABC would sell the footage to the BBC, which could cull out highlights of the hometown hero.

Luckily, I didn't have to fiddle with tape. The network's sports department put it all on laser discs, cross-indexed and catalogued. Couple of clicks on the control panel and I could instantly call up whatever we wanted to look at. We watched Wickenhampshire play a few holes. He was teamed with Mr. Wizard himself.

"So what is it, Eddie?" I asked him lightly. "You tryin' to learn something from the Wizard?"

Eddie didn't react. "He barely shot par that day."

"I shot a sixty-nine!" Markovy protested with mock indignation.

"I know. I meant Wickenhampshire. Let's see the Open. Round Two."

So I put that up. What the hell, we weren't really doing any analysis anyway, just watching. Wickenhampshire was teamed with Scott Bradman, a pretty decent top-thirty player. "Same thing that day," Eddie said. "Came in with a seventy-three."

We waited, watching Wickenhampshire play as I clicked my way through his holes.

Eddie got up and went to the front of the room, standing and watching the screen with his arms folded. Half to himself and half to the rest of us, as though just musing out loud, he said, "Is there anything about Bradman's and Markovy's games that might have thrown him off a little?"

"Yeah," came Fleckheimer's voice without hesitation. "They both play like a pair of fuckin' machines, is what threw him off!"

That got a big laugh, including from Markovy. Eddie smiled as well, then suddenly sobered up. "That's it, Joel. Alan, let's see number seven at the Kemper again."

I cued it up. "That was some shot I hit!" Markovy said as it began rolling.

"Never mind you," Eddie admonished lightly. "Watch Wickenhampshire's face. Can you play it again?"

Three clicks and Markovy's tee shot came back up. We all did as instructed, watching Wickenhampshire's face.

" 'Ey, wha-waz dat?" Senzamio called out. "Dad little-a smile, what, whadda you call it?"

"A smirk?" Asphal offered.

"A grimace?" Merriwell suggested.

Eddie shook his head. "See him take a deep breath, look up at the sky while letting it out?"

Everybody could see that this is what he had done.

"He was ridiculing you, Jon," Eddie pronounced. "That was contempt on his face."

"Me? Why? Whud *I* do to him?"

"Not a thing. But you were being so methodical, so effective . . . so goddamned *boring.*" Everybody laughed, and Eddie waited for it to die down. "The guy thought to himself, probably without even realizing it, he thought, Is this fucker gonna play some golf here or what?"

"But I was even with him at that point," Markovy said, puzzled but completely intrigued. "I was playing as good as him."

Eddie nodded vigorously. "Yeah, but it's like a tennis player who keeps dropping these namby-pamby little touch shots just over the net 'stead of whacking the shit out of 'em the way God intended." He pointed to the screen. "I think Wickenhampshire was pissed off because he was playin' real golf and you weren't and he still couldn't get ahead of you."

Markovy had begun nodding his head halfway through Eddie's explanation. "So he wanted to teach me a lesson? Is that it?"

"Something like that. Here, watch his shot. And watch his face before he hits."

I played the scene again. There was a definite indication of annoyance or impatience in the tautness of Wickenhampshire's mouth as he took his place on the tee box. "He used to be in the Army, this guy, right?" Eddie said. "Tough-guy left-tenant or whatever the hell they call 'em over there? Watch his face, watch his body . . . see? Man's got his dander up. Setting up not relaxed, stiffer than usual, now watch . . . jumped at it much harder than he usually does, and see what happened?"

The camera followed the ball as it took off straight ahead and then began turning sharply right as the whirling dimples dug into the air. "Came right out of the shot and sliced it," Eddie said as the ball sailed off into the trees. He signaled me to pause it, then turned away from the screen.

"You give this guy a little macho golf, hand-to-hand combat, that Lawrence of Arabia kind of no-prisoners, win-for-the-queen shit, he gets high off it. Settles him down, lets him get into his game. But you pull this robot shit, this safety-first number, and it throws him off."

Heads were nodding throughout the room. "Whoever plays him," Eddie continued as he started walking toward his seat at the back of the room, "play for the safest, dullest, most boring goddamned pars in the world. Even if he gets two or three up on you, keep hitting the same crap-ass shots over and over."

It was so obvious, everybody wondered why they hadn't seen it. Thing is, they hadn't been looking. I'm not sure many of us in the room had ever really stopped to take stock of the human being we were fighting down the stretch, only looked to see what scores he was managing. But Eddie'd spent a lifetime studying his opposition. And how stupid could *I* be? Here I had the greatest hustler on the planet right on my team, and it never even occurred to me to get his opinion on how to play this tournament.

"What if you're wrong, Caminetti?" It was Carmichael, his voice dripping derision and disdain.

Eddie looked at the screen, which I'd put back into play mode. It was showing Wickenhampshire walking from the tee down to the fairway, lips pressed together, eyes fixed on the ground, not talking to anybody. It looked to me as if he blamed Markovy for his lousy tee shot.

"Trust me on this one," Eddie said to me. "But only for his singles match Sunday."

"Some kind of foxhole-loyalty notion?" Asphal asked.

"Yeah. This *left-tenant* may shoot himself in the foot, but he's less likely to take a playing partner down with him."

Carmichael got ready to say something back, but I stepped in. "Let's move on, guys. No sense overanalyzing this stuff."

We watched for several more hours, everybody deferring to Eddie as he made observations. When we got to the European captain, Jacques St. Villard of Belgium, Eddie said, "This guy's got his head screwed on real tight. There's no dickin' with him. You gotta beat him playin' golf, and that's all there is to it, 'cuz he keeps his *cojones* out of the game."

Having played against St. Villard many times, I knew Eddie was right, and we moved on to Helmut Braunschweiger of Germany. "Same deal," Eddie said. "Don't bother playing with this guy's head."

"He's so together, how come he hasn't won any big ones?" Carmichael asked, still determined to bait this presumptuous interloper who had suddenly grabbed everyone's attention.

"He's got a loft problem."

"What the hell is a loft problem?" Carmichael asked.

"LOFT," Eddie replied. "*Lack Of Fucking Talent.*" As we laughed at Eddie's joke, all of us except Carmichael, the almost alarming insight of this simple truth he'd uttered was not lost on us. Braunschweiger may have had one good season but, when you got right down to it, he wasn't that good a golfer. It was just that we tended not to say things like that about fellow professionals.

Eddie waited for the laughter to die down and added, "His skills matched his brains, he'd blow everybody else out of the water."

"Who could ever do that?" Merriwell asked rhetorically.

"Derek could."

The room fell into an eerie silence.

Without anybody quite having noticed it, Eddie had become some kind of focal point around which each of us had begun to arrange our perceptions of the game and its practitioners. He was one of the most cynical human beings I'd ever met, cutting hardly anybody any slack if they tended in the slightest to drift off into anything less than pure rationality. He had built-in radar designed to spot hyperbole and self-aggrandizement at a thousand yards, and he'd just spent the afternoon reducing almost the entire European Ryder Cup team, consisting of some of the best players in the world, into nothing more than a sludge pot of exploitable human foibles.

And here was that same misanthropic curmudgeon telling us, point-blank, that sitting right in this room was a young man with the potential to become the greatest golfer who ever lived.

I don't know if I can explain this properly, but it was one of the most electric moments of my entire life. I think most of my teammates felt it, too. Anouilh sat there, staring at Eddie without moving. He'd had so much praise, envy, money and attention heaped on him that he hardly noticed any of it anymore, practically yawning through the endless honorary degrees and televised testimonials his sponsors insisted he accept. And yet, somehow, this observation from a crusty old fart of an ordinary citizen of uncertain origin floored him, and I think that, for the very first time, it sank into The Kid that maybe he really was something quite special in the universe beyond the heaps of bullshit manufactured by his aunt and his handlers.

Anouilh looked at Eddie and said, "But you whupped my ass." It was as if he needed to eliminate any uncertainty that had surrounded Eddie's comment by bringing it up himself.

"It didn't count, so you didn't give a shit."

"Played for ten grand, didn't we?"

"Time it took you to lose that ten grand, you probably made twenty from your Purina contract."

Everybody laughed, nervously, but Anouilh looked serious. "How long'd we play?"

"Four, four and a half hours," Eddie answered.

"Uh-huh." Anouilh thought about it for a second, then said, "More like thirty grand." This time the laughter was genuine.

"So, Caminetti," Fleckheimer said when it started dying down, "tell us about *our* games."

"Say what?"

"Us. What are the Euros sayin' about us?"

Eddie looked around the room: *You sure you all want to hear this?* I inclined my head toward him: *Let's have it.*

"They'll know you as a risk-taker, Fred," he said to Asphal. "They know that if you see a fifty-percent shot to make birdie, you'll take it over a ninety-percent sure par." He waited to see if Asphal would protest, but as no opposition seemed forthcoming, he continued. "Let's say the other guy's about to hit his second shot before you hit yours, and he sees you got a Rambo opportunity for birdie. If he's heads up and payin' attention, he's gonna go for a safe par, knowing sure as shit you're gonna take the risk, and also knowing you're likely gonna blow it. And if he's *really* smart, even if you make that birdie, he'll play you the same way the next hole, and every hole, because you'll fuck it up more times than you'll make it, and if he's patient over eighteen holes, he'll beat you."

It was devastating, even brutal, but it was dead on. We knew it; Fred knew it. From a career perspective, it didn't make any difference. With that style of play, he'd win plenty of money and even one or two events every year, which was enough to put you over the top in a sport that simply could not be completely dominated by any single individual anyway, the way tennis could. But there was only one Ryder Cup every two years, and it was an all-or-nothing kind of thing. There was no coming back next week to try to do better.

I stood up and pretended to stretch some kinks out of my back. "How 'bout a break, fellas? I'm gettin' stiff."

Amid the discomfort we all felt, everybody thought it a good idea. Eddie, Fred and I walked together toward the driving range.

"So what should I do?" Asphal asked Eddie, trying to keep his voice level and not bothering to argue.

"Tee off to a spot that'll make the other guy think you're going for the heroics on your second shot."

"Then what?"

"Then go for par."

Asphal blinked at him. "Then we'll both simply trade pars all day. How am I to gain the advantage?"

"Wait for him to realize that he's the one's gotta start taking all the chances. You try to get your birdies on the holes where there's less risk. They'll be there, and all the other guy has to do is fuck up once or twice, and the match is yours."

"Doesn't that depend upon whom I'm playing?"

"Sure does. Play a guy like Wickenhampshire and he'll be dead in fourteen holes."

"Ah, I don't know, Eddie . . ." I said skeptically.

"Hey, Al," he said, "you wanna go out right now and play me straight up for a hunnerd grand?"

"How many strokes you gonna give me?" I asked with a grin, but Eddie just stared at me until I finally said, "No, Eddie, I won't play you straight up."

"Why not?"

" 'Cuz you'll kick my ass, is why not."

"Right. So shut the fuck up and listen."

I shut the fuck up and listened.

"What you're after," Eddie said, "is consistency. Never hitting a shot unless you know precisely what it's gonna do."

We pulled up alongside his bag, and he took out his driver. "See that?" He showed us the face of the club, pointing to a worn spot right in the middle about the size of a half-dollar.

"What's that?"

"It's where I hit the ball."

"Which ball?"

"All of 'em."

He stood and walked over to my bag, pulling out my driver. Normally I go for a guy's throat he even walks near my bag, but right now I stayed put.

Eddie looked the driver up and down. "How far you usually hit this?" he asked without looking at me.

"Uh, two-eighty, two-ninety depending. Sometimes I manage three hundred yards."

Eddie nodded, as though he'd expected me to say something like that. "I hit mine two-fifty," he said, dropping my club back into the bag, less gently than I would have liked. "Plus or minus five yards, I hit it two-fifty every time. Know why?"

"Why?"

"Because I can. Every time. Sure, I can belt it a lot farther than that, but not every time, not nearly, and not with any real accuracy. So I don't try."

Some of the Euros on the range had turned as they heard us talking, so we walked over to an umbrella table set up just back of the range. "I *can* hit it close to two-ninety," Eddie said. "But if I have two-sixty to clear some water, I'll lay it up every damned time, because at two-fifty I'll put it where I want it and I can't do that at two-ninety or even two-sixty." He looked out toward the far end of the range. "The secret to my game is never hitting a shot that I don't know for a dead certainty I can make."

"But what about that retriever shot?"

"What retriever shot?" Asphal asked.

"Hitting it out of a bunker and right onto the green with a ball retriever," I answered. "I saw him do it."

Eddie told us that it was amazing the crazy things you could do just by practicing them, like hitting perfect drives with a paper cup over your ball or putting with a three-wood. He said he got so he could pretty consistently hit a putter just about any distance up to 180 yards, which meant he could play an entire round with just that club and do fairly well. He tried to make it look as if he just sauntered onto the first tee willing to do any wacky thing in the world that happened to come up, but the fact is that he had a dedicated work ethic and spent countless hours on the range, putting green and practice bunkers. Of course, part of the effort involved traveling for at least an hour each way to a distant driving range, since he didn't want to be seen practicing anywhere near where he was known.

"Besides, it's not *any* retriever," Eddie said. "It's this one." He pulled it out and handed it to me.

I looked at it. "Looks to me like a Nakashima, right off the shelf."

"It is. But it's a helluva club. Perfectly balanced, good length, and see the head here? Part that gets the ball? You couldn't design a better sand club if you tried."

He took it back and returned it to his bag. "If I'm one down on the eighteenth, or if I find the ball sitting against a railroad track or on top of a rock or halfway down a dead duck's throat, well, there's simply no alternative and I have to go for it. Otherwise, I never hit shots I'm not sure of."

"I'll wager you miss a great number of birdie opportunities that way." Asphal said what I'd just been thinking.

"You're gonna miss a lot more hero shots and end up with bogeys. Look, pars are what keep you in the game until you can make enough birdies to win. Doesn't sound like much, but it's everything. Hit the shots you know, and maybe one out of every three times, you'll find yourself with a makable birdie opportunity that's risk-free. Let's say you make two out of every three of those.

"Now, if you've been parring everything else, you just shot yourself a sixty-eight. But if you tried to be a hero and bogeyed as many as you parred, you're slammin' your trunk on Friday afternoon instead'a playin' on Saturday morning."

He sat back and looked out at the first-hole tee box, scratching his chest as though he'd rather be out there playing than sitting here yakking at us. "And four sixty-eights in a row, maybe a sixty-seven thrown in, well"—he turned back to me—"that there'd win you damned near any tournament in the world."

It dawned on me that two sixty-sevens and two sixty-eights added up to Derek Anouilh's record-setter at Augusta, but before I had a chance to really think that over, I blurted out, "But who's that consistent they can rely on shots like that?" *Except you*, I didn't add out loud. *Who hits a driver 250 dead straight every time?*

Surprise: Eddie actually seemed to think this was a reasonable question. "When you go out to the range," he said, "working on your wedge or whatever, whaddaya do? You stand there, hit two, three hunnerd wedge shots?"

Reluctantly, not knowing where this was leading but knowing I was going to answer wrong, I nodded.

"Groove that old muscle memory right in there, eh?" He nodded back, but it quickly turned to a shake. "All you're doing, you're teaching yourself to hit a perfect wedge shot after you've just hit two hunnerd of 'em in a row without a break. The hell's that got to do with playing golf? You ever find yourself hitting two hunnerd wedges in a row out on the course?"

He was tampering with ancient wisdom now, and Fred wasn't buying it. "You don't believe in muscle memory?"

" 'Course I do. Think I'm stupid? But muscle memory doesn't start at your takeaway or your backswing. Look here."

He stood up. "When you use that wedge, whaddaya do, stand in one place and keep hitting it?" Teacher that he was—or could be, if he wanted to—Eddie didn't demand that we dutifully answer dumb, obviously rhetorical questions. "No. What you do, you take a long walk . . ." He began walking. "Then you reach into your bag . . ." He reached into my bag and pulled out a club. "Take one or two practice swings and then go for it. *That's* what you do in real life." He slammed the club back into my bag and pointed at me. "*That's* what you want to have in your muscle memory!"

"So what are you telling me?"

"I'm telling you to go to the range, hit the wedge a few times, then put it down and hit a seven, a three-wood, whatever, then pick the wedge up again, take a few practice swings and hit it once. Then put it down again and hit a couple other clubs, then the wedge again, then put it down."

He resumed his seat opposite me. "That's what you're trying to burn into your brain, that feeling of picking up a cold club with complete confidence. You don't have time to wear in a groove when you're on the course. You don't want it to feel strange when that wedge first touches your hand. You want to get used to that sensation of coming to it cold and sudden-like, and being comfortable with that. You gotta make it *normal*."

He held out his hands and then gripped an imaginary club. "You want, in that moment, the same feeling you built up on the range, to have that club come to you new and immediately turn into an old pair of slippers like it did a hunnerd times when you practiced it, y'see what I'm sayin' here?"

I did. I saw everything that he was saying. It's why I won the British and three other tour events the following season, with top-five finishes in a bunch of the others, including second at the Masters (which Fred Asphal won). I got flak for playing it safe, playing it boring, but the heroes were always below me on the leader board. People watched what I was doing on the range in complete mystification. Usually, when a golfer practices, he starts with a short iron and works his way up to the driver. Me, the very first shot I hit on the range now is the driver. First I do my stretching religiously, then grab the big dog and swing it a few times, then I step up and whack the hell out of it, just to get used to that feeling of stepping up to the real tees with a driver in my hand and whacking the hell out of it there. Before, even if I'd just been on the range finishing up with the driver right before my tee time, it was always weird feeling it in my hands on the very first shot.

No more. Now when I pull it out of the bag, it's like an old friend come back to where it belongs. I don't so much hold it as wear it, and it happens fast, because that's what I trained myself to expect out on that range.

I forgo the heroics now, making pars while I wait patiently for those birdie opportunities to present themselves. Amazing how many more of them there are when I don't try to force them. I seem to get luckier all the time but, as Ben Hogan himself once put it—or maybe it was Gary Player—the more I practice, the luckier I get.

Fred was nodding. Thinking. Of course, you already know what *his* next year on tour was like: He made more money than The Kid. But that's another story.

Eddie helped me out with the pairings, too, but we did that out of earshot of the rest of the guys.

One of the things you had to consider in managing the team was the interaction of the various personalities. They're like thoroughbreds, these professional athletes who live or die by margins so slim as to be nearly imperceptible, where the difference between being number one or number ninety on the money list might be an average of fewer than two shots per round. You need to worry about who gets paired up with whom in practice rounds, how you phrase things if you need to be critical, stuff like that.

And when you make up the pairings for the doubles rounds on Friday and Saturday, it isn't just a question of skill. It has as much to do with how well two unique individuals are going to play together. Is one guy willing to hold back and tee off safely so his partner can risk whaling the driver? Depends on who "the other guy" is. And not everybody gets to play every round or even every day, so you have to worry about who gets offended easily and who puts the good of the team above his own ego. All of which is a whole lot less predictable than I'm making it sound.

The captains have no say in who plays against whom, which turns out to be a pretty random process. For the first two days, where teams of two play each other, I will give the officials a sheet showing the four pairs of American players I'm putting up in the morning and the four in the afternoon, along with which of the eight preset tee times each of them will be taking. Jacques St. Villard will do the same for the Europeans. Only then do the officials post the matches. There is no way for one captain to predict whom the other captain will be teaming together or what tee times they'll be assigned to. It couldn't be more fair, or more exasperating. Ryder captains long ago gave up even trying to guess, and just did the best they could in trying to match personalities and optimize order of play. And just when you think you have it nailed, or at least as nailed as humanly possible, something unforeseen was probably going to come up and put all your analysis right in the Dumpster.

Each of the pairs matches was worth one point to the winning side, for sixteen points in all over the first two days. In the case of ties, which were typically plentiful, each side got a half point. Adding in the twelve individual matches on Sunday, there were twenty-eight points available in the whole tournament, so whichever side got fourteen and a half points was the winner. And if the whole thing was a dead heat, fourteen points each, the side that had been in possession of the Cup from the last Ryder got to keep it. That would be us. But I didn't want a tie, not when we were playing on American soil. I wanted an out-and-out win. I also wanted to hit the lottery jackpot and vacation on Jupiter, but those things were about as likely as us winning this Ryder.

Anyway, the four matches in the morning on both Friday and Saturday would be alternate shot, a really wild and entertaining format. Let's suppose Mack Merriwell and Derek Anouilh would be playing together as one of our four teams, which in fact they would be. Anouilh would start off hitting the tee shot on the first hole. Then Merriwell would play Anouilh's ball from wherever it ended up, then it would be Anouilh's turn to take the next shot, and so forth, until the ball was holed out. For scoring purposes, they would essentially be one player: Add up the strokes and that's it. Anouilh would tee off on all the odd-numbered holes, Merriwell on the evens, regardless of who hit last on the previous hole. Interestingly, this game is never played in the States, and yet we always did well in this format in past Ryder Cups.

"Craziest damned thing I ever heard of," Eddie said. "Sounds like fun."

"So who do you think ought to play together?"

"No idea."

Eddie Caminetti had no idea?

"Could sit here all day and think about it," he explained, "but I never seen it done. I'm guessing there's all kinds of weird shit, things to take into account you can only know if you been there. You have. I haven't. You figure it out." The only suggestion he came up with was that I list the demands of the odd versus the even holes so I could optimize who played which shots based on their skills. For example, if the toughest greens were mostly on the even holes, and most of those were par-fours, the best putter should be teeing off on the evens because he'd most likely get the first putt. That kind of thing. I ended up discarding all the ideas for pairings I'd been working on and starting from scratch, which took me most of the night, because the various combinations of demands and skills seemed almost infinite.

But that I did alone later on. Right now it was on to the "best ball" matches in the afternoon. Same deal, two-man teams, except each man would play his own ball, and whoever had the lowest score—the best ball—that would be the score for the team, and the higher score on each team would be discarded. So if Merriwell got a five and Anouilh a four, the team score was the four. The other team did the same, and the winner of the hole was the team whose best ball was lower. Very often, one player wouldn't even bother to finish. If Merriwell and Anouilh were both lying three on the green and Anouilh sank his putt, they'd just go with his total of four, since there was now no way Merriwell could beat it. Two-man "best ball" was something Eddie could relate to, as it was the single most popular amateur game in the United States for team play, which didn't explain why the Europeans typically dominated this portion of the Ryder Cup.

"Markovy and Asphal," he said as soon as I asked him for his thoughts.

"Already figured that one out," I told him. I'd figured it out based on Eddie's little tutorials while we were watching footage of the Euros. "But we got a problem with Senzamio."

"We do? Pretty much thought he could fit in anywhere."

"Thing is, Fabrizio Migliore hates him, on account'a Rico's a U.S. citizen now, and playin' for us. Migliore won't even refer to him by name. Calls him *Il Disertore*."

"Meaning . . . ?"

"The Defector. They end up playin' against each other, there's gonna be a lotta pasta flung around the course." Migliore's temper was legendary, one of those things they'd be laughing about in twenty years but about which there wasn't a damned thing funny right now. Some people get mad, they throw clubs. Others, like Boom-Boom Harriman, they throw whole bags into water hazards. Fabrizio Migliore's been known to set fire to his caddie.

"Well, put him with me, then. See what I can do to keep a grip on things."

"Okay. What about Carmichael?"

"Don't play him till Sunday."

"Jesus, Eddie! I can't do that!"

There were only eight two-man matches on Friday and eight on Saturday. That meant places for sixteen players from each side, so of my twelve guys, four of them would have to play both the morning and the afternoon rounds.

But there was nothing that said I couldn't play *more* than four guys twice in one day, and nothing that said I had to play everybody at least once. Eddie was suggesting that I keep Carmichael out of team play altogether, and only let him play his individual match on Sunday when everybody on both sides played.

"Sure you can. You're the captain."

"That's not what I meant. Technically, sure, I can bench him. But—"

"But you want to do the right thing."

"Course I do."

"Uh-huh. For one guy, or for the other twelve?"

"You mean the other eleven."

"I'm including you. Look, there's no way in hell that guy's gonna do well in team play."

"You're just pissed 'cuz he stiffed you fifty large."

"Do I look pissed?" No, he didn't. He never did, not so's you'd take it seriously. "Our deal says I gotta help you keep this cockamamy Cup, right? Okay then: Only reason I played that match against Carmichael was to make sure you didn't play him the first two days. You understand what I'm sayin' here?"

I did. It was the same reason he sabotaged Boom-Boom Harriman. It wasn't that he was afraid Harriman might take away his slot; he was savvy enough to know his place on the team was already assured. He did it to show me that Harriman didn't have the right stuff, so I wouldn't spend the whole tournament wondering if I'd done the right thing. But now, was I going to humiliate a fellow pro, who had secured a legitimate spot on the team according to the rules, based on the say-so of a guy I hardly knew?

"Man's on the team, damnit! I'm gonna tell him to warm a bench while everybody else is out playing?"

"Like I said, why not? You don't got a choice, him being on the team, but it's your call when he plays." When I didn't respond, he said, "Al, lemme ask you something: If you had the right not only to pick two guys at your own discretion but to knock two off as well, who'd be the first to go?"

"You know damned well who."

"Then what is your *problem!*"

"Just not easy, is all."

Eddie snatched the pairing sheet out of my hand. On top were listed all twelve players' names. On the bottom were the pairs matchups and their tee times. He took a scoring pencil off the table, scratched out the name Robert Carmichael and slapped the paper down on the table. "You're right," he said. "It was a bitch."

"Very funny. You know exactly what I mean."

Eddie looked at his watch, sighed and leaned back on his chair. "Here's what's gonna happen, okay? You're gonna moan and groan and scratch your balls for a few hours, bring in a couple other guys to witness your agony for the record, and then you're gonna bench Carmichael for the first two days."

He put his elbows on his knees and leaned forward, holding out his hands imploringly. "Now I could really use a beer, so could you gimme some kinda time frame on all this breast-beating and I'll meetcha after, or we can finish this up now and *then* you go drive some nails through your hands. Shit, tell Carmichael *I* did it!"

"I don't even want him to know you were in here." I picked up the pairing sheet and fiddled with it for a few seconds. "No, I'm the captain. I'll tell him. But what if it screws him up so bad it throws him off his game for Sunday?" Everybody plays on Sunday. Nothing I could do about that.

"Then you hope he plays the best guy the Euros've got."

"Why?"

"'Cuz Carmichael's gonna lose, and that's one point gone. Might as well lose to their best player so that guy can't beat another one of our guys who might have a chance of winning against somebody else. A sacrificial lamb, kinda."

"What makes you so damned sure he's gonna lose?"

"Wanna lay ten grand on it?"

"You'd bet against one of your own teammates?"

"Don't see you takin' the bet, *Captain* . . ."

"Fuck you."

And so it went, but we got it done, and I think, all in all, the pairings we came up with couldn't have been any better thought out.

That evening, I laid it all out for the guys, one on two instead of at a group meeting. My conversation with Markovy and Asphal was typical of how it went.

"You're the anchor, Jon," I said to Mr. Wizard. "Your job is to make pars all day. No matter what, you play it safe, get on the greens in regulation and don't take any chances trying to tuck in too close to the flag. You got a short putt, go ahead and try to make birdie. But if you're way out, get the first one close and sink the second. And don't go for the par-fives in two, either: Use all three shots, and just make sure you get there safe for a two-putt. Got it?"

"And I?" Asphal asked.

"You smack the living shit out of everything, Freddy. Go for birdies, eagles, what the hell ever."

"He'll bogey all over the place," Markovy protested. "If he's lucky."

"Who gives a shit?" I said, which was just what Eddie'd said to me earlier in the afternoon. "Taking chances like that, maybe he'll make three, four birdies, and it won't matter if he takes twelves on the rest if you keep getting those pars, Jon."

"Three or four under won't win it, Alan," said Asphal skeptically. "Not in 'best ball.' Not with this class of player."

I was hoping one of them would say that. I tried not to look too excited. "That's the beauty part, Freddy. If Mr. Wizard here plays it safe all day, relaxes and doesn't lose his cool, my guess, he's gonna get seven or eight birdie opportunities. Say he makes half of 'em. You figure eight or ten under'll win it for you?"

"What if I get mine on the same holes Freddy gets his?" Markovy, ever the scientist, but I was ready for him.

"Here's the thing: If Freddy's in birdie country, you can both go for it. That'll only add to the pie, see what I'm sayin'?"

"But what if we're both on in regulation, Alan, and we both must take a chance attempting a birdie, and let us further suppose—"

"Freddy. Listen. I can't play the game for you, 'kay? What I'm doing, I'm giving you the strategy. You and Jon, you gotta handle the tactics when shit comes up. Don't think about what I might say later. Just do what you both feel is right, the way you see it."

They nodded in unison. I couldn't tell if they were happy, but they both bought into the philosophy. There was great risk for both of them. If Markovy failed to make the pars, he would never forgive himself. And if Asphal didn't make enough birdies with all the leeway I'd just given him to go for broke, he wouldn't be able to live with himself either. But there was no way I could protect the guys from the pressure. It was, simply, their problem, and they knew that going in.

Needless to say, I'd asked Eddie all the same questions that Markovy and Asphal were asking me. He'd told me one thing I decided not to share with the two players: He was guessing that Asphal would be raining birdies all day, maybe seven or eight of them, because he'd have less pressure knowing that the team could always fall back on Markovy's pars if he screwed up. "Trust me on this one, Al," he'd finally said. "It's a lock, so put it in the bank and let's move on."

I also had to tell Carmichael I wasn't playing him at all on Friday. Or Saturday, either, even though I didn't have to make that decision just yet. The conversation that ensued was an ugly one, but I'll forgo telling you about it so I don't have to relive it myself. Let's just say that the resultant effect on his head pretty much guaranteed he wouldn't win on Sunday if he ended up playing Helen Keller and she spotted him two a side.

I took the pairs sheet to the PGA of America on-site office. The European captain, St. Villard, had arrived just a few minutes before. As soon as I handed the official my sheet, he made a photocopy of it and handed me a copy of St. Villard's. The two of us tried not to appear too anxious to figure out who would be playing against whom prior to the PGA guy taking all of three minutes to produce the official starting sheets. Then St. Villard emitted a low growl from the back of his throat, which quickly rose in pitch until he yanked the paper up in front of his eyes to start doing it in his head. Laughing, I did the same thing, and within seconds we were alternately groaning, cheering and commiserating with each other as the pairings fell into place. I wondered if we'd be such good buddies this time tomorrow.

Nothing left for us to do now but play the tournament.

CHAPTER SIXTEEN

Friday Morning

The first person I saw on my way out of the clubhouse on Day One was Fabrizio Migliore, the mercurial Italian whose on-course antics made Boom-Boom Harriman look like a priest quietly administering benedictions. He'd brought his entire hometown soccer team over to watch the Ryder and cheer for him. Right now he was absolutely subdued as he trudged off the practice green.

"Fabrizio!" I said, trying to use my best Italian accent, a good trick for an Arizona native with all the ethnic sensibility of a dust cover. *"Come sta?"*

I hadn't seen him in almost six months, not since the Insta-Flush Invitational in Akron, where he'd planted himself in the middle of the eighth fairway after he was refused a free drop from what he insisted was casual water and the official seemed to think was just dew. The rest of the players had to play around him all afternoon, and when Juan Castillo Licenciados of Spain hit him in the leg from the tee and the ball ricocheted off into the rough, Migliore was declared to be part of the playing field and Licenciados was told to play it as it laid. I liked Migliore and expected a typically ebullient greeting, complete with a kiss on each cheek.

He looked up at me with weary eyes and said, *"Vugganeeta."*

That was a new word to me. "What's that mean, *vugganeeta?*"

Migliore inhaled heavily and looked away, shaking his head. *"Vugganeeta,"* he muttered once more, and walked away.

The next person I saw was Eddie's assigned caddie, sitting alone, smoking a cigarette, no bag nearby. Caddies guard bags the way mother lions guard cubs, so something wasn't right.

"Why aren't you gettin' ready?" I asked him.

"Ain't goin'." He took a final drag on his cigarette and flicked it away.

"Where's Caminetti's bag?"

He pointed somewhere off to his right, got up and walked off. I looked over and saw a familiar face standing near the practice green; then I spotted Eddie practicing putts. I walked over to him. "What's Fat Albert doin' over there?"

Eddie didn't look up from the green. "Carryin' my bag."

"Get atta here." He didn't respond. He was serious. "He doesn't know the greens, doesn't even know the damned *game*! How's he gonna help you with club selection and reading putts and—"

"Right." He drained a four-footer. "So he'll keep his yap shut when I'm tryin' to play." I was about to tell him that in this heat the kid was probably gonna be comatose by the third hole when I saw Fat Albert swing the fifty-pound tour bag up onto his shoulder like it and the clubs within were made out of helium. He didn't even lean to one side to compensate for the weight. Which made me take a closer look at the bag.

Earlier in the week the vendor reps showed up with their vans full of gear, ready to give any player anything he wanted, trunkfuls of stuff just for the asking. When they discovered that Eddie didn't have any sponsors and no pending commitments, they descended on him like locusts on a wheat field. I asked him, for form's sake, to at least grab himself a new bag. The Kmart logo peeking out from beneath the bag on Fat Albert's shoulders showed me he hadn't taken this to heart. ("It's a goddamn *bag*, Al. You put shit in, you take shit out. What, new one gonna improve my score?")

"Kid can bench press two-eighty," Eddie was saying as he tapped another ball. "Don't worry about it." The ball dropped into the cup with a satisfying clatter. Eddie looked up and leaned on the putter, waving to his new caddie. "He dies, I get another one. Grandmother lives right near me, in Lauderdale, so I'll give her the bad news myself. That be okay, Captain?"

At that point, Andrew Firth of Scotland made his appearance. To say this was one of the more obnoxious guys in the game would be like saying Liberace had an occasional lapse of good taste. Firth had all the social grace of an overheated wasp, and nobody could stand to play with him. He was the type of guy who considered everybody else on the

course to be his mortal enemy, and I'm not talking about during tournaments, just friendly rounds at the local club. He'd bitch and moan about
how slow those sons'abitches in the group ahead were but would never
let a fast twosome play through. He was capable of great charm and wit
in the postgame press conferences, but his on-course misbehavior had
been witnessed by too many in the age of television for him to fool
people anymore. Basically, he felt that Scotland had invented the game
and nobody else had much of a right to play it, least of all the upstart
North American colonists who had come to dominate the sport.

"Jayzus, Bellamy!" he said as he walked up to the putting green, a
nasty smile on those puffy lips buried in the middle of his florid face.
"Yer callin' this freakin' lamb chop a toof course, are ya?" He pulled up
in front of me, not caring that he was standing right in Eddie's putting
line. "I'll tell ya toof, laddie." By now Fred Asphal and Mack Merriwell
had wandered over, along with Juan Castillo Licenciados and Jürgen
Kurzer.

"Once at Auchnafree," Firth went on, "I took me a drop in the gorse
on the hole they call Switham Bairn. Held me hand out shoulder high
like so, I did, and let the thing drop straight doon." He turned to the
others. "Hoonted high and low for the little booger and never found the
bleedin' thing." Returning to me, he poked me in the chest with his
putter. "Now that's toof, sonny, noot like this fair lassie of a track you're
so bloody proud'a!"

"One time, up in Washington State?" It was Eddie, standing behind
the bunch of us, unable to putt because of where Firth had taken up
residence. "We were playin' this bitch of a course carved out of an old
Indian burial ground." Everybody turned, Firth only reluctantly, not
pleased at losing his audience. "I hit into this weird, tangly kind of shit
and couldn't find the ball, so I set my bag down and took a drop. Fifteen
full minutes three of us looked around for that damned thing."

"But ya found it, nay?" Firth asked.

"Yeah, we found it," Eddie admitted, setting the putter down and
bending over his ball to resume practice. As the Scotsman's lip began
to curl in contempt, Eddie added, "Lost the bag, though." Then he hit
the ball, hard, and Firth had to jump quickly out of the way to avoid
getting cracked in the ankle.

I left them all standing around laughing at Firth's expense, and as I
walked over to where Fat Albert was posted, I couldn't tell if the ripples

surrounding him were heat-wave mirages or his body fat jiggling as he stepped impatiently from foot to foot.

"Yo, Mistuh Bellamy, whassup!"

"Whaddaya say, Albert."

"Kick some ass today!"

"Yeah. Listen, Eddie tell you anything about how this works? Raking traps, fixing divots? Taking the flag out, where to stand . . . ?"

Fat Albert rolled his eyes up at the sky. "Been at it since four, Mr. Bellamy. Lotta weird shit I gotta do, I don't even getta hit the damned ball!"

"But you do understand what you gotta do."

He looked at me sideways. "Ain' ezzackly nuke-ular physics, Mr. Bellamy . . ."

Enrico Senzamio walked by. "Hey, Rico," I said. "What the hell's *vugganeeta* mean?"

"Inna wot language?"

"Whaddaya mean, what language? In Italian!"

"Italian, *mi culo*. Where you hear?"

I reminded myself who I heard it from, Senzamio's mortal enemy Migliore. "Forget it. Where's Ezio?"

Eddie was teamed with Senzamio for the morning alternate-shot matches, and I went to have a word with Ezio Morricone, Rico's nephew, who would be caddying for him. I asked Ezio to keep an eye on Fat Albert, help him out, but mostly make sure he didn't do anything stupid. Morricone observed, as I had, that there was no way this kid was gonna be breathing without a respirator by ten o'clock.

Mack Merriwell came off the green. "Hey, Al," he said to me. "You speak a little Italian, right? What the hell's *vugganeeta* mean?"

"Where'd you hear it?"

"Migliore. I ask him how's he like the hotel, the food, the course—all he says, *Vugganeeta*. Fuck's it mean?"

"Go ask Rico," I told him. "He'll know."

Things were moving slowly, which was unusual in the minutes before the tee-off of a major event such as this. The fact that it was ninety-two degrees at six forty-five in the morning may have had something to do with it.

Migliore wouldn't speak to Senzamio, so I asked Ezio Morricone to try to find out what the hell he was talking about. Ezio came back and said, " 'E say-a, *Vugganeeta*."

"I already knew that, goddamnit!" I was starting to get irritated. "I don't understand what it *means!*"

He looked at me the way an impatient schoolteacher would look at a retarded first-grader and pronounced each word carefully, thumb and forefinger pressed together and bouncing up and down with each sylla- ble: " 'E . . . don' . . . like . . . da . . . *Vugganeeta!*"

I stared at him in total confusion. Then Uncle Enrico came around from behind me and said, "I think he don' like the *fokkin' heat*, Alonzo."

Oh. Well, the guy had a point. We knew some of the Europeans from the colder climates were going to be uncomfortable, but this heat was ridiculous. Physical conditioning was going to make a difference, and some of our guys were a lot more out of shape than their guys. You can play pro-level golf with a pot belly and poor aerobic fitness, but in conditions like these, being overweight or short-winded would take its toll.

First tee-off was scheduled for seven-thirty. The network guys were in full swing, buttonholing everybody they could, loosening up with some perfunctory banter before getting down to the only two questions really on their minds: What about this Caminetti guy, and why is Robert Carmichael not playing on the first day?

I let it be known that my players were strictly off-limits prior to their matches. It was tough enough trying to warm up on the range and get in some putting practice in this heat without having microphones and cameras shoved up their nostrils. As a quid pro quo, I promised Bob Muesli of ABC a couple of minutes with me that he would then pool to the others. So the reporters ran around trying to cadge wives, girlfriends, caddies and, in one case, a gardener mistaken for a PGA official, while I did my on-screen with Muesli. I knew when we were hot without even looking at the little red light on the camera because his normally dour expression instantly exploded into an im- possibly huge smile as soon as he got the word through those absurdly large headphones.

"Hi, Bob Muesli right here on ABC with an exclusive pre-tournament interview with the captain of the U.S. team, my good friend and three-time Player of the Year Alan Bellamy, who's agreed to give only ABC this exclusive interview, live from La Quinta, California where— What? What? Ah, gimme a fuckin' break, Dick! Shit. Okay. *Okay*! Hi, Bob Muesli here, with an exclusive— Goddamnit to hell, Dick, we got three fuckin' minutes with the guy! Whuwuzzat? So get a *new* goddamned cable, what the hell are we, fuckin' Fox? Jesus H— Hi, Bob Muesli here, and we've got an exclusive pre-tournament interview with the captain of the U.S. team, my good friend and three-time Player of the Year Alan Bellamy, who's agreed to give only ABC and me, Bob Muesli, this exclusive interview, live from La Quinta, California. Ha ya' doin', Al?"

"Great, Bob. You know, it's—"

"Great, great! So tell me Al, how do you see it? What kind of player's gonna have the advantage on this beast of a course?"

"Well, I'll tell you, Bob, I think the guy that can hit long and keep it on the fairway, has good distance and accuracy with his irons, the guy who can get up and down from the sand, tuck those approach shots in nice and close, not make any mistakes through the green, and one-putt most of his holes—guys who can put all of that together, I think they're gonna do well out here."

"There you have it, folks," Muesli said, beaming, "right from the man who should know! Thank you for that insight, Al . . ."

"You bet, Bob."

". . . and good luck out there today!"

I touched my cap in a two-finger salute and walked away, having pretty much given Muesli the exclusive inside scoop that the matches were likely to go to the guys who shot the lowest scores.

The first foursome would be a good matchup. It was Jon Markovy and Fred Asphal versus Juan Castillo Licenciados of Spain and Andrew Firth of Scotland. Even though personality-wise Licenciados and Firth was like teaming up a Benedictine monk with Dennis Rodman, the two Europeans were very solid, all-around players, whereas we had a machine and a random-miracle generator. Since this was alternate shot, though, Markovy and Asphal wouldn't be doing their I'll-hit-it-safe-

and-you-whack-the-bejesus-out-of-it number. I put them together in the
morning just to get them the feel of playing as a team, trying to get some
idea of what the other was capable of before the afternoon's "best ball"
matches.

Markovy was up first, and hit a perfectly fine 240-yard three-wood
onto the fairway midway between two bunkers. Licenciados hit a similar
shot, but about 20 yards longer. Because they were the opening shots of
the tournament, both received rousing ovations from the gallery, or at
least as rousing as this semi-somnambulant crowd seemed capable of.

Then it was Derek Anouilh and Mack Merriwell versus Fabrizio
Migliore and Eric Swenborg of Sweden. Migliore led off with a tremendous—and risky—drive that started well right and drew back beautifully for a picture-perfect fairway landing, which the crowd appreciated.
Anouilh, hearing something that might pass for cheering, took his driver
out of his bag. I walked up next to him, grinning like an idiot for the
cameras, leaned in, and said out of the side of my mouth, "Don't you
even think about it!"

Derek smiled back, and the whole gallery thought I had just given
some piece of humorous encouragement to one of my guys. He threw
back his head and laughed and tried to be discreet as he slipped the
driver back into the bag and took out the three-wood instead. I clapped
him on the back as he, still laughing, mouthed, "Eat my shorts,
dickwad," and then I got out of his way. Derek nearly came out of his
shoes as he whacked the three-wood a whole lot harder than he normally did, blasting it about 270 but setting it down against the side of a
hillock that he could have avoided if he'd eased off a bit. The crowd, of
course, went (relatively) cuckoo, and as Derek turned to shoot me a look
clearly directing me to stick it in my ear, I saw him scratch his nose
with the middle finger of his right hand, his cute way of telling me I
might want to reconsider coaching him hole by hole. It was going to be
a long day.

As the foursome left the tee box I got a call over the two-way radio
strapped to my belt that the first group had halved the hole with pars.
Good sign: Fred must have hit a nice, safe second shot, setting up a
two-putt par. If he did that all day, the birdies would come eventually.

A couple of people in the gallery looked a little startled, and there
was some whispering going on, which was strange when nobody was
getting ready to hit. I clipped the radio back onto my belt and turned

just in time to see the next foursome coming up to the tee. The most visible member of the entourage, and apparently the cause of the strange looks, was a profusely sweating brown beach ball with Eddie Caminetti's golf bag hanging off its shoulder. Ezio Morricone looked at me and then at the sky as he slipped Senzamio's bag off and set it down. I got on the radio again and alerted the clubhouse to make sure another caddie was on standby. The reply directed me to look at a tournament official standing on the other side of the tee box. I noticed it was a young kid, in contrast to the other officials, all of whom were of a certain age. The voice on the radio told me that he was the backup caddie, and that he would be sticking with this group throughout, ready to take over from Fat Albert at a moment's notice.

Eddie and Senzamio were up against Jürgen Kurzer of Germany and Charles Woolsey of England. Playing it safe as everybody else had today, Kurzer put a three-wood to the safe spot 240 out, and Eddie did the same. I decided to walk along with this group.

"How you makin' out, Albert?" I asked as we walked off the tee and down to the fairway.

"Good. Yo, Eddie, drink summa this here." He held a water bottle out toward the side opposite me.

"Not thirsty," Eddie replied.

"You thirsty, be too late. Drink the shit, man."

Eddie accepted the bottle and took a sip, then started to hand it back. "More," Albert commanded.

"Gonna hafta pee every hole," Eddie objected, but drank some more anyway. "Florida, I don't hardly drink at all."

"Yeah, Florida," Albert said, taking the bottle back. "Drown walkin' down the street, that boggy shithole. Play some B-ball here, twenty minutes you head bustin' open, you don't suck down some water."

"I ain't playin' B-ball," Eddie pointed out.

"But you walkin', aintcha?"

It looked to me as if Albert himself was going to need an IV drip just to replace all the perspiration pouring off his face. But it didn't look as though the golf bag was giving him any trouble. Without missing a step, he swung it around in front of him, zipped the bottle into a pocket and then swung it back behind him.

"Whatcha want?" he said as we pulled up to Eddie's ball. He was pointing back at the bag with his thumb, asking what club he should take out.

"Cold beer," Eddie said. "Ain't my shot."

"Oh, yeah. Whatsisface."

Whatsisface was Senzamio, who would take the team's second shot. With 190 to the center of the green, Morricone started to pull out the five-iron, but Senzamio waved it back. "Gimme six."

Morricone got the club and said, "Sure she's enough, *Zio*?" *Zio* is Italian for uncle.

"Green, she's-a like olive oil," Senzamio replied.

It was a good call. He set the ball down just in front of the green, taking nearly all of its speed off by the time it bounced across the remaining few feet of fairway grass. But after it reached the green it still covered a surprising amount of distance, stopping about twenty feet before the pin.

Watching the shot, Woolsey and his caddie exchanged some mutterings, and then he, too, swapped clubs. His ball was too short, though, and came to rest ten feet in front of the green. It would be a difficult approach shot for Kurzer, who would have to hit it practically vertically into the air so it dropped straight down and stopped where it landed.

Albert hadn't bothered taking the bag off his shoulder as those shots were hit. He had no notion of how to conserve his energy early on so he'd have something in reserve later. I checked on the radio as we headed for the green. Pars on both sides for Anouilh/Merriwell and Swenborg/Migliore on this hole, same for Markovy/Asphal and Licenciados/Firth on number two. No blood yet.

We paused before the green for Kurzer to take his shot. Using a sand wedge with the face so open it was just about parallel to the ground, he took a full swing and hit the ball nearly ninety degrees straight up. It fell less than three feet from the pin and didn't roll an inch, a truly superb and gutsy shot.

"Holy shit!" Albert exclaimed as the crowd roared its appreciation. "Howda hell he do that!" He looked from the ball to the flag and back again, then over to the U.S. team's ball six times farther away, concern written all over his face.

"Seventeen more to go," I reassured him. "Don't worry yet."

Kurzer marked the ball and picked it up. I nudged Albert to give

Eddie his putter, telling him next time to hand it to him as they walked toward the green, and to go tend the flag now. "Hold on to it until he tells you to pull it out. If he doesn't tell you, stand there until he hits, then pull it out once the ball's on its way."

Albert nodded and did as he was told. If he was bothered by the crowd as he took center stage in the middle of that green, he didn't show it, intent as he was on watching Eddie's every move.

Without taking his eyes off his line, Eddie stuck his thumb in the air, and Albert smiled and gave him thumbs up right back. "Pull the flag out!" I hissed at him as giggles spread through the gallery. The smile disappeared as Albert nervously yanked the flag out with a clatter. Then I motioned to him to get out of the way.

Eddie had his spot in the grass picked out and stared at it as he stood up and took his position over the ball. He got his putter lined up, then took one last look at the hole to confirm the distance in his mind's eye, checked on his target spot and finally settled his gaze on the ball itself. He brought the putter back and swung it smoothly toward the ball, following through after making contact. He didn't lift his head until the ball was a few feet from the hole. It was a fast, assertive putt that lost hardly any speed during its travel over the slick green. It rolled over the hole, hit the back of the cup and popped a few inches into the air, came down and hit the back again, this time ricocheting off into the front lip and then down into the hole. It was a birdie, and Woolsey wouldn't even bother to take his putt. Lying three already, the best score the Euros could make was four, so that was the end of this hole.

The desultory crowd was moved to some cheering, America having gone one up for the first time after three tied holes so far. But their cheering was short-lived, because Eddie's wonderful birdie putt soon took second place to a different show.

Remember when the Lakers won their first game with Magic Johnson on the team, him running all over the court like a madman, jumping up and hugging Kareem Abdul Jabbar, the least huggable man in the NBA? You would've thought they'd just won game seven of the championship instead of only the first of eighty-five regular-season games, and nobody knew quite what to make of Magic's uninhibited jubilation.

As Eddie picked his ball up out of the cup, Fat Albert threw his hands in the air and let out a raucous war whoop, then began dancing some kind of weird, robotlike thing, moving back and forth across the green with his hands and arms making like a hula dancer's. The reserved crowd wilting in the heat was shocked at first, but then they started laughing as the beach ball's spontaneous and unrestrained explosion of pure joy caromed around the green, and they marveled at how this first cousin to Jabba the Hut could be so light on his feet that he didn't seem to be leaving footprints on the grass. It was a good thing the Euros had putted first, because things didn't settle down on that green until Ezio Morricone picked up Eddie's bag, handed it to Fat Albert and pushed him toward the next hole.

I was going to say something admonishing to him until I noticed that the formerly languorous gallery had suddenly become animated and invigorated, applauding even as they walked with us toward the next tee. Besides, Albert was beaming so happily at Eddie that even that confirmed fusspot couldn't prevent a mild blush, so I just let it go.

They halved the next two holes, once with pars, once with birdies, and then the Euros birdied number four while our guys only parred. All even after four. A larger crowd than I would have expected was now following us.

"What, we gonna play feetsies widdese guys a whole day?" Senzamio said to Eddie as we moved to number five.

"Whud you rather do, Rico?" Eddie asked.

"Make-a some birdies, that's what!"

"So who's stoppin' you?"

"Don' be wise-a guy. What else, maybe shoot Kurzer? Gotta take-a some risk here."

Eddie stopped suddenly, and we all drew up behind him. "Trust me, Rico. Okay? We're not up two by the fourteenth, you do what you want. But trust me until then."

Senzamio stared at him for a few seconds, then sighed deeply and clapped him on the shoulder. "Sure, Eddie. Hokay." I nodded my approval, and we walked on to number five.

Both teams parred the next two holes to remain even. Frustration was evident on both sides, caddies and players, and among the gallery as well. Only Eddie seemed calm and untroubled.

On the seventh hole, Kurzer and Woolsey had already holed out for another boring par, and Eddie was trying to line up a putt. Some guy in a red tank top who was standing on the edge of the green directly in his line of sight fidgeted as Eddie took the putter back, so he aborted the shot. Swinging the club a few times, he once more took his position over the ball, went through his routine and again brought the putter back. This time the guy scratched his nose with big up-and-down movements, and for the second time Eddie stopped in mid-putt.

I saw Fat Albert, puzzlement on his face, look from Eddie to the guy in red and back again a couple of times as he caught on. He stomped over to the guy—I could swear I felt the ground shake—stuck a finger in his face and yelled, loud enough to be heard in Phoenix, *"GIT YO' ASS OUT THE MAN'S WAY!"*

The guy in red got his ass out the man's way. Fat Albert glared at him as he slunk off, then turned back toward Eddie and planted his feet, folding his arms across his chest and smiling his permission for Eddie to continue. Eddie raised his eyebrows at this picture of his own personal Budweiser genie single-handedly doing crowd control for him, then hunkered back down and sank the putt. Fat Albert nodded his approval and, with one last glower at the poor guy with the red tank top who was suddenly beset with visions of his own mortality, hoisted up Eddie's bag and opened a swath in the crowd for his man to walk through.

So far there were no breakthroughs anywhere. Markovy and Asphal were dead even with Licenciados and Firth. Anouilh and Merriwell were one up on Swenborg and Migliore, and Fleckheimer and Paul DeMonte in the group behind ours were one down to Wickenhampshire and Villard. Net net, we were up one hole overall, but this early it was meaningless and could change in seconds.

Eddie was doing a pretty good job of keeping a grip on Senzamio, but it was easy to see that Kurzer and Woolsey were getting upset with the lackluster play. On the ninth hole, an absurdly difficult par-four with only water where grass should have been, Jürgen Kurzer, scowling, leaned hard into his driver and cracked it more than 290 yards toward a piece of dental floss passing itself off as a fairway, a truly dumb, stupid, needlessly risky shot that plunked itself down on the only square foot of safe turf anywhere in the vicinity. In the time it had taken that ball to leave the teeing area and make its way over that treacherous stretch of real estate, the normally reserved Charles Woolsey had gone from rage to religious hope to near-lethal exultation, actually going so far as to clap Kurzer on the back as the crowd boomed out its stunned delight.

Calming himself during the long walk to the ball, Woolsey was composed by the time he arrived and lofted a seven-iron in a high arc to a pinpoint landing, giving Kurzer an easy putt for birdie.

Our guys made par, losing the hole. Senzamio, seeing how pumped the Euros had become, started in on Eddie again about going for some gold, but Eddie held him to his fourteen-hole deal. On number ten Woolsey, still stoked, gleefully clobbered his driver in a gorgeous, soaring arc that came down so straight it hardly left a ripple in the surface of the water it disappeared beneath.

Senzamio, thoughtful now, played it safe. But after what looked like a perfect shot from Eddie, the ball hit something hard near the edge of the green and took an awful bounce, landing twenty feet to the left. Kurzer took a drop next to the water and landed a four-iron the same distance on the opposite side of the green, a pretty good shot considering where he'd started from. Both balls were about equidistant from the pin, but the Euros were lying three to our two, owing to their penalty stroke for the water shot.

Senzamio took a seven-iron and gently tapped the ball toward the flag, such a gem of a chip that even while it was rolling Woolsey snarled, "Pick the fooker up!" and began stalking off without ever setting foot on the green. Eddie walked over and retrieved the ball as the nonplussed Kurzer, standing well off the green, yelled, *"Was passiert hier!"* at his partner's having conceded the hole without even consulting him, but Woolsey just waved a dismissive hand at him without looking back. *"Verdammter Scheisskopf!"* Kurzer muttered angrily as he threw his wedge to his caddie and proceeded toward number eleven. Ezio, Senzamio's caddie, let out a labored breath, having been robbed of the opportunity to take a rest while the teams putted. With some difficulty, he hoisted the bag and began trudging to the next tee.

The two Euros stood far apart, glowering at each other as Eddie teed off with his usual shot. Then Woolsey grabbed his driver out of the bag without talking to Kurzer or his caddie and stepped up to the tee. It's generally not a good idea to get mad at your ball, but Woolsey got mad at his and punished it, but good, blasting a magnificent shot that surprised even him and made him momentarily forget his irritation with Kurzer, who became so emotional he turned the sides of his mouth down and nodded in grudging approval.

Senzamio looked puzzled, and started to say, " 'Ey—" but I turned toward him and whispered with as much urgency as I could muster, "Shut the fuck up, Rico!"

"But—"

"Quiet!"

He shrugged but complied, and we trooped off down the fairway. Senzamio hit a nice second shot for the team, then Kurzer hit a gorgeous one right to the green. Eddie chipped on and both sides prepared to putt, the United States lying one more than the Euros. Senzamio looked at me pleadingly, and I moved my head back and forth as discreetly as I could: *No!*

"Hey, wait jus' a damned minute!" Fat Albert exclaimed, and I sighed in relief. "How come Wooly went first?"

I cleared my throat loudly, and Senzamio turned to me. *Now, Rico!*

He conferred with Eddie, and then the two of them waved the Euros over to where an official was standing. I joined them as Albert stood alone, frowning.

"I think was da wrong guy tee off, no?" Rico said.

"Fook you talkin' about?" Woolsey said suspiciously.

"Was? Was?" Kurzer asked.

"Think it mighta been your partner's turn, Charles," Eddie explained helpfully, real pain on his face at having to deliver the awful news.

Woolsey stared at him. "Ballocks," he said. "We'll go back and do it right."

"I'm afraid that won't be possible, Mr. Woolsey," the PGA official said. "Once you struck the ball instead of Mr. Kurzer, your team was in violation."

Woolsey, aware of the cameras, tried to be sportsmanlike. "Fair enough." He turned to Kurzer and began to explain, using a combination of hand signs and the eight words of German he knew, that they had to tee off again and would be lying three because of the penalty.

"Ah, well . . ." the official began again, so apologetic he looked as if he were telling them their hometowns had been carried away in a typhoon ". . . I'm afraid that won't be possible either. Actually, um, you lost the hole as soon as the wrong man hit the ball."

In their anger with each other, the Euros had gotten confused. Since it had been Woolsey's turn to hit when he suddenly conceded the hole, he must have figured he was up first on the next tee, forgetting that tee shots are alternated regardless of who hit the team's last shot on the previous hole. Kurzer was supposed to start all the even-numbered holes. I had told Senzamio to stay quiet because I didn't want it to look as if we were jumping on a technicality to gain an advantage. I was hoping somebody else would notice. We had until the hole was played out to make a protest, and I would have, had Albert not blurted out the error in time. Now, nobody could point a finger at the rest of us for being cheesy about pointing out a rules violation. We were now up two after eleven holes, and Senzamio was doing a good job of hiding his delight. Eddie was his usual inscrutable self. I learned by radio that both matches ahead of ours had ended in ties, a half point for each side.

Kurzer's and Woolsey's vexation with each other turned to desperation, which led to sloppy play. After fifteen, they were down three with three holes to go. The best they could do was halve the match, and they'd have to win all three holes to do it. Drawing on some inner reserves, they rallied to win the next two with birdies against our pars, Fat Albert scowling so menacingly that the crowd was intimidated into only perfunctory applause. Senzamio started yammering away at Eddie again to try a risky play on eighteen.

Woolsey teed off with a terrific drive that visibly disheartened Senzamio, but he pulled himself together and matched it with one of his own. As we got to the ball, it was clear that Kurzer was going to attempt a huge draw shot that would put him in spitting distance of the green. If Eddie didn't try something spectacular, we could easily lose the hole and have to settle for a tie instead of a win. But if Eddie screwed it up, we were equally as dead. Everything rested on this decision, and none of us seemed willing to make it.

"Man can't go to his left," we heard from behind us.

We turned. Fat Albert stood with a golf bag on either shoulder and a contemptuous sneer on his face. "Whud you say?" I asked him, annoyed at the intrusion. "And how come you got two bags?"

Albert pointed back at the tee box, where Ezio Morricone was sitting on his haunches, a tournament aide holding a cold towel to his forehead. Albert was carrying Senzamio's bag in addition to Eddie's. "Man can't go to his left," he said again, indicating Kurzer with his chin. It was a basketball term for a player who couldn't suddenly whirl on a defenseman and drive around his left side toward the basket.

"What do you mean?" I asked him.

"I mean," he answered, as though it should have been obvious, "every time he puts one high 'n' outside, it gets away from him."

Baseball, this time, meaning when Woolsey tried to hit a high draw, it was like a pitcher throwing a curveball away from a right-handed batter and overdoing it, spinning it out of control. I thought back to some of the long draw shots Woolsey had tried today. I have a near-perfect memory of every golf shot I see.

"Play it safe," I said to Eddie. "Let's get on in three." He was nodding his agreement before I finished. I held up my hand as Senzamio started to protest, and he stayed silent. Eddie hit a very sweet shot that set up perfectly for an easy approach to the green. Woolsey and Kurzer sneaked small smiles at each other, friends again. They had predicted that Eddie would play it safe, and now Woolsey was ready to crack a big one that would demoralize us completely.

A big one it was, Woolsey grunting as he came through the ball and sent it skyrocketing off at tremendous velocity. It started off to the right of the green, just as he had intended, then started coming back in beautifully, then its curvature increased and it crossed the centerline and then increased some more until it was perfectly clear that this one was headed for a watery grave. What had started off as an Atlas missile landed in the drink with an embarrassingly pathetic little *kershplunkt.*

As Kurzer began hissing at Woolsey in unintelligible but obviously not laudatory German and went off to take his drop, Senzamio hit his lob wedge to within five feet of the pin. Kurzer's recovery shot was pretty marvelous, too, and landed about eight feet from the hole. But we were lying three, and they were lying four. Woolsey made their putt, then Eddie made ours, and the crowd immediately turned away from the golfers and toward Fat Albert, who didn't disappoint them. It was the New York City Ballet meets Howdy Doody and was replayed countless times that night on all the networks.

A full point for us, the only one of the four matches that didn't end in a tie. So after the first morning, it was United States 2½, Europe 1½.

Fat Albert was still high-fiving spectators twenty minutes later, both bags dangling from his massive shoulders, while Ezio Morricone was getting rehydrating glucose infusions back at the clubhouse. I went with Rico to see him, and asked Ezio what had happened.

"*Vugganeeta,*" was all he could manage by way of reply.

CHAPTER SEVENTEEN

Friday Afternoon

The second round of matches didn't go our way. I kept two of the teams the same, Eddie/Senzamio and Markovy/Asphal, and paired August Hookstratten with Derek Anouilh and Archie McWhirter with Tal Thomashow.

Eddie acquitted himself beautifully, staying cool and making pars and birdies all over the place. The four times he bogeyed, Rico was there with pars to back him up and save the holes. They played well together, acting as a team unmindful of individual credit, but so did their opponents, Eric Swenborg and Jacques St. Villard. It was an exciting match, the lead flip-flopping all during the round, but it finally ended in a tie. Hookstratten's and McWhirter's teams were also all square, the former largely because of some weak putting by Anouilh.

The only loss came from Markovy and Asphal, and I think it had to do with their heads getting rattled early in the round. From then on it became a comedy of odd occurrences and rules interpretation. In golf, those kinds of situations would drive a Supreme Court justice blind.

They were up against Jürgen Kurzer and Fabrizio Migliore, "best ball" format. The whole mess started when Migliore was late, probably after visiting his nephew in the clinic. Normally this would involve a penalty or a disqualification, but in "best ball," Kurzer could start playing without Migliore, and whatever score he got playing alone would be the team's score. Theoretically, he could play the whole round himself, but winning would be virtually impossible because he'd have to consistently outshoot both Markovy *and* Asphal.

Markovy teed off first, hitting a beauty about 270 to the middle of the fairway and slightly left, just where he wanted it, taking the bunker on the right front of the green out of play. Kurzer also hit well, fifteen yards shy of Jon but well placed nonetheless, and Fred's was fairly close to that one. Kurzer was away and went for the pin, but his angle was too shallow and the ball skittered across the green after landing and rolled off the back. Fred, according to our plan, also went for the green, hitting up high so the ball would plant itself where it landed instead of rolling. It planted itself all right, but in the sand, not on the green.

Markovy then took the conservative approach, hitting in front of the green, where the slightly taller grass would stop the ball. Even so, it somehow managed to dribble on, leaving him about a twenty-footer for birdie. Asphal and Kurzer both hit back onto the green, Kurzer about fifteen feet out, Asphal about twenty-five.

At that point, two golf carts with flashing lights and nonstandard motors came roaring up the cart path, disgorging a harried Fabrizio Migliore and a new caddie, the same guy that Eddie had replaced with Fat Albert that morning. We smiled our hellos and got down to the business of lining up our putts. Asphal was away and hit a nice one, but it ran past the cup, and he holed it out for a bogey. Markovy was next, and put it within one inch of the cup, tapping in for a nice par, which was according to our strategy: Asphal takes the risks, Markovy saves the par, and that par was now the "best ball" score for the U.S. team.

Kurzer got down on one knee to read the green. Lying three, he needed this one to halve the hole. Anything else and the hole would go to us. It was a tricky putt that Markovy and Asphal, having been on the other side of the hole, hadn't had to deal with. The green sloped to Kurzer's right, but there was a slight hump that would send the ball leftward, and the putt would have to be at just the right speed to ride both curves successfully to the hole.

As Kurzer dangled his putter to plumb-bob the line, Migliore walked to the opposite side to check it out from another angle. Markovy and Asphal looked at each other but didn't say anything yet. Then Kurzer said, "Vot you t'ink?" and Migliore replied, "I think is gonna slide left."

"Hey, you can't do that!" Asphal said.

Kurzer looked up in surprise. "Do vot?"

"You can't get advice from him. He's not in this hole!"

"But he iss mein partner!" Kurzer said, annoyed at his concentration being disrupted.

"Not on this hole, he's not," Asphal said. "He's not playing it."

"I'm not playing," Migliore said. "I give advice."

Markovy shook his head. "He played this one alone. You can't give him advice."

"*Mi culo*," Migliore said. *My ass.*

Markovy waved over the PGA official and made his protest. The official didn't take any time at all to formulate his reply. "It makes no difference if he played the hole or not. He could have elected not to play it even if he had been here on time. He's still Mr. Kurzer's partner for the round and entitled to give advice. Please proceed, gentlemen."

And proceed they did, Kurzer draining the putt to halve. There may have been no blood on the hole, but there was some in the air, and it stayed there for eighteen holes.

The next incident came on number three, a 470-yard par-four whopper called the Crescent for a moon-shaped sand pit protecting the left side of the fairway. The bunker was about 80 yards long and stretched from 225 to 305 yards away from the tee, the exact range of distances covering decent tee shots. You couldn't leave the drive short, because that would give you at least 245 to the green, which was fronted by a big, oddly shaped bunker, and trying to hit past it on the fly and stay on the green was all but impossible. The only par-saving shot was to keep the ball to the right of the moon bunkers on a piece of fairway less than 40 yards wide. The farther you tried to hit the ball, the tougher that would be.

Migliore, with little warm-up time, missed badly, ending up in the rough about 240 out. Markovy, acutely aware of the difficulty of this hole, made the smart play, hitting a three-iron about 225, just short of the crescent-moon sand. He would lay his next shot up in front of the green, then try to chip close over the protective trap and one-putt for par.

Kurzer, frustrated that the score was still all square after three holes, went for it. Even I had to suppress an appreciative cry as his drive sailed off to the right and drew back perfectly for a touchdown between the moon bunker and the right rough that would leave him 210 to the green. Asphal, as I suspected he would, nearly came out of his shoes trying to outdrive Kurzer, and he did, except that his ball landed in the crescent sand instead of the fairway. It looked as if Kurzer and Mr. Wizard would be duking it out for this hole.

Markovy hit first, nicely laying a five-iron up about 50 yards short of the green. Migliore hit a hell of a shot off a bad lie in the rough, but it came down in the bunker guarding the front of the green. At that point Kurzer realized that his outstanding drive actually didn't do him all that much good, because the odds of his keeping a ball on that narrow, slippery green from this distance weren't promising. He couldn't roll it up because of the front bunker. And in order to carry the bunker and still have the ball stick when it landed, he'd have to hit way up in the air so the ball came down at a steep angle. Trying to do that from 210 yards away was not going to be easy. The wise move at this point would have been to do as Markovy had done, and lay up.

But I could see Kurzer wasn't interested in that. He conferred with Migliore, who assured him he could get up and down from the sand for par. So Kurzer took a three-iron and opened the face wide, in the hopes that the sky-high trajectory would be compensated for by the overclubbing. Damned if it didn't do just that. Kurzer gave it a mighty whack, and the ball lofted skyward about as steeply as I've ever seen a three-iron intentionally hit. Everyone watching knew it was a brilliant shot, and the applause was long and sustained as the ball drilled into the green about fifteen feet from the flag, hopped back into the air and came back down practically in its own pitch mark.

Asphal, a club already in his hand, pursed his lips and looked down, flipping the clubhead back and forth on the turf. Then he turned and headed for the moon bunker. He had to take a lot of sand in order to clear the high wall of the bunker, and his plan was to hit as hard as he could with a seven-iron to make the distance. But he underestimated his own strength, and his wonderful shot airmailed the green and came to rest in the rough behind it. Markovy then pitched onto the green, but not as well as he would have liked. He had eight feet to putt.

Migliore's sand shot also wasn't as accurate as it could have been, and he nearly hit his partner's ball as his came out too hot and rolled way past the pin. The two Euros were about thirteen feet from the flag, with Migliore's ball about three inches behind Kurzer's. Asphal's pitch from the rough behind the green was terrible, and he was effectively out of the hole.

So here was the situation: Markovy was lying three and would very likely make par. Migliore was also lying three but with a difficult putt for par. Kurzer, on the other hand, was only lying two, also with a tough putt, but if he sank it, it was a bird and the Euros would win the hole.

Markovy beckoned Asphal over, and the two of them spoke quietly for a few seconds. I know exactly what Markovy was proposing, which was to concede Migliore's par without making him putt.

The reasoning was pure Mr. Wizard: The Euros were sure to make at least a par. But if Migliore putted, even if he missed, he would be showing the line to Kurzer, vastly increasing his chances of making his birdie. By conceding Migliore's putt, our guys would be making it much tougher for Kurzer, who would have to make his birdie attempt without seeing how Migliore's ball moved on its way to the hole.

Asphal saw it right away, and as Migliore set up to putt, said, "Pick it up!" and started to walk off the green. Markovy turned to step out of Kurzer's line of sight. But when he turned back, Migliore was still poised over the ball, moving his head back and forth between the ball and the hole.

"Hey, Fabrizio," he called out, "we gave it to you. Pick it up!"

Migliore shook his head. "Gonna putt."

"Whaddaya mean, you're gonna putt?" Asphal yelled from the edge of the green. "We gave it to you!"

Migliore, an exasperated look on his face, stepped away from the ball and turned to Asphal. "*Basta*, Freddy! I gotta right to putt if I wanna!"

"The hell you do!" Asphal retorted, and started to walk back onto the green. But Migliore was lining up again, Kurzer kneeling behind him to watch the ball's path, and Asphal stopped. Whatever else, he wouldn't dare interfere while a man was getting ready to hit.

Migliore uses a pendulum putter, one of these things that look more like a vaulting pole than a golf club. You hold the end against your chest with one hand and swing it with the other. Migliore's ball looked as if it was going to go in, but veered slightly with about a foot remaining and slid past the cup on the left. Kurzer nodded knowingly, and Markovy held up his hand to stop Asphal from saying anything else. Migliore tapped in for his bogey five, then it was Kurzer's turn. Now armed with the knowledge he gained from going to school on his partner's putt, he struck the ball confidently and drained it for a birdie, much to his and Migliore's delight.

Markovy took his time with his putt and sank it as well, for a par and a seemingly lost hole. But before any of them left the green, Markovy called over the PGA official and lodged a claim, demanding a ruling. The official put his chin in his hand and thought about it for a long time, then said, "The U.S. team is correct. Mr. Migliore should not have putted his ball. As the beneficiary of that violation, Mr. Kurzer is disqualified from this hole, and his score doesn't count."

Trying not to gloat, Asphal put out his fist and Markovy tapped the top of it with his own, then Asphal did the same to him. "Finally put up a damned score," Markovy said.

"Fuckin' A," Asphal replied.

"Excuse me?" the PGA official said.

"We halved the first two," Asphal explained. "Finally advanced one up on them."

"How so?" the official inquired innocently.

Markovy frowned. "My par against Migliore's bogey, that's how so."

The PGA official, a thin little man with thick glasses, blinked rapidly. "Oh, I shouldn't think so, Mr. Markovy. The hole has been halved. No blood a'tall."

Markovy stopped walking. "What the hell are you talking about? Since when does a bogey tie a par!"

The official, somewhat nonplussed at Markovy's uncharacteristic outburst, stammered as he said, "But the European team scores a par as well, sir."

"How!" Asphal demanded, stepping into the man's face.

The official's minor surprise was short-lived as he asserted himself right back. "Mr. Migliore made par, Mr. Asphal!"

"He took a *five*, buddy! You been counting?"

"I most certainly have. As I recall, you conceded his putt. Wasn't that the basis of your claim?"

"Conceded his— What're you, nuts? He putted anyway and *missed*!"

"It didn't count!" the official retorted. "His play ended when you conceded! That's why Mr. Kurzer was disqualified. Now, you either gave him the damned putt or you didn't! Which is it?"

Well, they certainly couldn't take it back, and anyway, the rules would speak for themselves regardless of what they said. Migliore had scored a legitimate, conceded par, and that was that. The bottom line is that halving this hole was all my guys had been going for in the first place, and that's what they ended up with, but the whole thing left a sour taste in everybody's mouth.

They were all square after three holes. Things only got worse after

that. On number seven, Asphal moved his ball on the green to make
way for Markovy's putt. Apparently he never replaced the ball but
putted from its temporary location, making birdie and winning the hole
for the United States. On number nine, Migliore gleefully went up to the
PGA official, Dickie Paettersen, and told him about it, laying claim to
the win on that hole because of Asphal's violation. He waited until this
hole because that's where the television control barn was located, and
he dragged Paettersen over to watch a replay.

"Yup," Paettersen said to Asphal, taking off his boater and scratching his head, "you sure did screw that one up."

Asphal, aghast, watched the screen, and the official watched Asphal.
Kurzer and Migliore attempted some European version of a high-five,
but Paettersen ignored them as he kept his eyes on Asphal, who eventually dropped his head and said, "I never put it back." He looked up.
"They're right, Dickie. What can I tell you?"

"You can tell me if you knew, Mr. Asphal," Paettersen said.

Asphal shook his head. "I don't even remember it now." Realizing
that this would mean the loss of number seven rather than the win they
thought they had, he looked over at Markovy and started to apologize,
but Markovy firmly let him know it was unnecessary.

"They're only one up, Freddy. Lotta golf to go."

"No, they're not," Paettersen said as he replaced his straw hat and
began walking out of the control barn. Kurzer and Migliore glanced at
each other and were soon on Paettersen's heels like hungry wolves,
demanding an explanation or his head.

Paettersen calmly looked at his watch and waited for them to calm
down. "You've got to make your claim prior to teeing off on the next
hole following the alleged violation, which would have been number
eight. Here we are on number nine already, so it's too late."

"But he play frumma wrong-a place!" Migliore protested.

Paettersen looked at him as if he'd just been told two and two make
four. "I *know* that, Mr. Migliore. Nobody's arguing about it. But you
can't save up your claim for when it's convenient. The only way I could
uphold you is if Mr. Asphal did it intentionally." He looked over at
Asphal. "And it's my judgment that he didn't." Turning once more to
the two Euros, he said, "Do you wish to dispute that?"

Calling Asphal a liar would have been too much even for this carnival of bad feeling, especially since the incorrect location had given Freddy no advantage, and they let it go, still down one after eight holes. The angry Euros then won number ten to tie it all up.

On number eleven—called Eternity, and they're not kidding— Kurzer, ungodly pissed by now, walloped an astounding drive of over 300 yards, then hit an equally monstrous driver off the deck, plopping his ball into a greenside pond. This is a 618-yard slaughterhouse of a hole, and Kurzer had just come 570 yards in two shots. Even with a one-stroke penalty for the lateral hazard, he could still make par with a good chip and a one-putt.

Kurzer had to take his drop within two club-lengths of the water. He could see that such a drop would keep him in the rough, the smooth fairway just a tantalizing foot or so away. As he held the ball at shoulder height ready to let it go, he backed off and walked over to Migliore's bag, pulling out the Italian's pendulum putter. Smiling, he used this railroad track of a club to remeasure his two club-lengths, which would place him squarely on the fairway.

Asphal, laughing good-naturedly, called out, "Give us a freakin' break, you German gerbil!"

Kurzer smiled back, held out his hand and dropped the ball onto the smooth grass. Asphal stopped smiling and waved the official over.

"He took his partner's putter to measure, f'Chrissakes!" Asphal said, folding his arms and waiting for justice.

"So what?" the official said. Aware that many pros don't know all the rules and variations, he explained that Kurzer could use any club he wanted, no matter whose it was, as long as he had the owner's permission. As Asphal walked away, Kurzer pitched up and almost holed it, settling for a par but winning the hole anyway. The Euros were now one up, and it stayed that way for the next six holes.

On number eighteen, still down one, Asphal and Markovy had no choice but to go for it. This is truly a one-of-a-kind hole. Imagine a bowling lane 440 yards long. As you look down toward the pins, the right one third of the lane is grass, and the left two thirds is water, and it's like that for its entire length. That's the Coliseum. The gutsiest way to play this hole is to smack the longest drive you possibly can, straight out over the water with a slight fade. Theoretically the ball will drift right and settle onto the grass at whatever distance you managed, so long as it curved enough to clear the water.

If Kurzer and Migliore had been playing with their heads instead of their testicles, they would have gone for the easy par on this hole and let Markovy and Asphal take all the risks. But Kurzer tried to come out of his shoes again and sliced his drive, coming to rest on the cart path running along the right side beyond the rough. Markovy, knowing that playing conservative wasn't going to win this hole, figured he might as well let the big dog loose, too, and wound up in a fairway bunker. Migliore, well aware that there were hero points to be had if he outdid everybody else, also went for the glory and wound up in the same bunker as Markovy.

Which left Asphal, who chose this moment to unleash all the pent-up hostility he'd been trying with only partial success to suppress since the first hole. With a backswing as deep as I've ever seen him take, he hit a thunderous shot that blew out over the water with a riffling sound not unlike that made by an incoming mortar shell. It was easily the longest drive of the day, and we watched, hypnotized, as the ball began to come back to the right. But Freddy had hit it so far that it was beyond the point where the water actually makes a slight incursion toward the land. Had it been thirty yards shorter, it would have landed safely on the fairway. As it happened, it hit the rocky bank and bounced into the water.

Asphal hung his head as the crowd groaned. The other three players managed recovery shots that set them up nicely for short approaches to the green, although no one had actually managed to get on. Asphal realized that, after his drop from the lateral water hazard, he had an opportunity to be on the green in three, which would be no worse than any of the other guys.

As we trooped up to where his ball had gone in, we were amazed to find him in the same situation Kurzer had been in on number eleven: A standard two-club drop would put him in the rough, but another foot would get him out onto the fairway with a pretty easy 125 to the green and a par opportunity.

Asphal chuckled and walked over to Migliore's caddie. Reaching out for the pendulum putter in the bag standing on the grass, he turned and said, with exaggerated formality and a deep bow, "Signor Migliore, may I have the pleasure of borrowing your putter?"

As Asphal's hand closed around the club, Migliore, with an equally florid gesture, replied, "No."

Asphal froze, the smile still on his face. "Come again?"

"I say . . . no." Migliore shrugged, indicating some sort of help-lessness about his decision.

"No," Asphal echoed mindlessly.

"No."

"You're kidding, right?" Markovy said.

"I'm kidding, no right," Migliore answered.

And we lost the match. At the end of the first day, Friday, it was all square, 4–4.

CHAPTER EIGHTEEN

Saturday Morning

Nobody was in a good mood. We all realized that a tone had been set for the tournament that had little to do with civility and the grand traditions of golf sportsmanship and more to do with the Marquess of Queensberry rules that governed boxing matches. There didn't seem to be anything that could be done about it, either, just as nobody could do anything about the unconscionably boorish behavior of the American crowds at Kiawah Island in 1991; that Ryder event was already being called The War by the Shore even before the first ball had been struck. While some sense of gentility had been restored in 1993, there seemed to be little doubt that we were about to set the clock of propriety back to sometime during the Inquisition.

About two thousand spectators had turned up just after sunrise to watch the players warming up on the driving range. I stood off to the side watching as Derek Anouilh started with a nine-iron and gradually worked his way up to longer clubs. He'd only hit about two dozen shots before he pulled out his driver.

How that skinny kid could hit a ball so far was a real mystery. At least it had been until Eddie had offered up a theory that, the more I thought about it, made sense. It was after the two of them had played Eddie's "audition" round. Even though Anouilh had lost, the talk around the clubhouse centered mostly on those flabbergasting drives he'd gotten off.

"Swing easy, hit hard," Mack Merriwell had mused, reciting a standard golf aphorism as we watched Anouilh on the Crystal Canyon range some weeks before. His drives were landing on the tee box of the fourth hole on the Mountain nine.

"Hanged if I could tell you why," Fred Asphal chimed in. Anouilh

coiled into a deep backswing that brought the club all the way around
his neck, then let loose another screamer of a shot.

"Technique," Eddie said as he watched the ball fly. "Hitting it
square."

"Doesn't tell me anything," Merriwell said. "Seems to me, the faster
the clubhead's going, the harder you're gonna hit the ball and the faster
it's gonna go. Simple physics, not magic."

I had to agree with him. I knew the standard stuff about letting the
clubhead do the work, but all of a sudden I couldn't see what that had
to do with how fast the ball got off the face.

"And you're right," Eddie continued, "but here's the thing. Let's say
the clubhead is moving ten miles per hour faster than your usual swing.
Then the ball ought to fly off the face ten miles per hour faster too,
right?"

"Sure would seem that way."

Eddie nodded. "Obvious. But let's say your usual swing catches the
ball right on the sweet spot of the club. If you try to put ten more miles
per hour on the swing and that makes you contact the ball *off* the sweet
spot, or at some angle other than square, well, that's not only gonna
wipe out those extra ten per, it's gonna end up at even less than your
usual swing. The point of hitting easy isn't because of some wild-ass
theory of alternative physics, it's just to make sure you stay in control
and hit the ball sweet and square."

He looked out to the range where Derek Anouilh was now whacking
his three-wood farther than many of us could hit a driver. "You think he
has the highest clubhead speed on the tour?"

"He doesn't?" Asphal said.

Eddie shook his head. "Guarantee you Harriman's clubhead speed is
faster. The big secret is that Derek hits every ball perfect. I mean *dead*
perfect. If he could swing at full speed and still hit the ball that perfect,
they'd have to redesign every golf course he played on. Be like having a
nine-foot guy on your basketball team."

He pulled out his own driver and hefted it before teeing up a ball
and addressing it, standing farther back than he usually did. "Swing
easy . . ." he said, then went into his backswing, paused at the top
and came back around with very little apparent effort. The sound the
clubhead made as it struck the ball was about the purest little *tink* I
ever heard, and the ball sailed off only to be lost in the setting

sun. ". . . hit hard," he concluded, still holding his finishing position.

I wondered how he could be following that ball straight into the sun. Then I noticed that his eyes were closed.

Here at PGA West, the protective net at the back of the range was about 240 yards away and at least forty feet high. Shortly after Anouilh whacked his first drive, a little puff of dust popped off the net about twenty feet from the top. It was a place so rarely touched that dirt had been accumulating there undisturbed since the last rains six months before. His second drive produced a puff five feet higher than that one, as did his next shot, and pretty soon he was coming within ten feet of the top. It was a spectacular display.

Sometime in the past few minutes, Eddie had come up and joined me. As another smasher cracked off into the distance, he frowned and said, "The hell's he playing with his driver for?"

"He can put it out three-thirty and straight when he's on like this," I said.

"So what? Think his score'd be any worse if he only put it two-ninety?"

I didn't answer. After another minute of listening to the devotional chants emanating from the spectators, Eddie said, "Man took thirty-four putts his last match."

I was getting a little annoyed at his carping over Anouilh's performance. "What's your point, Eddie?"

"Point is," he answered, as though he'd been waiting for me to ask, "you shoot a regulation round, half a all your shots are gonna be putts. That's three times as many as you'll take with your driver. So why's he out there walloping drivers when he should be on the practice green trying to get down to twenty-eight putts instead of thirty-four? Which one you think is gonna be better for his score?"

I didn't have a snappy comeback for that. "He's just trying to groove himself, Eddie. Make sure he's got the feel of the club."

We watched a little while longer. Oddly, four of Anouilh's next five shots produced no telltale puffs of dirt, and it took me a moment to realize that this was because he was now going *over* the net. Onlookers with binoculars had already seen this and were dumbstruck.

"I'd say he was pretty much grooved now," Eddie said as he turned to walk away. "Get his ass on the putting green."

Eddie'd said this before, in different words—"Practice the worst part of your game, not the best"—but what struck me now was that he all of a sudden seemed to care about how Anouilh was going to do in his match. That was something new.

The morning's alternate-shot matches were uneventful, and it was still all tied up afterward. The only thing that got the press excited was trying to figure out why I still hadn't played Robert Carmichael, and they hung around the locker room hoping to grab him as he came out to watch the afternoon rounds. As of yesterday afternoon I hadn't told anyone that he wouldn't be playing in those, either, and when the tour officials announced the best-ball pairings last night, reporters started going crazy to find out what was going on.

"Don't read anything into it," I kept repeating. "It's just part of our overall game plan." Nobody was buying it. What kind of game plan kept a team member in the locker room for two days? It might not have been that big a deal, except that reporters have a special gland located far from their hearts that squirts venom into their brains whenever it detects an opportunity to create a scandal. What else would you expect from a press that gave more column inches to President Eastwood's dick than it did to the threat of nuclear annihilation? Acutely aware of what an unpleasant character Carmichael was, the scandal gland must have been spraying like a fire hose.

It was starting to get to the rest of my guys, too. Not keeping Carmichael out, but the constant harping on it by the press, which naturally spread to the PGA officials, caddies and VIP guests who on their own might not have given it much thought except that the media were always the ones responsible for deciding what everyone thought was important.

It was time for a pep talk, not just to pump the guys up but to get their minds back on the game. Pep talks in golf are kind of tricky. In football or basketball or marathon running you say something inspirational to get the adrenaline flowing, but adrenaline is the most dangerous substance in golf, a sport in which you can't dig down for an extra burst of strength. You can't use that deeply hidden reserve that squeezes the very last modicum of power and endurance out of your muscles, the kind that lets you keep a full-court press going for two more minutes or chase down a fresh-legged reserve running back at the end of the big game or cover that last quarter mile to the finish line before collapsing in exhaustion. Try to do something like that in golf and you might as well head for the parking lot and throw your clubs in the trunk.

In golf you have to do the exact opposite. You have to make absolutely sure to keep the adrenaline at bay. Not to get mystical on you, but it is somewhat Zen-like: *To win, you have to put winning out of your mind.* You have to concentrate on each individual shot as though it were the only thing in the universe that existed right now, or would ever exist. You don't think about the consequences—"If I hit it well, I win; if I screw it up, I lose"—you think only about how you're going to hit *this* shot. You know for sure you're getting your mind right when you look up from a well-struck ball and it takes a half second to remind yourself why you even bothered to hit it in the first place.

There's so much ego involved in the game, you have to get your ego out of it to play well. "I just gotta beat this guy!" is the worst kind of thought to harbor in your brain, and it seemed to be the only thought in my players' minds. It's not easy to try to forget for a moment the weight of your team and your country on your shoulders as you stand hunched over the ball with a five-iron in your hands. Bottom line, though, it does you no good to think about that even if you're in a two-dollar Nassau down at the local muni; it's sure as hell not going to help you hit the ball any better.

I try to tell this to amateurs during corporate outings, when they're shaking and sweating and muttering to themselves about how they just gotta get this one right, they just gotta. Don't the pros often rise to the occasion, playing beyond their abilities when the big one is on the line? Don't you hit better, knowing what's at stake?

I try to tell them that what they should be doing is playing every shot, of every round, as though it were the deciding ball on the eighteenth at Augusta. That way they get used to the feeling of making them all count. And I also tell them that what the pros are doing when the big one is on the line is concentrating even harder to kick that fact out of their heads. Because if you think about the big one being on the line, what you're really doing, without your even knowing it, is trying desperately not to lose rather than trying to win. Hoping that this shot makes it to the green is a lot different from hoping that you don't screw it up.

I explained all of this to the players as we sat in the locker room. When I was finished there was a respectful silence, and I knew I had gotten to them.

Joel Fleckheimer folded his arms across his chest. "Jesus, you suck at this, Bellamy," he said with heartfelt derision, shaking his head.

"Hey, tell us that part about the Zen shit again!" Mack Merriwell yelled out.

"Yes," even Freddy Asphal agreed loudly, "what shall we do, master: contemplate our penises and chant *Om?*"

"Hey!" Markovy shouted over the hubbub. "Whud the Zen master say to the hot-dog vendor?"

Merriwell yelled back, *"Make me one with everything!"*

They were unable to stop laughing as I stood there like a schmuck, red-faced. "Fuck everyone'a you assholes," I eventually mumbled, and that only made them laugh even harder, real tears flowing down a few faces, until I had to smile myself, wave a dismissive hand at them and go meet the press. What the hell, at least I managed to loosen things up a bit.

There's something I need to mention about Fleckheimer. All that stuff about holding the adrenaline at bay, putting emotion out of your system and forgetting your personal feelings about what's going on in a golf match? It's all true. Every bit of it. Except when it came to Joel Fleckheimer.

Fleck is the only golfer I knew of who cranked his game up to new levels whenever he got really angry, and the more enraged the better. Damned if I know how, but over the years his mind had figured out some way to channel his fury into a purity of swing and a stolidity of approach that were positively eerie. The last thing in the world you wanted to do if you were playing against the Fleck was piss him off.

At the last Masters, the one Derek Anouilh won, Joel was in a foursome with the Romanian national champion Mieczyslaw Piranewski. On the tenth tee, the up-and-coming self-professed descendant of Vlad the Impaler (a dubious claim considering Piranewski had been born in Poland) scratched his nose and sniffled loudly in the middle of our boy's backswing. Fleck being Fleck, he managed to abort the shot and throw Piranewski a cold look just to make sure he'd understood what he'd done, however inadvertent it might have been.

Then Piranewski did it again, this time too far along in Fleck's backswing for him to do anything about it, and he shanked the ball badly. Piranewski, without apologizing or even acknowledging his unforgivable gaffe, walked off the tee box as though nothing had happened. Fleck stood still and stared at him until he was about thirty yards away, the onlooking gallery certain he was going to throw his driver at the guy's head. But Fleck got hold of himself and turned to an official, asking him to radio in for the standings. At that point, the Romanian was in fifth place, Fleck in fifteenth.

I've seen the tapes. A muscle in Fleck's jaw had been working like a bilge pump, but by the time he walked off the tee box, it was perfectly still. Joel never said a word to Piranewski. In fact, he never said a word to anybody for the remaining eight holes. He just proceeded to take Piranewski apart with methodical and ruthless precision, responding to the poor man's every shot as though it were match play with a million bucks on the line. If Piranewski hit a drive 270 yards, Joel hit it 280. If Piranewski dropped it onto the green eight feet from the pin, Joel got it within six. It went like that for the rest of the afternoon, Fleckheimer casting murderous glances at the Romanian that were so potent they must have physically scrambled some of the guy's brain cells. By the time the day was over, Fleckheimer had moved from fifteenth to fourth place, and the badly rattled Romanian had dropped back to twenty-seventh.

Fleckheimer fell out of the zone only when network commentator Bob Muesli came running up to him and said breathlessly, "I'm here with Joel Fleckheimer! Joel, how'd you do it, fella! What turned it all around?"

Fleckheimer, blinking and frowning in confusion, looked at him for a few seconds and said, "How'd I do what?"

Saturday Afternoon

As much crap as I took after my lecture, I sensed new resolve in the guys as they trooped out for the day's "best ball" rounds. I sensed a similar mood among the Euros, though, and suspected that Jacques St. Villard had also done something to get his team inspired. I wondered how he did that with all the different languages he had to cope with.

I kept the teams pretty much the same as yesterday's. The results were different, though. For one thing, Eddie and Senzamio were playing against the Grand Teutons, Helmut Braunschweiger and Jürgen Kurzer. Eddie was playing quite well, but Senzamio was just plain out of his mind, hitting magnificent drives and delicate approach shots that were well above his usual game. On number eight, The Links, an ogre of a 557-yard par-five that tempts the unwary to try to reach the green in two, Rico *did* reach it in two and eagled the damned thing, somehow avoiding all the sand, craters, bushes and other crap that course designer Pete Dye had thrown in there to try to stop him. They were two up on the Germans, the crowd audibly praying for the Americans to win more holes so they could watch Fat Albert do the South Central two-step.

Then, on number ten, Rico hauled off on the tee and nearly came out of his shoes. It was a slight fade, starting out over the water and drifting right, but it didn't get over quite far enough and landed in the lake less than five feet from land. Senzamio, shaken, looked down at his driver and immediately began to think about what had gone awry and how he was going to fix it.

"What I do wrong, Eddie?" he said as they began walking off the tee.

Eddie stopped walking and looked at him. "What're you, kiddin' me?"

"I put in the fokking water!"

"So what?"

"Wha' you mean, so what—I gotta fix it!"

"Fix it?" Eddie repeated in utter astonishment. "Fix what! You just hit ninety percent of your tee shots smack down the middle of the fairway! S'matter, ninety percent not good enough for you?"

They resumed walking, Senzamio unmollified by Eddie's reaction. Eddie saved the half with a par, and they were still up two holes as they stepped up to number eleven.

"But whuh hoppen on tha' last-a one?" Senzamio insisted, still unwilling to shake off the water shot.

Eddie walked up to him until they were toe to toe, grabbed the driver out of Rico's hand, and shook it at him. "You *missed* it, that's what happened, you dumb guinea bastard! The hell's a'matter with you!" He opened Rico's hand and slapped the club into it. "Don't you *dare* screw around with that shot!"

Senzamio looked at Eddie like he'd just landed from Mars, but he was so intimidated by his fierce demeanor and authoritative manner that he just stepped up to the ball, gripped it and ripped it, about 310 yards and so straight the ball might as well have been on rails. Once the shock began to fade, a big smile slowly split his face and he turned to Eddie grinning like an idiot. Eddie just spread his hands and raised his eyebrows: *See, you big dope?* and I think Rico's game changed forever.

They won the hole on Rico's birdie, putting them three up, and it stayed that way until number sixteen. With three holes left to play, the United States was dormie, meaning we couldn't lose the match. The worst we could do was tie, and then only if the Euros won all of the last three holes.

The sixteenth was called The San Andreas Fault, and for good reason. Two bunkers lined the left side of the 571-yard fairway, the first about 175 yards long, the second 165. But these were no ordinary sand traps. They were so deep that there were long wooden ramps every fifty yards so you could get in and out without mountaineering gear should your ball wind up in one.

Eddie and Braunschweiger were both lying three on the green after matching each other's shots all the way up the fairway. Senzamio and Kurzer were essentially out of it, Rico having farted around in the second bunker trying to clear the fifteen-foot-high wall with a seven-iron and failing miserably, the German equally frustrated in a stand of trees way off to the left.

Braunschweiger was putting for the team's birdie, a tricky but certainly makable putt. Fat Albert was shaking his head. "Every time he's got one'a them things, that grass pointin' caddy-whampus like that?" He flapped his hand at the ground, as though directing the air to move to the left. "He miss it on that side. Watch this shit here."

Braunschweiger hit the ball. As I thought it would, it took a basically straight bead, and about halfway there, some subtle shift in the green's topography tried to grab hold of it and start moving it left a little, then abruptly quit as the surface leveled out to dead flat. The ball was headed directly for the heart of the hole, an apparent great putt, but then the grain of the grass, "pointin' caddy-whampus," as it were, came into play and subtly began guiding the ball to the left, where it wobbled past the hole and came to rest six inches away.

"Dumb muthafuck'," Fat Albert muttered, shaking his head in disgust. "Where his brains at, he don't see that shit, he done it fi'ty times already!"

Senzamio, still puffing after climbing his way out of the bunker, arrived just in time to see his partner concede the par. Eddie began lining up his putt, an eight-footer from the side of the hole opposite where Braunschweiger's ball had been.

"Now, watch this shit *here*," Fat Albert said approvingly, nudging me in the ribs so hard I almost fell over. I thought Eddie would take it to the same side of the hole as Braunschweiger, only more so, but he hit it straight for the cup instead. "Got this little hill," Fat Albert whispered to me, "so the grass don' mean shit." The *little hill* canceled out the effect of the grain, and Eddie sank the putt for a team birdie.

It was over, a statement as much as a victory, our guys winning four and two. Fat Albert went into his dance, the lopsided blimp of a Rockette nothing but arms and legs and toothy grin as he crabbed sideways all over the green. Rico grabbed Eddie in a bear hug and kissed him violently, Eddie shaking him off and threatening to belt him if he didn't quit it, and the crowd ate it all up, screaming their happiness and trying to imitate Fat Albert to hideous effect.

Then Archie McWhirter and Tal Thomashow lost their match, and August Hookstratten and Derek Anouilh tied theirs. The only match still out there was Markovy and Asphal versus Firth and Luc van Ostrand, a twenty-two-year-old Belgian playing his first round of the tournament and amply demonstrating why. According to my radio reports he hadn't hit a noteworthy shot all day, and Firth was carrying the team single-handedly while brutally humiliating van Ostrand at every opportunity. Maybe the hapless Belgian had been destined to hit only a couple of lousy shots on the first few holes and then pull himself together, but any hope of that had been dashed by the force of Firth's verbal hazing while the cameras were watching. Van Ostrand, a fitness fanatic and part-time ascetic with the kind of emaciated physique and wispy beard usually found on people who worked in health-food stores, was a vulnerable type not amenable to the kinds of interpersonal confrontations that were Firth's stock in trade. St. Villard would tell me later that he had paired them believing Firth could protect van Ostrand in the event of some usually harmless trash-talking from us Americans, never dreaming that it would be Firth himself who would pummel the kid's fragile ego into fine dust.

I headed back out to the course to watch, but they were nowhere to be found. That was because Freddy and Jon had stuck to Eddie's strategy and stomped the Euros into the ground, ending it on the fifteenth hole after an absurdly risky but ultimately successful birdie by Asphal. They'd been in the clubhouse for the past half hour.

We ended the day ahead, 8½ to 7½.

CHAPTER NINETEEN

Saturday night before the final day I arranged for a quiet, early dinner at the Ritz-Carlton in Rancho Mirage, one of the most beautiful hotels in the desert, or anywhere, for that matter. Something about the place relaxes you the minute you walk onto the premises. It's set on a bluff overlooking the whole valley, with spectacular views, and that feeling of floating serenely above everything adds to the peacefulness.

They had the kind of service where everything got done right away but you hardly ever noticed anybody doing it, which is perfect when you're trying to relax. Wives and girlfriends attended as well, and we had a private dining room arranged with four tables, although nobody paid much attention to staying in their own seats. The idea was just to hang out together and take it easy for a few hours, and it was working, especially since we were up a point and Robert Carmichael hadn't shown up for dinner.

Eddie Caminetti and Enrico Senzamio were the toasts of the evening, their spectacular victory over the Grand Teutons the biggest highlight of the day. Forgotten was my earlier altercation with Eddie, back at the course after the afternoon's matches were concluded. I had tried to escort him to the press conference, but he refused to go. When I told him it was mandatory he replied, "What're they gonna do—take away my tour card?" I should have known better.

"We need to get punched up," Archie McWhirter was saying, twirling an asparagus spear in his fingers, "get some motivation for tomorrow. Maybe you shoulda hired us a sports psychologist, Bellamy."

That got a nervous chuckle from some of the women present, but not from the players, who knew McWhirter was serious. He was always reading the kind of pop-psychology books that spewed philosophies and theories unsullied by anything so repulsive as hard data.

"You not motivated enough, Arch?" Fleckheimer asked. "You figure maybe tomorrow's just another corporate outing?"

"Nah, okay, maybe not motivated, maybe that's not the right word. But you know what I mean: some pumping up, something to help us focus on our personal goals, give us that winning edge, awaken the beast within so we can reach out to our inner . . ."

I got a little nervous, wondering which of a half dozen candidates would be the first to demotivate McWhirter in a profoundly personal way, when Eddie, sitting to my left, began speaking in a quiet voice. There were five of us within earshot at the moment, all players, and as Eddie spoke, the lingering aftereffect of McWhirter's comment dissipated slowly as it became clear that the full-group conversation was over and we could go back to our more private chats. I breathed a sigh of relief, then tuned in to what Eddie was saying.

"Trouble with all these psychologists, telling you to forget mechanics, forget everything, clear your mind and be one with the fucking dimples? The trouble is, a guy gets up there and does all that stuff and still can't hit the ball, not only does he feel like a duffer, he feels like a failure as a human being, like he's got brain damage or somethin' on account of he can't hit like Nicklaus by emptyin' out his brain. Only time that psychoshit works is when the brain's already burned in the right swing after four million shots and now all it can do is get in its own way. Some guy, he don't have the fundamentals down yet, playing golf with an empty brain's the same as flyin' an F-15 on Thorazine."

He paused momentarily to begin unwrapping one of the cigars that had been passed around a few minutes earlier. "They make you feel like there's something wrong with you if you get upset over a crappy shot, like it's some kind of deep failing if you curse or smack your club into the ground, like you should always be playing with this dumb-ass smile on your face and stay perfectly calm and relaxed, and if you can't, you better read their newest book and cut that shit out."

Fleckheimer reached for a cigar, as did Asphal, and a waiter came up with a fancy lighter, but I waved him away.

"Well, fuck them," Eddie said after he bit the end of the cigar off and spit it out angrily. "What the hell's the sense of playing if you don't care enough to get pissed off at yourself every so often? How do they figure you're gonna get one'a them religious highs they keep yappin' about if you don't get yourself bent outta shape once in a while!"

He pulled a tattered book of matches out of his pocket, struck one and held it to the tip of the cigar, cooking it a little before drawing in the flame and speaking around the smoke. "Hey, I wanna feel like a human when I play, not some blissed-out endorphin junkie. Get happy, get pissed, amaze yourself, hate yourself—run through the whole freakin' menu."

He waved the match to put it out, drew on the cigar and looked up, blowing a great cloud of bluish smoke toward the ceiling. Then he looked back down and tapped two fingers on the table. "Then you know you played yourself a goddamned round of golf."

Silence ensued as everybody thought about that. Then Fleckheimer said, "You don't think the mental aspect is important?"

Eddie tapped some ash into an elegant china ashtray. "It's damned near the only thing that is, Joel. But only once you've got the fundamentals down. After that, the most important single factor in a golf shot isn't your grip or your stance or the shoulder turn or take-away or follow-through or swing plane. It's knowing for a damned certainty that you're gonna hit the ball perfectly. If you stand up there and the only thing in your head is a prayer that you don't fuck the shot up—guess what? You're prolly gonna fuck it up."

"Amen, brother," Merriwell affirmed.

"And the second most important thing, if you *do* fuck up the dead-certain shot, is still believing for dead certain the next one is gonna be perfect anyway."

"But that doesn't make any sense!" Mr. Wizard objected.

"Whole damned *game* doesn't make any sense, Jon! It did, we woulda called it bowling!"

The rest of us laughed, except Markovy, who said, "But that's all in your head, Eddie."

"Doesn't make it any less real. Sometimes the things that are only in your head are the realest things of all."

Markovy waved it off. "I don't hold a lot of truck with all this psycho-mumbo-jumbo golfers are always blaming their troubles on. I got a problem with my swing, I fix it. I don't have slumps, I have mechanical problems that may take me a while to figure out."

Eddie nodded his appreciation of Markovy's point. "You're a lot tougher mentally than you give yourself credit for, Jon. Maybe that's why you're one of the best in the world. You play your own mind games, you just don't realize that's what you're doing."

One of the waiters had come to the table while the conversation was in full swing, standing discreetly aside and waiting for a lull. Now he leaned down to whisper in my ear that Jerome Bushnell was waiting for me in the bar. Bushnell was an official with the PGA of America, which ran the tournament. He was a good guy, a former pro, and his coming to the Ritz on the night before the final day, knowing full well that we were here for a little R&R to stay loose, was not a good sign.

I smiled and excused myself, then made my way to the "bar," which is really a kind of second lobby that looks out over the pool and down into the valley. They serve afternoon tea there, and it's one of the most popular afternoon gathering spots for those who can afford the prices. Bushnell sat alone at a table for two, staring out at the view and nursing a cranberry juice.

"Lookin' to pick up a date, Jerry?"

Bushnell turned toward me and grunted. "What they pay me, I'd be lookin' down the Motel Six, not here."

"Keep refusing bribes, you're never gonna rise above your station." I sat down and waved off the waiter who'd materialized at my side. "What's up?"

"Nothin' much, but I figured I'd tell you early in the evening so's you'd have time to think about it, maybe chat it up with your boys. One'a the Europeans, van Ostrand? He got hisself, uh, what the docs're callin' *gastric distress*."

"The trots?"

"Big time. What I hear, hotel's plumbing may not take the strain. Also cramps, that kind of thing. Prolly somethin' he ate."

"Where'd he eat?"

"Big Louie's."

"Figures." One of the best things about international travel for a golf pro is getting to sample the local cuisine, especially the off-the-path stuff. Texas-style barbecue holds a particular fascination for a lot of Europeans, but for guys like van Ostrand who watched themselves carefully, usually eating things like stump paste and bumblebee droppings or what-the-hell-ever, the sudden excursion into hot sauce and smoked meat can have a profoundly disorienting effect on their untrained digestive systems. In van Ostrand's case, combine that vicious blow to his intestines with the drubbing he took earlier in the day from Markovy and Asphal as well as his playing partner, Andrew Firth, and it ought not to have been a surprise that he was sick as a dog. "So he's out tomorrow?"

"Looks that way. No way to know for sure, so you gotta be prepared. St. Villard wanted me to let you know. Spirit of sportsmanship and all that."

If a player was unable to make his individual match for a legitimate reason, such as illness or a family emergency, the other side had to choose a player to sit out as well, and the match was an automatic draw, half a point to each side. If it happened a second time to the same team, they forfeited the second match.

"St. Villard said he'd get your message light turned on as soon as they made a final decision one way or t'other. That way you could pick it up whenever you got up tomorrow morning."

I nodded. Bushnell was implying that I might want to wait until morning before I informed whoever on my team would be sitting out, not to hurt the guy's feelings in case van Ostrand somehow was able to play and there was no need to have said anything in the first place.

I would like to have invited Bushnell in to have coffee with us, but we both knew it wouldn't look right for an official to be hanging with one of the teams. He wouldn't even have let me pick up his cranberry juice, so I didn't offer, just thanked him and went back to the dinner.

"Hope that one doesn't make it rain!" I heard Mack yell across the room. I looked toward where he had shouted but saw nothing to have warranted the outburst, just Derek sitting there with a loopy grin on his face.

"Tee 'em high and let 'em fly!" Derek called back.

"Grip it and rip it." Fred, from somewhere off to my left.

"Let the big dog eat!" Mr. Wizard, by way of an answer.

"Swing easy, hit hard!" Fleck.

"Keep it in the short stuff!" Paul DeMonte.

"Shank you very much! You're on the dance floor! That won't hurt you! That'll play! You gonna like-a dat! Splashomatic! Hit a house! Hit a brick! Get legs! Plenty'a room on the green!" Hookstratten. Thomashow. McWhirter. Wizard again. Enrico.

"What the hell's going on?" I whispered to Juliette Merriwell.

"Keep swinging—maybe the breeze'll get it off the tee! Next time you see that ball its picture's gonna be on a milk carton! Like it was on rails, baby! Time to get my retriever regripped! Even God can't hit a one-iron! Fairway was so tight, we hadda walk single file! Drive for show, putt for dough! Breezy? Swing easy!"

"I think they're getting them all out of the way before tomorrow," she whispered back between giggles.

"Right in the heart! Nice lag, Alice! Get it close! Is there really a hole there? It's a speed putt! Swear to God that broke uphill! What kept that out of the hole! Never up, never in! Miss it on the pro side! If I couldn't putt, I couldn't play! That one get caught in your skirts? Your husband play this game? Don't give away the hole! It's still your turn! Lotta chicken left on that bone! Hike up your skirt and tap the rest of it in!"

"The rest of what?" They were into responsive chanting now, like the mating calls of loony birds.

"I think he's DWS . . ."

"Driving while spastic!"

"It was an SBU . . ."

"Shitty but useful!"

"A South American putt . . ."

"One more revolution!"

"Like an elephant's ass . . ."

"Up high and stinky!"

"Ever play with those two Chinese guys . . . ?"

"Tem-Po and Ti-Ming!"

"Every freakin' cliché in the book, that's what," Eddie said. I hadn't noticed him coming up to me from the side opposite Juliette. "Anything up that high . . . !" he called out.

"Oughta have a stewardess on it! Should be serving drinks! Gonna burn up on reentry!"

"How long's this been going on?" I asked.

"Since you left," Juliette told me.

"USA!"

Silence. Nothing. All eyes turned to Derek, who'd shouted the letters only to receive nothing by way of reply.

"What the devil is USA?" Fred finally ventured.

Derek looked around, blinked his eyes a few times, then shrugged. " 'You still away!' "

I quietly passed word to Asphal, Merriwell and Eddie, the guys who had become sort of my executive committee, to meet me after we got back to our hotel.

"That's an easy one, Al," Eddie said.

"Carmichael."

"Who else?"

We were in the living room of my suite rather than the meeting room that had been serving as the U.S. team's headquarters. My bride, Louise, and some of the other wives and girlfriends were using that room to watch a movie video on the big screen, Louise acting as a kind of social host for significant others during the tournament.

Merriwell puffed out his cheeks and shook his head. "Technically that's maybe what we should do."

"Whaddaya mean, technically?" Eddie asked.

"What he means is," Asphal said, "how can one in good conscience keep one of the crew from participating, not allowing him to play a single round? He's a legitimate member of the squad, and he has a right to play."

"And Al's got a legitimate right to do what he's gotta do to make sure the team wins."

"That's very businesslike thinking, Eddie," Asphal said.

"So what'sa matter with that?"

"What'sa matter is, this ain't business." Merriwell stood up and went to the bar, reaching for a bottle of scotch and then thinking better of it, settling for a caffeine-free diet cola. His comment had brought Eddie up short. Meaning no disrespect, he was pointing out that Eddie was the only guy here for whom this *was* business.

Eddie thought about it as we stayed silent, then said, "Y'know what, Mack? You're right. Dead right. Me, I'm just a hired gun, working for money, and I shouldn't be pokin' my nose inta stuff that ain't my concern."

He looked startled when the rest of us started to protest, then caught on. "Hey, wait a minute!" He held up his hands defensively and smiled. "That wasn't sour grapes I was throwing. That's just the way it is, and I don't got a problem with it. Sometimes you gotta do what's right even if it's not the right thing to do, and that's your call, not mine."

We got past it, and I framed the question for them again. "Given I'm not gonna bench Carmichael, who should sit out?"

As they shifted around uncomfortably, there was a knock at the door. I opened it to see Jon Markovy standing there. Looking past me, he saw his three teammates inside and beckoned me into the hall.

"I know what's going on, Al," he said. "Van Ostrand being sick and all. Put me in the envelope." He was referring to the procedure that would be used to designate which of our players would sit out. I would put one name in an envelope and turn it in to the PGA. If van Ostrand wasn't able to play the next morning, the envelope would be opened just before the match and the name revealed. That prevented the other side from playing fast and loose with just how "sick" their guy was, depending on whom he might no longer have to play. I asked Markovy why he thought he should be the one in the envelope.

"I got an any-given-day game, Al. We both know it. If I keep cool, follow my game plan, I hit pars all day and maybe get a few lucky birdies, and usually finish in the top twenty. I make good dough, even win one once in a rare while if everything breaks my way and I don't make too many mistakes."

I nodded. "Not a bad way to make a living, pal."

"Sure isn't. But this? The Ryder?" Markovy leaned against the wall and folded his arms. "No sense me playing in an emotional game like this, the Euros knocking themselves out to go one up on me. They'll probably do it, and if I respond, I'll screw up completely and lose. If I don't, I'll lose anyway."

We stood there, awkwardly, until Markovy forced himself to brighten. "Listen, don't worry about it, I'm okay with this. I'm up on the board, I had two damned good days. Fact is, I'm just not a match player. Do me a favor, don't embarrass me in front of the whole country by making me go toe to toe with one'a these guys."

He was really something, Mr. Wizard, but as I started to slobber some heartfelt sentiment, he said, "Oh, give that shit a rest, Al. You're no damned good at it anyway. I'll help you out tomorrow from the sidelines, all right?"

I went back in and said, "Well, the problem's just solved itself. Markovy's volunteered to sit out."

"How 'bout that guy," Merriwell said, and Asphal grunted his agreement.

"No!" Eddie nearly shouted, rising up out of his chair. "Are you guys crazy? Jon's one of the best bets we got tomorrow!"

"You gotta be kidding," Asphal said.

But Eddie wasn't kidding. "You think there's a single guy on the European team doesn't think getting beat by Robby the Robot would be an embarrassment? All Jon's gotta do is play his regular old game, go for those pars, drive the other guy crazy and suck him into taking stupid chances!"

"But what about the pressure?"

"You serious, Mack? Pressure? The guy's number four on the goddamned money list! Look at his play with Fred. It was the worst drubbing the Euros took all weekend!"

"But van Ostrand was useless," Mack pointed out. "Firth practically played by himself."

"Forget how *they* played, Mack. Look at how *Markovy* played! Man was sensational."

"But he had a partner, Eddie," I protested. "He fucked up a hole, there was always a chance Freddy's game would be there to save him. He gets behind tomorrow, he's gonna feel like he's gotta go for it."

"Then tell him he can't." Eddie turned to me. "You're the captain, Al. Tell him how he has to play. That'll even take some of the pressure off. If he loses, he can always tell the world he was just doing what he was told to do."

"And I get the heat."

"It's your *job* to take the heat, f'Chrissakes, what the hell else're you good for! You can't win any damned matches if you ain't playin'!"

Merriwell put a hand over his mouth to keep from laughing, but Asphal was too late to stop a mirthful snort from escaping. "Fine bunch'a fuckin' friends you guys are," I said. I exhaled and dropped into a chair. "So who *should* go in the envelope?"

"Maybe me, Al," Merriwell offered.

Eddie shook his head. "Nope."

"Come on. I played like shit for two days. We all know that."

"Played like shit 'cuz you were confused. Didn't know how to use your partner, couldn't look beyond the hole you were playing. It was all tactics and no strategy."

It was getting late, and Eddie had no time to be diplomatic, assuming he even had the capacity. It was probably for the best. Merriwell knew he was right, but he wasn't sure what it meant and why Eddie thought he should still play on Sunday.

Eddie didn't wait for him to ask. "You gonna be the man tomorrow, Mack."

Merriwell looked up, and it was amazing to see the amount of deference he was paying this nobody from Hallandale, Florida. "Tomorrow it's just you," Eddie was saying to him. "Gonna be so happy settling back into your own game, you'll be unconscious by the third hole. Poor bastard playing you won't even know what hit him."

Merriwell lit up like a thousand-watt bulb. But Eddie wasn't making a prediction, he was making it *happen*. That image he was telegraphing right into the middle of Mack's brain, backed by the faith Mack had come to have in his insight? He wouldn't be able to sleep that night, he'd be so excited to get the hell up, get the hell out and do just as Eddie had practically guaranteed him he would. As you already know, that's exactly what he did.

But I'm getting ahead of myself. We were still faced with the problem of who to knock out.

"Do me any good bringin' up Carmichael again?" Eddie asked, resuming his seat.

Before anybody else could respond, I said, "No. I believe you, he's going to lose, but we'll live with it."

"Losing's one thing," Eddie said. "What if he embarrasses the whole team, makes you all look like jerks?"

Now it was *you* instead of *us*. "It's my call, Eddie, and that's the way I'm makin' it." I needed to lighten this up. "Listen, maybe he'll get matched up with Firth and they'll kill each other before they finish the round and make it a tie!"

Everyone laughed but Eddie, who said, "Fine. Then take me out."

The ensuing silence was awkward. I don't know what Mack and Fred were thinking, but I personally thought Eddie was the last guy I'd bench. Singles match play was his life's blood.

"With me, it's just business," he explained. "If I was captain, I would never dream of jeopardizing something I thought was important by playing a guy who didn't belong in it. Since you guys think that's more important than winning—"

"Hey, wait a minute—"

"Didn't mean that as a criticism, Fred."

"But it's not true."

Eddie looked at him sternly. "Carmichael's gonna lose tomorrow, and you're playing him anyway. So take me out. Let the guys who really give a shit have a go, because it doesn't mean squat to me. I get paid anyway, right?"

"That's true," I confirmed. It was the first time the matter of Eddie's compensation had come up with him present.

Asphal stood up and bent way over, touching his toes to loosen up his back. "You know, you're being a tad too black-and-white about this, Eddie."

"Am I."

"Yeah." He straightened up and did some side bends. "Just because we're playing Robert doesn't mean we don't care about winning. All it means is that there's a line we won't cross to do it, that's all."

Eddie seemed to consider this. "But you're willing to knock out another one of your deserving teammates, hurt a guy who's been looking forward to this for a year, so you can put in some unknown schmuck from Florida who has no right to be here?" Asphal had paused in mid-bend as Eddie spoke. "Can't have it both ways, Fred."

"We would choose a man who's already played several matches this weekend," Asphal said, straightening up. "Carmichael would be the only healthy player in Ryder Cup history not to play a single game. There's a difference."

Before Eddie could argue any further, I said to him, "Look, Carmichael's in, somebody else is out. So who's it gonna be?" Either nobody noticed, or nobody saw fit to comment on, the fact that I'd just asked Eddie to make the call.

He was a good soldier. Once he lost the argument, he put it aside and jumped easily into going along with my command decision. He spent a few moments in thought, rubbing his chin with his thumbnail as usual, then said, "Fred."

It wouldn't have been seemly for Asphal to question that, so Merriwell did. "Why Fred?"

" 'Cuz he's the biggest risk."

And that was it, right there. That was how I really screwed up, by playing Robert Carmichael on the last day when I had the perfect gift-from-heaven opportunity dropped right into my hands to pull him. My teammates, all of them except Eddie, agreed with how I handled it, but it was my decision. I was the captain, and I take full responsibility.

CHAPTER TWENTY

Sunday

What can I say about Sunday that hasn't been said already? Probably a lot.

The final day of the Ryder Cup is the most exciting, grueling, exhilarating and depressing day in all of professional golf, one of those Super Bowl–like events that guarantees an equal distribution of ecstasy and misery. It's impossible to pull back psychologically and try to tell yourself that it's only a game. Instead you feel as though the entire fate of Western civilization is hanging in the balance.

The format is the simplest of all: twelve individual matches, twelve points at stake. Nobody knows until the night before who is going to be playing against whom. Each captain submits the order of play for his own guys, and trying to guess who the other captain is going to assign to which tee times is a waste of energy, because he's doing the same guessing about you, and so the pairings are as random as can be. The best you can hope for is to place each guy where he's comfortable and where he's likely to do the most good. If a player is the kind who thrives on pressure and pulls out his best game when all the chips are in the pot, you put him toward the end. If pressure makes him too nervous, send him in early when matters seem less urgent and mistakes are more quickly forgotten.

A few weeks ago I tried to warn Eddie, who'd never played in a major pro tournament, about the pressure.

"What pressure?"

"It makes some guys puke."

Eddie looked at me in real confusion. "It don't cost nothin' to play. You lose, it still don't cost you, right? So where's the pressure?"

"Believe me," I said, surprised at his naïveté. "It's there."

He shook his head, amazed at mine. "I line up a twenty-footer for ten grand, knowin' I'm out the dough if I miss—that's nerves, Bubba. I line up the same putt and I ain't out a thing if I miss?" He shrugged. "Who gives a shit?"

Sure enough, Eddie had started out playing the Cup as cold as dry ice. It wasn't until the last day that he started to show some yips, and then he showed them big time. I thought when it happened that maybe he had gotten into the spirit of the thing and it surprised and scared him at the same time. But things aren't always what they seem, are they?

Once again I'm getting ahead of myself. Going into Sunday morning, we were up by a point, a state of affairs that had made headlines all over the world given the original odds against us. But it had become 9–8 instead of 8½–7½ because Luc van Ostrand really had gotten ill and wouldn't be playing, and therefore his non-match against Fred Asphal counted as a tie. Now there were only eleven points left rather than twelve, and since we were starting out up by one, we could halve every single match and still get the fourteen and a half necessary for the outright victory. We could also halve ten of them and lose one, tying the Euros 14–14 and retaining the Cup. Normally, I'd be tempted to say I'd rather lose the damned thing outright than slink home with the trophy by default, but this year, given how heavily the Euros had been favored at the beginning, a tie would be treated as a resounding, indeed miraculous, victory for us. Even today, despite our one-point lead, the bookies in London had the Euros at 5–2 to win, and it had nothing to do with local pride. London bookies don't *have* any local pride and would take bets against England in a nuclear war if their analysis showed the Queen a few megatons shy.

Since tying every match would win it for us, the order of the day was conservative play, no heroics, which was roughly tantamount to asking a serial killer to play nice with his neighbors. My only prayer was that nobody would do anything completely stupid in the hopes of pulling off some potentially legendary feat à la the 1993 Ryder, where rookie Davis Love III, with the rest of the matches far enough along to guarantee at least a tie, came up to the eighteenth dead even with Costantino Rocca and won the hole, giving the United States the definitive victory. That had been only the most visible feat, though. Earlier in the day, with the United States already down two points in the tournament, Chip Beck was trailing Englishman Barry Lane by three after the thirteenth hole. His ever-sunny smile never fading, he won three of the next four holes, one of them with an eagle, halved the other one and then won the eighteenth for the match victory. And that was just a day after his and rookie John Cook's remarkable victory over Nick Faldo and Colin Montgomerie that was considered the psychological turning point of the tournament for the United States.

We didn't need any of that today. What we needed was for everybody to put the team ahead of themselves and manufacture a nice boring bunch of all-square matches. First up to the tee at seven-thirty that morning was Robert Carmichael, playing against the Englishman John Wickenhampshire. I put Carmichael up first because it was kind of an honor, which didn't cost us anything but might help to soften some of the embarrassment he was probably feeling over not having played the first two days.

Things started off well enough. Carmichael stuck to the plan for the first few holes, going for the safe pars, waiting for birdie opportunities without straining to make them happen. Wickenhampshire did the same, and they were all square through the first five holes. Checking in on them occasionally, I sensed some restlessness in the crowd, and I thought some of it was starting to get to Wickenhampshire as well. It probably didn't help anybody's disposition much that an incredibly loud roar could be heard from somewhere about three or four holes back at roughly fifteen-minute intervals. That meant that something extraordinary and exciting was going on back there, in stark contrast to the forced march *this* round was fast becoming.

On number six, a fiendishly tricky par-three of 255 yards, Carmichael made another par, keeping his ball well to the left of the green because the right border consisted entirely of water. Going directly for the pin on this hole was a very low-percentage proposition, owing to the difficulty of tucking it in close without hitting the drink.

But Wickenhampshire apparently felt it was time to get a little aggressive, taking dead aim for the flag and hitting a truly splendid three-wood to within twelve feet, then sinking the putt for a birdie to go one up. Coming off the green, he shot Carmichael a look, something clearly meant to communicate contempt for the American's conservative play. It was a pure sucker gambit, the kind of blatant baiting nobody in his right mind would go for, especially considering that both of them had been playing the same way for the first five holes.

It pissed Carmichael off. He hit a monster drive on the next hole, when a three-wood or even a long iron would have been the prudent play. Wickenhampshire did the same, and suddenly the fight was on. And it was very, very personal.

Wickenhampshire cranked up his game about six notches and began hitting the ball better than I think he ever had in his professional life. Carmichael, for his part, began to play as though he were having an out-of-body experience. Something in his brain that usually controlled his style of play had somehow stepped aside and let something else take over, and the result was a game vastly better than he was generally capable of. What followed had a chance of becoming one of the all-time classic duels of golf, a display of shotmaking ability unlike anything most of us had ever seen before. I began to get a glow from my decision to play Carmichael, and I could hardly wait to rub it in Eddie's face. The glow lasted for eight more holes, of which Carmichael won an extraordinary three, going two up on Wickenhampshire by the end of thirteen. It was a virtual lock if he stayed calm and simply nursed it home for the last five holes. He could phone this one in for the win, and nobody was paying any more attention to the crowd noises periodically wafting across the desert from one of the matches behind us.

On the underrated fourteenth hole, The Cavern, Wickenhampshire hit a mind-boggling five-iron to put his second shot onto the smallest green on the course. Trying too hard to match the feat, Carmichael ended up in the bunker that gave the hole its name, a pit so deep and steep I wasn't sure enough daylight could drip its way down to make the ball visible. Remarkably, he managed to spit the ball up and out, landing it on the green about six feet closer to the flag than Wickenhampshire's. Nevertheless, he was lying three and the Englishman two.

Contemplating his fifteen-foot putt, Wickenhampshire casually strolled to a point halfway between his ball and the hole and bent over to fix something on the grass, then straightened up and walked back.

"Hold it!" Carmichael yelled, startling his opponent, and walked toward him from the opposite side of the green. He stopped at the spot where Wickenhampshire had made a repair and pointed to it. "That was a spike mark," he said, with much the same implication as Zola's "*J'accuse!*"

Wickenhampshire, disbelieving, said, " 'Twas a pitch mark, my good man."

I once asked Jon Markovy if he could explain why golf is so addicting, and somewhere in the middle of an extended discourse he'd said, "As you like to say, Al, it'd be like trying to explain sex to someone who's never done it. On the face of it, both activities are equally absurd to anyone who isn't doing them, and describing them in terms of mechanics would sound even more ridiculous and invite endless cynicism. Even describing the rules of golf would sound more like a Monty Python sketch than anything in real life." And right here on the fourteenth hole was a perfect example: It's illegal, prior to putting, to fix a mark left by an earlier player's shoe, but perfectly all right to repair one caused by a ball's landing on the green. Why one and not the other, I have no idea—maybe something to do with the speed of play—but that's how it is.

"The hell it was," Carmichael shot back.

"See here, you were ten yards away, sir!" Wickenhampshire replied.

"Yeah, well I walked past it when we got to the green."

Wickenhampshire's eyes grew wide. "And you *remembered* what kind of mark it was?"

"Sure did. You lose this hole, Wickem."

"That's Wickem-*shire*, and I can't lose it till I've putted. Now kindly stand aside!"

"You lost it already, on account'a the penalty!"

"There is no penalty," Wickenhampshire sniffed confidently. "I repaired a pitch mark, and that is perfectly cricket."

"Cricket, my rosy ass."

And with that, Carmichael called over one of the officials who is assigned to each hole. This turned out to be Desmond Grant, an upper-crust Brit, one of the grand old men of the game and probably its foremost rules authority as well.

Carmichael explained the situation, none too diplomatically and at some length. When he paused for a breath, Grant turned to Wickenhampshire for his side.

"Quite simple, umpire: I repaired a pitch mark."

"A pitch mark."

"Precisely."

"I see."

"Quite."

"It was a goddamned *spike* mark!" Carmichael roared.

Grant, in no hurry, turned to him. "Mr. Carmichael, if you have something new to add, please do so. Otherwise, kindly desist." He kept looking at Carmichael until it was clear that he'd gotten the message, then said, "What do you propose? Other than my simply ruling your way, of course."

"Look at the damned thing!" Carmichael said, pointing toward the offending spot.

"Certainly," Grant answered, tugging the knees of his pants upward and kneeling down, peering at the ground with his head tilted back slightly in order to bring the bottoms of his bifocals into play. "It appears a pitch mark," he announced. He would tell *Newsweek* two weeks later that he couldn't see a blessed thing.

"Well, how the hell can you tell that after the guy's already fixed it!" Carmichael demanded angrily.

Grant stood back up and straightened his trousers. "Then why did you ask me to look at it?"

Carmichael, undeterred by any demonstrations of his own illogic, said, "I'm telling you, it was a spike mark!"

"I appreciate your concern, Mr. Carmichael," Grant said quietly, "but your opponent has told me it was a pitch mark."

"My opponent's full'a shit!"

"That's as may well be, sir, but in the event of a dispute involving the absence of any physical evidence, as you yourself just pointed out, word against word, as it were—"

"Precisely," Wickenhampshire added.

"Quite. Er, as I was saying, in the event of a dispute involving the absence of any physical evidence, the personal integrity of the player vulnerable to the infraction carries the day. The assumption is that he is conducting himself honestly."

"That's complete bullshit."

Still unruffled, Grant said, "With what would you replace it, Mr. Carmichael?"

"Listen," Carmichael replied, showing not a modicum of respect for this venerated official who was straining to be tolerant of his boorishness, "I'm not here to debate policy with you, buddy."

"Ah! Quite right, sir!" Grant stepped back and called to the scorekeeper, loud enough for the crowd around the green to hear, "No penalty!" He turned back and said, "Kindly resume play, gentlemen."

Carmichael, shaking with anger, stomped back to the opposite side of the green. "I'm filing a goddamned protest," he said.

Wickenhampshire's caddie for this tournament, a three-handicap high school kid from a bad section of Liverpool, said, "Fook *me*, Mister! Two up and five to go and you're in me lad's face? Give it a fookin' rest, why don'tcha!"

If Carmichael's caddie was required to come to *his* lad's defense, he didn't, just stood there trying to look elsewhere. As Carmichael prepared to deal with Wickenhampshire's caddie himself, a stern "Quiet on the green!" sprang from one of the marshals positioned in front of the crowd, an admonition normally reserved for spectators, not players.

Thirty feet away, Wickenhampshire stood staring at Carmichael. The Brit appeared expressionless but in reality was shaken and disoriented. There was only one thought remaining in his mind as he walked toward his ball, but it occupied all the available space: Beat this American degenerate into the ground! Standing over the ball, he'd never wanted anything so bad in his whole life as to drain this one, and you could see it in every muscle and his twitching jaw, the way his tense body seemed to hang by taut cables connected to an invisible puppeteer.

There was no way in hell he was going to make this putt. He stood up suddenly and backed off, resting the putterhead on the ground and closing his eyes.

As I mentioned before, it's one thing to put circumstances out of your mind in a regular tour event, and it's quite another to try to forget for a moment the weight of the team and your country on your shoulders as you stand over the ball with a putter in your hands. But the hardest thing of all is to try to completely forget the maddening outrage you feel toward the sonofabitch bastard standing right over there, the one who essentially accused you of cheating. It was hard, but Wickenhampshire did it. Everybody could see him do it. The lines in his forehead disappeared, the clenched jaw relaxed along with the rest of his body, and his hands loosened their death grip on the putter. Eyes still closed, he exhaled one long breath, and the transformation was complete.

There is really only one way for a golfer to take revenge for a perceived wrong, and that is to forget about it and play his best. When Wickenhampshire finally opened his eyes and walked back to the ball, his posture was so casual it looked as though he didn't care if he sank it or not. He aligned himself over the ball, took one last look at the cup and, with barely a moment's hesitation to make sure the clubface was square to the line, drew it back and swung with utter confidence. His head didn't come up until he heard the unmistakable *ploink* of the ball banging into the bottom of the cup.

Carmichael, still so pissed you could see veins pulsing in his temples, picked up from his now-useless lie and stomped off the green. He looked in danger of becoming even more unglued, so agitated I wouldn't have been surprised to see smoke coming out of his ears.

For the rest of the match he hissed, spat, threw clubs to the ground and cursed to himself. He complained loudly of too much crowd noise, partisan tendencies on the part of the PGA officials—even when they weren't European—and anything else that came to mind. Worse, his temporarily magical golf game went completely down the shitter, and he started screwing up all over the place.

Actually his game didn't go down the shitter. It just wafted over to Wickenhampshire, who didn't so much walk the last four holes as glide over them, so serene and self-possessed he might have been a Buddhist monk moving among the faithful in a temple. Every new outburst from Carmichael only added to his tranquillity. He won the next two holes with pars against Carmichael's bogeys, going one up at the end of sixteen. When he took the seventeenth as well, the match was over, Wickenhampshire winning it two and one. Only then did the spell break, as the Brits among the onlookers rushed to hoist him onto their shoulders amid an outpouring of unrestrained joy and amazement. The normally reserved and proper Wickenhampshire looked as if he was trying to stop himself from crying, and even the highly partisan American spectators, although not quite sure exactly how this had happened but knowing it had been significant, heaped adulation on him while their own Robert Carmichael slinked off unseen, as did my fantasies of rubbing a Carmichael victory in Eddie Caminetti's face. We were back to all even for the tournament, ten matches still out on the course behind us.

She's a hard teacher, experience: gives the test before she gives the lesson. Christ Almighty, was I going to suffer for this one.

CHAPTER TWENTY-ONE

The crowd of delirious Brits finally cleared off to let the next match through, August Hookstratten and Eric Swenborg equally annoyed at the delay as they stood, steaming, out on the fairway of number eighteen. You couldn't blame them: They'd just played one of the dullest matches in history, neither one of them able to get anything going. The only thing that distinguished their round was that they had both shot the exact same scores on every single hole. Nothing changed on the last one, either, a pair of desultory pars ending it with half a point for each side.

Paul DeMonte and Charles Woolsey also tied about ten minutes later, although they at least had seesawed the lead a couple of times. I was starting to wonder if the boys were taking this conservative-play business a little too literally. Hell, I'd almost rather see a Carmichael blow a gasket but at least get passionate about things, rather than keep watching this kind of plodding ditch-digging. Emphasis on the *almost.* I could tell from the radio chatter that the next two matches, Archie McWhirter versus Eero Tukinen of Finland and Tal Thomashow versus Mieczyslaw Piranewski, were also nothing to write home about. So I flagged down a passing beverage cart, normally not seen at tournaments but supplied here because of the desert conditions, and rode back to see how Derek Anouilh was doing against Juan Castillo Licenciados.

Now, *that* was almost worth having to listen as Twinkie McDaniels, the spray-painted, gum-snapping beverage lady, shared with me her ambition to nail every golfer on the top-twenty money list now that astronauts were no longer de rigueur. "And I'm like, should we do the top ten? And my girlfriend? Buffy? From the snack bar? She's like, why not the top twenty? And I'm all, are you serious? And she's like . . ."

Truth be known, The Kid hadn't really been on his game during the opening matches. His partners, Mack Merriwell and August Hookstratten, had pretty much carried him, barely managing to tie their rounds, never mind win any of them. I had spent a good part of the past two days worrying if he was in a slump.

Eddie told me not to concern myself. "Biggest factor in a slump is the slump itself. If we woke up some morning and somehow just forgot we were even in a slump, it would disappear."

"Yeah, well," I responded sarcastically, "barring some miracle of sleep therapy, what d'ya do when a guy's really in one?"

"Change something," he answered.

"Change what?"

"Doesn't make a shit-ass bit'a difference. Just change anything."

"And when he slumps again?" As we all inevitably do.

"Change somethin' else."

"What?"

"Anything. Make him pay attention." He could tell I wasn't following. "Look, remember how easy I told you it was to sell your driver if you don't like it? Just hand it to a guy on some long hole and tell him to belt it a good one? The thing is, putting a new club in somebody's hand, they're so aware that something's changed, they concentrate and focus automatically, with no effort at all."

What he was describing was the well-documented Hawthorne effect, the favorite scam of high-priced management consultants everywhere. Change anything, and things will improve long enough for you to collect your check and clear out of Dodge before they get back to normal.

"So what do I change for Anouilh?" I asked him.

"Not a damned thing. Work's been done for you already."

I asked him what he meant.

"Gonna be playing all by hisself tomorrow," he explained. "No partners to share the spotlight, no strategy conferences, no getting *permission* from any other assholes before he can take his shot. Just the cameras and The Kid. Trust me, Al, that's all the change the boy needs."

Truer words was never spoke. I caught up to Anouilh and Licenciados coming off the fifteenth, and I could tell at fifty paces that some kind of transmogrification had already occurred. The Kid had that air of otherworldly quiescence you rarely see on a golf course, especially remarkable given that, as the little posters carried around by barely clad Twinkie McDaniels clones revealed, he and Licenciados were in a dead tie. That's when I noticed that Licenciados also had "the look," and then I glanced at the poster boards again, craning my neck to try to read the little handwritten numbers on the back. I had to blink to make sure I wasn't seeing things.

As I said, the match score—who was up or down in terms of holes won and lost—was even, as indicated by a little minus sign. As to the raw gross scores, which were irrelevant but tracked anyway just to keep the record complete, Licenciados was at seven under and Anouilh one under that. On the TPC Stadium course, playing from the tips, this was almost more than I could assimilate. The only reason the match was all square despite Anouilh's lower gross was that he had beaten Licenciados with an eagle on number five to the Spaniard's par, and it doesn't matter in match play by how much you win the hole; the one hole is all you win.

I must have had a visibly shocked expression on my face as I ran up to the sixteenth teeing grounds, because the PGA official standing there smiled at me and nodded, as if to say, *Yes, it's true*, even before I could ask for verification. Now I knew where all that crowd noise had been coming from.

As phenomenally as these guys had been playing all day, they both knew that one of them had to bust it open in order to win it. Neither of them would forgive himself if he let an exhibition like this end in a tie without pushing the edge of the envelope as hard as he could. As Austrian downhiller Franz Klammer said before his now-legendary second run at the Innsbruck Olympics in '64: To win, you have to risk losing.

A fairly stiff wind had kicked up right into our faces. It would make this 571-yard hole seem like well over 600, and the extreme tee box placement and a flag well to the back of the green would make it even longer. Licenciados was first up, and I thought he was in danger of pulling half the muscles in his back as he swung so hard I swear I could feel the breeze coming off his club. He watched his ball soar into the stratosphere and come to rest about half an hour later in the middle of the fairway some 290 yards away. On a calm day, it would have been good for over 310. Only then did he stoop to retrieve his tee and smile at Anouilh, who said, "Not bad, J.C. I think you're starting to get the hang of this."

"Then give us a lesson," the elegant Spaniard said, holding a hand out toward the tee box.

Anouilh nodded and called for his driver, which his caddie slapped into his palm like a scrub nurse handing over a scalpel. He took a few steps forward, knelt to tee up his ball, then stepped back and worked the grip a few times before he cast a first look out at the target. I noticed a large crowd gathered around the green way off in the distance, and I think Anouilh must have noticed it, too. His thin frame, reedlike in the freshening wind as he moved into position over his ball, seemed to fill out before my eyes as he grew quiet, the clubhead falling slowly until it was poised about a half inch above the ground, as steady as if it were resting on a stand.

Then he wound up and let go. The sound was like a bullet striking sheet metal, and it didn't seem possible that the cover could remain on the ball after such abuse. It looked from my perspective as if it might catch Licenciados's shot on the fly before starting its ground roll, but that quickly became academic, because as soon as the ball touched down, it bounced back into the air at a crazy angle that sent it sharply to the left. Really sharply. As in right for the sand if something didn't stop it.

We watched, bewildered, as the ball hit the grass and bounced again, clearing some of the rough that might have stopped it had it been running along the ground instead of back up in the air. Then it disappeared completely, Anouilh still holding his follow-through position, staring at where the ball had initially dropped back to earth and wondering what had made it bounce like that.

Three or four figures began running toward the spot where the ball had last been visible. Finally bringing his club back down, Anouilh watched them, trying not to betray any emotion as he waited to see if they were going to stop at the lip of the massive bunker and gather there, staring down the fifteen-foot wall and shaking their heads at his rotten luck.

But suddenly the front-running spectator stopped and whirled around to face us. He thrust his hands high into the air, and both The Kid and I, as well as about two thousand of our closest friends around the tee box, did the same. It was probably a totally shitty lie in the rough, but at least the damned thing was up at sea level instead of at the bottom of that Marianas Trench of a sand trap.

Licenciados patted Anouilh on the back as he walked past him, and the assembled multitudes began the trek out to see just how much trouble The Kid was in. The prevailing sentiment was that this might be the decisive hole of the round. They were not going to be disappointed.

While the crowd walked toward his ball, Anouilh walked directly to where it had originally landed, as did I. There we discovered what had happened.

The Stadium course uses the kind of sprinklers that sit flush to the ground when not operating. When the automatic timers send water down the pipes, the pressure causes a brass head to rise up about an inch, exposing the nozzles that spray water in a wide arc. A common problem is a piece of debris jamming itself beneath the brass head while it's in the up position, preventing it from dropping down when the water is turned off.

That's what had happened to the sprinkler we were looking at right now. We could even see a kind of notch in the mud-encrusted surface where Anouilh's ball had hit the thing. His caddie began picking the gunk off as we turned to walk over to the ball.

The good news was that Anouilh actually had a decent lie on some low rough. The bad news was that the sprinkler head had not only knocked the ball somewhat sideways but at a right angle, so what should have been about 320 yards was almost 30 less than that. He was only a few inches farther out than Licenciados. Worse news was that he was also about 20 yards to the left.

As Anouilh and I looked over the situation, we didn't need any discussion to know exactly what he was facing. While Licenciados had a straight-on shot up the fairway toward the green, Anouilh would have to carry the second fairway bunker to get to the same place. That bunker didn't even start until 200 yards from here and then ran all the way up to—and past—the green. It was nineteen feet deep, and if he hit into it, he might as well concede the hole right there. If he decided to lay up and play safe instead, he'd have a third shot of about 165 yards to the back of a green only forty feet long. A par might be possible, but Licenciados had a chance to birdie the hole if everything went right for him.

"Good thing he hits first," I said to Anouilh. He could hold off on a decision until we saw what Licenciados would do on his second shot.

He nodded, arms folded across his chest as he squeezed himself to try to relieve some tension. "Didn't know he could play this good, Al."

"Neither did he."

Licenciados had his own decision to make. Obviously he wanted to get his second shot as close to the green as possible. But the second bunker running along the left reduced the fairway to a strip less than thirty yards wide, and it got narrower the closer you got to the green, where it was down to less than fifteen. The longer you try to hit a ball, the less accurate it becomes, and so the trade-off on this hole was length versus safety. My guess was that Licenciados would hit an iron about 190, putting it just past where the bunker started and leaving himself an easy 100 or so to the green. He knew Anouilh couldn't do any better than that, so why risk a crash-landing in that sand-laden gorge? It would be a sure par and a possible birdie, since the headwind would help to bring the ball straight down onto the green without too much roll.

Licenciados pulled a club out of his bag, and I had to rub my eyes to make sure I was seeing it right. "He takin' a wood?" I heard Anouilh say.

It sure looked that way. "He's crazy. Five-wood off the grass to that ribbon of a fairway . . . ?"

"It's a three."

I turned toward Anouilh's caddie. "Whud you say?"

"It's a three-wood."

"Horseshit."

The caddie nodded vigorously. "I reccanize it from before. Got that piece'a metal behind the head?"

I could see it from here, shining in the sun, a weight mounted on the rounded back of the clubhead. "Nuts. Totally." I looked at Anouilh. He wasn't agreeing with my assessment as I expected he would. He was just staring intently at his opponent's back as Licenciados got into position and took his time getting lined up.

The crowds following these two players all day had grown so large that total quiet was an impossibility. What most people don't realize is that it isn't noise per se that disturbs golfers; it's sudden, *unexpected* noise. In truth, most pros would prefer it if the crowds looking on jabbered away softly. That kind of relatively constant white noise is not disturbing in the slightest, and it even helps to mask any individual sounds that might be obtrusive on their own. It's when, out of total silence, you hear a camera snap or somebody sneeze that you get thrown off balance.

Right now there was none of that. Right now, if I closed my eyes, I wouldn't have any auditory evidence at all of three thousand people with their eyes glued to Juan Castillo Licenciados as he took an unusually long time over his ball. I remember thinking that he'd better hit pretty soon or people were going to start fainting from forgetting to breathe. And then he did.

You can tell the idiots from the sophisticated fans easily. The idiots start screaming, "Get in the hole!" before the ball has barely left the clubface on a forty-foot putt. Knowledgeable fans yell too, but only when the ball is just a few feet from the hole and has a chance of going in. Raucous yelps of *You da man!* don't even bother me so much if I whack a truly immense drive and the ball has gotten far enough away so everybody can tell that a safe landing is assured.

This was a good crowd. Nobody said a word as the ball left the clubface, although hundreds gasped as they realized early on what kind of shot Licenciados had just hit. You couldn't see the actual surface of the green from where we were because of a slight rise about 100 yards in front of it, but the flag was visible and everyone knew that the ball's trajectory was as laser-perfect as it could be. There was no question that it would end up in the middle of what little fairway was available between the trap and the rough, only how far it would go before stopping. We had the answer a few seconds later as some people ran toward the mounds on the right to get a better view.

Licenciados was less than forty yards from the green, an easy birdie opportunity, as good as he was with his wedge. His shot was so dazzling that even the distinctly pro-American gallery was moved to lusty yells of admiration and respect, causing the normally reserved and aloof Spaniard to blush and turn away in pleased discomfort.

As he turned in our direction, Anouilh applauded as well, and Licenciados gave him a quick wave before returning the three-wood to his bag. Anouilh took a deep breath and looked once more toward the green, only the very tip of the flag visible from our vantage point. He then walked forward to where Twinkie McDaniels had parked her beverage cart.

She flashed him a bright smile and began licking her lips, but he didn't even seem to notice. As she got out of the cart to see what he needed, Anouilh grabbed hold of one of the supports holding up the cart's flat roof and swung himself up onto the back bumper and then onto the top of the compartment where the cold drinks were stored. Hanging on to the roof to keep his balance, he surveyed the landscape lying between his ball and the green, taking his time even as Twinkie frowned at the scratches his spikes were making in the metal cooler covers. Had she been thinking about her wallet rather than The Kid's *schvanz*, she could have taken those covers off later and auctioned them off for a small fortune.

After a minute or so, Anouilh jumped down off the cart and walked back to where we were standing near his ball. We backed off to give him some room, and as he came closer he veered off toward his bag, grabbed a three-wood on the fly and kept walking.

My jaw must have dropped open or something, because as he pulled up to his ball Anouilh looked me in the eye and said, "Not one word, Al." Then he kept staring at me until I took a few more steps backward toward the fairway.

When he was sure I was safely away and thoroughly disabused of any notions of interfering with his intentions, he hunched over his ball, three-wood in hand, jaw muscles working rapidly. I could sense tension all over him as he got ready to pound the hell out of that poor, unsuspecting ball. He looked toward the flag, then back at his ball, then at the flag once more and back down again, waggling his legs and tush back and forth as he put the target out of his mind and settled in over his shot, and he hung there, unmoving, for what seemed like ten minutes.

Then he did something I hadn't seen him do even once in the three years I'd known him. He stood straight up, lifted the club so the head was in front of his eyes and then backed up. Staring down at the ball for a few seconds, he walked over to his bag, dropped the three-wood in and grabbed a different club without a word to his caddie.

That wasn't it, though, the new thing I'd never seen him do, nor was it that the club he had taken was a driver, a totally demented choice. But as he stood over the ball and lined up his shot once again, looking from the green to the ball and back again, he paused and glanced up, just slightly, just from under the hood of his cap. Directly at me.

And smiled. Understand, Derek Anouilh does not stop in the middle of a shot to smile at anybody. Not that it was much of a smile, mind you, just the kind of devilish, shit-eating quarter-smirk a boxer might give you in the thirteenth round a split second before he breaks three of your ribs.

And then it ended, just as quickly as it had begun, so fast I wasn't even sure it had really happened at all. I blinked, and there he was, poised over the ball again, all his back-and-forth looking completed, concentrating so fiercely on that dimpled sphere that I doubt he would have noticed a thermonuclear weapon detonating on the next fairway.

Before I could recompose myself, he was taking the club back. Anouilh normally has a pretty extreme backswing, often bringing the club so far back behind his neck that it points toward his left foot before he reverses direction, but this time it seemed almost like it had gone all the way around practically back to its starting position, pointing to his *right* foot. His torso was so twisted it must have been painful, but his head, as immobile as a cheetah's doing sixty-plus across the savannah, was still directed squarely at the ball, and then the club began its journey back around, picking up speed so rapidly it was a complete blur by the time his hands were over his right shoulder, and still it kept accelerating.

When, after what seemed to me an interminable interval, the clubhead finally whipped its way into the ball, it transformed it into a Sidewinder missile rocketing away so fast I swear to God I saw smoke trailing behind it. It made the same sound as an Olympic ski jumper leaving the ninety-meter ramp, a sort of ruffling, crackling *rhhummpp* that faded into the distance, leaving behind only the faintest suspicion that it had ever really been here at all.

As soon as the ball had shrunk so small I couldn't follow it any longer, I looked at Anouilh, a piece of sculpture standing perfectly balanced at the end of his follow-through. His eyes were closed, and a look of radiant bliss suffused his face. He didn't need to watch the shot; every strand of muscle in his reedy body knew with faultless precision exactly where it was going.

I heard a new sound cranking up in the distance, somewhere in the direction of the green. It sounded like a tidal wave gathering force just before it slammed into the beach. It was unmistakable, that sound, the decibel-laden jet-engine scream of maniacal fans witnessing something

they were not likely to see again in their lifetimes. The roar crescen-
doed impossibly, and kept on rising until it suddenly shot up to a
deafening peak that simply wouldn't quit until three thousand throats
and diaphragms had wrung themselves out so thoroughly that it was
either take a breath or turn blue, and even then the lingering cacophony
still carried all the way back to where we were standing.

Anouilh let his back and shoulders relax, then turned back to me all
lit up with a full-wattage grin. Behind him, Juan Castillo Licenciados,
standing on a mound to watch Anouilh's shot, had hung his head and
was rubbing the bridge of his nose between thumb and forefinger, handing his club back to his caddie with his free hand and then folding his
arms across his chest. Gathering himself and trying to play the good
sport, he came toward Anouilh on unsteady legs to squeeze his shoulder
in acknowledgment of he knew not exactly what, only that this match
was probably over. It was a gracious gesture, especially in light of the
total demoralization etched deeply into his face.

Even Anouilh and I didn't know at that point that his 300-yard shot
off the deck had landed about twelve feet from the pin. We walked up
with Licenciados, Anouilh so zoned out I don't think he was leaving
spike marks, and waited politely for the Spaniard to hit his wedge,
which he did with his customary precision, putting the ball six feet
inside of Derek's own. An easy birdie opportunity, truly awesome in its
own right for this unforgiving Gorgon of a hole.

Anouilh was lying two to Licenciados's three. Since The Kid hadn't
three-putted since the earth cooled, it was dead certain the worst he
could do was tie this hole, even if Licenciados holed his putt. But
Derek was putting first.

He tried to put the memory of that second shot out of his mind so he
could concentrate, but he was only partially successful, and it looked to
me as he connected with the ball as though he may not have hit it hard
enough. Licenciados must have seen it too, because he suddenly
straightened up as the ball headed for the hole. I saw him look rapidly
from side to side, trying to project the ball's trajectory and gauge it
against the slant of the green, the grain of the grass and, for all I know,
the effect of Saturn's gravitational pull as well.

The ball kept rolling and decelerated less rapidly than I thought it
would. With two feet to go, it seemed almost out of steam, but still it
kept turning and proceeding forward until it reached the very lip of the

cup, hanging there, no more movement apparent but balanced so precipitously on the edge of the hole that it seemed to defy the laws of physics, but still it didn't drop in. I tried to watch even harder, as though the force of my gaze might supply the last, tiniest quantum of force required to disturb the ball's exquisite equilibrium and let it fall into the hole. The rules allowed a normal walk to the ball plus ten seconds before Anouilh would have to tap it in and take the extra stroke.

Just then somebody in the crowd started jumping up and down. Then somebody standing next to him did the same thing, and before too long several thousand pairs of feet were pounding furious hell out of the ground in a frantic effort to start a small earthquake.

The Kid smiled and finally stood straight up, resting his putter on his shoulder and beginning his painful walk toward the hole, glancing at his opponent's ball marker to assess the likelihood of Licenciados's sinking his putt for a birdie to halve the hole, when the ball suddenly disappeared. Just like that. First it was there, then it wasn't. Anouilh stopped dead in his tracks and stared at the hole, not quite sure what had happened, seemingly unmindful of the deafening screams and yells coming from the delirious crowd surrounding the green. A stupid look on his face, he walked up to the hole and slowly, very slowly, like a poker player peeking under his last down card to see if God was smiling on him this hand, brought his face over the cup and looked down into it. He reached over and picked the ball up, examined it to make sure it was his, then held it up in the air for all the world to see.

A few seconds later, as Anouilh tossed the ball to a young kid clapping madly beyond the ropes, Licenciados came up from behind, turned him around and kissed him on both cheeks. "Two holes to go, *señor*," he said with a smile, but somehow I could tell he knew it was all over.

I was proud of The Kid, not for eagling the fourth-toughest hole on the course but for keeping his wits about him for the two that followed. Both players dropped their tee shots onto the green and made birdie on number seventeen, Alcatraz, a par-three consisting of nothing more than a tiny island in the middle of a lake. In one last desperate attempt to tie the match, Licenciados overdid his tee shot on number eighteen and went into the water while Anouilh played it safe, and several minutes later it was over.

I believe it will go down in golf history as one of the greatest matches of all time, the kind that would get replayed on television during rain delays at the Masters decades from now. I don't even think it much mattered to the people who witnessed it which side would eventually win the Ryder Cup.

It mattered to me, though. Bottom line, The Kid's performance had merely nullified Robert Carmichael's loss, so we were back to a one-point lead with six matches still to be completed. As I walked Anouilh back to the clubhouse and the waiting throng of reporters, the radio on my belt crackled. I picked it up.

It was Freddy Asphal, telling me that Jon Markovy had just lost his match to Fabrizio Migliore by one hole, down two with one left to play after the seventeenth. Mr. Wizard had lost two balls in the rough despite frantic searches by a horde of concerned spectators, and it had cost him both the holes it had happened on. The tournament was back to even with five matches left.

CHAPTER TWENTY-TWO

Amazing, isn't it, how the highest highs can dramatically metamorphose into the lowest lows?

I'm not even talking about Markovy's loss to Migliore. A blow, certainly, but not a total disaster, even though it proved that Eddie's judgment wasn't infallible, which I found somewhat comforting. It put the tournament back to even so it wasn't like we were suddenly losing, but it didn't end there.

I rushed back to the eighteenth green to watch just as Mack Merriwell and Helmut Braunschweiger were hitting up, Merriwell in the lead by one hole. This time, as Eddie had predicted, Merriwell was having a career round that on any other day would have made headlines. But at this weird tournament, his thunder had been muted by the equally sterling play of Braunschweiger, who had risen to the occasion and shot the lights out of the course. The lead had changed five times already, but I watched it end in a victory for Merriwell as both men made par on the last hole, Braunschweiger missing a birdie putt. As he stooped to pick up his ball without bothering to tap in for a meaningless par, Merriwell walked up to shake hands with the normally reserved German and tentatively risked clapping him on the shoulder as well. Braunschweiger, to everyone's amazement and delight, grabbed him in a bear hug and pounded his back, and the two of them walked off the green arm in arm, Braunschweiger rightly convinced that he had done everything he possibly could to win and satisfied with the one-hole loss owing to the stout response of his opponent.

Far be it from me to downplay the significance of this grand display of mutual respect and admiration, or of the absolutely impossible reality that we were now up a full point on the Euros with only three matches left to complete, but the fact was that their wonderful bonding experience hadn't done anything to make me relax despite our single-point lead. Asphal had just told me something over the radio that was so absurd I was tempted to break down laughing, except that it wasn't really all that funny. Well, actually, it was kind of funny, but funny in the way that slipping on a banana peel would be funny when you talked about it years later, even though you'd fallen down a flight of stairs and broken both legs.

It had happened on number twelve, The Moat, just after Enrico Senzamio had gone one up on Jürgen Kurzer on number eleven. The Moat, contrary to its moniker, had no water on it. The name referred to a sand trap that wrapped around the green on three sides, including the front. Although short at 360 yards, this hole required two extremely accurate shots to get to the green, the first one dangerously toward the right rough so you could barely even see the green at all, and then another one onto the twelve-yard-long dance floor without landing in the bunker.

They'd both managed to get on in two, and Kurzer had just parred the hole with a two-putt from twenty-five feet away. Senzamio had only a ten-footer for his birdie, but he took so much time reading the green and getting himself lined up that he forgot how hard he needed to hit the ball, leaving it an embarrassing twelve inches short. Angry with himself, he walked forward and tapped the ball with only one hand on the putter.

And missed. Not even a lip-out. The ball just slid past the hole and came to rest six inches behind it, for a bogey and the loss of the hole. Stunned and then enraged, Senzamio slammed his putter into the ground with such force that the shaft snapped cleanly in two.

Senzamio's anger, having been spent on the blow he dealt to the green, gave way to a sheepish smile as the crowd laughed. He walked over to the PGA official stationed on the green and asked him to radio the clubhouse for a new putter. The official, Phil Stimson, just stood there looking uncomfortable, making no move to take up the two-way radio clipped to his belt.

"Hey, s'matta for you?" Senzamio prodded. "Gotta be onna tee in like-a ten minutes, 'ey?"

Stimson cleared his throat. "Uh, I'm sorry, Mr. Senzamio, but you're not entitled to replace that club."

"Scusi?" Senzamio leaned forward and put his ear near Stimson's face. "What you say?"

Trying not to stammer, Stimson replied, "Well, uh, you see, you didn't break the putter in the normal course of play. What I mean to say is, um, it didn't break while you were, uh, while you were *putting*, as it were. You broke it in . . . ah . . . while you were, uh . . ." Stimson took a breath and sighed. "You got pissed off and smashed it into the ground, is what you did, Rico. Not exactly the normal course of play."

Senzamio straightened up, took a step backward and looked the man square in the face. "You tell-a me I no getta new putter?"

Stimson gulped. "Not as such."

Rico stared at Stimson for another second or two and then went for the luckless official's throat, only the quick thinking of his and Kurzer's caddies preventing him from making contact and doing some real damage both to Stimson and to Senzamio's own future on the pro circuit. Stimson, sympathetic to Rico's predicament, declined to make an issue of it and helpfully suggested using his driver as a putter from that point forward.

Senzamio chose his three-wood instead and tried to make a go of it on the next few holes, but the level of play in this contest left no room for any compromise. He managed to stay afloat until number seventeen, aided by some dumb mistakes on the part of the suddenly overconfident Kurzer, but it was no use, and he lost the match.

We were even once again, with only two matches left: Eddie Caminetti versus Jacques St. Villard, the European captain, followed by Joel Fleckheimer versus Andrew Firth.

CHAPTER TWENTY-THREE

I enjoy joshing with the crowds on the sidelines, the good-natured ones. If not for them, I'd be mowing the grass on some local muni.

On the sixteenth at the last U.S. Open, I smacked one of the longest, straightest, sweetest drives I've ever hit in my whole life. As our group began moving up the fairway, a guy walking along with us on the sidelines called out, "Didn't get all'a that one, didja, Al!" I recognized him because he'd been following me all day, going through the same gamut of emotions as I did, shouting "Well struck!" when it was well struck, shaking his head and looking glum when I screwed up. He was as thrilled with that drive as I was, and I called back, "Maybe get me some lessons later!" The guy smiled and then dropped it, asking nothing else of me, and is probably still telling his kids that story to this day. Just as I'm telling you.

Problem is, sometimes you mix it up a little and they think they own you, demanding your attention as if it were more important than playing golf, getting offended or even sinister if you refuse them. I was in no mood for either protocol today, and I'm afraid I rudely ignored the spectators as I madly careened back and forth between the last two matches riding in a souped-up golf cart I begged from the course superintendent. Eddie was one up on Jacques St. Villard coming off the fifteenth, and Joel Fleckheimer was teeing off against Andrew Firth on thirteen, their match even. There was a one-hole gap between them because Enrico Senzamio had no need to finish out his bizarre loss to Jürgen Kurzer and Eddie and St. Villard were playing fast.

By the time I got over to number sixteen, Eddie was nowhere to be seen. I groaned out loud as I saw a mass of spectators five deep lining one edge of the first of the two huge sand traps running along the left edge of this par-five hole. Sure enough, there was Eddie down at the bottom, trying to decide what club to hit that would give him some respectable distance while at the same time providing enough loft to get over the wall towering above his head. St. Villard's ball, on the other hand, was sitting impressively close to where Juan Castillo Licenciados's drive had landed earlier in the day in his match against Derek Anouilh.

Jacques St. Villard was inarguably the best golfer in Europe, and arguably one of the best three in the world. He was higher up on the European Order of Merit than the next three guys just below him would have been had they been combined into one player. When I heard he was to be named captain of the European team, I thought it a really dumb move. Sure, St. Villard was one of the best-liked figures in the sport and a man of enormous personal integrity, but why take your best player out of Ryder contention by making him the captain?

I suppose I shouldn't have been surprised when he announced his decision to play as well as serve as captain. I imagine that was probably part of the deal, although nobody was saying. It also shouldn't have come as a surprise that he would not give himself the last tee time on the last day of competition. That might appear as though it was the tactic of a man looking to be a hero by bringing in the gold, even though the real reason might be that he was just trying to save a teammate potential humiliation in case the whole tournament rested on the final match and an American should win. But that rationale would have been tough to get away with, considering that nobody with at least a double-digit IQ thought the Americans *could* win. So he put himself third from last.

I had put Eddie up in the same spot for two reasons. One was that I thought he would be less visible if, owing to some providential intervention not witnessed since the parting of the Red Sea, we had held our own and it all came down to the final twosome. None of us needed for the already controversial unknown to have all that attention focused on him. The second reason was that, should we end up losing before the last match was even played, it wasn't fair to let one of my regular guys get robbed of a full round and a possible Ryder Cup match victory despite the overall loss.

It had never occurred to me that Eddie would be up against St. Villard himself, but there it was. And what do you know? He was beating him through fifteen holes, up one with three to go.

As I peeked over the edge of the bunker watching him try to select a club, Fat Albert standing nearby looking worried, Freddy Asphal sidled up, a little out of breath. "My Lord," he wheezed, looking down into the pit.

He told me that he'd been following this match around most of the day and that it had started off pretty dull, both players going for the safe pars. All of a sudden, around the eighth hole, both guys had begun taking risks, making either birdies or bogeys, a kind of hell-or-high-water approach I wouldn't have expected from either Eddie or St. Villard. But it made for some mighty exciting golf, and the crowds had built up accordingly. A lot of the people who had been following Anouilh around all day had made a beeline for this match, word apparently having gotten out that it was something worth watching.

"What the devil happened to Carmichael?" Asphal asked.

I shrugged and shook my head. "Not everybody's gonna win, so let's just make sure the last two guys do their bit."

"Not winning is one thing," Asphal said. "But from what I heard, he must have swallowed a grenade. What got into him?"

I had no rational answer for him. Asphal clenched his jaw and took a deep breath, letting it out slowly. "Eddie was right, goshdarn it."

"Of course he was right. We knew that going in."

"No, I mean he was *really* right. Not just that Carmichael was going to lose, but that we shouldn't have played him even conceding that. He made us all look bad." Appearances being what they were to Frederick Olmsted Asphal III, I suspect that the unseemly aspect of Carmichael's loss was particularly galling.

It looked like Eddie had finally settled on a four-iron, which I wouldn't have thought lofted enough to do the job, but this was Eddie Caminetti, after all, and he picked the ball cleanly without appearing to have touched a single grain of sand. Even though he was now less than 100 yards past St. Villard's ball and lying two, it was a wonderful clutch shot, and the onlookers loudly applauded the feat.

"How's it goin'?" he asked casually as he came up the ramp and out of the bunker.

"Not so hot," I answered. "We're down one."

"Carmichael, okay. Who else?"

I filled him in, and then I told him only one other match was under way, Fleckheimer versus Firth somewhere on fifteen by now, all tied up.

A few minutes later, they were back in play. St. Villard wisely laid up short of the green, and so did Eddie, whose only chance now was to chip up close enough for a one-putt and hope that St. Villard would take two, but it wasn't to be. Eddie's par after that hideous tee shot was impressive indeed, but St. Villard got his birdie, and the match was back to even.

I made a conscious decision not to worry, because I remembered something Eddie and I had spoken about once during our practice sessions at Crystal Canyon. The hardest part of his hustle was keeping the margin thin, he'd said. He never wanted to get out too far ahead of his opponent, or he would quickly find his action drying up as people realized how good he really was.

Along those lines, the dumbest thing he ever did turned out to be about the smartest. Early in his "career," he'd been playing The Links in Athens, Georgia, against some heavy money from Tennessee in front of a crowd of onlookers. One of the men on the losing side offered to bet him he couldn't knock a ball over the dilapidated sixteen-story Trafalgar Hotel on the east side of the course. They agreed he'd get five tries, but they had to wait nearly ten minutes, because that's about how long it took for all the side bets among the crowd to get laid off, the odds running heavily against Eddie.

He took his three-wood, opened the clubface and whaled away. It was a huge shot, but it peaked short of the building and ended up hitting somewhere along the third floor. So he took his driver, teed the ball up as high in the air as he could without the tee falling over from lack of support, then hit it with everything he had. This time he managed a boarded-up window on the tenth floor. At that point he realized he would never come close, and he walked away without using up the rest of his shots and having given back all the money he'd just won on the course and then some, not to mention whatever the pissed-off spectators had dropped on the side.

Dejected and miserable, not for missing the shot but for falling for such an obvious sucker bet, he limped back to his home course in Spencerville, only to find that he'd suddenly become the most sought-after money player in southern Georgia. Every duffer with a spare dollar wanted to play the chump, the loser, forgetting about the rest of his accomplishments in light of his one dumb play. Eddie made more money in the next six months than he had in the previous six years and learned an important lesson to boot. That's when the final transformation of his ego was completed, and he learned how to cut his victories razor thin so people wouldn't realize how good he really was and refuse to bet with him.

That was the best thing that ever happened. The worst was when one of those two-bit local television newsmagazines did a film-at-eleven-you-won't-believe-it-startling-exposé-etc. on "Gambling in Georgia: The Hidden Menace." Not knowing in advance what the story was about, one of Eddie's admirers wound up on camera telling the whole state about a guy named Caminetti who was probably the greatest golfer who ever lived and rarely lost a bet.

The action for Eddie at Spencerville dried up faster than a speakeasy after a raid. He couldn't get a two-dollar Nassau if he spotted a scratch player three a side. Even guys he'd been playing with for ten years wouldn't give him a game, as though that one comment on a sleazy television show had somehow changed everything. And that's how Eddie wound up in southern Florida, another lesson learned.

Of course, walking that fine line for bets on the local muni was a far cry from managing your margin at the Ryder Cup, but I knew that the last damned thing Eddie Caminetti needed was to go home a big hero. He'd never get another money game going as long as he lived. He'd have to win this one thin, and make it look almost like an accident.

But as he handed his putter back to Fat Albert coming off sixteen, I knew this was not a good time to have that conversation with him. Not that he'd have it with me anyway.

Jerome Bushnell, the official who had brought me the news at the Ritz the night before about Luc van Ostrand being sick, was standing near the seventeenth tee as I came up with Eddie and St. Villard. He motioned to me and I walked over, following him as he moved us away from the gallery.

"Gonna take long, Jerry? Wanna watch my boy tee off."

He shook his head. "Could actually wait, but I thought you might like to know." Did he always have a pained expression on his face, or did I see him only when he had bad news? I asked him what was going on, hoping he'd tell me quickly.

"That match between Markovy and Migliore? The one your boy lost?"

The one Eddie practically guaranteed me Mr. Wizard would win. I nodded for him to go on.

"Tell you in advance, there's nothing to be done about it, but I thought you'd want to know. Just got finished watching some tapes the network boys handed me, the parts where he lost those two balls in the rough."

I twisted around to look at the tee box, seeing that Eddie and St. Villard were getting ready to tee off. I didn't want to rush Bushnell, but he could tell I was anxious and only listening to him with half my attention, so he got right to it.

"We're pretty convinced some guys picked up those balls and pocketed them, although we'll never be able to prove it."

I turned back, now fully his. "Some guys . . . ?" I managed to croak.

"Somebody said they were soccer players. From Italy."

The team Migliore had brought over. I was reeling, unable to speak.

"Only thing I know for sure," Bushnell went on quickly, "Fabrizio didn't know about it. When I asked him, he damned near fainted, and he wasn't faking it, believe me."

I managed to take a couple of breaths, then said, "Anybody confront them?"

"Can't find 'em, Al. My guess, next time anybody hears from 'em, they'll be back in Italy. Probably for them it was just some screwing around, like throwing dog shit onto the field at a European soccer match."

He patted me on the back and left his hand there. "Awfully sorry, bud. Hadn'a happened, Cup'd already be yours, a real goddamned miracle, you ask me."

I wasn't thinking about miracles. I was thinking about how Eddie had made the right call about Markovy after all. The stolen balls had cost him two holes, yet he'd lost by only one.

CHAPTER TWENTY-FOUR

I got back to the tee box just as Eddie and St. Villard were getting ready to go for the tiny island green of Alcatraz. I watched as both of them landed within fifteen feet of the flag, then walked down to see them each one-putt for birdies. The match was still all square, meaning that the entire tournament now depended on only three more holes, Fleck and Firth on seventeen and eighteen and Eddie and St. Villard on eighteen. I thought there was a real possibility I might have a full-blown anxiety attack in front of the cameras.

"He is amazing, Alan," St. Villard said to me softly as he passed by on his way to eighteen, pronouncing my name Ah-*lain*.

If he's so fucking amazing, I thought, *why isn't he winning?* It wasn't a rational thought, really, and hardly charitable. Here was one Eddie Caminetti, a complete unknown, a virtual street urchin in the world of our sport, who had just gone one on one with the Vladimir Horowitz of golf and was still all square at the end of seventeen holes. Viewed from afar, this state of affairs was such a patently ridiculous proposition that I wouldn't have blamed anyone who wasn't there for refusing to believe it. And I was all ticked off because he wasn't in the lead.

Which was about the time I noticed that Eddie didn't look so good. He was licking his lips and moving his head around as though something was cramping his neck. Even Fat Albert looked concerned, and he thought Eddie was the god of golf made manifest and totally indestructible.

Seeing me near the eighteenth tee box, Eddie gave me a look I couldn't read but which said worry all over. Asphal, standing next to me, said, "It *is* rather nice that he finally seems to be feeling the pressure, don't you think?"

To which I responded, "Well I'm so pleased you're touched, Freddy. Really, it restores my faith in humanity. And if he loses, I'm gonna wring his fucking neck, and then you can wring mine."

Eddie was up first and hit his tee shot into the water.

That's it. There's no way of saying anything positive at all about that crappy shot. We didn't need any heroics out of him, just a plain old par, and yet he cranked up and overhit the ball, something I'd never seen him do before. With all his authoritative lecturing about consistency being the very soul of his game, why the hell did he have to pick this particular moment to violate the canon that had worked for him so successfully all those years? And it wasn't as if it was even close. That thing was so far out into the lake the next set of eyes to see it would probably belong to an archaeologist from Neptune a thousand years from now.

Seeing that shot, St. Villard put back the driver he'd been holding while awaiting his turn and took out his three-wood instead. Maybe Eddie could put his next shot on the green and maybe he couldn't, but either way, he was going to be lying three and St. Villard two. A par for Eddie was highly doubtful, so the Frenchman knew he could play it ultra-safe and still win the hole and the match.

"Rats," Eddie said as he stepped off the tee.

Rats? My bowels were doing the Montezuma mambo and that's all he had to say, *Rats?* He was carrying cool just a bit damned far for my taste, but rather than take the time to point out his titanic ignorance of all that was holy and sacred about the Ryder Cup and how it was supposed to be played, I turned away, just in time to see St. Villard smoothly spank the three-wood to a pinpoint landing about 200 yards from the green. What he would try to do on his next shot would depend entirely on what Eddie did with his.

"Jesus H, this guy is good," he said.

He seemed to be forgetting my incipient panic, or maybe he was trying to get me to forget it. "You thought, what, the number-one ranked golfer in the world was gonna be a pushover?"

"Wonder what's happening on sixteen?" Asphal said, jiggling his two-way radio in his hand. "Nobody's answering."

"Go have a look," Eddie said before I could stop him, then called over to his left, "Yo, Jack!" He put his thumb toward his mouth and stuck his pinky out in the other direction, then waggled his hand: *Something to drink?*

"*D'accord!*" came St. Villard's reply, and before I could do anything about it, the PGA official on the hole radioed in for Twinkie, and Asphal hopped in the super-cart to head for seventeen to see what was going on over there.

"Are you nuts, Eddie?" I asked in astonishment, knowing that all of this was going to delay things at least ten minutes and maybe more. "Let's get this goddamned thing over with!"

"Relax, Al." He grinned at me as he tore off his sweaty glove. "S'matter, you worried?"

Was I worried?

As Eddie blew some air out of his mouth and put his hands on his hips, all traces of his earlier sickly look completely gone, St. Villard began doing stretches, bending over with a club clutched in both hands until his knuckles touched the ground. "What got things moving?" I asked, as long as I was unable to do anything about getting things rolling here anyway. "Back on eight?"

"Huh? Oh, that. I bet him fifty large I could beat him."

Eddie turned away to grab a towel and couldn't see the look of shock that invaded my face, but Fat Albert did. "Yo, Mistuh Bellamy. You okay?"

I barely heard him as I stepped to the side to face Eddie over his bag. "You *bet* him? You made a *bet* with St. Villard?"

He pulled the towel away from his face. " 'Course I bet him. So what?"

"So what? *So what?* This is the goddamned Ryder Cup, f'cryin' out loud! You don't bet guys at the Ryder Cup!"

"Says who?"

Who, indeed? There was no sense giving him grief over what had already happened, and while I wanted to get back to the subject of why the hell he seemed so bent on slowing things down, just then Asphal came bouncing back over the fairway, a grin on his face as he shook his head. "You won't believe this," he said, getting out of the cart. "Fleckheimer's mother's here."

That was a surprise. I knew Frieda, and I had no idea she was coming. "And that caused a delay?" I asked him.

He held up a hand. "Not in and of itself. But as they're all walking up after their tee shots, she starts yakking away at Fleck. In Yiddish."

I still didn't see where this was going, and Asphal seemed to relish taking his time to tell the story. "Get to the point, Freddy," I said.

"The point is, Firth grabbed an official and told him Joel was receiving outside assistance."

Now I know why Asphal had been grinning like that. "He claimed Frieda Fleckheimer was giving her son golf advice?" It would have been a clear violation of the rules, but the image of that dowdy Jewish mother telling her son how to hit his shot was absolutely riotous, the perfect capper to a far-from-riotous day. She was probably just giving him *tsuris* about drinking enough in this weather and not wearing enough sunscreen, which was perfectly legal so long as she didn't add anything about whether he was making sure his clubface was square to the target or something like that.

But that wasn't the important part. The important part was that something had gone and gotten Joel Fleckheimer righteously pissed off. It was the best news I'd had all day.

"The *vugganeeta* must have gotten to Firth," Asphal said by way of explanation. "By the time I arrived, he and Frieda were screaming bloody murder at each other."

"Should I go over there?"

Asphal waved me off. "I shouldn't think so. Desmond Grant's got it well in hand. Appears he's going to allow Firth to blow off some steam and then get on with things."

While everybody else was laughing, Eddie was listening intently, a serious expression on his face. He turned away just as I noticed it, then waved at the oncoming beverage cart to get Twinkie's attention. A minute or so later, Asphal said, "I suspect that the altercation back on sixteen has not concluded."

"How you know that?" Fat Albert asked him.

"Would have been some noise by now, my dear fellow." Asphal pulled out his radio to check on the situation.

He was right. The altercation was apparently not over. We huddled around him as he told us what was going on.

It turned out that there had been some additional delay as the television people repositioned cameras brought in from other holes. There were no stands of trees on this wide-open course in which to hide platforms, so the place was dotted with cranes and cherry pickers that

made it look like an oil field. I wondered if the network already had
tapes of the earlier incident between Mrs. Fleckheimer and Firth.

Fleck had real fire in his eyes, incensed over the embarrassment
Andrew Firth had caused his mother. He had a decent lie after what
had been a nice drive off the tee. But while the flag was only about 170
away, Joel was sitting well left of the fairway centerline with only the
most precarious line to the small, water-bounded green. He would have
to land on the green itself to have any hope of making par, but it would
be like setting a fighter plane down on a rowboat. Even though Firth
hadn't driven his ball as far, he was now situated at the very rightmost
edge of the fairway with a small but playable grass gateway up onto the
green.

Firth was away and was first to hit. Jon Markovy, who was watching
the match now that his had ended, tried to take advantage of the few
extra seconds to get Fleck calmed down, but Joel was having none of it,
even ignoring Frieda, who was busy staring daggers at Firth and making
some kind of Eastern European hex signs at him with her fingers. The
Scotsman, apparently still rattled by the tasteless confrontation and
aware that the real grief was yet to come when the media got hold of it,
decided to play a conservative iron, landing his ball in the widest part
of the fairway between the sand and the water, some thirty yards short
of the green, from which it rolled up almost to the edge of the frog hair.
An accurate chip up and a one-putt would get him his par.

Fleckheimer had no room at all for error. Not only did he have to
start the ball out over the water and bring it back in, he had to touch
down on the green and then stop the ball dead to keep it from rolling
off. There was no way to land it short and let it roll up as Firth had,
because the only thing short of the green from his position was liquid
fairway.

It was an extremely difficult shot. But Fleck was extremely pissed.
He grabbed a four-iron and waved everybody back. He was so furious
he may not have realized he had taken a club he could easily hit over
200 yards. Since Markovy knew there would be no talking to him, he
hung back and hoped for the best, but at that point Fleck put back the
four and took a *three*. Frieda, clutching a handkerchief to her bosom,
looked as worried as Markovy must have, even though she didn't know
a three-iron from a curling iron.

Her son's eyebrows, still knit in anger, began to relax as he positioned himself over his ball. Willing himself to calm, he opened the clubface wide until it looked more like a sand wedge than a three-iron, then hauled off and whacked it as hard as he could.

I watched it later on the network pool tapes. The last time I saw a ball go that high into the air off a long iron was when Eddie had hit a similar shot during his round with Anouilh, and that had been just a seven-iron. Fleck's ball looked as though it might achieve escape velocity and leave our planet altogether. I had no idea how something hit that high could have any sort of accuracy, but before long the ball was hanging in the air over toward the green and started its downward plunge. The reentry angle was so steep it seemed to come down in an absolutely vertical drop until it thudded onto the green and stuck there, six feet from the pin.

Before anybody could react, Fleckheimer yelled loudly, "Thanks, Mom!" and Frieda yelled back with equal volume, "Dun' mention it, *boychik!*" Firth, scowling darkly, tried his best to ignore the howling from the gallery, but he could no more do that than ignore the devastating blow Fleck's majestic shot had just dealt him. How he managed to compose himself for his chip to the green was beyond me, but he did, getting it to within four feet of the pin for a near-certain par.

On the green, Fleck bent to his mother as she whispered something in his ear. Straightening back up, he announced to the crowd, "She just wished me good luck, swear to God!" Even Desmond Grant turned away to hide a smile as the spectators roared their approval. Andrew Firth stood stoically neutral, betraying nothing as Fleck left Frieda on the sidelines to walk to his ball.

Changing his entire personality in some sort of mental phone booth, Fleck grew calm, trying to make himself forget the reason he wanted this putt so badly. He analyzed the green until there was no more data to be wrung from it, positioned himself over the ball and lined up his putter. When there was nothing left to do but hit, he looked straight down, took his arms and shoulders back while holding them as a single entity shaped like an unwavering triangle, and struck.

He closed his eyes without watching the path of the ball, relying on the swelling cry from the gallery to tell him that his line was holding steady as the shot progressed toward the hole. He never heard the ball drop into the cup over the noise of the crowd.

Birdie. Fleck was up by one, with only two holes left to play.

Asphal stowed the radio and jumped back into the cart to watch them tee off on seventeen.

Eddie having taken an inordinate amount of time just to select some mineral water, we were back in gear on the eighteenth.

The water played as a lateral hazard, so Eddie dropped his ball perpendicular to where it last crossed land on its way into the drink. Fortunately he'd hit a hook, not a slice. Had it gone the other way, his drop area wouldn't have been much past the tee box.

His drop put him about 250 yards from the green. Going for it would be suicide, given the extreme difficulty of hitting that dime-sized green butting right up against the water.

Not going for it would be suicide, too. While laying up had a better chance of keeping him dry, the best he could do after that would be on the green in four, to St. Villard's two or three.

There was no decision, really. Eddie couldn't hit 250 off the deck. At least he never had, or not that I'd seen. And while I was doing all of this analysis for him, Eddie had already selected a club and was addressing his ball, and while I was being offended by his not consulting me regarding this crucial shot, he hit it.

Thousands of spectators thronged the side of the fairway opposite the water, and thousands more jockeyed for viewing position near the little green. There were at least five television cameras looking down from cranes, and two more in the blimp hovering overhead, the one with the dog painted on its side. I don't know exactly how many people in the United States and Europe were watching that shot, but it had to be over a hundred million, and years later all of them would recollect it in its infinite perfection.

Eddie's intention was to hit the ball just as straight as physically possible, directly toward the green, with as much power as he was capable of generating. It was about the only way available to get as close as he could without needing to be precise about the distance. As long as the ball's trajectory remained a beeline for the target, no matter where it finally touched down it would be dry and safe, and the farther the better.

But hitting a ball very long and very straight is one of the most difficult feats in golf, especially off the grass instead of a tee. In order to go straight, the ball can't spin left or right. Try to picture a clubface slamming into a golf ball at some 115 miles per hour and doing so with such total precision that no sideways force at all is applied. Players generally count on a fade or draw of varying severity, it being a hell of a lot easier to control the amount of sidespin than to eliminate it altogether. That was especially true if you hit it as hard as Eddie just had.

I'm guessing that the same dimples on Eddie's ball that were facing forward when it took off were still facing forward when it landed. It was a low shot that kept continuing to rise, a suborbital missile seeking a celestial target and only reluctantly sinking back to earth. The shallow angle allowed the ball's momentum to be conserved as it touched down lightly on the hard, dry grass and continued to roll at high speed, slowing noticeably only as it approached the boundary between fairway and frog hair, slowing still more as it crossed over, really dying now as it trickled onto the green and finally gasping the last of its kinetic energy as it wobbled to a stop less than eight feet from the flag.

There was a split second before the gallery erupted into pandemonium, as though some other source of verification was needed before they were willing to believe what they'd just seen with their own eyes. I turned to see Eddie's reaction, fully expecting to find him with the stick still over his shoulder and his right foot still pointing straight down, but the club was in Fat Albert's hand, and he and Eddie had already covered some ten yards on their way up the fairway to get abeam St. Villard's ball.

I jogged to catch up and said to Albert, "Whud he hit?" The caddie held the club out for me to see: It was the driver. How many more surprises were there to be on the last holes of the tournament?

St. Villard waited for the noise to die down before setting up for his shot. He had what looked like a four-iron. Eddie had a certain bogey and a possible par, and St. Villard had no choice. He had to go for the green.

It wasn't that difficult a shot, to be candid, but I felt that the crowd could have been a little more generous and a little less partisan when the European captain nailed the damned thing, leaving himself a fifteen-foot putt for birdie. Some of his teammates who were standing nearby began to run toward him, but St. Villard waved them back. I wonder if the same Yogi Berra–ism that was in my mind was also in his: *It ain't over till it's over.*

As we walked toward the green, my radio crackled, and I quickly took it off my belt to kill the noise. Who the hell would be calling me on the eighteenth hole?

It was Asphal, on his way back from seventeen. Fleckheimer and Firth had both hit terrific tee shots and landed in the shadow of the flag, Fleck about seven feet from the hole, Firth about nine. They were already on their way to the green when Asphal had left them to return to eighteen. Seeing him in the distance, I said, "Stay on the horn and tell me what happens," then turned off the power on my radio and put it away for good.

Asphal caught up and slowed the cart. I got in while it was still moving. "So . . . ?"

He took the radio away from his ear. "Firth missed his birdie putt, and Joel just conceded the par."

Neither of us was willing to say out loud what we both dared to think. If Fleck sank his birdie putt, he'd win his match and we'd be up a full point for the tournament, with only this one last match left. The worst we could do then was tie; there'd be no way for us to lose.

St. Villard was away, so he was first to putt. I admired the fact that he didn't take any more time or do anything different for this shot than he usually did. He was averaging twenty-four putts per round, so why mess with a good thing?

Maybe he should have. He was smart enough not to leave the winning putt short, but he overdid it and took out just enough of the break to miss the hole and end up about eighteen inches past it. I prayed that Eddie wouldn't signal him to pick it up but would make him putt it out instead—hey, you never knew—but Eddie brought the fingertips of his right hand together facing downward, then flipped his hand over. St. Villard nodded at him in appreciation of the gesture and picked up his ball, holding it aloft as the crowd politely applauded his par and got it over with quickly so they could turn their attention to Eddie, lying just one stroke away from *his* par, only eight feet standing between him and the eternal gratitude of a nation perpetually in need of external validation.

I had no way to know at the time what was happening back on seventeen, but here's how it went, as we would learn later:

Fleckheimer forgot about Firth as he considered his putt, which wasn't a particularly tricky one, just long. Knowing how much was riding on this one shot, the crowd grew eerily still as Fleck bent over the ball and got lined up, bringing his putter back and forth several times to try to groove the swing path into his body.

Finally he stopped moving the putter and held it motionless behind the ball. With one last look at the hole to check the distance, he turned his face down and hung there, still as death. His form and concentration were admirable.

Until he looked up at Firth.

"And then the Lord said . . ." he intoned, drawing the putter back and holding it stopped in the air, ". . . *the Firth* . . ." He let the putter swing back toward the ball without ever taking his eyes off the Scotsman. Hundreds gasped involuntarily as the putter struck the ball, Fleck still looking straight at his opponent. ". . . *shall be latht.*"

Fleck still didn't look even as his ball took off, never turned to watch as it sped irretrievably away . . .

Fat Albert looked ready to explode. I suspect that he didn't have a really clear sense of why this shot was so important, but he knew it was. Eddie was doing more investigatory fieldwork for this putt than he had for his last ten combined. His oversized bonbon of a caddie couldn't keep still, rocking from one foot to the other, until Eddie began dispatching him to various corners of the green to help him read the surface. St. Villard tapped his foot repeatedly while the crowd fidgeted and created a background murmur not unlike that of a hornet's nest.

But the crazier everybody around him seemed to get, the calmer Eddie grew. He was cloaked in the same kind of oblivious tranquillity that suffused religious martyrs about to be burned at the stake, as if all was finally right with the universe and any impending catastrophe was of vanishingly small consequence. Fat Albert was bouncing around all over the place, taking inventory of the exact height, angle and thickness of every single blade of grass between ball and hole, seemingly unaware that his man was standing still, arms folded and one thumb scratching at the bottom of his chin, ignoring him completely.

Unhurriedly, mindless of the cameras, the softly droning blimp and the escalating anxiety of thousands of spectators, Eddie began walking toward me. His composure was maddening and fascinating at the same time, giving me the uncomfortable feeling that he knew everything and the rest of us knew nothing. My febrile imagination was even starting to conjure up the distinct impression that light from the sun was converging into a kind of aura around him, and I had to mentally smack myself back to reality.

Then he was at my side, both of us looking at the green, me trying to pretend everything was normal, Eddie just plain not giving a shit. I made a few feeble hand and facial gestures to give everybody the impression I was consulting with him on the putt, and whispered, "For the love'a Pete, Eddie, why aren't you putting the goddamned ball!"

I wasn't sure he'd heard me. Then he put a hand on my arm and squeezed. "You worried, Bubba?"

Again with the *was I worried.* Was he totally deranged?

"The Cup is yours, buddy."

What? What'd he say? *The Cup is yours*? I didn't get it. The words made no sense. What did that mean, *The Cup is yours*?

"Start polishing up the mantel, Al. Go have a beer and work on your speech."

"What are you talking about, Eddie?" I somehow managed to squeak.

He turned to me, smiling, light beams radiating from his face. "Not that difficult a concept."

No, it wasn't. Not in and of itself. But in the present situation such definitiveness was not only inappropriate, it was downright cruel. Yet this was Eddie Caminetti talking, and if there's one thing I'd learned over the past few months, when Eddie Caminetti spoke, I listened.

Or maybe it was just hopeful desperation that made me think that way at this moment, wishful thinking of the most juvenile sort. Eddie

must have read that in my face, because he laughed, joyfully, and
squeezed my arm again. "Trust me on this one, Al," he said, then
walked away.

All the looking and reading and surveying and analyzing had clearly
crossed the threshold into the theater of the ludicrous, so Eddie waved
Fat Albert out of his line of sight and finally walked up to the ball, took
his position, and began carefully getting himself aligned. The crowd
started to simmer down as he took one last look at the hole and then put
it out of his mind, concentrating only on the ball between his feet. He
wiggled his knees and went still, then drew the putter back and held it
in the air.

And held it some more. It just hung there forever, and I thought I was
going to throw up.

The sound of a four-engine jet aircraft taking off suddenly screamed
in from somewhere in the distance. Or maybe it was a tidal wave crashing onshore from the ocean a hundred miles to the west, or a volcanic
eruption . . . ?

The sound soon resolved itself into the deranged screaming of thousands of people suddenly gone totally berserk, the kind of sound you
might hear if a comet were spotted heading toward earth or the Cubs
won the World Series or it was discovered that french fries and Häagen-
Dazs rum raisin in sufficiently massive quantities prevented all known
forms of cancer.

Or maybe . . .

Eddie had looked up from his ball and was staring at me with an
impish, mischievous grin. Even in the harsh sunlight his features shone
with a light of their own. Again I felt as if I were being left out of
something everyone else understood, so I looked elsewhere and saw
Fred Asphal facing away from me, bent over, a finger in one ear and his
two-way radio pressed tightly against the other. He bobbed forward
slightly, probably trying to hear the radio better over the noise, then
straightened up slowly and turned until his eyes found mine.

I tried to read his expression—all I could tell for sure was that he
was startled—but a slight movement caught my eye from the middle of
the green and I reflexively turned toward it, just in time to see Eddie's
putter thaw out and start its downward trajectory, Albert kneeling on
the grass about fifteen feet back to try to see what the surface was
doing, frowning and jiggling his shoulders and moving his head back

and forth to improve his depth perspective. Before I could even get myself reoriented away from that sound still crashing in from somewhere behind me to focus on what was happening here on eighteen, Eddie had taken his shot.

I was instantly aware of the dizzying loss of connection between player and ball as the latter's journey got under way and it was no longer subject to any human influence. Only the gods and the surface of the green could now affect its path, and as soon as the leading edge of Eddie's putter undocked from the ball, my coaching job had ended and I, like thousands of others, could only sit, watch and pray as the difference between the heights of victory and the depths of despair was reduced to a silly little object full of cute little dimples rotating its way clumsily across the grass.

The ball hadn't gone two yards when Fat Albert jumped to his feet with astonishing quickness and shrieked, *"That grass be caddy-whampus, Eddie!"*

As though there were anything his man could do about it now. I frankly didn't see a problem, the ball rolling with perfect speed on an accurate line to a delicious par. But Fat Albert had seen something in the grass the rest of us hadn't, some tiny defect somewhere or the grain inclining in a way only visible from a very specific angle or Lord only knew what.

The huge kid had his face buried in his hands, unable to watch, and sure enough, the perfect line began to disintegrate as the ball, for no easily discernible reason, veered ever so slightly to the right. "Ever so slightly" at three feet translated into about two inches by the time the ball neared the cup which, being only four and a quarter inches in diameter to begin with, imposed definite limits on allowable discrepancies. Maybe if Eddie's ball had started off slightly faster, it could have rolled through the tiny break and plunged into the heart of the hole, but the grain was winning this battle.

The ball finally made it to the cup and entered along the right lip, sinking into the waiting maw of the hole, where the last bit of forward momentum, assisted by the pull of gravity at the bottom of the cup, sped it up just the smallest fraction. It rode around the rear edge and right back out of the hole, leaving the same way it had entered and coming to rest less than two inches away.

He missed.

CHAPTER TWENTY-FIVE

Eddie having lost his match, the Euros were up a point, 14–13, and I had just seen my entire life swirling down the vortex of an industrial toilet. Honest to God, in that moment I would have swallowed hemlock had it been available.

Eddie was standing with the putter resting on his shoulder, a hand in his pocket. When he saw me looking at him, he shrugged and pursed his lips in an *oh-well-what-the-hell* kind of way, but he was still smiling. Then I saw that two fingers of the hand holding his putter were raised in a V, and he was waggling them to make sure I noticed.

Victory? I wasn't sure if the sun had finally fried his brain or mine, but for damned certain it was one of us.

Whatever shock and depression clamped down on my heart quickly gave way to terror as the thought that the spectators might actually kill me popped into my head. Behind the profound silence that had gripped the immediate vicinity, we could still hear the mob back on seventeen, the roar only now beginning to dissipate. Then a ripple became visible among the crowd here on eighteen, an actual physical thing running its way in and through the massed bodies much as a wave on a watery surface might. It seemed to emanate from several points, each of which was occupied by someone with either a portable radio or a cell phone, alternately gesticulating wildly and then trying to wave everybody into silence while straining to hear. The ripple bounced around and doubled back on itself, increasing its speed and intensity with every ricochet. Then, as one, the entire collection of sweating, vibrating bodies began to move, and I realized that a number of people were in danger of fainting dead away and getting crushed by the frenzied hordes that seemed to be heading, uh . . .

. . . heading my way. Jesus! They *were* going to kill me! Nearly paralyzed with fright now, I twisted back and forth to see if there was any means of escape, but all I saw was PGA official Jerome Bushnell coming at me from the side, a feral expression on his face that was completely at odds with a personality normally so placid even news of an alien invasion probably couldn't crack it. It was hopeless, totally hopeless, and I jumped to the edge of the green to grab a club out of Eddie's bag to defend myself, an irrational notion in the face of so many attackers, but I had to do something. Before I could wrap my hands around a five-iron, Bushnell was on me, his surprisingly strong arms wrapped around my head like a pair of hose clamps, choking off the scream that was welling up from deep in my chest, which is when I felt his lips on my cheek and realized he was actually going to Tyson me and there was nothing I could do about it. Other arms gripped me until I was pinned into complete immobility, and all I could do was wait for Bushnell's teeth to tear into my face, but somebody managed to pull him away, the guy screaming, "Let me! Let me!" and then a strange face swung into view and a strange mouth was covering my forehead and cheeks with blubbering kisses.

"What the hell . . . !" I managed to sputter, but got the breath knocked out of me before I could finish as I was suddenly shot into the air, catching a momentary, eagle's-eye view of the crowd below me until I came back down to find myself sitting on the shoulders of two huge guys wearing Hawaiian shirts emblazoned with images of tropical fruit. Bushnell was weeping openly now, his hand locked onto my thigh, and I was dragging him along with me as the pineapple-and-coconut shirts began bouncing me up and down while parading me around the green to the rapturous delight of the crowd. From my vantage point above the desert floor I could see a second Mongolian horde sweeping in from the direction of the seventeenth green, carrying aloft another poor soul, along with a woman. An elderly woman.

I blinked to try to fight back to some kind of normality and looked over to where I'd last seen Fred Asphal. He was still there, and he had a smile on his patrician puss, a quiet, supremely contented one, the kind you see on the faces of saints in Renaissance paintings.

Fleck? I mouthed at him silently, hopefully, while pointing to his radio. Asphal pressed the antenna back in and stuck the two-way in his pocket, folded his arms across his chest and nodded back at me.

Joel Fleckheimer had sunk his birdie putt on seventeen. He must have done it about two seconds before all that noise started, because that's how long it would have taken the sound of the hysterical mob to reach us. Sinking that putt won him his match with no need to play the last hole, and it had put us one up on the Euros, 14–13, which became 14–14 a few seconds later when Eddie missed his putt. Impossibly, *absurdly*, the Cup was still ours despite Eddie's blown match, and bookies all over London were probably already slashing their wrists over their huge losses as the Ryder ended in a dead tie.

Eddie's putt had been irrelevant. He'd waited until he knew that Fleck had closed out his match, until he knew that the Cup was ours for certain, before putting his own ball.

But *why* had he waited? Why not just get up there and take the shot? There could only be one explanation . . .

"Fuck *me*, Al!" Bushnell was yelling at the top of his lungs so he could be heard above the din. He must have seen confusion and uncertainty on my face, because he said, "You know what Fleckheimer did on seventeen?"

I did know, and that's what the crowd had found out about from all those radios and cell phones, too, because a chant of "We keep the Cup!" had spontaneously arisen from God-only-knew-how-many throats. "We keep the Cup!" they bellowed, and the coconuts bounced me hard with each repeated syllable. In a handful of seconds they'd gone from the black pit of Eddie's missed putt to the radiant heights of an overall draw, and they were going to wring from the moment every ounce of pure exultation they possibly could.

"You da man, Al!" Bushnell was shouting at me, all pretext of PGA of America impartiality thrown to the winds. "You. Are. The. Fucking. MAN!"

"God bless you, Alan Bellamy!" a woman whooped from somewhere off to the left. "You're a genius, Bellamy!" someone else yelled in from the right. The man and woman surfing the crowd in from seventeen shimmered in the waves of heat rising from the desert but soon coalesced into Joel and Frieda Fleckheimer. Groups of spectators from here on the eighteenth green peeled off like squadrons of F-14s and headed out to the fairway to heap adulation on the man who'd sealed the next two years of the Ryder Cup's continued occupation of a trophy case on U.S. soil.

Eddie was nowhere in sight.

———

A little while later, after the crowd had spent its frenzy and gotten back to realizing that it was over 108 degrees out here, I found myself sitting on the grass with Fred Asphal, Joel Fleckheimer and Jerome Bushnell, a line of security guards shielding us from the blitzkrieg of reporters trying to get at us. We were laughing as Bushnell told us the rest of what had happened on seventeen.

Fleck never did look at his ball, but he knew it had gone in, not by the unearthly caterwauling of the swooning crowd but by Firth's eyes closing in dismay as he saw that nothing short of a tornado was going to keep it out of the hole. Frieda Fleckheimer flipped Firth the bird in front of a hundred million television viewers and, unbeknownst to any of us up at eighteen, we had the lead, 14–13, and a lock on the Cup. Then all we'd needed from Eddie Caminetti was to tie his match with St. Villard and we would be the creators of the biggest upset in Ryder Cup history. I stopped laughing at that point and sobered up.

"Why'd Eddie take so long with his putt?" Asphal asked me.

I turned my hand up helplessly by way of an answer.

Bushnell couldn't stop shaking his head in wonder and amazement. "Not a soul alive thought you'd get within four points of those guys, Al. Not the network talking heads, not the PGA office—" I looked up at that, and he nodded. "Nobody." He heaved a great sigh and patted the surface of the green affectionately. "Not even you."

"We only tied them, Jerry. I mean, come on . . ."

He laughed and wiped a bead of sweat from his brow as Asphal said, "You can be so beastly thick, Bellamy."

Bushnell wiped his hands together and got slowly to his feet, grunting and stretching his back as he stood upright. He looked over at the reporters who'd begun buzzing when they thought they might finally get their shot at us. "It's the biggest goddamned victory we've ever had, Al. Far and away. Shit, I heard about Fleck's putt, I got wood." He knelt back down and looked me in the face, jerking a thumb past the security line, wearing his official PGA face now. "So don't make yourself look like the world's biggest asshole by treating it as anything but when you talk to those guys."

I wasn't thinking about *those guys*. I was thinking about Eddie Caminetti, about how he had realized before I did that the Cup was back in our hands.

I was thinking about how he'd missed his last putt on purpose.

CHAPTER TWENTY-SIX

I had to get away to breathe before the shit hit the fan, and sitting in the golf-cart storage barn with Eddie seemed as good a place as any. The steady hum from the overhead charging units drowned out much of the commotion coming from outside, a good deal of it having to do with the PGA's public-relations people trying to find me in order to get my canonization in front of the media started. Talk about a country starved for heroes.

Eddie didn't seem particularly troubled as we sat in a cart side by side, but he knew I was. I needed to talk, but I had no idea what about, too confused and upset to sort my thoughts out. How could I just come out and ask him if he'd purposely thrown his match?

"So how come you agreed to do the Ryder Cup, Eddie?" I asked, only to make conversation. "Just the money?"

"*Just* the money? Boy, you guys really do get rich off this game. Me, I never made three hunnerd grand in one week before, that's a damned fact."

"Three hundred? We're only paying you a hundred."

"Yeah, but the Europeans're paying me two hunnerd."

The hum coming from the ceiling got louder. Or maybe it was just my brain suddenly starting to vibrate, too, in preparation for a full-blown psychotic episode. "For what?"

"For blowing my match and making it look legit. Or I *guess* it was two hunnerd. How much is a million francs in English?"

"About two hundred grand. And you're full'a shit."

"You think so?"

If I said anything now, it would just be blabbering while I tried to buy some time to absorb this, so I stayed quiet. Eddie pulled out a pack of cigarettes and shook two out. He lit his and then mine. "Whether or not you think I took a dive, why're you here talking to me, I blew my match and almost lost the tournament for you?"

"Coulda happened to anybody." It was hard to speak while trying to catch my breath.

"Not to me."

"It *did* happen to you!"

"The hell it did. I was paid to lose."

"Horseshit. You were losing, and St. Villard had you beat."

"Really." He tapped some ash from the end of his cigarette. "What makes you say that?"

Was he trying to get me to believe he really could have beaten St. Villard? "He was a stroke up on you at the eighteenth green!"

"I was two down to you with three to go, first time we played. Remember who won that one?" He didn't wait for an answer. "I was *behind.* I wasn't losing. I didn't lose until I made myself lose."

I wasn't buying it. "Even you couldn't purposely keep it that thin on this track, Eddie, staying that close and losing by a stroke. Not on the Stadium. So don't bullshit me."

"Same three hunnerd grand says I go out there tomorrow and shoot sixty-six." He took a deep hit off the cigarette. "Whaddaya say?"

He couldn't intimidate me with that crap. "What do I say? Same three hundred says you can't get that ball to go in and out of that hole again from the same distance!"

Eddie, startled, stared at me for a second then threw back his head and laughed, which quickly turned to coughing as he tried to talk through the smoke he'd forgotten to exhale. "Are you fucking nuts?" He hacked a few more times, then swiped at his eyes and started laughing again. "I missed it too damned close! Almost had a heart attack, I saw that thing headin' for the cup!"

That grass be caddy-whampus, Eddie!

Why was I arguing with him, when I knew it was true? I didn't say anything, preoccupied as I was with trying to keep from soiling myself. The initial shock was passing, and I began thinking about the details, trying to find a way to prove he was making this up. "How come you won your rounds on Friday and Saturday, if you were on the Euros' take?"

"Hadda make sure I was playin' on Sunday, or the deal was off. I'da blown those early ones, you woulda benched me, right?"

"How could I bench you? Everybody plays on Sunday."

He smiled slyly. "Ah, c'mon, Al, I told you plenty'a times: Never bullshit a bullshitter. You tellin' me you wouldn'ta made up some story about me gettin' an attack o' the shits the same way Jack Villard made one up about that Belgian guy?"

Oh, Lord . . . I took a deep drag on the cigarette and asked him how come he slowed things down so much on the sixteenth hole, when all he'd had to do was finish up and lose and he'd have his two hundred thousand.

"Just trying to make everybody think I was freaking out, make the loss look a little better. I didn't know who'd be hitting first on eighteen. If it was me, I wouldn't be able to see what Jack was going to do first, and I'd have to put on the big choke without being able to see if I really needed to. And that's just what happened, but nobody was too surprised when I hit it into the water, 'cuz they'd already seen me getting all nervous."

"You don't *get* nervous."

"You know that, but they don't. Part of keeping a low profile, like I told you. Then when I get all nervous again on eighteen, nobody's surprised anymore."

"But—"

"Hey, c'mon Al, lighten up a little. Like I said, your side got what it wanted, so why—"

"*My* side? Shit, Eddie, *you're* an American, it was your side, too!"

"Horseshit!" he spat with real anger. "It was a goddamned golf game, not a holy war! What, Joe Sixpack gives a shit if twelve multimillionaires in funny-looking pants lose a golf game to a bunch of foreigners? You figure maybe the Third World ain't gonna buy Coke and Marlboros from us anymore?"

"But losing a golf match on purpose, Eddie. Holy shit . . ."

He couldn't see it. He'd lost hundreds of times on purpose. When he was playing low-stakes games against people with half his talent, he'd frequently dump the round to boost his action. Nobody was stupid enough to bet against somebody who never lost, and Eddie was like those professional poker players who thought nothing of occasionally folding with a winning hand just to make it easier to pull off the big bluff later. Back in Georgia, before he'd had to leave on account of that dumb television show, he'd made the mistake of winning so often nobody would play him straight up and he'd had to start inventing crazy-ass games just to get a bet going. He'd offer to play one-handed, or from inside the golf cart, or using ladies' clubs, or even to play left-handed using right-handed clubs, holding them upside down to get the shaft above the club head.

Eddie especially loved cross-country, where he would bet guys he could bogey a hole starting from the roof of the clubhouse or the parking lot or even the men's crapper. One time he played a guy a single hole for a thousand dollars, except that the tee was on the eighth hole at Shandin Hills and the green was the fourteenth at Riverdale. Eddie shot a 24 against his opponent's 25, the other guy having lost a stroke when he failed to make his first try over the I-70 and his ball landed in an open-backed truck hauling onions. How could I give hell to a hustler like that for taking a dive that still allowed us to keep the Ryder Cup in the United States?

"Ah, what the hell, Al," Eddie said, slapping my thigh and getting out of the cart. "You're getting your damned Cup, I'm getting my dough, the press is gonna make you out to be Jesus Christ hisself for holding off the foreigners—everybody's happy, so why're you so freakin' glum?"

Because if you had won your match, I would have made history. I didn't want to talk to him anymore, but I wanted even less to have to go outside. It wasn't the press beatification I was afraid of. It was the crucifixion I was facing from my teammates. All the overheated praise that was about to rain down on them couldn't get their minds off their having smelled an outright victory and seen it slip away.

And they didn't even know Eddie'd blown it on purpose.

"Maybe was da *vugganeeta*," Enrico Senzamio suggested, trying to lighten the atmosphere following Eddie's loss to St. Villard.

The broadcast guys were already calling this the greatest Ryder Cup ever, an awesome display of skill and mental toughness not seen elsewhere in anyone's memory, punctuated by enough colorful behavior to make it the stuff of legends. Left and right, American golfers rose above their games to play against the vastly superior Europeans at levels nobody would have thought them capable of, and to end in a dead heat after such magnificence seemed only fitting and an awesome achievement for our boys. We as Americans should be goshdarned proud of blah blah blah . . .

Right. Try telling that to the ten dejected men sitting in the PGA

West locker room, Robert Carmichael and Eddie Caminetti wisely having chosen to be elsewhere.

"Caminetti blew it."

There. Mack Merriwell had voiced what most of them were feeling.

"It only seems that way," I pointed out, "on account of he went last. All the other lost matches counted just as much."

"That's true," said Jon Markovy, who had lost his Friday pairs match along with Fred Asphal as well as his one-on-one against Migliore today. I hadn't yet told him the true story behind that last one. "I coulda been last and looked like the goat."

"It was Carmichael," Joel Fleckheimer said. "At least you tried, Jon, you and Freddy. At least you played your best, and you killed 'em on Saturday. Carmichael, that horse's ass, he tried to play with his fat fuckin' mouth and lost one he didn't have to." The bitterness and venom in his voice were palpable, and he was trembling with the force of it. He was also conveniently forgetting that Markovy and Asphal had lost their first match largely as a result of their sophomoric psyche war against Jürgen Kurzer and Fabrizio Migliore, which didn't seem to me all that different from why Carmichael had lost to John Wickenhampshire.

"Let's not change the subject, Fleck," Asphal said. "Carmichael didn't have a contractual obligation to us. But we *hired* Caminetti, to play for money. We were paying him to win, to help *us* win."

"Which he didn't," August Hookstratten threw in.

"The hell he didn't!" I didn't at all like the way this was going. "Think about all the stuff he—"

"I'm not payin' him, Al," Merriwell said. "I'm not kickin' in."

I could hear a fly buzzing all the way in back of the room. "What do you mean, you're not paying him?" I said in disbelief. "We had—"

"Neither am I," Asphal said.

As I whipped my head around to look at him, Fleck said, "Same here. We didn't win, that was the deal, and that's all there is to it, far as I'm concerned."

I didn't need to hear from anyone else to know this was a universal sentiment. I was sure they hadn't had this conversation before we convened in the locker room, but somehow they'd all come to focus their frustration and anger on Eddie. For some final confirmation I swiveled around to look at Derek Anouilh, who only shrugged, but whose face made it clear he was standing with his teammates.

I was the only one in the room who knew that Eddie, more than anyone else, had put the Cup back on our mantel. But I couldn't tell them that without also telling them that he'd taken a dive once he knew it was all right to do so. "We still have the Cup," I offered feebly, sorry the instant the first word came out, but I felt I had to try to do something.

"Pure symbolic horseshit and you know it," the normally sunny Merriwell said. "Only reason we have it is on account of us winning it two years ago. Got nothin' to do with what we did this weekend."

Merriwell pretty much summed up how everybody felt, including me, despite the news commentators' hyperbolic blaring about all the great play and the hands-across-the-water bullshit. I'd been excoriated in the papers for the past two days for not playing Robert Carmichael in the doubles rounds, and tomorrow, when the excitement of our "awesome achievement" died down and the Monday-morning second-guessing began in earnest, they'd tear me apart with equal glee for not having benched him or Eddie instead of Asphal on Sunday.

If there's one thing I pride myself on, it's confronting problems head on. The first one was meeting the reporters who were swarming outside the clubhouse, desperate to make their deadlines and crazed that we were taking so long.

The second was delivering the bad news to Eddie.

I hadn't been this tense and anxious since before my final match two years ago when I'd last played in the Ryder, the one we'd won to retrieve the Cup from the Europeans on their own soil. I'd come through, which was probably one of the main reasons I was chosen as captain for this one.

I picked Eddie's room to get together in rather than mine so I could terminate the meeting by leaving whenever I wanted to rather than have to kick Eddie out. He didn't look all that upset when he opened the door for me, maybe just a little pensive. But for someone so consistently authoritative and self-confident, this alteration in his demeanor made him look like a different person.

We sat on opposite sides of a round table near the window. I tried to make it sound like it should have been obvious that he wasn't going to get his money. "Sorry this didn't work out for you, Eddie. You got enough to cover the bet with St. Villard?"

He scratched at his chin with his thumb, not responding immediately. "What're you talkin' about, Al."

It wasn't a question, but a demand for me to explain myself. "I'm asking, do you have enough cash to pay him off. Those checks you carry around with you, will they cover it?"

He stopped scratching. "You telling me you don't have my money with you?"

"What money?" I said, all innocence and sincere puzzlement.

He didn't insult my intelligence by explaining what he meant, but leaned forward and said very slowly, "Tell me what the fuck you're talking about, Al, and quit bullshitting me, okay? You're no damned good at it."

I considered continuing the sham, but trying to put one past Eddie Caminetti made about as much sense as sneaking a pound of Limburger past a bloodhound. I let out a sigh and slumped back in the chair. "We're not paying you, Eddie." Good team player that I was, I didn't tell him that I disagreed with the guys. I wasn't sure I did.

"That much I already figured out. Why not?"

"The deal was, you were going to help us win the Cup."

"The hell it was."

"Now what're *you* talkin' about!"

"Your exact words, Bellamy: *You play every match I put you in, you get paid, win or lose, but only if we keep the Cup.* Don't bother to argue, either. I can remember every detail of every bet I ever made going back to grade school." He waited to see if I was going to contest the point, and when I didn't, he went on. "Every time we talked about it, you used the same words: *Keep the Cup,* you said. *Help us keep the Cup.* That's all anybody ever said. Not win it; *keep* it."

"It was just a goddamned expression, Eddie! F'Chrissakes, of *course* we meant to win!"

"So you want to renegotiate the deal now? Is that it? Change the terms after the fact?" I had no answer for him. I was no Robert Carmichael, easily able to ignore logic and blithely argue pure nonsense in the face of facts to the contrary. I also think that he'd figured out by now that my heart really wasn't in this, that I was just playing the good manager and it was all out of my hands, and the reason he continued to argue anyway was probably just to give me ammunition in going back to the team one more time. Maybe he thought that their initial response was just an overreaction to the shock of not winning the Cup flat out when it had been so close, and that they would be more amenable to persuasion once that wore off a little.

But his anger was no act. "I helped you keep it, Al, and I did a helluva lot more than just play my matches. You want me to run down the list, shit that wasn't even in our deal?"

"Jesus, Eddie, you lost your last match!"

"I'd already done my part. You gonna tell me I didn't help you keep the Cup?"

"You were supposed to help us *win!*"

"Don't start that shit again, and don't blame me." He paused, making sure I was paying complete attention, then pointed a finger at me and said, "*You* fucked it up, Bellamy! You and your bleeding-heart team-mates!"

"What the hell are you talking about!"

"I told you for a dead damned certainty Carmichael was gonna lose on Sunday. You played him anyway, and he lost. You'da done it my way, you would'a had your precious point!"

"What we did was the right thing to do. You said so yourself."

"It was right for everybody's *conscience*, not for winning. I told you in that meeting I was a hired gun. Shit, you didn't ask for Carmichael, you got stuck with him, but you *hired* me! For me it was business, and you had as much responsibility to me as you did to Carmichael!"

I didn't understand that last part, and said so.

Eddie cleared it up for me. "You thought our deal was that I didn't get paid unless you won, right?"

"Right . . ."

"Then you had no right to fuck with my money by playing Carmichael! You were a *fiduciary*, Bellamy, and you had an obligation to me to do everything you could to win. Far as I was concerned, soon as you failed to keep your part of the bargain by benching Asphal and playing that flaming asshole instead, I was free and clear of our contract."

"So if you thought the deal was off, how come you're still asking for the hundred grand?" Hah! I had him!

"*Fuck* the hunnerd, Al!" He waited until the self-satisfied smile left my face, then added, "Won't be the first time I got stiffed."

I thought my heart would break right on the spot. After all my cajoling to get him to play in the Ryder, after all he did for us and me believing with all my heart that he would have given up two hundred thousand dollars if Fleckheimer hadn't won his match, to him I was now just another cheap welsher refusing to pay up. I was nearly speechless under the weight of that shame, but I wasn't about to leave this room just to carry it around with me for the rest of my life. "We had a contract, Eddie. A contract! We give you a hundred grand, you help us win. You broke the contract, and you don't get paid. Now, maybe there's some disagreement over the interpretation of that contract, and maybe you got a little technical about just what I meant by *keeping the Cup*—"

His look told me I needn't bother to finish that line of thought, but I had one last round in the clip. "Least none of them took a dive."

He smiled for the first time since I'd walked into the room, but it wasn't pleasant, just grim. "Don't come over all self-righteous with me, Bubba. *You* were the guys ready to pay a hunnerd grand to bring in a ringer and *I'm* the cheatin' bastard?"

"There was nothing unethical or illegal about that!"

"Good. Then you won't mind my calling up the *New York Times* and telling *them* about it." That was my cue to stay quiet for a while.

Eddie folded his arms and shook his head. "I told you flat out I play for money, and I don't give a rat's ass how I look or how the team looks, 'cuz it wasn't my team. I was the hired help; have club, will travel. I do the job, I get paid. I don't, I don't."

This wasn't going well. I made one last attempt to put some positive spin on it for him. For my conscience, really. "What the hell, Eddie, you got your two hundred large from the Euros." Which was a hundred better than he thought he'd get when he agreed to participate.

"No I didn't. Way they figured, it was a throwaway, on account of it didn't give 'em the win. So they stiffed me, too."

I just sat there, staring at him stupidly, no idea what to say, as if there were any words I could conjure up to take the sting off this situation for him. Eddie Caminetti, the greatest con artist in history, wasn't going to make a dime off the Ryder Cup he hadn't wanted to play in the first place.

Resigned now to not getting paid by either side, Eddie stood up and turned toward the window. "I always told you, Al, like I tell 'em all: Anybody thinks I put one over on him, they don't gotta pay." *Which makes you no better—he didn't have to add out loud—than that piece of shit Carmichael who didn't pay me either when I beat him fair and square.*

We weren't friends anymore but I had to ask him, so I'd know for sure. "Tell me the real reason you slowed it down on sixteen, Eddie, and why you waited so long to putt on eighteen."

He hadn't needed to do anything to make his dive look good; he was a nobody playing against the best golfer in the world, and all he needed was to get on the eighteenth green in three and then two-putt against St. Villard's par. All this stuff about looking nervous and jumpy, freaking under the pressure? Baloney. He may have slowed things down, but he looked just as ice-cold and nerveless as he ever had, so I wasn't buying his nonsense explanation. I *had* to know if he was really preserving the Cup for us, but not admitting it for fear of my thinking he was at heart a softy after all.

"I told you already," he said, fatigue lacing his voice. "I had to make it look like I was falling apart, like—"

"Now *you* don't bullshit a bullshitter! We both know that's a crock, so why don't you just—"

"Excuse me!" he said, whirling away from the window to face me, his eyes flashing. "Do I owe you explanations now, Bellamy? You maybe want to get some more golf advice outta me while you're kickin' me in the balls?"

He wasn't going to answer. Or he already had and didn't see any need to repeat it, even though his answer didn't make sense to me. Either way, my license to continue this conversation had just been revoked.

"Win the Cup," Eddie said half to himself, repeating my words but with such disdain they sounded silly, like some high school football mantra chanted by perky blond cheerleaders while their team was down forty with two minutes left to play. He put his hands on the table and leaned across it, into my face. "Tell me you went into this believing you had a holy chance in hell of even coming close to the Euros, Al. Tell me that and you can walk out of here with a clear conscience."

Fifty different possible comebacks ricocheted around my brain, some of them pretty good zingers, but only one came out. "I can't do that, Eddie."

He just stared at me without speaking, but I could hear what he was thinking anyway: *Bet your ass you can't. Because you never believed for one goddamned second you'd come home with that Cup.*

I looked away, and that's when I noticed that his bags were already packed and sitting by the door. Without another glance at me, he turned and walked across the room, opening the door and holding it with his foot as he picked up the bags. Then, just like that, Eddie Caminetti walked out of my life as abruptly as he'd walked in.

I could hardly eat for days, I was so torn up about how we'd treated him at the end. Eddie Caminetti robbing the United States of its out-and-out win? That's like blaming Merriwell for our loss in Italy six years ago just because his missed putt came at the end, when it was really my fault but my screw-ups got buried much earlier in the tournament. If it weren't for Eddie, we would have lost this one by at least four full points, as everybody expected we were going to because of how much better the Europeans had been playing for the past two tour seasons than we had. All the pairings were his, he scoped out the whole European team and told us exactly how to play them, and he was the real winner of his two team matches. He made sure we didn't let Boom-Boom Harriman on the team, and he tried as hard as he could to keep Robert Carmichael from playing as well. All because he'd made a deal and that was the kind of guy he was. As opposed to the kind of guys we were.

Eddie earned his money, even if he did take "keep the Cup" a little too literally. I dragged him kicking and screaming into a tournament he didn't want any part of, made a deal to pay him for it, then threw him out into the street without a dime.

So much for the most honorable sport in the world.

Part 3

....

CHAPTER TWENTY-SEVEN

It haunted me, this business with Caminetti, and for months I wasn't able to let go of the unanswered questions that insisted on swirling their way through my brain, but at least I had them narrowed down to just a couple of possibilities.

One was that the unthinkable had happened to him, that he got a bad case of Ryder Cup syndrome and crumbled as the enormity of it all finally struck him. Maybe he hadn't ever intended to make good on his deal with the Euros to take the dive, not wanting to look like a schmuck in front of the entire world, but really and truly fell apart, brought to his knees by the kind of pressure that makes grown men upchuck in the middle of a round. No way he'd admit that to me, so he figured he might as well tell me that he dumped it on purpose.

Or maybe he just plain got beat. Yeah, something as simple as that. No nerves or shakes, he just couldn't pull it off against someone as good as St. Villard.

Then again, maybe he had told me the complete truth, that he lost his last match for no other reason than because he felt obligated to make good on his deal with the Europeans, free to forget about *our* deal because we'd forgotten about *him* when we put Carmichael in on Sunday.

There was a correct answer in there somewhere. But there were some things that didn't jibe at all, such as how could he tell me he broke our contract because I broke it first, and in the same breath tell me we owed him his money because he'd actually *fulfilled* the contract? I chalked it off to just Eddie being Eddie and trying to have it both ways, depending on which particular line of reasoning happened to suit him. So that one didn't bother me all that much, although I wish I had thought of it while we were arguing.

But here's the one that was really killing me: What if we really had needed him to tie or win his match in order to keep the Cup?

What if we had been even or behind in tournament points instead of ahead, and the Cup had come down to his round against St. Villard? Would he have gone ahead and won it, getting our hundred grand for himself but sacrificing the two hundred from the Europeans? Or was he truly the ultimate hustler, and would have gone down regardless, without caring what anybody thought of him? Would he really have thrown us to the dogs like that and allowed himself to become the most reviled American in all of sports?

I don't think he would have. And while I prefer to think maybe there was some tiny modicum of honor somewhere in his moth-eaten conscience, there was another, more practical reason. After all, how much action would he get back on his home turf if everyone in the country despised him? It wouldn't take much to hate him. Hell, they ridiculed Nick Faldo half into the ground because he hadn't won a major, even though he was the tour's leading money-winner. One of those fish-wrapping British tabloids even called him Nick *Foldo*. So what would it take to get everybody in the United States to hate Eddie Caminetti for blowing the Ryder Cup and humiliating his home country? Who would lay any action with him after that?

There was no way to know what he would have done in that situation, so eventually, albeit slowly, I got past the point where it troubled me on a daily basis, and soon I stopped thinking about it altogether.

Both Jacques St. Villard and I had played extremely well at Augusta the following spring. We were neck and neck down the stretch, battling for first place in the most prestigious tournament in the golfing world, at least for individual play. Neither of us would have guessed that Fred Asphal would come tearing up the fairways behind us, taking insane chances, making birdie on five of the last seven holes and winning the damned thing, St. Villard and I tying for second place. It would probably go down as the most exciting Masters ever, and it wiped out any lingering memories of Asphal sitting out the last day of the Ryder Cup.

That night, after our mandatory appearances at the post-tournament press conference, St. Villard and I and our wives had dinner together. The string of occurrences at the Ryder had been so bizarre that, somehow, most everybody on both sides had come to the conclusion that it had been too complex a web for anybody to successfully sustain any assessment of blame against anybody else. So we just kind of collectively said *what the hell* and forgave one another en masse so we could all be friends again, much to the relief of everybody, especially the wives and girlfriends.

At dinner, we talked about some of the unusual things that had happened to people we both knew. Stephen "Boom-Boom" Harriman wrote his autobiography, *The Longest Drive*, and now lectures to schoolchildren on the horrors of substance abuse. Hey, if it keeps him on the wagon . . .

Robert Carmichael, after fighting exercise and everything else his string of eventually fired doctors told him to do, finally found a solution for his back problem. The one doctor who managed to last more than three months broke down and reluctantly sold him some weird and terribly expensive concoction he'd found in Mexico, telling Carmichael to rub it into his lower back vigorously for ten minutes prior to beginning a round of golf and then ice down afterward to "leach the near-toxic stuff out once it had done its job." Miraculously, it eased the awful inflammation and reduced the pain so much he was soon playing thirty-six holes a day. When he insisted on knowing what was in it, the doc confessed that it was a harmless mixture of silly herbs with a dash of some exotic-smelling stuff he got from his daughter, a flake of the first water who instantly latched on to whatever the macro-kablotto fad of the week was, the wackier the better, and that particular week it happened to have been some kind of voodoo involving smells.

Before Carmichael could haul him up on ethics charges, the doc explained that all he was trying to do was get Carmichael to give himself a vigorous lower-back massage to stimulate the area and get some blood flowing to his muscles, then ice down after the round to reduce inflammation. Carmichael thought about that for a good ten minutes, then formed a partnership with the physician to manufacture and sell Flame-Out, an astounding remedy the government doesn't want you to know about because it would throw the entire twenty-billion-dollar back-care industry into turmoil and destabilize the American medical infrastructure, but you can have it direct from the manufacturer for the incredible low price of $19.95. The directions called for the user to rub it robustly into the lower back until it disappeared, but for no less than ten minutes, then ice down afterward to leach out the etc., etc.

Although getting off to a vigorous start by claiming that Flame-Out helped the United States win the Ryder Cup, the company went belly up after its star athlete and endorser, Robert Carmichael, who never revealed that he owned the company, failed to make the cut in the next four tournaments and couldn't get another pro to stand up for the miracle cream. Worse, even though the FDA hadn't been able to stop him from purveying the worthless stuff because it didn't contain any medicine and was therefore not under their jurisdiction, the FTC brought suit against him for fraudulent claims of health benefits and deceptive packaging, serving formal notice on the PGA that any winnings of his were to be forwarded forthwith to an escrow account pending the outcome of the proceedings, which were estimated to last at least seven years.

Frieda Fleckheimer got her own talk show, a midday slot during which she interviewed the parents of celebrities and got them to reveal embarrassing secrets about their illustrious progeny. The show was partially financed by Joel Fleckheimer, who'd had it written into his mother's contract that the show would be terminated should she make good on her promise to show baby pictures of her son on the pilot or any other segment.

Talk eventually turned to The Kid, who disappeared from the golf scene as abruptly as he had entered it. Remember earlier when I told you Fred Asphal made more money on tour the next year than Anouilh did?

During the lull following the Ryder, the swirl of publicity surrounding Derek Anouilh and his extraordinary achievements devolved from the heady and pulse-quickening to the crazy and downright stupid. Here was the top money-maker in the world, by a record-setting margin, a guy on his way to becoming the greatest golfer in history, but no matter what he did, there seemed to be some kind of weird compulsion to crank up the expectation level even further.

Things began to tip over into the realm of total lunacy when sportswriters who should have known better started talking about Anouilh winning all four majors the following season: that's the British and U.S. Opens, the Masters and the PGA Championship. This, of course, is essentially an impossibility, owing to the genetically baked-in fickleness of golf, which has no rival in any other sport. Just ask Tom Kite, 1989 Player of the Year, 1997 Ryder Cup captain and number two on the *all-time* money list, who won only a single major in his entire storied career. Or Lee Janzen, who won the PGA in 1993 and then couldn't make it into the top twenty in a single tournament the very next year. Or Nick Price, who won the British and the PGA barely a month apart, but only after completely missing the cut at the U.S. Open.

Winning a single major in a career is a wondrous achievement. Winning two in a year is monumental. More than that is a miracle and is rarely even whispered about in polite company. There are only four golfers in history ever to have won each of the majors during *different* years in their multi-decade careers, something even the immortal Arnold Palmer didn't do, and yet here were these experts burning up their word processors with talk of Anouilh taking them all in one season, the Grand Slam of golf.

The worst part of it was, Anouilh wasn't denying he could do it. To sportswriters sick of their columns reading more like police blotters than sports news, this was like pouring a boatload of cattle entrails into a swimming pool full of starving sharks. The resulting frenzy made him scared even to get out on the course. Whenever he failed to birdie a hole and produced only a lousy, stinking par, on-course television commentators would groan their anxiety about whether this was the beginning of the end, and was Derek Anouilh finally washed up.

He decided to take a few weeks to relax, in itself an extraordinary occurrence: The missed tournaments were one thing, but it probably cost him ten million in lost outings and other non-tour income. As a favor to his agent, though, whose wife was on the board of about four thousand charities, he agreed to appear in a public-service announcement being filmed at a racetrack in Mississippi, something about him exhorting frantically horny teenagers not to have sex because it was bad for them. They stuck him in an Indy car, gave him a few pointers and turned him loose, talking him through his first few laps over a two-way radio while the film crew set up their gear.

After getting the feel of the thing, he cranked it up a little, his agent watching nervously behind the rail as his meal ticket zoomed around at close to a hundred miles per hour. The agent started palpitating visibly as The Kid's speed kept climbing, and he practically begged the track superintendent watching from the tower to order him back to the pit over the radio. But Anouilh ignored him and kept notching it up, and one of the local racing veterans got on the horn to talk him through it so at least he wouldn't kill himself, because if he did, his agent would probably end up owning the track once all the lawsuits were settled.

Don't worry. It doesn't end the way you think.

Before too long even the pros watching the action started to look a little pale. Here was the most popular athlete on the planet—maybe the most popular human being—taking turns so fast his tires were hanging just on the edge of breaking free, squealing frighteningly and flirting so closely with catastrophe people started to wince and turn their heads away.

About two laps later, every eye was back on the track. The tires still squealed around the turns, but The Kid never lost it, staying right on the verge but never slipping over. It was as if Anouilh had some kind of disaster meter mounted on the dash and he was hugging the redline but never quite hitting it. He kept it up for nearly fifteen minutes, during which the course superintendent signaled frantically for someone to for God's sake get a goddamned timer going on this lunatic.

Anouilh may have been watching the disaster meter, but he wasn't watching the gas gauge, and somewhere on the back S-turn he ran out. He'd only had a small amount of fuel to start with, to keep down the flames in case he wrecked the car. As the onlookers began running and driving to the far side of the track to pick him up, Anouilh slowly squirmed his way out of the cramped cockpit, took off his helmet and just stood there staring at the car, one hand on a support strut, his jaw hanging open.

He was so blissed out, I'm told, so completely amped, he literally couldn't speak for several minutes. He motioned everybody away, and while they drifted off in confusion and eventually returned to the pit area by cutting across the infield, he walked back along the full length of the track. By the time the onlookers arrived, somebody was coming out of the control shed scratching his head in wonderment and looking at a piece of paper.

With Anouilh still a quarter mile away, the man came up to the group and said, "Who the fuck was that? The golfer kid?"

"Why?" asked Anouilh's agent.

The man looked down at the paper he was holding. "Sumbitch came two seconds from breaking the course record. How long's he been driving?"

" 'Bout twenty minutes," the agent said.

"No, shithead. What I meant, how long's he been driving race cars?"

"I *know* what you meant," the agent said, "and I'm telling you: about twenty minutes."

Which is how Derek Anouilh came to quit the tour and devote himself to auto racing with the same passion we all thought exclusively reserved for golf.

The rest is the history that was likely to be made in the next few years.

As I said, there was a general air of forgiven bygones surrounding us veterans of the last Ryder. Which is not to say that we didn't throw a few friendly jabs whenever the opportunity presented itself.

"I know what you did at the Ryder, Jacques," I said slyly to St. Villard when Louise and Nicolette had gone off for one of those mysterious communal bathroom trips that seem to be for women what bowling night is for men, a bonding kind of thing the other side couldn't hope to fathom.

"Did? What I did?"

"Come on." I smiled to let him know I wasn't angry. "Mrs. Bellamy may've raised some ugly kids, but she din't raise no stupid ones. With Eddie Caminetti?"

He continued to stare at me in confusion, then broke into a sheepish grin of his own as he saw that further evasion would be fruitless. "Ahhh . . ." He flapped his hand at me dismissively. "Was a, what you say, a harmless little *pronque*, no?"

"*A harmless little prank?*" I echoed incredulously. "You call two hundred grand a harmless little prank?"

"What is a *grand*, Ah-*lain?*"

"Dollars, Jacques." I puffed out an exasperated breath. "You know damned well what it is. Two hundred thousand dollars. A million francs."

His smile was replaced by a puzzled frown. A real one. "What two hundred thousand dollars? What are you speaking about?"

It was my turn to be confused. "What are *you* speaking about?"

"I am talking about Braunschweiger! You know what a jokester he is, that Bavarian buffoon." I just stared at him, and he looked down in embarrassment. "Ah, so he makes a small phone call to your Monsieur Caminetti." He looked up at me with a mischievous grin. "At three in the night! He wakes him up, so what? Just was a joke!" He clapped me on the shoulder several times to get me to lighten up.

"A phone call?" I felt my eyes growing wide of their own volition. "What about you paying Eddie Caminetti to lose his match!"

It took a moment for that to sink in, then *his* eyes started expanding. *"Merde!"* he exclaimed, banging his fist on the table, then drew slowly back, snarling, "You dare to accuse *me* . . . ?" in Gallic indignation.

I watched in amazement as his face grew red. The sonofabitch wasn't kidding. "You mean you didn't . . ."

He looked away, snatched the napkin from his lap and slapped it down on the table. He pushed his chair back, and as he tried to stand up, I grabbed his arm. "Jacques, please, sit down! Please . . . ?"

He paused in mid-rise, and I nodded hopefully toward his seat. He must have seen something pleading and vulnerable in my look, because he slowly sat back down, but the scowl didn't leave his face. When he had calmed slightly and settled in tentatively against the seat back, I leaned in toward him and said, "Jacques, please, listen'a me." He didn't respond. "Don't get mad, okay? But I gotta know something." He still wasn't responding. *"Okay?"* I demanded.

He gave me one of those noncommittal European shrugs: *So far I'm not moving, but no promises.*

"Jacques, just between you and me, did you guys have any kind of, uh, any kind of an *arrangement* with Eddie Caminetti?" I could see him start to get his dander up again, and I pumped my open palms at him to keep him calm. "Take it easy, Jacques. I'm not accusing you of anything. Just tell me, f'Chrissakes!"

Perhaps seeing some real pain in my expression, he softened noticeably. "I swear to you, I never spoke weeza man, eh? Only to tell him a putt wass good, or nize shot, or go fuck yourself, you American peegdog." I kept peering into his eyes, not laughing at his joke. "I swear, Ah-*lain,*" he said sincerely. "On my honor."

Louise and Nicolette were returning to the table. We both leaned back in our chairs and tried to act normal. Jacques, shaken as he was, managed to pull it off, but it took Louise, in her quiet wisdom, less than five minutes to read me, gracefully extricate us and get me the hell out of there.

It was killing me. Like finding out after fifty years that you were adopted or that your wife was a foreign spy or that those awful headaches you suffered for half your life were just because of tight underwear. When assumptions so basic that you don't even think about them are suddenly overturned, it's disorienting and frightening, and it makes you start to wonder about other things you've maybe taken for granted.

Eddie's account of a bribe from the Euros to take a dive had been complete bullshit. I was convinced of that now. In a subsequent conversation with St. Villard, I told him the entire story of how we had paid Eddie to play for us. He took it in stride after he thought about it carefully, because there was really no reason it would have been improper for us to have done so. All the other U.S. players had plenty of money and could take time off for no pay to participate in the Ryder. Eddie was a working-class stiff, so what was the big deal? In this spirit of openness, St. Villard would have told me if they had tried to pull something as well.

I know what you're thinking. Paying a guy to win is one thing, but bribing an opponent to dump a match was a whole 'nother smoke. Had they really done it, there's no reason St. Villard would have admitted it to me, right? Right. But as Eddie liked to say, *Trust me on this one.* It never happened.

So what did? Why did Eddie blow his last match when he could have won it and gotten our hundred thousand?

Now you're thinking, maybe he didn't dump it. Maybe he just plain lost it, and made up this ridiculous story so I wouldn't think he hadn't been good enough to win. And I told you a little while ago that this possibility had occurred to me as well.

But come on. You figure he'd rather have me think he betrayed his team than just made a lousy putt? Eddie didn't pride himself on being a good golfer, he prided himself on being an honest one. So much so that he always offered to call off a bet, no questions asked, if the other guy thought he'd been misled. None of this *Tin Cup*, Hollywood-style bullshit where I bet you I can hit it farther than you and then I knock it onto a paved road and watch it roll for two miles. Not Eddie Caminetti.

Which, of course, didn't answer any of my questions, only added a whole stack of new ones.

I had to go see him.

CHAPTER TWENTY-EIGHT

July in southern Florida is a distinctly unfortunate confluence of time and place. Being native to Arizona, I was used to dry air, and here on the outskirts of Fort Lauderdale, as Fat Albert had put it, it felt like you could drown just walking along the street.

I went to the Embassy golf club in Hallandale and drove into the near-deserted parking lot. A black teenaged boy on the practice green was alternately putting and swatting at the flies that buzzed around lazily in the late-morning heat. He didn't even look up as I walked into one of the doors of the shabby, low-slung building that stretched from the putting green to the first tee. The room was empty except for a thin guy wiping glasses behind the bar and two men talking down at the far end. One of them, exceptionally well dressed in expensive country-club clothes, turned at the sound of the screen door slamming shut behind me. He tilted his head to one side to get the sun from the window behind me out of his eyes.

"Al!" he called out, then mumbled something to the other guy and walked toward me.

"Danny," I said back to him. "Whaddaya say?"

As we shook, he put one hand on my arm, like a professional politician or a corporate CEO at an investors' meeting. "Good to see you, fella! C'mon over here 'n' siddown!"

We took a table off toward a corner and made a minute or two of small talk, then I asked him if Eddie was anywhere around. His previously animated features suddenly quieted, and he furrowed his brow. "Jeez, didn't you know?"

My heart sank. "Don't tell me he moved again."

"He's dead, Al."

The first time I'd been in this place I hadn't noticed the four, old-style fans that hung from the ceiling. They didn't seem like much, turning so slowly they hardly called attention to themselves, but they did move the air around a bit, just enough to keep the interior from becoming intolerable. They were comforting in a way, too, maintaining their constant motion even as the world immediately around them seemed determined just to give up and skid to a halt in the stultifying heat. Maybe that was why I liked grandfather clocks so much, their faithful pendulums seeming not only to track time but to actually keep it going. No matter what lay ahead, moving forward was still preferable to stopping.

It was a heart attack or a stroke or something, Danny explained, three months before. He shook his head as he told me that hardly anybody had even noted his passing other than a prefab, eight-line obit in the local rag.

I had trouble accepting that Eddie Caminetti was dead. It was like hearing that Gandhi or Churchill had died; you'd never felt that they'd been real, living human beings in the first place, so how could they die? "Guy was barely in his late forties, looked pretty healthy . . ."

"Ah, way we figure it, musta been the excitement."

"What excitement?"

"You kidding? The guy got home from that Ryder thing, you never saw so much action in your whole life. Linin' up twelve deep to play him, they were. Play the loser, the big choker, the *patzer* who couldn't handle the pressure." Danny smiled broadly and some life began to creep back into his face. "He musta been clearin' ten, twenty g's a week, guys happy to give it to him just so they could tell their grandkids or sumpin', I guess. Fifteen, sixteen hours a day he's playin' golf. Got so's he wasn't even enjoyin' it, like he didn't even wanna play. But guys—hard-lookin' guys—they come eight hundred miles to play, prob'ly wasn't smart he tells 'em to piss off, so he played." Danny pulled a pack of Dunhill cigarettes out of his pocket, lit up with what looked to be a solid-gold lighter and blew a cloud of smoke into the still, sultry air. "You ask me, s'what killed the poor bastard."

He held out the pack and I took one, trying to keep my hand steady as he lit it for me. He clicked the lighter shut, and I inhaled deeply. *They die young, those who burn too bright,* I thought to myself.

"Huh?"

I must have mumbled it out loud. "Nothin'. Where's he buried, Danny?"

He told me, then I nodded dumbly, excused myself and stepped out into the sun, walking to the bench where Eddie and I had sat and talked so many lifetimes ago. I looked at the spot he'd occupied, pictured him jumping up to grab a club so he could make a point, accidentally getting excited and then catching himself in the nick of time, to make sure I didn't think he really gave a shit.

Just remember one thing, Al: I'm a hustler, plain and simple. Not a glory boy playin' for God and country. So don't be makin' any assumptions about what you think I might or might not do, see?

You should see his grave. It didn't have a regular headstone, but one of those fancy granite slabs the golf courses with upscale pretensions put on the tee boxes to tell you the yardage. EDDIE CAMINETTI, it said in simple carved letters. LYING ONE, UNDER THE GREEN. Lying one. A pun?

Sitting there on the cool grass, my back against a tree, it crept up on me again, that question: Would Caminetti have gone ahead and blown his match had it really counted? I could practically hear him answering me from beneath the ground: *I'm a hustler, Al, not a patriot, so quit blowin' smoke up both our asses and just deal with it!*

Don't understand why I'd agree to lose in front of all those millions watching? Hah! Be a hero at the Ryder Cup, who in his right mind would play me for money again? This way, everybody in the country figures I choke on the big ones. Know how much money I won since I got back home? From complete strangers?

Okay, Eddie, I get it now. Quit beating on me already. But if you slowed down on sixteen to look nervous, why the hell didn't you *act* like you were nervous? There was a full hole open between you and number eighteen and no excuse for the delay, so why didn't you at least pretend to look as though you were about to toss your cookies? Why'd you let Fred Asphal go back and check on how Fleckheimer was doing, promising you'd wait until he got back before hitting your next shot? Why didn't you sweat or frown or bend over and puke or— Wait a minute.

Wait just a goddamned minute! Let Asphal go see what was doing? What was the point of that?

It came to me then, all of it, and I let my head drop back hard against the tree trunk, not even feeling the pain of the bark biting into my scalp.

Eddie didn't want to tee off on eighteen until he had a better handle on what the outcome of Fleckheimer's match was likely to be. That's why he dragged his ass on sixteen. It had nothing to do with waiting to see if he really had to fake the big choke and certainly nothing to do with all this bullshit about needing a drink or pretending to have a sudden case of Ryder Cup yips. It had to do with stalling until Fleckheimer's match ended.

Because he wasn't going to let us lose the Cup. It's what I'd always wanted to believe, but I couldn't prove it to myself. If Fleckheimer had tied his match against Firth, Eddie would have tied his against St. Villard. If Fleckheimer had lost, Eddie would have won. Either way, he wasn't going to let us lose, even though it would have cost him a lot of action back home.

But Joel did win, and Eddie was free to dump his match and *still* give us the Cup.

When Asphal returned and recounted what was going on back at sixteen, Frieda Fleckheimer going toe to toe with Andrew Firth, everybody laughed but Eddie. To him it wasn't funny. He needed for it to *end*, and here were Fleckheimer and Firth still farting around in the middle of the fairway while he and St. Villard were practically done. He found himself in a desperate situation: What the hell was he supposed to do now, having run out of ways to delay his match? He had to make a quick decision and get on with play.

Instead of going for a birdie, he'd set up for a par instead by dumping his first shot in the water and then getting to the green on his next shot. Why? To keep the match even, rather than getting ahead of St. Villard. If he was in the lead and Fleckheimer won, he'd have to play worse than a blind man in order to lose the hole, and nobody was going to believe it was an honest loss after the way he'd been playing all day.

But if he let St. Villard go up a stroke, Eddie could then make the match go either way afterward by making par or bogey, which wouldn't raise suspicion. That was the safest way to get off the eighteenth tee and still have his options open depending on Fleckheimer's match, and that's exactly what he did. Then he'd stalled again on the green with all his surveying bullshit and pretending to come consult with me. Even as he set up to make his putt, he didn't strike the ball until hearing the noise that told him Fleckheimer had just won his match. At that point, relaxed and confident, smiling that shit-eating smile at me, he'd blown his putt, losing the match by a single shot. Nobody in the world questioned the outcome, and Eddie thought he had still had his hundred grand from us. And, as the icing on the cake, he had the whole planet believing he was a world-class choker and rushing to his door to take his money, leaving behind huge donations to his bank account instead.

Now, in case you don't think what Eddie did on those last holes was all that impressive from a golf-skill point of view, let me digress and fill you in on something: There are no certainties in this game. It's like a quantum effect. I can pretty much predict within four strokes what a pro golfer is going to shoot in a particular round. That's less than a 6-percent error, and I'm willing to lay money on it. But I wouldn't bet two cents on exactly what will happen on an individual shot unless it's a putt within three feet.

The definition of a good golfer is one whose probability of hitting his next shot well is high, but that tells you little about what *will* happen when he hits that shot, only what is *likely* to.

Take a top-notch pro who's played his home course three times a week for ten years. He's birdied every hole countless times and even eagled a bunch. But has he ever birdied every one of them in a single round and shot a 54? Never. Not even once. I doubt anyone ever has on a regulation course. That would pretty much be a perfect round, even though a lower score is theoretically possible, and in the entire history of the sport—and we're talking *billions* of rounds of golf here—it's never happened.

That's how flaky golf is. And yet there was Eddie, banking on the fact that he could control the outcome of a match to within a single stroke. I'll be honest with you and tell you that I truly don't believe he could pull that off again even one time out of three. He was good, but nobody could be *that* good. There's just too much uncertainty inherent in the game, like the wind, temperature, humidity, the surface of the grass— and that's not even mentioning the eight hundred separate internal factors that affect the player himself.

No, that strategy of Eddie's was not evidence of his skills. It was a testament to his extraordinary self-confidence. He hadn't been kidding during that dinner at the Ritz when he spoke about believing, deep down, that the next shot he hit was going to be perfect, even if that mind-set had just failed him ten times in a row. For him there was no contradiction, no dereliction of logic. Eddie didn't just believe it would be perfect, he *knew* it would be, and no amount of screwing up could dissuade him from that abiding conviction for the next shot.

Danny's description of the aftermath of "Eddie's big choke" at the Ryder started to fall into place now. People figured that the way to beat him was to make the bets so big he got scared and crumbled under the pressure. And every time he beat them anyway, they assumed it wasn't that Eddie was really immune to the pressure, it was just because the stakes weren't big enough, so they raised them higher still, and when he won again, they just threw even more money into the pot. Eddie was getting absurd breaks on strokes, people wanted to play him so bad. Not just to win money, but to show this unpatriotic sonofabitch what it was like to get beat by a *real* American! He dumped matches all over the place just to keep them all guessing, but that was pure investment money, and the returns had been astronomical.

Okay, here's what I'm left with: Am I now supposed to believe that Eddie Caminetti, of the Embassy Golf and Mud Club of Bumfuck, Florida, manipulated the greatest golf tournament in the world just to boost the bets when he got back home? That he deliberately made himself look as if he had cracked under the pressure in order to draw in the big fish who were too damned stupid to smell a con when they saw one?

Just as stupid as I had been?

Who knows. Fact is, Eddie loved the game of golf. Hell, he was probably the first person in the world to literally golf himself to death, if you don't count the two-legged bags of cholesterol who finally blow their tickers walking from the tee back to their carts.

Well, so what if Eddie had pulled the ultimate hustle, opening up a nearly unlimited spigot of cash without ever having violated his deal with us, thereby remaining a man of his word, which was the only thing more important to him than the game. As far as he was concerned, his job was to help us retain the Cup. Once we had it in the bag, his responsibility ended, so he lived up to that contract. But rather than tell me how he'd dumped the match with St. Villard to boost his action at home, he'd chosen instead to let me think he had a separate deal on the side with the Euros. And I now knew why.

If I suspected that he had planned all this out from the get-go, I could claim that he hadn't taken our arrangement seriously and instead had tricked me into it just so he could work the big con. That would mean it wasn't a legitimate deal but part of some other, hidden agenda, and I could make a valid claim under his ironclad don't-pay-if-you-think-I-misled-you warranty. But if I thought that he had gone into this just as we had discussed, and only afterward did someone else come along and make a better offer that would still let him fulfill his obligations to us, then I should understand that this was the normal course of business and I ought not to have a problem with it. In Eddie's particular method of accounting, there was nothing worse than being a welsher, but there was nothing wrong with sticking to the letter of a deal, even if the spirit perhaps wasn't quite in sync with that letter. That was just business, a trickier variation of *caveat emptor*. He hadn't cared a lick about our hundred grand, and only put up an argument to deflect me away from the truth.

Bottom line, Eddie did right by everybody. But mostly, he did right by himself.

And now he was lying one, under the green, with a clear conscience. How many of us truly know if we parred life before we die? I'll have to ask him when I get there. Assuming, of course, hustling's allowed in heaven.

Otherwise, Eddie'd probably just take a pass.

I had all the answers I needed, or was ever going to get, so I said good-bye to Eddie, got into my car and drove off. I didn't feel like leaving the area just yet, so I headed back to the Embassy, thinking about how Eddie, who had pulled off the ultimate hustle, the big con, had died alone. What was the point of it all if there was nothing to show for your life after you've gone, nothing of yourself left to carry on?

Hoping I wouldn't have to explain to Danny why I was still here, I walked into the bar.

"Hey, Al. You see Eddie's grave?"

"Yeah."

"Siddown, take a load off." I took off my cap and dropped gratefully into a chair by a window table. "You want a drink?" Danny asked, coming over to the table.

As I was about to tell him what I wanted, he sat down himself and signaled to the thin guy behind the bar, who came over to us.

"Glenlivet for me. Al?"

"Uh, same. Neat."

The other bartender nodded and went off to get the drinks. I looked around the near-empty room and said to Danny, "What, they got so much business here they need two bartenders?"

He reached for his cigarettes. "Actually, I own the bar now." He smiled at my surprised look and added, "And a chunk of the course, too."

"Jeez. You don't mind my asking, where'd you get that kinda scratch?"

"From Eddie. In his will. Even left the hospital a Pontiac Catera unit, or sumpin' like that."

A Ponti— "You mean a *cardiac catheter* unit?"

"Yeah, 'at was it."

The same kid I'd seen earlier on the practice green walked in at that moment, blinking to try to adapt his eyes to the dim light. "I seen that kid somewhere," I said quietly to Danny. "Looks so familiar . . ."

"Him? That's—"

"Fat Albert!" I yelled before I could stop it coming out.

Startled, the boy snapped his head toward me, blinked some more and then smiled as he recognized me. "Yo, Mistuh Bellamy! Whassup?"

"What the hell are you— Hey, I'm sorry. I didn't mean to call you—"

He was grinning broadly now, and held up his hand. "No problem."

Now I realized why I hadn't recognized him at first: Fat Albert wasn't. Fat, I mean, at least not like before. He was stocky, sure, and pretty thick around the middle, but barely an abbreviation of his former self.

" 'Bout sixty pounds," he was saying. "Mebbe fi'teen, twenty more to go."

"Good for you. How?"

"Exercise, eatin' right. Usual bullshit, you know."

"What got you to do it?"

Albert put his hands together and brought them around behind his right shoulder. "Couldn't make a full turn. Kept my distance down."

Danny excused himself and then got up to see about something behind the bar, leaving Albert and me alone.

Albert had a grandmother down here—I remember Eddie's mentioning something about that at the Ryder—and came to live with her while he earned money for college by working at the Embassy, a job Eddie got for him.

"Thing is," Albert said, "I knew all along it was Eddie paid my salary, but din't say nothin', you know? Woulda embarrassed the shit outta him."

I told him I knew what he meant. He said Eddie gave him golf lessons in exchange for caddying for him and driving him around to various money matches, doing odd jobs here and there on account of Eddie got these headaches and didn't feel so hot sometimes.

"I was with him when he fell down," he said, jerking a thumb over his shoulder. "Right there on number sixteen." He looked away and shook his head. "Man never got up."

"He have any last words?" I didn't know why he should have, but it seemed worth asking.

"Yeah." Albert's smile came back. "Said, *'I'm up three with four to go, how the fuck can I die now!'* "

As we laughed, a voice rang out from somewhere near the pro shop. "Albert!"

He wiped something away from an eye and stood up, extending his hand. "Gotta go now, Mr. Bellamy. Sure good to see ya, man."

I shook his hand, and he walked off. Twisting in my chair, I called out, "Hey, Albert!" He stopped in the doorway, the light from outside framing him in silhouette, and I said, "You up for a game?"

He stared at me for a second, then leaned against the doorjamb and rested his arms across his chest, rubbing his chin with his thumbnail.

"For how much?"

EPILOGUE

The hustler kept a stone face, betraying nothing of what he was thinking.

The mark eyed him warily. "What you're telling me, you're gonna hit your tee shot at least a hunnerd yards farther than mine?"

The hustler did nothing for a second, then glanced at the other two in the foursome, friends of the mark, who smirked openly. After all, their man had just hit his drive over 220, a downright miracle in light of the butt-ugly shots he'd been spraying all over the course thus far. And did this little pecker think he could hit 320, and do it with only one try, right this very minute? He'd already taken them to the cleaners on this round—they'd just paid him five hundred dollars each—but he never hit one over 250, and even those had looked like a strain.

"You're thinking this is a trick, right?" the hustler asked. "You're thinking, what's this guy got in his bag, he thinks he can hit that far."

"Somethin' like that, yeah."

The hustler sniffled and looked up at the Oklahoma sky for a second, then back down. "Okay, let's make this real simple." He looked at the other two again, as if to recruit them as official verifiers, to underscore that he wanted all three of them to be in on it so no tricks were possible. "I swing, I hit the ball, it lands, and fifty bucks says it's at least a hunnerd yards from yours."

The mark saw the simplicity, but was still hunting for loopholes. "You gonna hit from right here?"

"Yep."

"With a golf club?"

"Completely legitimate shot, 'cording to the rules a'golf."

"Huh." Getting drawn in now.

"I don't hit a legit shot, bet's off. Better yet, you win."

"How do we measure?"

"You pace it off. You 'n' your buddies here." *The shit-kickers with their cowboy hats and boots with golf spikes. Oklahoma. Christ . . .*

"You gonna trust us?"

"Your call. I'll believe you."

"Fuck, Stewie," one of the buddies said. "What's the man gotta do, sign a freakin' afferdavit?"

The mark was still uncomfortable. "All's you're sayin', your ball's gonna be at least a hunnerd yards from mine."

"You got it."

"Huh."

"Chrissakes, Stew!" the other buddy said in irritation, pushing the cowboy hat with the OK CORRAL GOLF AND CC logo farther back on his head. "Shit er get off the pot!"

"Maybe he can hit that far," the mark said, with no real conviction.

Before the buddies could start in ridiculing their chickenshit friend, the hustler nodded, as though he'd just heard a rational concern. "I'll use a three-wood."

"Fuck, Stewie!" the first buddy said, in agitated disbelief that such an offer could be refused. "Stewie" could tell he was agitated because he was twirling the silver-and-turquoise ring the size of a tangerine around and around on his finger.

On the verge of real humiliation, the mark stood up straight and nodded. "You're on, pal! One shot!"

He stepped aside to let the hustler take the tee, but the smaller man turned to the ball pocket of his bag and began to unzip it.

"Hey!" the mark yelled. "No trick balls! You said it's gonna be a legitimate shot, and it ain't legitimate if you use a—"

"Gimme one'a yours," the hustler said calmly. Buddy Two immediately tossed him one. "Thanks."

Without examining the ball, the hustler grabbed his three-wood, teed up and stepped back, flexing his club and massaging the grip. He took a few big practice swings, which made the other guys a little nervous, then eyed the fairway and stepped up to the ball. A few waggles and then he had the clubhead settled behind the ball. The mark and Buddy One began to sweat, despite the absurdity of this pathetic twerp trying to hit a fairway wood so far, then sweated a little harder as the twerp did nothing. A ray of sunlight glinted off the steel shaft of the club and momentarily blinded them.

"Shit!" Buddy Two whispered hoarsely. "He's waiting for the tailwind to pick up!"

At that moment the hustler turned ninety degrees and, before any of the others could assess what the hell was going on, hit the ball straight over the stand of trees that sat off to the left of the tee box.

He stayed poised at the end of his follow-through for a moment before bringing the club to rest on the ground. The mystified trio, trying to make sense out of a senseless situation, watched as the ball disappeared toward the wrong fairway.

The hustler folded both hands over the top of the club and turned back to them.

"What the fuck . . . ?" the mark finally said.

"You wanna pace it off?" the hustler asked. "Or do you figure it's over a hunnerd yards from your ball?"

Comprehension dawned, and anger followed milliseconds later.

"You tricked me!" the mark howled.

"How?" the hustler asked.

"You said— You said—!"

"I said what?"

Reason was wasted on the irate and humiliated mark. *Ah, shit,* the hustler thought. All the way to Okla-goddamned-homa to get his head kicked in by three unemployed roustabouts upon whom logic was lost in favor of fisted persuasion. *I'm gonna hafta lay down clutching my chest again! Endow another freakin' cardiac-cath unit . . .* He could sense silent and potentially lethal transmissions flashing among the three as they tried to agree on a course of action without actually appearing to discuss it.

The hustler shook his head and leaned down to pick up his tee. "Forget it," he said dismissively, turning away to shove his club back in his bag. "Go ahead and finish the round."

"Ain't you gonna tee off?" Buddy One asked, not embarrassed in the slightest at having so casually abetted the welshing of a bet.

The hustler didn't bother to answer, but unstrapped his bag from the golf cart, hoisted it onto his shoulder and began walking off.

"Hey!" Buddy Two yelled. "That was my ball you hit into the trees!"

The hustler paused in disbelief, then slowly turned. "You want it back?"

The mark grabbed Buddy Two's shoulder and turned him back

toward the tee box. "Forget it, forget it." He waved at the hustler. "It's okay," he called out magnanimously. "Don't worry about it!"

"Gee, thanks, pal. Sure you don't want two bucks for it?"

As he turned away again, the hustler could sense a hard look or two but started walking anyway, hoping nothing would hit him in back of the head.

And he smiled to himself, enjoying the weight of the bag and that dumb Okie sun beating down on his bare head.

"How'd it go, boss?" the course manager asked as the hustler walked into the office behind the pro shop and settled heavily into a chair.

"Assholes," the man replied, trying to sound weary and disgusted. "Nobody's got any sense of honor anymore." He sighed and reached for a manila folder on the desk, opened it and looked at the sheet of paper inside. "How's it look?"

"Good day. Hunnerd and thirty players out."

The hustler ran his finger down the sheet, counting to himself. "And maybe a third of 'em actually paying full bore."

"Fucking coupons."

"Whaddaya gonna do?"

"You make a living."

"Not off'a this piece'a shit course," the hustler replied, throwing down the report. "Anything on?"

"Those two guys from Tulsa."

"Tulsa. Jesus."

"Whadda you give a shit, long's they got dough in their pockets? Anyways, tomorrow morning, they say you give 'em two a side, a grand each."

The hustler thought it over. "Tell 'em five grand, three a side."

"Jeez." The manager sat up straighter, smelling his 15 percent going down the drain. "Not sure they're gonna buy it."

"Then the hell with 'em. Too damned hot to sweat around eighteen for peanuts." *But drier than Florida, that's for damned sure.*

"Peanuts." The manager snorted and shook his head. "Peanuts, he says, God help me! Okay." He reached for the phone and peeled a sticky note off the receiver.

The hustler stood and stretched his back, raising his arms high overhead. "You tell Jake, make sure there's no water when we get near a hole's got a cooler on it."

The manager brightened immediately, visualizing the marks wilting from dehydration halfway through the round, the hustler drinking from squeeze bottles stashed in his bag. "Something tells me," he said, mostly to himself as he read the number off the note and began to dial, "gonna be steak tomorrow night."

The hustler, now rejuvenated with fresh prospects, dropped his arms and shook his shoulders.

"Trust me on this one, Bubba."

ACKNOWLEDGMENTS

The Green is a gift to the many hundreds of golfers
with whom nervous starters all over the country have
teamed me up over the last few years, and who
graciously ignored my atrocious handicap in deference
to our mutual love of the game.

I owe them an incalculably large debt of gratitude, one
that I hope to repay someday by being equally kind to
those even more swing-challenged than I after my own
game becomes somewhat less of an embarrassment.

With luck, that will occur not too deeply into
the next millennium.

Special thanks to Bill Atkins, the Beast, Shawn Coyne,
Nick Ellison, Bob Gumer, Susan Martin, Helen
Gruenfeld (she really said that), Hughes Norton,
rec.sports.golf and the world's greatest golfing buds:
David Brenner, Charlie Davis, Jimmy Doyle, Paul
Elieff, Marty Jacobson, Msgt Jamie Jamison, Greg
Klein, Ross Mack, Mark Mastalir, Mack and Julie
Mead, Tim Morris, Jeff Perlis, Dude Powell, Don Short,
Larry Simkins, the entire Shandin Hills Men's
Club . . . and the greatest of all, Pop.